Anita Shreve is the author of many acclaimed novels, including *Eden Close*, *The Weight of Water*, *The Last Time They Met*, *Light on Snow*, *Body Surfing*, *Testimony*, *A Change in Altitude* and most recently, *Rescue*. She lives in Massachusetts.

ALSO BY ANITA SHREVE

Rescue
A Change in Altitude
Testimony
Body Surfing
A Wedding in December
Light on Snow
All He Ever Wanted
Sea Glass
The Last Time They Met
Fortune's Rocks
The Pilot's Wife
The Weight of Water
Resistance
Where or When
Strange Fits of Passion
Eden Close

THE WEIGHT
OF WATER

RESISTANCE

Anita Shreve

ABACUS

This omnibus edition first published in Great Britain in 2011 by Little, Brown

First published separately:

The Weight of Water first published in Great Britain in 1997 by Little, Brown and Company
First published in paperback in Great Britain in 1998 by Abacus
Copyright © Anita Shreve 1997

Resistance first published in Great Britain in 1995 by Little, Brown and Company
First published in paperback in Great Britain in 1996 by Abacus
Copyright © Anita Shreve 1995

A CIP catalogue record for this book
is available from the British Library.

ISBN 978-0-349-12384-4

Printed and bound in Great Britain by
Clays Ltd, St Ives plc

Abacus
An imprint of
Little, Brown Book Group
100 Victoria Embankment
London EC4Y 0DY

An Hachette UK Company
www.hachette.co.uk

www.littlebrown.co.uk

The Weight

of Water

For my mother and my daughter

Author's Note

DURING THE NIGHT of March 5, 1873, two women, Norwegian immigrants, were murdered on the Isles of Shoals, a group of islands ten miles off the New Hampshire coast. A third woman survived, hiding in a sea cave until dawn.

The passages of court testimony included in this work are taken verbatim from the transcript of *The State of Maine* v. *Louis H. F. Wagner*.

Apart from recorded historical fact, the names, characters, places, and incidents portrayed in this work are either the products of the author's imagination or, if real, are used fictitiously.

The matter of who killed Anethe and Karen Christensen was settled in a court of law, but has continued to be debated for more than a century.

I HAVE TO let this story go. It is with me all the time now, a terrible weight.

I sit in the harbor and look across to Smuttynose. A pink light, a stain, makes its way across the island. I cut the engine of the small boat I have rented and put my fingers into the water, letting the shock of the cold swallow my hand. I move my hand through the seawater, and think how the ocean, this harbor, is a repository of secrets, its own elegy.

I was here before. A year ago. I took photographs of the island, of vegetation that had dug in against the weather: black sedge and bayberry and sheep sorrel and sea blite. The island is not barren, but it is sere and bleak. It is granite, and everywhere there are ragged reefs that cut. To have lived on Smuttynose would have required a particular tenacity, and I imagine the people then as dug in against the elements, their roots set into the cracks of the rocks like the plants that still survive.

The house in which the two women were murdered burned in 1885, but when I was here a year ago, I photographed the footprint of the house, the marked perimeter. I got into a boat and took pictures of the whitened ledges of Smuttynose and the black-backed gulls that swept and rose above the island in search of fish only they could see. When I was here before, there were yellow roses and blackberries.

When I was here before, something awful was being assembled, but I didn't know it then.

I take my hand from the water and let the drops fall upon the papers in the carton, dampened already at the edges from the slosh. The pink light turns to violet.

Sometimes I think that if it were possible to tell a story often enough to make the hurt ease up, to make the words slide down my arms and away from me like water, I would tell that story a thousand times.

IT IS MY job to call out if I see a shape, a rocky ledge, an island. I stand at the bow and stare into the fog. Peering intently, I begin to see things that aren't really there. First tiny moving lights, then minutely subtle gradations of gray. Was that a shadow? Was that a shape? And then, so shockingly that for a few important seconds I cannot even speak, it is all there: Appledore and Londoners and Star and Smuttynose — rocks emerging from the mist. Smuttynose, all of a piece, flat with bleached ledges, forbidding, silent.

I call out. *Land,* I guess I say.

Sometimes, on the boat, I have a sense of claustrophobia, even when alone on the bowsprit. I have not anticipated this. We are four adults and one child forced to live agreeably together in a space no bigger than a small bedroom, and that space almost always damp. The sheets are damp, my underwear is damp. Rich, who has had the boat for years, says this is always true of sailing. He gives me the impression that accepting the dampness, even taking a certain pleasure in it, is an indication of character.

Rich has brought a new woman with him whose name is Adaline.

Rich gives instructions. The sailboat is old, a Morgan 41, but well-tended, the teak newly varnished. Rich calls for the boat hook, shouts to Thomas to snag the buoy. Rich slows the engine, reverses it, guns it slightly, maneuvers the long, slim boat — this space that moves through water — alongside the mooring. Thomas leans over, catches the buoy. Adaline looks up from her book. It is our third day aboard the sloop: Hull, Marblehead, Annisquam, now the Isles of Shoals.

The Isles of Shoals, an archipelago, lie in the Atlantic, ten miles southeast off the New Hampshire coast at Portsmouth. The islands measure three and a half miles north and south by one and a half miles east and west. There are nine islands at high tide, eight at low; White and Seavey are connected. The largest island looked to its first residents like a fat pig wallowing in the sea, and hence the name of Hog. Smuttynose, our destination, derived its name from a clump of seaweed on the nose of a rock extending into the ocean. It has always been an off-putting name, though the others read like poetry from a ship's log: "We passed today the islands of Star and Malaga and Seavey and Londoners; and navigated to our success the treacherous rock of Shag and Eastern and Babb's and Mingo."

In 1635, the Isles of Shoals were formally divided between the Massachusetts Bay Colony, which included Maine, and the territory subsequently to be known as New Hampshire. Duck, Hog, Malaga, Smuttynose, and Cedar went to Maine. Star, Londoners, White, and Seavey went to New Hampshire. The division has always held. In 1635, when the ordinance was first declared, nearly all of the residents of Star fled to Smuttynose, because it was still legal to drink in Maine.

From the guidebooks, I read startling facts: On the island of Star, in 1724, a woman named Betty Moody hid herself and her three children from Indians in a cavern. She crouched near to the ground and held one of the children, an infant girl, tightly to her breast. Mrs. Moody meant to silence her baby to keep the child from giving away their location, but when the Indians had gone, she discovered that she had smothered the girl.

Rich looks like a wrestler: He is neatly muscled and compact. His head is shaved, and he has perfect teeth. I do not think he resembles Thomas at all — an odd, genetic quirk; there are ten years between them. Rich tickles Billie unmercifully, even on the Zodiac. She squeals as if she were being tortured, and then complains when he stops. Rich walks about the Morgan with athletic grace, and he gives the impression of a man for whom nothing has ever been complicated.

We have come only from Annisquam and arrive in the early morning. I watch Thomas bend over the stern to snag the mooring. His legs are pale with whorls of brown hair above the backs of his knees. Over his bathing suit, he has on a pink dress shirt, the cuffs rolled to the elbows. It is odd to see Thomas, my husband of fifteen years, engaged in chores upon this boat, a second mate to his younger brother. Without his pen or his books, Thomas seems disarmed, disoriented by manual labor. As I watch him, I think, as I so often do, that my husband looks too tall for his surroundings. He seems to have to stoop, even while seated. His hair, cut longish, now nearly colorless, falls forward onto his forehead, and he pushes it away with a gesture I am fond of and have seen a thousand times. Despite his seniority, or perhaps because of it, I sometimes see that Thomas is unsettled by the presence of Rich and Adaline, as a father might be in the company of a grown son and a woman.

What does Adaline think when she observes Thomas? My husband is a poet of the first tier, already a kind of emeritus at the university, even though he is only forty-seven. Adaline is not a poet, but seems to have great admiration for Thomas's work. I wonder if she knew Thomas's verse before, or if she has learned it for the trip.

When there is time, I read about the islands. I carry pounds of paper in my camera bag — guidebooks, accounts of the murders, a trial transcript — materials from Research, who seem to think that I am writing the piece. When the murders occurred, in 1873, the newspapers wrote of the crime, and later it was called in these same papers "the trial of the century." This is a familiar turn of phrase this summer as we witness a courtroom spectacle that has all but benumbed even the most avid observers. My editor thinks there is a link between the two events: a double murder with a blade, a famous trial, circumstantial evidence that hinges on tiny factual details. As for me, I think the similarities few, but a magazine will make of something what it can. I am paid to take the pictures.

My expense account is lavish, but Rich, who publishes technical journals, will not hear of money. I am glad that Thomas has thought of his younger brother and his boat: I would not like to be in such close quarters with a strange captain or a crew.

How long, I wonder, has Rich been seeing Adaline?

I read many accounts of the murders. I am struck most by the relativity of facts.

When I think about the murders, I try to picture what might have happened that night. I imagine there would have been a gale, and that the wind from the water would have battered against the glass. Sometimes, I can hear that wind and can see the wooden house under the high cirrus of a full moon. Maren and Anethe would have lain on their backs on either side of the double bed — or could it have been that they were touching? — and in the next room, Karen would have called out suddenly with fright.

Or was it that the dog barked first?

Sometimes I imagine the murders to have been a thing of subtle grace and beauty, with slim arms raised in white nightgowns against the fright, white nightgowns against the snow, the rocks sharp and the gale billowing the thin linen like sheets on a line. I see an arm raised along a window, the moon etching smudges on the panes, and a woman calling to another and another, while below them, at the waterline, the waves slap fast and hard against the dory.

I love to watch my daughter move about the boat in her bathing suit, the fabric stretched and limp, riding high over her butt, her body plump and delicious, often salty if I lick her arm. At five, Billie is entranced by the sloop, a space with lots of cubbyholes and clever places to store the few toys she has been allowed to bring along. She sleeps in the quarter berth beside the companionway. Adaline and Rich are in the forward cabin, the owner's prerogative. Thomas and I have less privacy, stowed amidships as we are, in the open, on a bed that is put away each morning to become a breakfast table.

Occasionally I find Billie's sandy footprints down below. Sand in the fridge. Does Rich mind? I think not. Billie's hair has lightened in the sun and curls continuously from the damp. More and more, I notice her enlarged pupils and the way they cause her eyes to appear nearly black. She has extravagantly long lashes that exaggerate every blink. The loss of her two top front teeth has widened her grin and produces a delicate lisp.

In the mornings, I can hear Adaline and Rich in the forward cabin: a rustle of cloth, a murmur, rhythmic movements. The sounds from Adaline are surprising — guttural and sometimes frantic. I begin to anticipate the sounds and to move away from them. I go above to the cockpit in my robe. I wonder if Billie would be afraid if she awoke — afraid that Adaline were being hurt.

I think that Evan, who was Anethe's husband, would have moved urgently toward the door on the morning after the murders, reports of the unthinkable pushing him forward in a kind of frenzy. The high cirrus would have blown out by then, and the sun would have been on the rocks, beginning to melt the snow. Evan would have been the first man inside the door. He would have insisted.

In 1852, Nancy Underhill, a schoolteacher, was sitting on a

ledge at Star when a wave washed her into the sea. Her body was found, a week later, at Cape Neddick, in Maine.

This morning, after we have tied up, Adaline stands in the cockpit, her hands at her waist, her eyes searching the shoreline of Smuttynose, as if something profound might reveal itself to her. When she speaks, she has a residue of an Irish accent, and her voice lends her an aura of authority I do not necessarily feel in myself. Her words rise and fall and dip some more, and then come back to where you can hear them — like soft church music, I often think, or like the melodious beat of water on the hull.

Adaline moves like a dancer, swaying for balance. In the mornings, when she comes up the ladder and emerges from the companionway, she seems to glide into the cockpit. She wears long skirts in thin cottons, with blouses that fall loosely around her hips. She wears a gold cross at her throat, jewelry that is somewhat startling in a woman of her age and stature. The cross draws the eye to the hollow above her clavicle, a hollow that is smooth and tanned. It is as though she once wore the cross as a girl and simply forgot to take it off.

Adaline, Rich tells me, works for Bank of Boston, in an international division. She never talks about her job. I imagine her in suits, standing at gates in airports. She has scars on her wrists, slightly crooked vertical threads in smooth flesh, as though she once tried to trace her veins with a razor or a knife. She has an arresting mouth, with full curved lips of even dimensions, and barely any bow at all.

Sometimes I imagine I can see Maren Hontvedt at the end of her life. In the room in which she is sitting, the wallpaper is discolored but intact. She wears an eyelet cap to cover her hair. I note the languid drape of the shawl folding into her lap, the quiescent posture of her body. The floor is bare, wooden, and on the dresser is a basin of water. The light from the window falls upon her face and eyes. They are gray eyes, not yet faded, and they retain an expression that others who knew her might recognize.

I think that she is dying and will be gone soon. There are thoughts and memories that she hoards and savors, holding them as one might a yellowed photograph of a child. The skin hangs from her face in folds, her skin a crushed velvet the color of dried hydrangeas. She was not beautiful as a young woman, but her face was handsome, and she was strong. The structure of her face is still as it was, and one can see the bones as one might be able to discern the outline of a chair covered by a loose cloth.

I wonder this: If you take a woman and push her to the edge, how will she behave?

After we moor the boat, Rich offers to take me over to Smuttynose in the Zodiac. Billie begs to go along. I shoot from the dinghy in a crouch, leaning against the side of the boat for balance. I use the Hasselblad and a telephoto with a polarizing lens. From time to time, I shout to Rich to cut the engine so that the vibrations will be lessened, or I gesture with my hand in such a way that he knows to push the throttle forward.

There are two houses on the island. One is a small, wooden-frame house called the Haley house. It is not habitable, but is of historic note and has a great aesthetic purity. The other is a shack with rudimentary supplies for shipwrecked sailors.

Rich beaches the Zodiac expertly inside the crumbled breakwater of Smuttynose. The beach is tiny, narrow, blackened by dark stones and charred bits of wood. The air is sharp, and I understand why years ago sea air was prescribed as a tonic for the body. Billie removes her life jacket and sits cross-legged on the sand in a lavender T-shirt that doesn't quite cover her belly. Rich is tanned already, an even red-gold on his legs and arms and face. There is a line at his throat. We have left Thomas and Adaline on the Morgan.

In the winter months on the Isles of Shoals, the windows were never opened, nor were the children ever let outside, so that by March the air inside the houses was stale and putrid and old with smoke, and the children could hardly breathe.

Rich takes Billie by the hand and guides her past the breakwater so that he can help her search for mussels among the rocks and put them in her pail. I heft my camera bag onto my shoulder and head out toward the end of Smuttynose. My plan is to turn around and frame a shot of the entire island. At my destination, the easternmost tip of the island, there is a rock shaped like a horse's fetlock. Inside the square-cut boulders is a sheltered space, a sea cave, that sloshes with water when the tide is high. It is slippery on the rocks, but after I have left my camera bag on a dry ledge and anchored it in a crevice so that the wind will not blow it away, I crawl like a crab to the sea cave and squat inside. On three sides of me are the shoals and roiling water, and straight out to the east nothing but Atlantic Ocean. Unlike the harbor and the place where we have landed, this side of the island is unprotected. There is lichen on the rock, and small flies lift in a frenzy whenever a wave crashes and sprays.

At the rock, which is known as Maren's Rock, I shut my eyes and try to imagine what it would be like to huddle in that cave all night in winter, in the dark, in the snow and freezing temperatures, with only my nightgown and a small black dog for warmth.

I crawl from the rock, scraping my shin in the process. I collect my camera bag, which has not moved from its notch. I take a roll of color slide film, thirty-six shots of Maren's rock. I walk the length of the island, the going slow in the thick, scratchy brush.

On January 14, 1813, fourteen shipwrecked Spanish sailors, driven to Smuttynose by a winter gale, tried to reach the light from a candle in an upstairs window of Captain Haley's cottage.

They died in a blizzard not forty feet from their destination and are buried under boulders on the island. One man made it to the stone wall, but could go no further. Captain Haley discovered him the following morning. Six more bodies were found on January 17, five more on the twenty-first, and the final body was discovered "grappled up on Hog Island passage" on the twenty-seventh. According to the *Boston Gazette* on January 18, the vessel, named *Conception,* weighed between three and four hundred tons and was laden with salt. No one in America ever knew the dead sailors' names.

When I find Rich and Billie, they are sitting on the beach, their toes dug into the sand. I sit beside them, my knees raised, my arms folded around my legs. Billie gets up and stares into her pail and begins to leap in stiff-legged jetés all around us.

"My fingers are *bleeding,*" she announces proudly. "We pulled off a million of them. At least a million. Didn't we, Uncle Rich?"

"Absolutely. At least a million."

"When we get back to the boat, we're going to cook them up for supper." She bends over her pail again and studies it solemnly. Then she begins to drag the pail down to the water's edge.

"What is she doing?" Rich asks.

"I think she's giving the mussels something to drink."

He smiles. "I once read an account of a pilot who said the most beautiful sight he'd ever seen from the air was the Isles of Shoals." He runs his hand over his shaved head. His skull is perfectly shaped, without bumps or dents. I wonder if he worries about sunburn.

"Adaline seems very nice," I say.

"Yes, she is."

"She admires Thomas's work."

Rich looks away and tosses a pebble. His face is not delicate, in the way that Thomas's is. Rich has dark, thick eyebrows that nearly meet in the center. Sometimes I think that he has Thomas's mouth, but he doesn't. Rich's is firmer, more pronounced in profile. "Childe Hassam painted here," he says. "Did you know that?"

"I wouldn't have thought that someone who worked for Citibank would know so much about poetry," I say.

"Actually, it's Bank of Boston." He tilts his head and looks at me. "I think poetry is something that's fairly universal, don't you? Enjoying it, I mean."

"I suppose."

"How is Thomas?"

"I don't know. I think he's convinced himself that each poet is given a finite number of words and that he's used up his allotment."

"I notice that he's drinking more," Rich says. Rich's legs are brown and covered with dark hair. Looking at his legs, I contemplate the trick of nature that has caused Thomas and Rich to receive what appear to be entirely separate sets of genes. I glance out toward the sloop, which floats four hundred feet from us in the harbor. The mast teeters in the chop.

"Adaline was married once," Rich says. "To a doctor. They had a child."

I turn to him. He must see surprise on my face.

"I think the girl must be three or four now. The father has her. They live in California."

"I didn't know."

"Adaline doesn't see the girl. She's chosen not to."

I am silent. I try to absorb this information, to put it together with the gold cross and the lilting voice.

"Adaline came over from Ireland for him," he says. "For the doctor."

He leans over and brushes a dried smear of muck from my calf. He smooths my leg with his fingertips. I am thinking that the calf is not a place that anyone touches much. I wonder if he shaves his head every day. What the top of his head would feel like.

"She's kind of detached," he says, withdrawing his fingers. "She doesn't stay with people long."

"How long have you two been together?"

"About five months. Actually, I think my tenure is almost up."

I think of saying to him that to judge by the sounds emanating from the forward cabin, I cannot agree.

In front of us, Billie lies down at the waterline. Mostly, I think, to get sand in her hair. I tense and begin to rise. Rich puts a restraining hand on my wrist.

"She's OK. I've got my eye on her."

I relax a bit and sit back down.

"Did you want something more?" I ask. "From Adaline, I mean."

He shrugs.

"She's very beautiful," I say.

Rich nods. "I've always envied you," he says. "You and Thomas."

He puts his hand to his face to shade his eyes, and he squints in the direction of the boat.

"I don't see anyone in the cockpit," I say.

A few minutes later, I take a photograph of Rich and Billie and her pail of mussels. Rich is lying on the small piece of rough beach, his knees raised, dark circles inside the wide openings of his khaki shorts. The eye is drawn to those dark circles. His arms are spread at his sides in a posture of submission. His head has fallen into a depression in the sand, so that his body seems to end at his neck. Billie is standing over him, perfectly bent at the waist, her arms stretched out behind her for balance, like two tiny wings. She is talking to Rich or asking him a question. Rich seems vulnerable under her scrutiny. Beside Billie is her green plastic pail of mussels, perhaps enough to make an appetizer for two. Up behind them both is the Haley house, small and old, the trim neatly painted in a dull brick red.

When I look at the photographs, it is hard not to think: We had seventeen hours then, or twelve, or three.

Immediately after the photograph is taken, Rich sits up. He remembers, he tells Billie, that a pirate named Blackbeard once buried his treasure on the island. He gets up and searches through the scrub, examining this branch and that, until he has made two forked sticks. He sets off with Billie while I wait on the beach. After a time — fifteen minutes, twenty? — I hear a cry from Billie. She is calling to me. I get up to look and then walk over to where she and Rich are standing together, about two hundred feet from the beach. Billie and Rich are bent over a hole they have dug in the sand. In the hole is a treasure: five quarters, two dollar bills, a gold-colored toothpick, a chain with a single key attached, a bracelet made of copper wire, and a silver-colored ring. Rich pretends to read the inscription under the band of the ring. "To E from E with undying love."

"What's 'E to E' mean?" Billie asks.

"Blackbeard's real name was Edward, which begins with *E*. And his wife's name was Esmerelda, which also begins with *E*."

Billie ponders this. Rich tells her that the silver ring belonged to Blackbeard's fifteenth wife, whom Blackbeard himself murdered. Billie is nearly levitating with excitement and fright.

The boundaries of the Hontvedt house — also known, before the murders, as simply "the red house" — have been marked with stakes. The boundaries delineate an area approximately twenty feet by thirty-six feet. In this small space were two apartments, separated by a doorless wall. The northwest side of the house had two front doors.

After the brief ride back, I step up onto the Morgan from the

Zodiac, Rich catching my hand. Thomas and Adaline are sitting opposite one another, on canvas cushions in the cockpit, seawater dripping from their bodies and making puddles on the floor. They have been swimming, Adaline says, and Thomas seems mildly out of breath.

Adaline has her hands up behind her head, wringing out her hair. Her bathing suit is red, two vibrant wisps of fire-engine red on glistening skin. Her stomach, a lovely, flat surface the color of toast, seems that of a young girl. Her thighs are long and wet and have drops of seawater among the light brown hairs.

She twists her hair and smiles at me. Her face is guileless when she smiles. I am trying to reconcile the image of her smile with the frantic, guttural sounds that emanate in the morning from the forward cabin.

I remember these moments not solely for themselves, but for the knowledge that beyond these memories lies an instant in time that cannot be erased. Each image a stepping stone taken in innocence or, if not in innocence, then in a kind of thoughtless oblivion.

Rich goes immediately to Adaline and puts a proprietary hand on the flat of her belly. He kisses her on the cheek. Billie, too, takes a step forward, drawn to beauty as any of us are. I see that Billie will find a reason to drape herself across those long legs. With effort, Thomas keeps his eyes on me and asks about our small trip. I am embarrassed for Thomas, for the extraordinary whiteness of his skin, for his chest, which seems soft. I want to cover him with his blue shirt, which is lying in a puddle.

On March 5, 1873, approximately sixty people lived on all the islands composing the Shoals: the lighthouse keeper's family on White; workmen building a hotel on Star; two families — the Laightons and the Ingerbretsons — on Appledore (formerly known as Hog); and one family, the Hontvedts, on Smuttynose.

We run the Zodiac into Portsmouth. We are hungry and want lunch, and we don't have much in the way of provisions. We sit in a restaurant that has a porch and an awning. It seems as close to the water as one can get in Portsmouth, though I think there is not much to look at beyond the tugs and the fishing boats. A sharp gust of wind catches the awning and lifts it for a second so that the poles that anchor it come off the ground as well. The awning tears loose at one corner and spills its wind. The canvas flaps in the breeze.

"The heavens rent themselves," Thomas says.

Adaline looks up at him and smiles. *"Uncovered orbs and souls."*

Thomas seems surprised. *"Mullioned waters,"* he says.

"Beveled whispers."

"Shuttered grace."

"Shackled sunlight."

I think of Ping-Pong balls hit hard across a table.

Adaline pauses. *"Up-rushed sea,"* she says.

"Yes," Thomas answers quietly.

At the restaurant, Billie eats a grilled cheese sandwich, as she almost always does. She is hard to contain in a restaurant, an effervescence that wants to bubble up and pop out of the top of the bottle. I drink a beer called Smuttynose, which seems to be a brand that capitalizes upon the murders. After all, why not name a beer Appledore or Londoner's? The drink is oak colored and heavier than I am used to, and I think I become slightly drunk. I am not sure about this. The boat itself produces a kind of inebriation that stays with you for hours. Even when you step foot on land, you are still swaying, still feeling the thump of water against the hull.

I read in the guidebooks that America was discovered at the Isles of Shoals, on Smuttynose, by vikings.

On Star Island, there is a cemetery known as Beebe. In it are

buried the three small daughters of George Beebe who died separately and within a few days of each other in 1863 of diphtheria.

At the restaurant I have a lobster roll. Thomas has fried clams.
There is a lull in the conversation, as though the strain of the trip
into the harbor in the Zodiac has drained everyone of words.
Adaline eats a salad and drinks a glass of water. I notice that her
back is straight while she eats. Rich, by contrast, is easily
slouched, his legs stretched in front of him. He pushes his chair
slightly closer to Adaline's and begins idly to stroke her arm.

Captain Samuel Haley settled on Smuttynose several years before the American Revolution. While he was building a seawall
to connect Malaga and Smuttynose, he turned over a rock and
discovered four bars of silver. With this money, he completed the
breakwater and built the pier. The breakwater was destroyed in
February 1978.

Edward Teach, also known as the pirate Blackbeard, spent his
honeymoon with his fifteenth and last wife on the Isles of Shoals
in 1720. He is said to have buried his treasure on Smuttynose.

"Don't tear your napkin."

Thomas's voice is ragged, like the bits of paper on the table.

Adaline gently removes the wad from Billie's fist and picks up
the debris around her plate.

"How did you get a name like Billie?" she asks.

"It's Willemina," Billie answers, the name spooling off her lips
in a pleased and practiced way.

"I named her for my mother," I say, glancing at Thomas. He
drains his wineglass and puts it on the table.

"My mom calls me Billie because Willemina is too old," she
adds.

"Fashioned," I say.

"I think Willemina is a pretty name," Adaline says. Her hair is
rolled at the sides and caught at the back with a clip. Billie stands

on her chair and tilts her head to examine the rolls and the way they seamlessly fold into the nape of Adaline's neck.

Smuttynose is twenty-eight hundred feet east and west, and a thousand feet north and south. It consists of 27.1 acres, almost all of which is rock. The elevation of the island is thirty feet.

Thomas is thin and stretched, and seems, physically, not to have enough leverage in life. I think that Thomas will probably be thin until he dies, stooped perhaps in the way some tall men become as they age. I know that it will be an elegant stoop. I am sure of that.

I wonder if Thomas is as sad as I am when he awakens in the mornings and hears Adaline and Rich in the forward cabin.

We are waiting for the check to come. Billie is standing next to me, coloring on a place mat. "Were you born in Ireland?" I ask Adaline.

"In the south of Ireland."

The waitress brings the check. Thomas and Rich reach for it, but Thomas, distractedly, lets Rich have it.

"This assignment you're on must be gruesome for you," says Adaline. She begins to massage the back of Billie's neck.

"I don't know," I say. "It seems so long ago. Actually, I wish I could get my hands on some old photographs."

"You seem to have a lot of material," Thomas says.

"It was foisted upon me," I say, wondering why my voice contains a defensive note. "Though I must confess I find the accounts of the murders intriguing."

Adaline reaches up and removes a gold hair clip from the back of her head. Her hair is multihued, a wood grain that curls slightly in the humidity, as does Billie's. On the boat, Adaline most often wears her hair rolled at the back of her head or at the nape of her neck in intricate knots and coils that can be loosened with a single pin. Today, when she removes the clip, her hair falls the length of her back, swaying with the fall. The settling of all that hair, the surprising abundance of hair springing from a knot no bigger than a peach, seems, at the time, like a trick, a sleight of hand, for our benefit.

I look over at Thomas. He is breathing slowly. His face, which normally has high color, has gone pale. He seems stunned by the simple fall of hair from a knot — as though the image itself, or the memories it evokes, were unwanted news.

I do not have many personal photographs of Thomas. There are dozens of other pictures of him, photos of a public nature: book-jacket portraits, for example, and formal snapshots in magazines and newspapers. But in my own collection, Thomas has almost always managed to avert his eyes or to turn his head altogether, as if he did not want to be captured on any day at any place in time. I have, for instance, a picture of Thomas at a party at our apartment after Billie was born: Thomas is stooped slightly, speaking with a woman, another poet, who is also a friend. He has seen me coming with the camera, has dipped his head and has brought a glass up to his cheek, almost entirely obscuring his profile. In another photograph, Thomas is holding Billie on a bench in a park. Billie, perched on Thomas's knee, seems already aware of the camera and is smiling broadly and clasping her tiny fists together with delight at this new activity, at this strange face that her mother has put on — one with a moving and briefly flickering eye. Thomas, however, has bent his head into Billie's neck. Only his posture tells the viewer he is the father of the child.

For years I thought that Thomas avoided the camera because he has a scar that runs from the corner of his left eye to his chin — the result of a car accident when he was seventeen. It is not disfiguring, in the way some scars can be, ruining a face so that you no longer want to look at it; instead, Thomas's scar seems to follow the planes of his face — as though a brush had made a quick stroke, a perfect curve. It is almost impossible not to want to touch that scar, to run a fingertip along its bumpy ridge. But it is not the scar that makes Thomas turn his face away from the camera; it is, I think, that he cannot bear to be examined too closely by a lens. Just as he is not able to meet his eyes for any length of time in a mirror.

I have one photograph of Thomas in which he is not turned away. I took it on the morning after we met. He is standing in front of his apartment building in Cambridge, and he has his hands in the pockets of his trousers. He has on a wrinkled white shirt with a button-down collar. Even in this picture, the viewer can see that Thomas wants to pull away, and that it is with the greatest of effort that he has kept his eyes focused on the camera. He looks ageless in the photograph, and it is only because I happen to know that he is thirty-two that I would not think he was forty-seven or twenty-five. In the picture, one can see that Thomas's hair, which is naturally thin and of no distinct color, has recently been cut short. I took the picture about nine o'clock in the morning. He looks that morning like someone I have known a long time — possibly since childhood.

We met for the first time, appropriately, in a bar in Cambridge. I was twenty-four, and worked for a Boston paper, assigned recently to Local Sports. I was on my way home from a shoot in Somerville of a high school girls' basketball team, but I needed a bathroom and a pay phone.

I heard his voice before I saw his face. It was low and measured, authoritative and without noticeable accent.

When he finished the reading, he turned slightly to acknowledge a nod, and I could see Thomas's face then in the light. I was struck by his mouth — he had a loose and generous mouth, the only extravagance in a spare face. Later, when I was sitting with him, I saw that his eyes were set closely together, so that I did not think he was classically handsome. His irises, however, were navy and flecked with gold, and he had large pupils, dark circles that seemed to have no protection.

I went to the bar and ordered a Rolling Rock. I was light-headed and hollow-stomached from not having eaten anything. It seemed that every time I had thought of eating that day, I had been called to yet another assignment. I leaned against the bar and studied the menu. I was aware that Thomas was standing next to me.

"I liked your reading," I said.

He glanced briefly at me. "Thank you," he said quickly, in the way of a man who has no skill with compliments.

"The poem you read. It was very strong."

His eyes flickered over my face. "It's old work," he said.

The barman brought my Rolling Rock, and I paid for the beer. Thomas picked up his glass, leaving a wet circle on the highly var-nished surface of the bar. He took a long swallow and set the glass back down.

"This is a reading?" I asked.

"Tuesday night. Poet's night."

"I didn't know."

"You're not alone."

I tried to signal to the barman, so that I could order a snack.

"Thomas Janes," he said, holding out his hand. I noticed the fingers, long and strong and pale.

He must have seen the confusion on my face.

He smiled. "No, you've never heard of me," he said.

"I don't know poetry very well," I said lamely.

"No apologies."

He had on a white shirt and a complicated cable-knit sweater. Dress slacks. Gray. A pair of boots. I told him my name and that I was a photographer for the *Globe*.

"How did you become a photographer?"

"I saw a show of AP photos once. I left the show and went out and bought a camera."

"The baby falling from the third-story window."

"Something like that."

"And you've been taking pictures ever since."

"It helped to put me through school."

"You've seen a lot of terrible things."

"Some. But I've seen wonderful things, too. I once caught the moment that a father lay down on the ice and pulled his son from a fish hole. You can see the clasped arms of the boy and the man, and the two faces with their eyes locked."

"Where was this?"

"In Woburn."

"It sounds familiar. Could I have seen it?"

"Possibly. The *Globe* bought it."

He nodded slowly and took a long swallow of his drink. "Actually, it's much the same, what you and I are doing," he said.

"And what would that be?"

"Trying to stop time."

The barman beckoned to Thomas, and he walked to a small platform at one end of the room. He leaned on a podium. The audience, to my surprise, grew quiet. There was not even the chink of glasses. Thomas pulled a piece of paper from the pocket of his trousers and said he wanted to read something he had written just that day. There were words that stayed with me: *Wainscot* and *redolent* and *core-stung*.

Later there were a great many glasses on the table, mugs of cut glass that refracted the dregs. There seemed to be endless circles of liquid oak. I thought that nearly half the people in the bar had come to the table to buy Thomas a drink. Thomas drank too much. I could see that even then. He stood and swayed a bit and held the table. I touched him on the elbow. He had no shame in his drunkenness. He asked me if I would help him get to his car. Already I knew that I would have to drive him home.

A sink with a rusty stain leaned along one wall. A small bed that sagged and was covered with a beige blanket stood in the center. Thomas lay on his back on the bed, which was too short for him. I removed his boots and sat on a chair by the desk. Thomas's feet were white and smooth. His stomach was concave and made a slight hollow under his belt. One of the legs of his trousers had ridden up to expose an inch of skin above his sock. I thought he was the most beautiful man I had ever seen.

When I knew that he was asleep, I slipped a hand into his trouser pocket and removed the folded piece of paper. I took it to the window, where there was a slit in the curtain. I read the poem in the street light.

After a time, I put a finger to the skin at his shin. I traced the scar on his face, and he twitched in his sleep. I put my palm on the place where his belly dipped. The heat of his skin through his shirt surprised me, as though he were running a temperature, as though the inner mechanisms of his body burned inefficiently.

I slipped into the bed and lay beside him. He turned onto his side, facing me. It was dark in the room, but I could see his face. I could feel his breath on my skin.

"You brought me home," he said.

"Yes."

"I don't remember."

"No, I know you don't."

"I drink too much."

"I know." I brought my hand up, as though I might touch him, but I didn't. I laid my hand between our faces.

"Where are you from?" he asked me.

"Indiana."

"A farm girl."

"Yes."

"Seriously?"

"I've been in Boston since I was seventeen."

"School."

"And after."

"The after sounds interesting."

"Not very."

"You don't miss Indiana?"

"Some. My parents are dead. I miss them more."

"How did they die?"

"Cancer. They were older. My mother was forty-eight when I was born. Why are you asking me these questions?"

"You're a woman in my bed. You're an attractive woman in my bed. Why did you stay here tonight?"

"I was worried about you," I said. "What about your parents?"

"They live in Hull. I grew up in Hull. I have a brother."

"How did you get this?" I reached up and touched the scar on his face.

He flinched, and he turned onto his back, away from me.

"I'm sorry," I said.

"No, it's all right. It's just . . ."

"You don't have to tell me. It's none of my business."

"No." He brought an arm up and covered his eyes. He was so still for so long that I thought he had fallen asleep.

I shifted slightly in the bed with the intention of getting up and leaving. Thomas, feeling the shift, quickly lifted his arm from his eyes and looked at me. He grabbed my arm. "Don't go," he said.

When he rolled toward me, he unfastened one button of my shirt, as though by that gesture he would prevent me from leaving. He kissed the bare space he had made. "Are you with anyone?"

"No," I said. I put my fingers on his face, but I was careful not to touch the scar.

He unfastened all the buttons. He opened my shirt and laid the white cloth against my arms. He kissed me from my neck to my stomach. Dry lips. Light kisses. He rolled me away from him, pulling my shirt down below my shoulders. He lay behind me, encircling me, pressing his palms into my stomach. My arms were pinned beneath his, and I felt his breath on the nape of my neck. He pushed himself hard against my thigh. I bent my head slightly forward, letting go, letting this happen to me, to us, and I felt his body stretch with mine. I felt his tongue at the top of my spine.

Sometime later that night, I was awakened by a ragged moan. Thomas, naked, was sitting at the edge of the bed, the heels of his hands digging angrily into his eye sockets. I tried to pull his hands away before he injured himself. He fell back onto the bed. I turned on a light.

"What is it?" I asked. "What's wrong?"

"It's nothing," he whispered. "It'll pass."

His jaw was clenched, and his face had gone a sickly white. It couldn't simply be a hangover, I thought. He must be ill.

He raised his head off the pillow and looked at me. He seemed not to be able to see me. There was something wrong with his right eye. "This will pass," he said. "It's just a headache."

"What can I do for you?" I asked.

"Don't go," he whispered. "Promise me you won't go." He reached for my hand, catching my wrist. He gripped me so tightly, he raised welts on my skin.

I prepared him an ice pack in the tiny kitchen of his apartment and lay down next to him. I, too, was naked. It's possible I slept while he waited out the pain. Some hours later, he rolled over, facing me, and took my hand. He placed my fingers on the scar. His color had returned, and I could see that the headache was gone. I traced the long bumpy curve on his face, as I was meant to do.

"There's something I want to tell you," he said.

In the morning, after our long night together, after the migraine, the first of dozens I would eventually witness, I persuaded him to get up and take me out to breakfast. I made him pose for a photograph at the front door of the apartment house. At the diner, he told me more about the scar, but the language, I could hear, had already changed, the telling of it was different. I could see that he was composing images, searching for words. I left him with a promise to return in the late afternoon. When I came back, Thomas had still not showered or changed his clothes, and there was an unmistakable exhilaration about him, a flush on his face.

"I love you," he said, getting up from the desk.

"You couldn't possibly," I said, alarmed. I looked over to the desk. I saw white-lined papers covered with black ink. Thomas's fingers were stained, and there was ink on his shirt.

"Oh but I do," he said.

"You've been working," I said, going to him. He embraced me, and I inhaled in his shirt what had become, in twenty-four hours, a familiar scent.

"It's the beginning of something," he said into my hair.

In the restaurant in Portsmouth, Thomas turns slightly and sees that I am watching him.

He reaches across the table. "Jean, do you want a walk?" he asks. "We'll go up to the bookstore. Maybe we'll find some old photographs of Smuttynose."

"Yes, that's right," says Adaline. "You and Thomas go off for a bit on your own. Rich and I will take care of Billie."

Rich stands. My daughter's face is serious, as if she were trying to look older than she is — perhaps eight or nine. I watch her smooth her T-shirt over her shorts.

"*Fat repose*," Thomas says. He speaks distinctly, but there is, in his voice, which is somewhat louder than it was, the barest suggestion of excitement.

At the next table, a couple turns to look at us.

Adaline reaches around for a sweater she has left on the back of the chair. *"Spaded breasts,"* she says.

She stands up, but Thomas cannot leave it there.

"Twice-bloated oaths on lovers' breath."

Adaline looks at Thomas, then at me. *"The hour confesses,"* she says quietly. *"And leaves him spinning."*

Thomas and I walk up Ceres Street to the center of the town. Thomas seems anxious and distracted. We pass boutiques, a microbrewery, a home-furnishings store. In a storefront window, I see my reflection, and it occurs to me there are no mirrors on the boat. I am surprised to see a woman who looks older than I think she ought to. Her mouth is pressed into a narrow line, as if she were trying to remember something important. Her shoulders are hunched, or perhaps that is simply the way she is standing, with her hands in the pockets of her jeans. She has on a faded navy sweatshirt, and she has a camera bag on her arm. She might be a tourist. She wears her hair short, hastily pushed back behind her ears. On the top of her hair, which is an indeterminate and faded chestnut, there is a thin weave of dew. She wears dark glasses, and I cannot see her eyes.

I am not, on the afternoon we walk up Ceres Street, or even on the evening I first meet Thomas, a beautiful woman. I was never a pretty girl. As my mother once said, in a moment of honesty that I used to resent but now appreciate, my individual features were each lovely or passable in themselves, but somehow the parts had never formed an absolutely coherent whole. There is something mildly disturbing, I know, in the length of my face, the width of my brow. It is not an unpleasant face, but it is not a face that strangers turn to, have to see. As Thomas's is, for instance. Or Adaline's.

Thomas and I do not touch as we walk up Ceres Street. "She seems a pleasant person," I say.

"Yes, she does."

"Billie likes her."

"And Rich."

"He's good with kids."

"Excellent."

"She has a beautiful voice. It's interesting that she wears a cross."

"Her daughter gave it to her."

At the top of the street, Thomas pauses for a moment and says, "We could go back." I misunderstand him and say, looking at my watch, "We've only been gone ten minutes."

But he means, *We could go home.*

There are tourists on the street, people peering into shop windows. We reach the center of town, the market square, a church, a tiny mall with benches. We round the corner and come upon the facade of a tall, brick building. The windows are long and arched, multipaned. There is a discreet card in the window.

"That was an interesting game you were playing with Adaline," I say, studying the card for a moment.

"Not really," says Thomas. He leans in toward the window and squints at the sign.

"THE PORTSMOUTH ATHENAEUM," he reads. "READING ROOM OPEN TO THE PUBLIC." He examines the hours listed. He seems to study the card a long time, as though he were having trouble understanding it.

"Who was the poet?" I ask.

"Fallon Pearse."

I look down at my sandals, which are spotted with drops of oil from cooking in the kitchen at home. My jeans have stretched and wrinkled at the tops of my thighs.

"If any place would have archival photographs, this would be it," he says.

"What about Billie?" I ask. We both know, as Rich and Adaline do not, that even a half hour with Billie can be exhausting. All those questions, all that curiosity.

Thomas stands back and scans the building's height. "I'll go back and find Adaline," he says. "I'll give her a hand with Billie. You see if they've got what you need, and we'll meet back here in, say, an hour?"

Underneath my feet, the ground seems to roll slowly up and away as it sometimes does in children's cartoons.

"Whatever you think," I say.

Thomas peers into the front window as if he might recognize something beyond the drapes. With a casualness and tenderness I suddenly mistrust, he bends and kisses me on the cheek.

Some weeks after Thomas and I met each other in the bar in Cambridge, we parked my car by the waterfront in Boston and walked up a hill toward an expensive restaurant. Perhaps we were celebrating an anniversary — one month together. From the harbor, fog spilled into the street and around our feet. I had on high heels, Italian shoes that made me nearly as tall as Thomas. Behind me, I could hear a foghorn, the soothing hiss of tires on wet streets. It was raining lightly, and it seemed as though we would never make it up the hill to the restaurant, that we were walking as slowly as the fog was moving.

Thomas pressed in on my side. We had been at two bars, and his arm was slung around my shoulder rather more passionately than gracefully.

"You have a birthmark on the small of your back, just to the right of center," he said.

My heels clicked satisfyingly on the sidewalk. "If I have a birthmark," I said, "it's one I've never seen."

"It's shaped like New Jersey," he said.

I looked at him and laughed.

"Marry me," he said.

I pushed him away, as you would a drunk. "You're crazy," I said.

"I love you," he said. "I've loved you since the night I found you in my bed."

"How could you marry a woman who reminded you of New Jersey?"

"You know I've never worked better."

I thought about his working, the dozens of pages, the continuously stained fingers.

"It's all your doing," he said.

"You're wrong," I said. "You were ready to write these poems."

"You let me forgive myself. You gave this to me."

"No I didn't."

Thomas had on a blazer, his only jacket, a navy so dark it was nearly black. His white shirt seemed luminescent under the street lamp, and my eye was drawn to the place where his shirt met his belt buckle. I knew that if I put the flat of my hand there, the fabric of the shirt would be warm to the touch.

"I've only known you for a month," I said.

"We've been together every day. We've slept together every night."

"Is that enough?"

"Yes."

I knew that he was right. I put the flat of my hand against his white shirt at the belt buckle. The shirt was warm.

"You're drunk," I said.

"I'm serious," he said.

He pressed toward me, backing me insistently into an alleyway. Perhaps I made a small and ineffectual protest. In the alley, the tarmac shone from the wet. I was aware of a couple, not so very unlike myself and Thomas, walking arm in arm, just past the narrow opening of the alley. They glanced in at us with frightened faces as they passed. Thomas leaned all of his weight against me, and put his tongue inside my ear. The gesture made me shiver, and I turned my head. He put his mouth then on the side of my neck, licking the skin in long strokes, and suddenly I knew that in that posture he would come — deliberately — to show me that he had become helpless before me, that I was an alchemist. He would make of this an offering of the incontinence of his love. Or was it, I couldn't help but wonder, simply the abundance of his gratitude?

I am trying to remember. I am trying hard to remember what it felt like to feel love.

I enter the building with the tall, arched windows and shut the door behind me. I follow signs upstairs to the library. I knock on an unprepossessing metal door and then open it. The room before me is calm. It has thick ivory paint on the walls, and heavy wooden bookshelves. The feeling of serenity emanates from the windows.

There are two library tables and a desk where the librarian sits. He nods at me as I walk toward him. I am not sure what to say.

"Can I help you with something?" he asks. He is a small man with thinning brown hair and wire glasses. He wears a plaid sport shirt with short, crisp sleeves that stick out from his shoulders like moth's wings.

"I saw the sign out front. I'm looking for material on the murders that took place out at the Isles of Shoals in 1873."

"Smuttynose."

"Yes."

"Well . . . we have the archives."

"The archives?"

"The Isles of Shoals archives," he explains. "They were sent over from the Portsmouth Library, oh, a while ago. They're a mess, though. There's a great deal of material, and not much of it has been cataloged, I'm sorry to say. I could let you see some of it, if you want. We don't lend out materials here."

"That would be —"

"You'd have to pick an area. A subject."

"Old photographs," I say. "If there are any. Of people, of the island. And personal accounts of the time."

"That would be mostly in diaries and letters," he says. "Those that have come back to us."

"Yes. Letters then. And photographs."

"Have a seat over there at the table, and I'll see what I can do. We're very excited to have the archives, but as you can see, we're a bit short-staffed."

I have then an image of Thomas with Adaline and Billie. Each has a vanilla ice-cream cone. The three of them are licking the cones, trying to control the drips.

Thomas said, "I'll go find Adaline." He did not say, "I'll go find Adaline and Billie," or "Adaline and Rich."

The librarian returns with several books and folders of papers. I thank him and pick up one of the books. It is an old and worn volume, the brown silk binding of which has cracked. The pages are yellowed at the edges, and a few are loose. Images swim in front of me, making an array of new covers on the book. I shut my eyes and put the book to my forehead.

I look at an old geography of the Isles of Shoals. I read two guidebooks printed in the early half of the century. I take notes. I open another book and begin to riffle the pages. It is a book of recipes, *The Appledore Cookbook,* published in 1873. The recipes intrigue me: Quaking Pudding, Hash Made from Calf's Head and Pluck, Whitpot Pudding, Hop Yeast. What is pluck? I wonder.

From the folders the library has given me, papers slide out

onto the table, and I can see there is no order to them. Some papers are official documents from the town, licenses and such, while others are clearly bills of sale. Still other papers seem to be letters written on a stationery so fragile I am almost afraid to touch them. I look at the letters to decipher the old-fashioned penmanship, and with dismay I realize that the words are foreign. I see the dates: April 17, 1873; November 4, 1868; December 24, 1856; January 5, 1867.

There are a few photographs in the folders. One is a portrait of a family of seven. In the photograph, the father, who has a beard and a full head of hair, is wearing a waistcoat and a thick suit, like a captain of a ship might have. His wife, who has on a black dress with a white lace collar and lots of tiny white buttons, is quite plump and has her hair pulled severely back off her head. Everyone in the photograph, including the five children, appears grim and bug-eyed. This is because the photographer has had to keep the shutter open for at least a minute, during which time no one is allowed to blink. It is easier to maintain a serious expression for sixty seconds than it is a smile.

In one of the folders, various documents seem interspersed with students' papers and what look to be, to judge from the titles, sermons. There is also a faded, flesh-colored box, a box expensive writing paper might once have come in. Inside the box are pages of writing — spidery writing in brown ink. The penmanship is ornate, almost impossible to make out, even if the words were in English, which they are not. The paper is pink at the edges, slightly stained in one corner. A water stain, I think. Or perhaps even a burn. It smells of mildew. I stare at the flowery writing, which when looked at as a whole makes a lovely, calligraphic design, and as I lift the pages out of the box, I discover that a second set of papers, paper-clipped together, is at the bottom of the box. These pages are written in pencil, on white-lined paper, and bear many erasure marks, which have been written over. They also bear one purple date stamp and several notations: *Rec'd September 4, 1939, St. Olaf's College Library. Rec'd 14.2.40, Oslo, forwarded Marit Gullestad. Rec'd April 7, 1942, Portsmouth Library, Portsmouth, New Hampshire.*

I look at the first set of papers and the second. I note the date at the beginning of each document. I study the signature at the end of the foreign papers and compare it to the printed name at the end of those written in English.

Maren Christensen Hontvedt.

I read two pages of the penciled translation and set it on my lap. I look at the date stamp and the notations, which seem to tell a story of their own: the discovery of a document written in Norwegian; an attempt to have a translation made by someone at St. Olaf's College; the forwarding of that document to a translator in Oslo; the war intervening; the document and its translation belatedly sent to America and then relegated to a long-neglected folder in the Portsmouth Library. I take a deep breath and close my eyes.

Maren Hontvedt. The woman who survived the murders.

Maren Hontvedt's Document

TRANSLATED FROM THE NORWEGIAN BY MARIT GULLESTAD

19 September 1899, Laurvig

If it so please the Lord, I shall, with my soul and heart and sound mind, write the true and actual tale of that incident which continues to haunt my humble footsteps, even in this country of my birth, far from those forbidding, granite islands on which a most unforgivable crime was committed against the persons whom I loved most dearly in all the world. I write this document, not in defense of myself, for what defense have those who still live, and may breathe and eat and partake of the Lord's blessings, against those who have been so cruelly struck down and in such a way as I can hardly bear to recall? There is no defense, and I have no desire to put forth such. Though I must add here that I have found it a constant and continuous trial all these twenty-six years to have been, even by the most unscrupulous manner of persons, implicated in any small way in the horrors of 5 March 1873. These horrors have followed me across the ocean to my beloved Laurvig, which, before I returned a broken and barren woman, was untainted with any scandal, and was, for me, the pure and wondrous landscape of my most treasured childhood memories with my dear family, and which is where I will shortly die. And so I mean with these pages, written in my own hand, while there are some few wits remaining in my decrepit and weakening body, that the truth shall be known. I leave instructions for this document to be sent after my death into the care of John Hontvedt, who was once my husband and still remains so in the eyes of the Lord, and who resides at Sagamore Street in the town of Portsmouth in the state of New Hampshire in America.

The reader will need sometimes to forgive me in this self-imposed trial, for I find I am thinking, upon occasion, of strange and far-away occurrences, and am not altogether in control of my faculties and language, the former as a consequence of being fifty-two years of age and unwell, and the latter owing to my having completed my last years of schooling in an interrupted manner.

I am impatient to write of the events of 5 March 1873 (though I would not visit again that night for anything save the Lord's admonition), but I fear that the occurrences of which I must speak will be incomprehensible to anyone who has not understood what went before. By that I mean not only my own girlhood and womanhood, but also the life of the emigrant to the country of America, in particular the Norwegian emigrant, and most particularly still, the Norwegian emigrant who makes his living by putting his nets into the sea. More is known about those persons who left Norway in the middle of this century because the Norwegian land, even with all its plentiful fjords and fantastical forests, was, in many inhospitable parts of this country, unyielding to the ever-increasing population. Such dearth of land, at that time, refused to permit many households even a modest living in the farming of oats, barley, mangecorn and potatoes. It was these persons who left all they had behind, and who set intrepidly out to sea, and who did not stop on the Atlantic shores, but went instead directly inland to the state of New York, and hence from there into the prairie heartland of the United States of America. These are the emigrants of our Norway who were raised as farmers in the provinces of Stavanger and Bergen and Nedenes, and then abandoned all that they had held dear to begin life anew near the Lake of Michigan, and in the states of Minnesota and Wisconsin and in other states. The life of these emigrants was, I believe and am sorry to have to write, not always as they had imagined it to be, and I have read some of the letters from these wretched persons and have heard of the terrible hardships they had to bear, including, for some, the worst trial of all, the death of those they loved most, including children.

As I have not ever had children, I have been spared this most unthinkable of all losses.

In our village, which was Laurvig, and which was well coasted and had a lovely aspect out to the Laurvigsfjord and to the Skaggerak from many vantage points, some families who made their livings from the sea had gone to America before us. These persons were called "sloopfolk," as they had sailed in sloops in voyages of one to three months, during which some unfortunates perished, and some new life was born. John and I, who had been married but the year, had heard of such folk, though we did not have the acquaintance of any of these persons intimately, until that day in the seventh month of 1867, when a cousin of John's whose name was Torwad Holde, and who is since deceased, set sail for new fishing grounds near to the city of Gloucester, off the coast of the state of Massachusetts in America, fishing grounds that were said to hold forth promise of great riches to any and all who would set their nets there. I must add at this point that I did not believe in such fanciful and hollow promises, and would never have left Laurvig, had not John been, I shall have to say it, *seduced* by the letters of his cousin, Torwad, in particular one letter that I no longer have in my possession but remember in my heart as a consequence of having had to read this letter over and over again to my husband who had not had any schooling because of the necessity of having had to go to sea since the age of eight. I reproduce that letter here as faithfully as I can.

20 September 1867, the Isles of Shoals

My Dear Cousin,

You will be surprised to hear from me in a place different from that where I last wrote to you. I have moved north from the city of Gloucester. Axel Nordahl, who you may remember visited us last year, came to Gloucester to tell myself and Erling Hansen of the fishing settlement of which he was a part at a place called the Isles of Shoals. This is a small grouping of islands nine miles east of Portsmouth, New Hampshire, which is not far north of Gloucester. I am now residing with Nordahl and his good family on the island of Appledore, and I can report that he has a trawler here, and that he has found a bounty of fish such as I have never seen before in any waters. Indeed, I do not think there are any waters on earth that are so plentiful as these in which he has set his nets. A man can put his hand into this sea and fetch up, with his hand only, more fish than his boat might bear. I am firmly of a mind to remain here through the winter with Nordahl and then burden his family no more as I will build my own cottage on the island of Smutty-Nose, which has a strange name and which is also sometimes known as Haley's Island. When spring comes I will have saved enough dollars from my work with Nordahl to begin such a project. This is a better life, Hontvedt, than that which exists in Laurvig, or in Gloucester, where I was lodged with fifty other fishermen of the fleet and where my wages did not exceed one dollar a day.

I beg of you, John, to share this bounty with me. I beg of you to bring your brother, Matthew, who may be as pleased as I am to fish in these fertile waters. I have selected on this island called Smutty-Nose a house for you to lease. It is a good house, strongly built to withstand the Atlantic storms, and I might have taken up residence there myself if I had already had a family. In the spring, if the Lord permits me to find a wife, I shall move from Appledore so that we may all be a family in the Lord's sight.

If you come, as I am hoping, you must go by coastal ferry to Stavanger, and thence to Shields, England. There you will take the rail to Liverpool where you will join a great flood of emigrants who will take passage with you on a packet to Quebec, where ships are landing now, preferring to avoid the higher tariffs charged in Boston and New York. For your voyage, you will want fruit wine to alter the taste of the poor water, and dried fish. Grind some coffee and put it in a box. You will also want to bake the flatbrød and pack it in the round tubs you have seen down at the docks, and also cure some cheese. If you have a wife and she is with child, then come before it is her time, as infants do not well survive the journey. Seven perished on my own passage, owing to the diphtheria croup which was a contagion on board. I will tell you in truth, Hontvedt, that the sanitary conditions aboard these ships are very poor, and it is too bad, but on my journey I was well disposed to prayer and to thinking of the voyage as a deliverance. I was seasick all but the last two days, and though I arrived in America very gaunt and thin, and remained so in Gloucester, now I am fat again, thanks to the cooking of Nordahl's wife, Adda, who feeds me good porridge and potato cakes with all the fresh fish you can imagine.

When you are here, we may together purchase a trawler in the town of Portsmouth. Send me news and greet all my friends there, my mother, and all soskend.

Your cousin and servant unto death, Torwad Holde

May God forgive me, but I confess that I have truly hated the words of Torwad Holde's letter and even the man himself, and I do so wish that this cursed letter had never come into our house.

It was an evil missive indeed that stole my husband's common sense, that took us from our homeland, and that eventuated in that terrible night of 5 March. Would that this letter, with its stories I could not credit, this letter that bore with its envelope strange and frightening stamps, this letter with its tales so magical I knew they must be lies, been dropped into the Atlantic Ocean during its transit from America to Norway.

But I digress. Even with the distance of thirty-one years, it is possible for me to become overwrought, knowing as I do what came later, what was to follow, and how this letter led us to our doom. Yet even in a state of distress, I must admit to understanding that a mere piece of paper can not be the instrument of one's undoing. In John, my husband, there was a yearning for adventure, for more than was his lot in Laurvig, desires I did not share with him, so content was I to be still near my family. And also, I must confess, there had been that summer, in the Skaggerak and even in the Kristianiafjord, a fish plague that had greatly lessened the number of mackerel available to the fisher-folk, and though not a consequence of this, but rather as a result of the importation of fish from Denmark, a simultaneous lowering of the price of herring in Kristiania, which caused my husband, in a more practical manner, to look toward new fishing grounds.

But bringing up a living fish with one's bare hands? Who could be such a blasphemer as to put forth such lies against the laws of nature?

"I will not go to America," I said to Evan on the landing at Laurvig on 10 March 1868.

I believe I spoke in a quavering voice, for I was nearly overcome by a tumult of emotions, chief among them an acute distress at having to leave my brother, Evan Christensen, behind, and not knowing if I would see him or my beloved Norway ever again. The smell of fish from the barrels on the landing was all around us, and we could as well distinguish the salted pork in wooden cases. We had had to step cautiously to the landing, as all about us the rod iron lay for loading onto the ship, and to my eye, this disarray seemed to have been made by a large hand, that is to say by the hand of God, Who had strewn about the pier these long and rusty spokes. I believe that I have so well remembered the sight of this cargo because I did not want to look up that day at the vessel which would carry me away from my home.

I must say that even today I remain quite certain that souls which take root in a particular geography cannot be successfully transplanted. I believe that these roots, these tiny fibrous filaments, will almost inevitably dry and wither in the new soil, or will send the plant into sudden and irretrievable shock.

Evan and I came to a stopping place amidst the terrible noise and chaos. All about us were sons taking leave of their mothers, sisters parting from sisters, husbands from young wives. Is there any other place on earth so filled with sweet torment as that of a ship's landing? For a time, Evan and myself stood together in silence. The water from the bay hurt my eyes, and a gust came upon us and billowed my skirt which had become muddied at the hem on the walk to the landing. I beat my fists against the silk, which was a walnut and was cinched becomingly at the waist, until Evan, who was considerably taller than myself, stayed my hands with his own.

"Hush, Maren, calm yourself," he said to me.

I took my breath in, and was near to crying, and might have but for the example of my brother who was steadfast and of great character and who would not show, for all the earth, the intense emotions that were at riot in his breast. My dress, I have neglected to say, was my wedding dress and had a lovely collar of tatting that my sister, Karen, had made for me. And I should mention as well that Karen had not come to the landing to say her farewells as she had been feeling poorly that morning.

The gusts, such as the one that had whipped up my skirt,

turned severe, spiriting caps away and pushing back the wide brims of the bonnets on the women. I could hear the halyards of the sloops slapping hard against their masts, and though the day was fair, that is to say though the sky was a deep and vivid navy, I thought the gusts might presage a gale and that I would be granted a reprieve of an hour or a day, as the captain, I was certain, would not set sail in such a blow. In this, however, I was mistaken, for John, my husband, who had been searching for me, raised his face and beckoned me toward the ship. I saw, even at a distance, that relief softened his squint, and I know that he had been afraid I might not come to the landing at all. Our passage had been paid already — sixty dollars — but I had, for just a moment, the lovely and calming image of two berths, two flat and tiered berths, sailing empty without us.

Evan, beside me, sensing that the fury had left my arms, released my hands. But though my wretchedness had momentarily abandoned me, my sorrow had not.

"You must go with John," he said to me. "He is your husband."

I pause now as if for breath. It is very difficult for me to write, even three decades later, of my family, who was so cruelly treated by fate.

In our family, Karen was born first and was some twelve years older than myself. She was, it must be said, a plain woman with a melancholy aspect, which I have always understood is sometimes appealing to men, as they do not wish a wife who is so beautiful or lively that she causes in her husband a constant worry, and our Karen was strong, an obedient daughter, and a skilled seamstress as well.

I see us now sitting at my father's table in the simple but clean room that was our living room and dining room and kitchen and where also Karen and I slept behind a curtain, and where we had a stove that gave off a great deal of heat and always made us comfortable (although sometimes, in the winter, the milk froze in the cupboard), and I am struck once again by how extraordinarily different I was from my sister, for whom I had a fond, though I must confess not passionate, regard. Karen had dun eyes that seldom seemed to change their color. She had had the misfortune, from a young age, to have fawn-colored hair, a dull brown that was not tinged with golden highlights nor ever warmed by the sun, and I remember that every day she fixed it in exactly the same manner, which is to say pulled severely behind her ears, with a fringe at her forehead, and rolled and fastened at the back of her head. I am not certain I ever saw Karen with her hair free and loose except for those occasions when I happened to observe her make herself ready for bed. Normally, Karen, who had great difficulty sleeping, was late to bed and early to rise, and I came to think of her as keeping a kind of watch over our household. Karen did have, however, an excellent figure, and was broad in her shoulders and erect in her posture. She was a tall woman, some five inches taller than myself. I was, if not diminutive, then small in my proportions. Like Karen, I too had broad shoulders, but perhaps a less plain face than hers when I was twenty. I did not possess, however, her obedience, nor her excellence as a seamstress. Though I would say otherwise at the time, I took a foolish pride in this when I was a girl, preferring the world of nature and imagination to that of cloth and needle, and I know that in my heart I set myself up as the more fortunate of us two, and I believed at the time that if ever I should have a husband, he would be a man who would be drawn to a woman not solely for her domestic skills, which has always seemed to be the measure of a woman, but also for her conversation.

In our family there was only the one other child besides Karen and me, Evan, my brother, who was two years older than myself, and so it happened that we were raised as one, so close were we in age, and so far from Karen. At that time, there were many deprivations visited upon the fisher-folk. Because of the shortness of the fishing season near to our home, our father, in order to feed his family, had sometimes to leave us for months at a time during the winter, to fish not by himself in his skiff, which he preferred and which better suited his independent nature, but rather to join the fishing fleets that sailed along the west coast and further north after the cod and the herring. When our situation was very bad, or it had been a particularly harsh winter, my mother and sometimes my sister had to hire themselves out for washing and for cooking in the boarding house for sailors on the Storgata in Laurvig.

But I must here dispel the image of the Christensen family in rude circumstances, hungry and in poverty, for in truth, though we had little in the way of material goods in my early childhood years, we had our religion, which was a comfort, and our schooling, when we could make our way along the coast road into Laurvig, and we had family ties for which in all my years on this earth I have never found a replacement.

The cottage in which we lived was humble but of a very pleasing aspect. It was of wood, painted white, and with a red-tiled roof, as was the custom. It had a small porch with a railing in the front, and one window, to the south, that was made of colored glass. In the rear of our home was a small shed for storing nets and barrels, and in front there was a narrow beach where our father, when we were younger, kept his skiffs.

How many times I have had in my mind the image of leaving Laurvig, and seeing from the harbor, along the coast road, our own cottage and others like it, one and a half stories tall, with such a profusion of blossoms in the gardens around them. This area in Norway, which is in the southeastern part of the country, facing to Sweden and Denmark, has a mild climate and good soil for orchards and other plants such as myrtle and fuchsia, which were in abundance then and are now. We had peaches from a tree in our garden, and though there were months at a time when I had only the one woolen dress and only one pair of woolen socks, we had

fruit to eat and fresh or dried fish and the foods that flour and water go together to make, such as porridge and pancakes and lefse.

I possess so very many wonderful memories of those days of
my extreme youth that sometimes they are more real to me than
the events of last year or even of yesterday. A child who may
grow to adulthood with the sea and the forest and the orchards at
hand may count himself a very lucky child indeed.

Before we had reached the age when we were allowed to go to
school, Evan and I had occasion to spend a great deal of time together, and I believe that because of this we each understood that
in some indefinable manner our souls, and hence our paths, were
to be inextricably linked, and perhaps I knew already that whatever fate might befall the one would surely befall the other. And
as regards the outside world, that is to say the world of nature
(and the people and spirits and animals who inhabited that tangi-
ble world), each of us was for the other a filter. I remember with
a clarity that would seem to be extraordinary after so many years
(these events having occurred at such a young age) talking with
Evan all the long days and into the nights (for is not a day actually
longer when one is a child, time being of an illusory and deceptive nature?) as if we were indeed interpreting for each other and
for ourselves the mysterious secrets and truths of life itself.

We were bathed together in a copper tub that was brought out
once a week and set upon a stand in the kitchen near to the stove.
My father bathed first, and then my mother, and then Karen, and
lastly, Evan and me together. Evan and I were fearful of our father's nakedness and respectful of our mother's modesty, and so
we busied ourselves in another room during the times when our
parents used the copper tub. But no such restraints had yet descended upon us as regards our sister, Karen, who would have
been, when I was five, seventeen, and who possessed most of the
attributes of a grown woman, attributes that both frightened and
amazed me, although I cannot say it was with any reverence for

her person that Evan and I often peeked behind the curtain and made rude sounds and in this way tortured our sister, who would scream at us from the tub and, more often than not, end the evening in tears. And thus I suppose I shall have to admit here that Evan and myself, while not cruel or mischievous by nature or necessarily to anyone else in our company, were sometimes moved to torment and tease our sister, because it was, I think, so easy to do and at the same time so enormously, if unforgivably, rewarding.

When our turn for the bath had come, we would have clean water that had been heated by our mother in great pots and then poured into the copper tub, and my brother and myself, who until a late age had no shame between us, would remove our clothing and play in the hot soapy water as if in a pool in the woods, and I remember the candlelight and warmth of this ritual with a fondness that remains with me today.

Each morning of the school year, when we were younger and not needed to be hired out, Evan and I rode together in the wagon of our nearest neighbor, Torjen Helgessen, who went every day into Laurvig to bring his milk and produce to market, and home again each afternoon after the dinner hour. The school day was five hours long, and we had the customary subjects of religion, Bible History, catechism, reading, writing, arithmetic and singing. We had as our texts Pontoppidan's Explanation, Vogt's Bible History and Jensen's Reader. The school was a modern one in many of its aspects. It had two large rooms, one above the other, each filled with wooden desks and a chalkboard that ran the length of one wall. Girls were in the lower room and boys in the upper. Unruly behavior was not allowed, and the students of Laurvig School received the stick when necessary. My brother had it twice, once for throwing chalk erasers at another student, and once for being rude to Mr. Hjorth, a Pietist and thus an extremely strict and sometimes irritating man, who later died during an Atlantic crossing as a result of the dysentery aboard.

In the springtime, when it was light early in the morning, and this was a pearly light that is not known in America, an oyster light that lasts for hours before the sun is actually up, and so has about it a diffuse and magical quality, Evan and I would wake at daybreak and walk the distance into Laurvig to the school.

I can hardly describe to you the joy of those early morning walks together, and is it not true that in our extreme youth we possess the capacity to see more clearly and absorb more intensely the beauty that lies all before us, and so much more so than in our later youth or in our adulthood, when we have been apprised of sin and its stain and our eyes have become dulled, and we cannot see with the same purity, or love so well?

The coast road hugged at times the very edge of the cliffs and overlooked the Bay, so that on a fine day, to the east of us, there would be the harbor, with its occasional schooners and ferries, and beyond it the sea twitching so blindingly we were almost forced to turn our eyes away.

As we walked, Evan would be wearing his trousers and a shirt without a collar and his jacket and his cap. He wore stockings that Karen or my mother had knit, wonderful stockings in a variety of intricate patterns, and he carried his books and dinner sack, and sometimes also mine, in a leather strap which had been fashioned from a horse's rein. I myself, though just a girl, wore the heavy dresses of the day, that is to say those of domestic and homespun manufacture, and it was always a pleasure in the late spring when our mother allowed me to change the wool dress for a calico that was lighter in weight and in color and made me feel as though I had just bathed after a long and oppressive confinement. At that time, I wore my hair loose along my back, with the sides pulled into a topknot. I may say here that my hair was of a lovely color in my youth, a light and soft brown that picked up the sun in summer, and was sometimes, by August, golden near the front, and I had fine, clear eyes of a light gray color. As I have mentioned, I was not a tall girl, but I did have a good carriage and figure, and though I was never a great beauty, not like Anethe, I trust I was pleasant to look upon, and perhaps even pretty for several years in my late youth, before the true responsibilities of my journey on earth began and altered, as it does in so many women, the character of the face.

I recall one morning when Evan and myself would have been eight and six years of age respectively. We had gone perhaps three quarters of the way to town when my brother quite suddenly put down his books and dinner sack and threw off his jacket and cap as well, and in his shirt and short pants raised his arms and leapt up to seize a branch of an apple tree that had just come fully into bloom, and I suspect that it was the prospect of losing himself in all that white froth of blossoms that propelled Evan higher and higher so that in seconds he was calling to me from the very apex of the tree. *Hallo, Maren, can you see me?* For reasons I cannot accurately describe, I could not bear to be left behind on the ground, and so it was with a frenzy of determination that I tried to repeat Evan's acrobatics and make a similar climb to the height of the fruit tree. I discovered, however, that I was encumbered by the skirts of my dress, which were weighing me down and would not permit me to grab hold of the tree limbs with my legs in a shimmying fashion, such as I had just witnessed Evan performing. It was, then, with a gesture of irritation and perhaps anger at my sex, that I stripped myself of my frock, along that most travelled of public roads into Laurvig, stripped myself down to my underclothes, which consisted of a sleeveless woolen vest and a pair of unadorned homespun bloomers, and thus was able in a matter of minutes to join my brother at the top of the tree, which gave a long view of the coastline, and which, when I had reached Evan, filled me with a sense of freedom and accomplishment that was not often repeated in my girlhood. I remember that he smiled at me and said, "Well done," and that shortly after I had reached Evan's perch, I leaned forward in my careless ebullience to see north along the Laurvigsfjord, and, in doing so, lost my balance and nearly fell out of the tree, and almost certainly would have done had not Evan grabbed hold of my wrist and righted me. And I recall that he did not remove his hand, but rather stayed with me in that position, his hand upon my wrist, for a few minutes more, as we could not bear to disturb that sensation of peace and completeness that had come over us, and so it happened that we were both late for school on that day and were chastised by having to remain after school for five days in a row, a detention neither of us minded or complained about as I think we both felt the stricture to be pale reprimand for the thrilling loveliness of the crime. Of course, we had been fortunate that all the time we had been in the tree no farmer had come along the road and seen my frock in the dirt, a shocking sight in itself, and which doubtless would have resulted in our capture and quite likely a more severe punishment of a different nature.

At school, Evan was well liked, but though he did join in the games, he did not take extra pains to become popular in the manner of some boys of the town. He was not a boy, or ever a man, who was filled with anger or resentments as some are, and if a wrong was done to him, he needed only to correct it, not exact a punishment for the crime. (Though I am sorry to say that Evan was eventually to learn, as were we all, that there was no righting of the ultimate wrong that was done to him.) In this way, I do not think I have measured up to him in character, for I have often felt myself in the sway of intense emotions that are sinful in their origin, including those of anger and hatred.

Evan was always substantially taller than myself, and for a time was the tallest boy in the Laurvig school. Although he had slightly crooked teeth in the front, he developed a handsome face that I believe resembled our father's, though, of course, I never saw my father as a younger man, and by the time I was old enough for such impressions to register, my father's cheeks were sunken and there were many wrinkles on his face, this as a consequence of the weathering that occurred at sea and was a feature of most fishermen of that time.

When our schooling was finished for the year, we often had the long days together, and this was the very greatest of joys, for the light stayed with us until nearly midnight in the midsummer.

I see us now as if I were looking upon my own self. In the woods, just west of where our home was situated, there was a little-visited and strange geographic phenomenon known as Hakon's Inlet, a pool of seawater that was nearly black as a consequence of both its extraordinary depth and of the sheer black rock that formed the edges of the pool and rose straight up to a height of thirty feet on all sides, so that this pool was, with the exception of a narrow fissure through which seawater flowed, a tall, dark cylinder. It was said to be twenty fathoms deep, and along its walls were thin ledges that one, with some practice, could navigate to reach the water and thus swim, or fish, or even lower a boat and paddle about. Yellow stone crop grew in the fissure, and it was altogether a most magical place.

At this pool, on a June morning, I see a small girl of eight years of age, who is standing on a ledge, holding her dress above the water, revealing her knees and not caring much, as there had not yet been between herself and her brother any loss of innocence, nor indeed any need for false modesty on the part of either, and beyond her, perched upon a nearby shelf of rock, with a rudimentary fishing pole in his hands, her brother, Evan. He is smiling at her because she has been teasing him in a pleasant manner about the fact that he has grown so tall that his pants rise a good inch above his ankles. He is, upon his rock, the embodiment of all that Norwegian parents might wish in their boys, a tall and strong youth, with the thin pale hair that we have come in this country to favor so, and eyes the color of water. Presently, the boy puts down his fishing pole and takes from his sack a small dark object that he quickly flings out over the water, and which reveals itself to be a net of the finest threads, intricately woven, a gauze, more like, or a web of gossamer, catching the light of the sun's rays that hover and seem to stop just above the surface of the pool. The girl, intrigued, makes her way to the ledge on which the boy is standing and sees that the net is large and comments upon this, whereupon the boy tells her that he has made it deep so that it will sink low into the pool and bring up from its depths all manner of sea creatures. The girl watches with fascination as the boy, who has had a not inconsequential amount of experience with fishing nets, and who has fashioned the present one from threads from his mother's sewing cabinet, expertly spreads the net over the surface of the black water and allows it, with its weighted sinks, to lower itself until only the bobbers at the four corners are visible. Then, with a deft movement of his body, and indicating that the girl should follow him, he hops from ledge to ledge, dragging the gathering net behind him. After a time, he lets the bobbers float closer to the wall of the pool, where he then snags them and slowly brings up the net. He hauls his catch up onto the ledge on which the pair are standing and opens it for their inspection. In the net are wriggling bits and sacs of color the girl has never seen before. Many of these sea creatures have lovely iridescent colorings, but some appear to her grotesque in texture, like mollusks without their shells. Some are translucent shapes that reveal working innards; others are heaving gills flecked with gold or round fat fish with bulging eyes or simple dark slivers the color of lead. Some of the fish the girl recognizes: a sea bass, a codfish, several mackerel.

But the girl is frightened by the grotesque display, and is fearful that the boy has perhaps trespassed in the unnatural world, and has brought up from the black pool living things not meant to be seen or to see the light of day, and, indeed, some small peacock-blue gelatinous spheres begin to pop and perish there upon the ledge.

"Maren, do you see?" the boy asks excitedly, pointing to this fish and to that one, but the girl is both attracted and repulsed by the catch, wanting to tear her head away, yet not able to, when suddenly the boy picks up the four corners of the net and upends the catch into the water, not realizing that the girl's foot is on a part of the net, whereupon the gossamer tears and catches on the girl's bare ankle, and with one swooping movement, she plunges into the water, believing that she might kick the net away whenever she wants to, and then discovers in a panic (that even now I can taste at the back of my throat) that both feet have become entangled in the threads and the skirt of her dress has become weighted with water. In addition, in her fright, she is surrounded by the sealife that had been in the net, some of which swims away, and some of which floats near to her face. She flails with her arms and tries to swim, but cannot find a suitable ledge to hang on to. And Evan, who sees that his sister is in great distress, jumps into the water after her, caring little for his own safety, but greatly concerned for hers. I can hear my voice that is filled with the utmost terror, calling out *Help!*, and then again, *Help!*, and Evan's voice, not yet broken and matured, a melodious voice that was most welcome at the Christmas Hymns each year, calling out, *I'll get you, Maren.* I remember now the strength of his hand under my chin, holding my mouth above the water so that I could breathe, while he splashed about most terribly and took in a great deal of water himself, and was as panicked as I, though he would never say so later. It was only by the greatest good fortune that we drifted, in this agitated state, across the pool, to a ledge a meter above the water and that Evan, by the grace of God and by a strength not commonly known to children of that age, grasped that ledge with his free hand and thus saved us both.

I remember that we lay upon the rocky shelf, clasped in each other's arms, for a long time afterward, and it was only after many minutes in such a position that I was able to stop shivering.

I think now upon that day and imagine another fate. A fisherman coming upon the inlet and seeing two children, locked together in embrace, floating just below the surface of the black water, forever free, forever peaceful, and I wonder now if that might not have been a more desirable end for both of us.

In our cottage by the sea, our mother had hung gay curtains of a red-checked cloth, and on our table, there was always, in season, a small glass milk pitcher of flowers that had come from the garden that surrounded the cottage, and for many years after our mother had died, I could not look at a vessel of flowers on a table without thinking of her. I am troubled now that I have primarily indistinct memories of my mother, whom I loved, but who was drawn in her aspect and often so tired as to be unwell. She was, like myself, a small woman who had a great many physical tasks to attend to, and who was not, I believe, of a sufficient fortitude to withstand these burdens. Also I believe that whatever love she did not reserve for her husband, she felt for her son, and in this she could not help herself.

In the evenings, I might be sent to bed while my mother spoke in low tones to Evan. About these talks, Evan would only say that they were often stories or homilies about virtues of character and defects of same, and that our mother had shown herself to be not religious in her beliefs, which at that time surprised me, as Evan and I and also Karen were required to spend almost all of Sunday in our church.

As to why I was excluded from these talks, my mother must have felt that either my character had already been formed and therefore such homilies were unnecessary, or that these talks in the night would be lost on a girl who would, by nature and by custom, submit herself to her husband's beliefs and character when she married. I am pleased to say that though marriage often constrained my actions, my character and my beliefs, both of which were molded by influences far stronger than the fisherman who became my husband, remained intact and unchallenged for the duration of my years with John Hontvedt. I will add, however, that an unfortunate result of these private talks between my mother and my brother was that I was hard-pressed to disbelieve the notion that of the two of us, Evan was the more greatly loved, and in some way I could not articulate or account for, the more deserving of this love, and thus my own affection for my brother was not compromised but rather enhanced by this exclusionary affection of which I so desperately wanted to be a part.

My mother sat by the table in the evenings when her presence was not required in town, and sewed or made bread for the next day. When I remember her in this way, I see her as in the thrall of a quiet sorrow, not the dreary if not altogether sour melancholy that Karen was sometimes possessed of, but rather a weight upon her spirit that she bore uncomplainingly and in an unobtrusive manner. Perhaps she was not ever really well and simply never told us this. When our father was home, he would sit near to her, mending his nets or just silently smoking his pipe, and though they seldom spoke, I would sometimes catch him regarding her with admiration, although I don't believe the possibility of romantic love between our mother and our father ever consciously occurred to me until I had occasion to witness our father's demeanor after our mother had died.

When I was thirteen years of age, and Evan just fifteen, our mother perished, giving birth to a stillborn child who was buried with her. It was in the worst winter month of 1860, and the environs of Laurvig, and indeed the entire coast region, had been buried with the snows of that year. On the day that my mother perished, there was, in the early hours of the morning, when she had just begun her labor, a wild blizzard of snow so thick it was impossible to see out the windows. My father, who had not been present for the births of his other three children, as he had been at sea during those occasions, did not feel qualified to attend to such an event, and therefore hastened, even in the terrible storm, to fetch the midwife who lived between our cottage and the town, and might be reached if the sleigh, belonging to our neighbor, Mr. Helgessen, could be fetched and could make the passage. Karen, who might have been able to help our mother, was residing that night at the boarding house for sailors, where it was thought she should stay during the storm. Thus myself and Evan, who were too young to help in this matter, except insofar as we could put ice on our mother's brow, wipe her head and arms when it was necessary, and hold her hand when she would let us, stood beside her listening to her terrible cries. I had had until that moment no experience of childbirth, and I had never seen such torment in any individual. I remember that in the candlelight Evan stood shivering with fear in his nightshirt, believing that our mother's agony was a certain sign that she would die. He began to cry out most awfully, although he wished that he would not, and I became distraught at the sight of Evan's crying, since he had always been a strong and undemonstrative boy, and I believe now that I was more distressed at the sound of his weeping, at least momentarily, than I was at the unspeakable rhythmic cries from our mother, and that I may have left my mother's side to tend to him, holding him with thin arms that barely reached around him, kissing his tear-ruined face to soothe him, to stop his shivering, so that when, startled by the sudden silence, I looked back at our mother, I saw that she was gone. A large pool of blood had soaked the bedclothes from her stomach to her knees, and I dared not lift the sheets for fear of what lay beneath them. I think that possibly I may have closed her eyes. My father could not reach the midwife and was forced to turn back. When he finally returned to our house, nearly dead himself, the event was finished.

I remember his hoarse shout when he entered the cottage and saw what lay before him. I remember also that I had not the strength to leave Evan, and that I could not go out into the living room to console my father. When finally our father came into our bedroom, with his face blasted by the sight of his beloved wife taken from him in such a violent manner, he found Evan and myself in our bed, holding each other for comfort.

I would not for all the world speak of such gruesome matters except that I have always wondered if I might not have attended to my mother in some better way and thus perhaps have saved her. And I have wondered as well if my memories of this terrible night, or my actions, have been the cause of my barren state in my own womanhood, as if I had been punished by God for not allowing the birth of my sibling.

I remained, for some months after this event, in an agitated state of mind. Indeed, I grew worse and was overtaken by a mysterious malady. I do not remember all of this time very well, but I was told about it often enough by Karen, who was, during those long and dark days, in despair over our mother's death and my illness. Unable to sleep at night, or if I did sleep, subject to the most excruciatingly horrible dreams, and without any medicines that might be a remedy to me, I became weakened and then ill, and from there slipped into a fever that appeared to all around me to have a psychic rather than physical origin. At least that was the opinion of the doctor who was fetched more than once from Laurvig, and who was at a loss to describe the root cause of my symptoms. I recall that for a time I could not move either my legs or my arms, and it was thought that I might have caught the meningitis, even though there were no other reported cases in our area that season. Because I was so incapacitated, I could not feed myself. Karen, having more than her share to do about the house as a result of my being bedridden, left this chore to Evan, who nursed me uncomplainingly, and I believe that he was in a kind of torment himself, owing to the events that had occurred on the night that our mother had died.

There were entire days when I could not speak and had to be held up in a half-sitting position just to take a sip of Farris water, which was thought to be therapeutic. I was moved for the duration of my illness to my father's bed near to the stove in the living room, while my father took up residence in the room that I had shared with Evan. My brother made a vigil at my bedside. I believe he sat there not speaking for much of the time, but he may have read to me from the folk tales as well. During this time Evan did not attend school.

I was not always lucid during my illness, but there is one incident I remember with absolute clarity, and which has remained with me in all its wonder and complexity.

I had just awakened from a dream-like state one morning some months into the illness. Karen was outside in the garden, and there were daffodils in a pitcher on the table. It must have been late April or early May following my mother's death. Previously, when I had awakened and was emerging from one of my dreams, I had felt frightened, for the feelings of the illness would flood into me and I would be visited by the strangest waking visions, which seemed very real to me at the time, and were all against the tenets of God. But that morning, though I was again beset with such visions, I did not feel fear, but rather a kind of all-encompassing forgiveness, not only of those around me, but of myself. Thus it happened that in the first seconds of consciousness that morning, I impulsively reached for Evan's hand. He was sitting in a wooden chair, his back very straight, his face solemn. Perhaps he himself had been far away when I awakened, or possibly he had been yearning to go outside on that fine day himself. When I put my hand on his, he flinched, for we had not willfully touched since the night that our mother had perished. In truth, I would have to say that he looked stricken when I first touched him, though I believe that this was a consequence of his worry over my health and his surprise at my awakening.

I remember that he had on a blue shirt that Karen had recently washed and ironed. His hair, which had been combed for the morning, had become even paler over the past year and accentuated the watery blue of his eyes.

His hand did not move in mine, and I did not let him go.

"Maren, are you well?" he asked.

I thought for a moment and then answered, "I feel very well indeed."

He shook his head as though throwing off some unbidden thought, and then looked down at our hands.

"Maren, we must do something," he said.

"Do something?"

"Speak to someone. I don't know . . . I have tried to think."

"I don't know what you mean," I said to him.

Evan appeared to be irritated by this admission.

"But you must do," he said. "I know you do." He looked up quickly and allowed his eyes to meet mine.

I believe that wordlessly, in those few moments, we spoke of many things. His hand grew hot under mine, or perhaps it was simply my own fever, and, just as I could not pull away, neither could he, and for some minutes, perhaps even for many minutes, we remained in that state, and if it is possible to say, in a few moments, even without words, all that has to be said between two individuals, this was done on that day.

After a time (I cannot accurately say how long this occurrence took place), I sat up, and in a strange manner, yet one which on that day seemed as natural to me as a kiss upon a baby's cheek, I put my lips to the inside of his wrist, which was turned upward to me. I remained in that position, in a state of neither beginning nor ending a kiss, until that moment when we heard a sound at the door and looked up to see that our sister, Karen, had come in from the garden.

I remember the bewildered look that came upon her face, a look of surprise and darkening all at once, so that she frightened me, and a sound escaped my throat, and Evan, leaving me, stood up. Karen said to me, although I think not to Evan, *What is it that you do?* To which question I could no more have made an answer than I could have explained to her the mystery of the sacraments. Evan left the room, and I do not believe that he spoke. Karen came to me and hovered over my bed, examining me, her hair pulled tightly back off her head, her dress with its shell buttons rising to her throat, and I remember thinking to myself that though the wondrous forgiveness I had so recently felt encompassed everyone around me, I did not really like Karen much, and I felt a pity for her I had not consciously realized before. I believe I closed my eyes then and drifted back into that state from which I had only a short time earlier emerged.

Not long after that incident, I recovered my health. Never was anyone so glad to greet the lustrous mornings of that spring, though I was quickly advised by Karen that my childhood was now over and that I would have to assume the responsibilities and demeanor of a young woman. Around that time, perhaps even immediately after my illness, it was decided that I would remain sleeping with Karen in the kitchen behind the curtain, and that our father would permanently take up the bed I had shared with Evan. This was because I had reached, during my illness, the age of fourteen, and that while I had been sick there had been certain changes in my body, which I will not speak of here, which made it necessary for me to move out of a room that Evan slept in.

Our mother having died, and our father out at sea for most of the hours in his day, I was put under the care of our sister, who was dutiful in her watch, but who I do not think was ever suited for the job. Sensing something, I know not what, a reluctance on her part perhaps, I was sometimes a torment to her, and I have often, in the years that have since passed, wished that I might have had her forgiveness for this. To her constrictions I gave protest, thus causing her to put me under her discipline until such time as I did not have so much freedom as before.

I would not like to attribute the loss of my liberty, my uncompromised happiness, to the coming of my womanhood, and I believe it is merely a coincidence of timing, but I was, nevertheless, plagued with extremely severe monthly pains, which may have had, at their root, the more probable cause of my barrenness.

I must stop now, for these memories are disturbing me, and my eyes are hurting.

WHEN I LOOK at photographs of Billie, I can see that she is there — her whole self, the force of her — from the very beginning. Her infant face is intricately formed — solemn, yet willing to be pleased. Her baby hair is thick and black, which accentuates the navy of her eyes. Even then she has extraordinarily long lashes that charm me to the bottom of my soul and stop passersby on the street. Our friends congratulate me for having produced such a beguiling creature, but inwardly I protest. Was I not merely a custodian — a fat, white cocoon?

In the first several weeks after Billie's birth, Thomas and Billie and I inhabited a blur of deepening concentric circles. At the perimeter was Thomas, who sometimes spun off into the world of students and the university. He bought groceries, wrote at odd hours, and looked upon his daughter as a mystifying and glorious interruption of an ordered life. He carried Billie around in the crook of his arm and talked to her continuously. He introduced her to the world: "This is a chair; this is my table at the diner." He took her — zipped into the front of his leather jacket, her cheek resting against his chest or her head bobbing beneath his chin — on his daily walks through the streets of the city. He seemed, for a time, a less extraordinary man, less preoccupied, more like the cliché of a new father. This perception was reassuring to me, and I think to Thomas as well. He discovered in himself a nurturing streak that was comforting to him, one that he couldn't damage and from which he couldn't distance himself with images and words. For a time, after Billie was born, Thomas drank less. He believed, briefly, in the future. His best work was behind him, but he didn't know that then.

In the middle circle were the three of us, each hovering near the other. We lived, as we had since Thomas and I were married, in the top half of a large, brown-stained, nineteenth-century house on a back street in Cambridge. Henry James once lived next door and e. e. cummings across the street. The neighborhood, thought Thomas, had suitable resonance. I put Billie in a room that used to be my office, and the only pictures I took then were of Billie. Sometimes I slept; sometimes Thomas slept; Billie slept a lot. Thomas and I came together in sudden, bewildered clutches. We ate at odd hours, and we watched late-night television programs we had never seen before. We were a protoplasmic mass that was becoming a family.

And in the center circle — dark and dream-like — was the nest of Billie and myself. I lay on the bed, and I folded my daughter into me like bedclothes. I stood at the window overlooking the back garden and watched her study her hands. I stretched out on the floor and placed my daughter on my stomach and examined her new bright eyes. Her presence was so intensely vivid to me, so all-consuming, that I could not imagine who she would be the next day. I couldn't even remember what she had looked like the day before. Her immediate being pushed out all the other realities, blotted out other pictures. In the end, the only images I would retain of Billie's babyhood were the ones that were in the photographs.

At the Athenaeum, I put the papers back into the flesh-colored box and set it on the library table. I fold my hands on top of it. The librarian has left the room. I am wondering how the material can have been allowed to remain in such a chaotic state. I don't believe the Athenaeum even knows what it has. I suppose I am thinking that I will simply take the document and its translation and then bring them back the following week after I have photo-copied them. No one will ever know. Not so very different, I am thinking, from borrowing a book from a lending library.

I put the loose letters, photographs, sermons, and official doc-uments back into the folder and eye it, trying to judge how it looks without the box. I put the three books I have been given on top of the folder to camouflage the loss. I study the pile.

I cannot do it.

I put the box back inside the folder and stand up. *Goodbye,* I say, and then, just as I am leaving, in a somewhat louder voice, *Thanks.* I open the metal door and walk evenly down the stairs.

When I emerge from the Athenaeum, Thomas is not on the sidewalk. I wait ten minutes, then another five.

I walk across the street and stand in a doorway. Twenty min-utes elapse, and I begin to wonder if I heard Thomas correctly.

I see them coming from the corner. Thomas and Adaline have Billie between them. They count *one, two, three,* and lift Billie high into the air with their arms, like a rope bridge catching a gust of wind. Billie giggles with the airborne thrill and asks them to do it again — and again. I can see Billie's small brown legs inside her shorts, her feet kicking the air for height. People on the sidewalk move to one side to let them pass. So intent are Thomas and Ada-line on their game that they walk by the Athenaeum and don't even see it.

Adaline lets go of Billie's hand. Thomas checks his watch. Adaline scoops Billie up into one arm, and hefts her onto her hip, as I have done a thousand times. Thomas says something to Ada-line, and she tilts her head back and laughs soundlessly. Billie pats her hair.

Moving fast, I cross the street before they can turn around. I reenter the Athenaeum and take the stairs two at a time. When I open the door to the reading room, I see that my neat stack of books and folders is exactly as I have left it. The librarian hasn't yet returned. I walk over to the long library table and remove the box from the folder. I put it under my arm.

I nearly slap the door into Thomas, who is looking up at the tall building, trying to ascertain whether he is in the correct place. Billie has climbed down from Adaline's hip, but is still holding her hand.

"Sorry," I say quickly. "I hope you weren't waiting long."

"How'd it go?" he asks. He puts his hands in his pockets.

"Fine," I say, bending to give Billie a kiss. "How about you?"

"We had a good time," Adaline says. She seems slightly flushed. "We found a park with swings, and we had an ice-cream cone." She looks down at Billie as if for confirmation.

"Where's Rich?" I ask.

"He's buying lobsters for supper," Thomas says quickly, again glancing at his watch. "We're supposed to meet him. Right now, as a matter of fact. What's that you've got there?"

"This?" I say, holding out the box. "Just something they lent me at the Athenaeum."

"Useful?"

"I hope so."

We walk four abreast along the sidewalk. I am aware of a settling of spirits, a lessening of exuberance. Adaline is quiet. She holds Billie's hand. That seems odd to me, as if she were unwilling to relinquish the tiny hand, even in my presence.

Rich is standing on the sidewalk and cradling two large paper bags. His eyes are hidden behind dark glasses.

We set off for the dock. The sky is clear, but the breeze is strong.

Rich and Adaline go ahead to prepare the Zodiac and to get the life jacket for Billie. I stand beside my daughter. Her hair whips across her face, and she tries unsuccessfully to hold it with her hands.

Thomas is staring into the harbor.

Thomas, I say.

Billie was six weeks old when she began to cough. I was bathing her in preparation for an appointment with the pediatrician, when I observed her — as I had not been able to when she was dressed — engaged in an awful kind of struggle. Her abdomen deflated at every pull for air, like an oxygen bladder on a pilot's mask. I picked Billie up and took her into Thomas's study. He glanced up at me, surprised at this rare intrusion. He had his glasses on, and his fingers were stained with navy ink. In front of him were white lined pages with unintelligible words on them.

"Look at this," I said, laying Billie on top of the desk.

Together we watched the alarming phenomenon of the inflating and deflating chest.

"Shit," Thomas said. "Did you call the doctor?"

"I called because of the cough. I have an appointment at ten-thirty."

"I'm calling 911."

"You think — ?"

"She can't breathe," said Thomas.

The ambulance driver would not let me travel with Billie. Too much equipment was needed; too much attention. They were working on her even as they closed the door. I thought: What if she dies, and I'm not there?

We followed in our car, Thomas cursing and gesturing at anyone who attempted to cut us off. I had never seen him so angry. The ambulance stopped at the emergency ward of the hospital in which Billie had been born.

"Jesus Christ," said Thomas. "We just got out of here."

In the emergency room, Billie was stripped naked and put into a metal coverless box that later Thomas and I would agree looked like a coffin. Of course, Billie was freezing, and she began to howl. I begged the attending physician to let me pick her up and nurse her to calm her. Surely the crying couldn't be good for the coughing and the breathing? But the young doctor told me that I was now a danger to my daughter, that I could no longer nurse her, that she had to be fed intravenously and pumped with antibiotics. He spoke to me as though I had been given an important assignment and had blown it.

Billie was hooked up to dozens of tubes and wires. She cried until she couldn't catch her breath. I couldn't bear her suffering one second longer, and when the doctor left to see to someone else, I picked her up, wrapping the folds of my quilted jacket around her, not feeding her, but holding her to my breast. Immediately, she stopped crying and rooted around for my nipple. Thomas looked at us with an expression of tenderness and fear I had never seen on his face before.

Billie had pneumonia. For hours, Thomas and I stood beside a plastic box that had become Billie's bed, studying the bank of monitors that controlled and recorded her breathing, her food intake, her heart rate, her blood pressure, her blood gases, and her antibiotics. There was no other universe except this plastic box, and Thomas and I marveled at the other parents in the intensive care unit who returned from forays into the outside world with McDonald's cartons and boxes from Pizza Hut.

"How can they eat?" said Thomas.

That night, Thomas was told that he had a phone call, and he left the room. I stood beside the plastic box and rhythmically recited the Lord's Prayer over and over, even though I am not a religious woman. I found the words soothing. I convinced myself that the words themselves would hold Billie to me, that as long as I kept reciting the prayer, Billie would not die. That the words themselves were a talisman, a charm.

When Thomas came back into the room, I turned automatically to him to ask him who called. His face was haggard — thin and papery around his eyes. He blinked, as though he were emerging from a movie theater into the bright sun.

He named a prize any poet in America might covet. It was for *The Magdalene Poems,* a series of fifty-six poems it had taken my husband eight years to write. We both sat down in orange plastic chairs next to the plastic box. I put my hand on his. I thought immediately of terrible contracts. How could we have been given this wonderful piece of news and have Billie survive as well?

"I can't digest this," Thomas said.

"No."

"We'll celebrate some other time."

"Thomas, if I could be, I'd be thrilled. I will be thrilled."

"I've always worried that you thought I was with you because of the poems. That I was using you. As a kind of muse."

"Not now, Thomas."

"In the beginning."

"Maybe, for a while, in the beginning."

"It's not true."

I shook my head in confusion. "How can this possibly matter?" I asked with the irritation that comes of not wanting to think about anything except the thing that is frightening you.

"It doesn't matter," he said. "It doesn't matter."

But of course it did matter. It did matter.

I learned that night that love is never as ferocious as when you think it is going to leave you. We are not always allowed this knowledge, and so our love sometimes becomes retrospective. But that night Thomas and I believed that our daughter was going to die. As we listened to the beeps and buzzes and hums and clicks of the machines surrounding her, we held hands, unable to touch her. We scrutinized her eyelids and eyelashes, her elbows and her fat calves. We shared a stunning cache of memories, culled in only six weeks. In some ways, we knew our daughter better that night than we ever would again.

Billie recovered in a week and was sent home. She grew and flourished. Eventually we reached the day when she was able to irritate us, when we were able to speak sharply to her. Eventually we reached the day when I was able to leave her and go out to take photographs. Thomas wrote poems and threw them away. He taught classes and gave numerous readings and talked to reporters and began to wonder if the words were running out on him. He drank more heavily. In the mornings, I would sometimes find him in the kitchen in a chair, his elbow resting on the counter. Next to him would be an empty bottle of wine. "This has nothing to do with you," he would say to me, putting a hand on the skirt of my robe. "I love you. This is not your fault."

I have sometimes thought that there are moments when you can see it all — and if not the future, then all that has gone before. They say this is true of the dying — that one can see a life — that the brain can perceive in an instant, or at most a few seconds, all that has gone before. Beginning at birth and ending with the moment of total knowledge so that the moment itself becomes a kind of infinite mirror, reflecting the life again and again and again.

I imagine that moment would be felt as a small billowy shock through the body, the *whoomph* of touching a frayed cord. Not fatal in itself, perhaps, but a surprise, a jolt.

And that is how it comes to me on the dock. I can see the years that Thomas and I have had together, the fragility of that life. The creation of a marriage, of a family, not because it has been ordained or is meant to be, but because we have simply made it happen. We have done this thing, and then that thing, and then that thing, and I have come to think of our years together as a tightly knotted fisherman's net; not perfectly made perhaps, but so well knit I would have said it could never have been unraveled.

During the hours that pass between our return from

Portsmouth and dinner, we each go our separate ways. Adaline shuts the door and reads Celia Thaxter in the forward cabin; Thomas dozes in the cockpit while Billie kneels beside him, coloring; Rich retreats into the engine compartment to fix the bilge pump; and I sit on Billie's berth with guidebooks and notes and the transcript spread all around me. I open the flesh-colored box and examine the penciled translation. I know that I will read it soon, but I am not quite ready. I feel furtive in the narrow berth, and vaguely ashamed of myself.

I tell myself that the reason for my theft is simple: I want to know how it was, to find the one underlying detail that will make it all sensible. I want to understand the random act, the consequences of a second's brief abandonment. I am thinking not so much of the actions of a single night as I am of the aftermath of years — and of what there would be to remember.

In the guidebooks, I read that history has only one story to tell about John Hontvedt, Maren's husband, at Smuttynose, apart from all the events attending the murders on March 5, 1873. On a frigid day in 1870, three years before the murders and two years after Hontvedt arrived in America, John left Smuttynose for fishing grounds northwest of the island. We are told it was a particularly filthy day, ice forming on mustaches and oilskins, on lines, and even on the deck of Hontvedt's schooner, which remains nameless. John stood on the slippery shingle of the small beach at Smuttynose, the sleet assaulting him from a slanting angle, trying to decide whether or not to row out to the schooner. We can only guess at what finally compelled Hontvedt to go to sea on such a day, among the worst the Atlantic had to offer that year. Was it poverty? Or hunger? Expensive bait that might rot if it wasn't used? An awful kind of restlessness?

After setting sail and losing sight of Smuttynose, John was surprised by a gale that blew up, creating heavy seas and blizzard conditions. The snow became so thick on the sea as the hours wore on that John could not have seen much beyond the boat itself. Perhaps realizing his mistake, John did try then to turn back toward Smuttynose, but the swells were so high and the visibility so poor that he could make no headway. He was instead forced to drift in an aimless pattern in a darkish, white blindness. The danger of being swamped or of the schooner being gouged open on unseen rocks and ledges was very real.

A number of the islanders, chief among them a man named Ephraim Downs, who lived on Smuttynose himself, and who would later live with his family in the Hontvedt house after the murders (the landlord refusing to clean away the bloodstains, he said, because he could get more money from souvenir hunters than he could from a higher rent), thought John mad for having set out that day at all, and watched for him to return. When it became apparent that Hontvedt's schooner must be lost, Downs set out in his own larger ship, aptly named the *White Rover*, to search for the disabled or stranded boat. Downs and his crew scanned the sea for hours until they themselves lost their bearings in the storm. After several hours, they finally caught sight of the smaller boat with Hontvedt aboard. Looping across fourteen-foot swells, Downs managed to collect the stranded seaman. After John was safely aboard the *White Rover*, Hontvedt's schooner drifted away and was never seen again.

For many hours, the *White Rover* rode the waves, the men aboard her becoming frozen and covered with ice until they could no longer move. When the boat finally beached herself — and history doesn't tell us where — the crew, who were able to use neither their legs nor their arms properly, hitched themselves over the prow of the boat and tumbled onto the sand. Several of the men from the *White Rover* had frozen their feet through and later had to have them amputated. John Hontvedt appears to have survived intact.

"Mommy, will you take me swimming?"

Billie tugs at my sleeve and rolls her head back and forth in the crook of my arm. I set my book down and lift her onto my lap. A small bit of crayon wrapping is stuck to her bottom lip, and I pick it off. She smells of shellfish and of sunblock.

"I don't know, Jean," calls Thomas from the cockpit. "It's awfully deep out there. I said she had to ask you. I don't especially want to go in again myself."

"She'll be all right if she wears her life jacket," says Rich, emerging from the engine compartment. "Anyway, *I* need a swim. I'm disgusting. If we both take her, she'll be OK."

"Please, Mom."

I look at Rich, whose hands are covered with grease, and then I look at Billie. "Sure," I say. "Why not?"

I am able to get over the side of the boat, but I am pretty sure they will never get me back in. Rich has left the swim ladder, which was being repaired, in his van at the dock. Billie cannonballs into the water and bobs straight up, her hair covering her face. I swim close to my daughter, never more than an arm's length away, while Billie flails her arms, barely keeping her mouth above water. The water is, at first, shockingly cold, but after a few minutes I begin to get used to it. From the waterline, the prow of the sailboat seems massive — that of an ocean liner. In the distance, without my glasses, the islands are indistinct shapes of gray and brown.

I give Billie a shove toward Rich, and she "swims" between her uncle and myself — a wriggly fish with no fear. Her mouth fills with seawater. She swallows it and she seems surprised by the taste. She begs Rich for a ride on his back, and when they swim near to me, Billie slides off and clutches me around my neck. Rich's leg is momentarily slippery against my own, and I grab onto his shoulder to keep from going under.

"Careful, Billie," I say, loosening her grip around my neck. "I don't have a life jacket on like you. You'll sink me."

From the bowsprit, Thomas watches us. He has a glass in his hand. I see him turn away and smile. He says something I cannot hear — it must be to Adaline.

When I let go of Rich, he dives deep into the water. He comes up about thirty feet away from me and begins to swim hard, his arms beating a rhythm to his kick. Billie and I paddle around each other until I see that she is tiring. Thomas reaches down, and between us we are able to get Billie easily back into the boat. As I anticipated, however, I am not strong enough to haul myself up and over, and there is an embarrassing and awkward pulling on arms and legs before I am able finally to flop into the cockpit. Billie wraps herself in a towel and sits, shivering, next to Adaline. When I stand up and put my glasses on, I see that Rich has swum all the way to Smuttynose and is sitting on the beach.

The Isles of Shoals derives its name not from the shoals surrounding the islands, but rather from the Old English word for *school*. As in schools of fish.

During the American Revolution, the Isles of Shoals were evacuated. Because the Shoalers had been trading with the British, the colonial leaders of New Hampshire and Maine ordered all residents off the islands. On January 5, 1776, eighty houses were dismantled, shipped to the mainland, and reconstructed all along the coast, from Massachusetts to Maine. A number of these houses are still standing.

"Loss. Abandonment. Castration. Chauvinism . . ."

"But think of Tom Moore, the charm."

"Melancholy. It's all melancholic," says Thomas. "Kavanaugh, Frost, MacNeice."

"You're forgetting Yeats. The celebration of the human imagination, the magician."

"Donnelly. Hyde Donnelly. Do you know him? *Gray light thieving, mother's grief / Steals by hedgerows —*"

"You're indicting an entire race," Adaline says lightly.

Thomas takes a long sip of scotch.

A thick, peasanty scent of fish and garlic spreads and settles over the cockpit where Adaline and Thomas and I are sitting. Rich is holding a plate of mussels he has just steamed.

"*I* picked them," Billie says, weaving through Rich's legs. She is trying to retain her pride in the mussels, though I sense she has been somewhat defeated in her attempts actually to like them. Just moments ago, going below to fetch the papers I took from the Athenaeum, I saw the partly chewed remains of a mussel stuffed inside a crumpled napkin. Billie has on clothes she particularly likes — a blue T-shirt with Pocahontas on the front and matching shorts — and I know she regards this small gathering as something of a party. As does Thomas. Billie has brought a sandwich bag of Cheerios, so that she can nibble with us. She comes and snuggles beside me, screwing her head up and inside my arm. Thomas and Adaline sit across from me. Within seconds, I know, Billie will ask me for a Coke.

"*Sons are leaving,*" says Thomas.

Rich sets the mussels on a makeshift table in the center of the cockpit, perches himself on the cabin roof, and dangles his legs over the opening. The air around us seems cleansed. Smuttynose is sharply etched and brushed with a thin wash of gold from a low sun. From the sloop, the gulls above the island are dark check marks in the blue dust. I am thinking that it is, possibly, the most beautiful night of the summer.

I have a photograph of the five of us in the cockpit of the Morgan the evening Rich makes the mussels and Thomas breaks the glass. I take the picture while the light is still orange; and, as a result, all of us look unreasonably tanned and healthy. In the photograph, Billie is sitting on Rich's lap and has just reached over to touch a gold wrist cuff that Adaline has put on a few minutes earlier. Rich is smiling straight at the camera, an open-mouthed smile that shows a lot of teeth, which look salmon-colored in the light. Beside him, Adaline has shaken out her hair so that the camera has caught her with her chin slightly raised. She has on a black sundress with thin straps and a long skirt; her cross gives off a glint of sunlight. The low sun is shining almost painfully into everyone's eyes, which is why Thomas is squinting and has a hand raised to his brow. The only part of his face that is clearly identifiable is his mouth and jawline. As for me, I have engaged the timer so that I have time to insert myself into the picture. I am sitting beside Thomas, but am slightly tilted, as though I am straining to be part of the composition. I have smiled, but my eyes are, at that instant, closed in a blink. Thomas has attempted to put his free arm around me, but the camera has caught him with it raised and crooked in the air.

"How exactly did you get the scar?" Adaline is asking.

"We really need to feed Billie," I say, talking as much to myself as to anyone. It has been an exhausting day, and I haven't thought about Billie's dinner at all. I know that Rich has bought lobsters for the rest of us, but Billie will not eat a lobster.

"Mommy, can I have a Coke?"

"In a car accident," Thomas says. "When I was a kid. The driver was drunk." Rich looks up quickly at Thomas, but Thomas turns his head away.

"Not now, Sweetie. It's almost time for supper."

"We have some tunafish," says Rich. "I'll make her a sandwich."

"You've done enough," I say. "The least I can do is make a sandwich." I start to get up.

"I don't want tunafish," Billie says. "I want a lobster."

"Billie, I don't think . . ." I start to say, but Rich stops me with a small shake of his head.

"Why don't you give the lobster a try?" he asks Billie. "And if you don't like it, we can make the sandwich then."

She closes her mouth and nods. I can see that she is slightly worried now that she has won her small contest. I doubt she really wants a lobster.

"Where are you from?" Adaline asks me. As she crosses her legs, a slit in the skirt of her black dress falls open, revealing a long, suntanned calf. Thomas looks down at Adaline's leg, and then away. I am wearing jeans and a sweatshirt. Thomas has a fresh shirt on, a blue shirt with a thin yellow stripe, and he has shaved.

"Indiana, originally," I say. "My parents are dead. I was born late, when my mother was forty-eight."

"Mommy, what do seagulls eat?"

"Fish, I think," I say to Billie. "They dive in the ocean for fish. If you watch them closely, I'll bet you can see them." Self-consciously, I look toward Smuttynose, at the gulls that loop in the air over the ragged shoreline.

"And you do this?" Adaline asks, gesturing with her hands to include the boat, the island, the harbor.

"When I can," I say.

"But, Mom, where do they sleep?"

"That's a good question," I say, turning to Thomas for help.

"Damned if I know," Thomas says.

"They must sleep on rocks," Adaline offers. "They put their heads under their wings, I think."

"Have you ever seen a seagull sleep?" Billie asks her.

Adaline purses her lips. "I must have done," she says. "But I can't think where."

"On the back of a garbage barge in the middle of Boston Harbor," Rich calls out from the galley.

"The rats of the sea," mutters Thomas.

Billie snuggles deeper into the cavity of my arm and chest and speaks into my rib cage. "Adaline is beautiful," she says shyly, not quite certain it is all right to say such a thing aloud.

"I know she is," I say, looking directly at Adaline, who meets my eyes.

"I love you, Mommy," Billie says.

"I love you, too," I say.

Early reports of the murders were hastily written and full of inaccuracies. The first bulletin from the *Boston Post* read as follows: "Two Girls Murdered on Smutty Nose Island, Isles of Shoals. Particulars of the Horrible Butchery — Escape of the Assassin and Subsequent Arrest in Boston — The Murderer's Object for Committing the Deed — Attempt to Kill a Third Person — Miraculous Escape of His Intended Victim — Terrible Sufferings from the Cold — Appalling Spectacle at the Home of the Murdered Females, Etc., Etc. — [SPECIAL DISPATCH TO THE BOSTON POST] Portsmouth, N.H., March 6. Our citizens were horror-struck soon after noon to-day, when a fisherman named Huntress, whose home is at the Isles of Shoals, by landing his boat at Newcastle, and taking them thence to this city, hastened to inform our police that murder most foul had been done at the Shoals."

According to the same report, a "rough young man named Lewis Wagner" was seen walking down to the wharf the previous night with an ax in hand. The next morning at seven o'clock, while Wagner and "Huntress" were "having breakfast together" in Portsmouth, Wagner told the unfortunate Huntress (who had not yet returned home and did not know of the murders) that something was going to happen to him (Lewis Wagner). Anetta Lawson and Cornelia Christenson were the victims. A third woman, Mrs. Huntress, had escaped. Portsmouth City Marshall Johnson was already on his way to Boston to try to apprehend the fugitive murderer, who had, earlier in the day, been seen boarding a train for Boston.

I go below to help Rich in the galley. He has a lobster pot on a burner on the stove, another on a hibachi on the stern. He is heating bread in the oven, and he has made a salad.

I begin to lay out the table. Rich and I move awkwardly about the cramped space, trying not to bump into each other or reach for the same utensil simultaneously. Through the companionway, I can see Billie lying faceup on the cushion I have vacated. She seems to be studying her fingers with great intensity. Across from her, framed in the rectangle, are Thomas's legs in their trousers, and his hand reaching for the bottle he has set by his right foot. The boat moves rhythmically, and through the west-facing portholes, watery reflections flicker on the bulkheads. I am searching for lobster crackers and picks in the silverware drawer when I hear three achingly familiar words: *Wainscot, redolent, core-stung.*

Adaline's voice is deep and melodious, respectful, forming words and vowels — perfect vowels. She knows the poem well. By heart.

I strain so that I can see Thomas's face. He is looking down at his knees. He doesn't move.

I remember the bar, the way Thomas read the poem. I remember standing at a window and reading it in the streetlight while Thomas slept.

"Thomas," I call. The edge in my voice is audible, even to me.

Billie sits up and leans on her elbows. She seems slightly puzzled. Adaline stops reciting.

Adaline's wrists are lightly crossed at her knee. In one long-fingered hand, she holds a wineglass. I am surprised suddenly to realize that this is the first time I have seen her drinking.

"Thomas, I need you," I repeat, and turn away.

I busy myself in the silverware drawer. He puts his head inside the companionway.

"What is it?" he asks.

"I can't find the nutcrackers, and I don't know what you've

done with the wine we're having for dinner." My annoyance — a weaseling, sour note — is unmistakable.

"I've got the wine right here," Rich says quietly next to me. He opens the tiny refrigerator door for me to see.

But it is too late. Thomas has already turned and walked away. He stands, looking out over the water. He holds his glass in one hand; the other he has in the pocket of his trousers. Adaline has twisted her body around, so that she, too, is gazing out over the water, but away from Thomas.

Rich goes above to put the corn into the pot on the hibachi. I see Thomas move aside and hold the lid for Rich. After Rich has dumped the ears into the steaming kettle, he wipes his hands on a dishtowel, and then bends and pours himself a glass of wine from another bottle on the cockpit floor. Thomas and Rich, their backs to me, speak a few words to each other, like husbands who have gone to stand by the grill in the backyard. I lean against the lip of the counter in the galley and sip my wine with concentration.

Billie looks at her father, then at me. She rolls over onto her stomach and puts her hands to the sides of her face, as if she were peering at something very tiny on the cushion. Rich turns around and gestures to Adaline to move over a bit. He sits next to her and rests his fingers on her thigh. He slips them in under the slit of her skirt, under the black cloth.

Thomas, who has made a half turn at that moment and is about to speak, sees Rich touch Adaline. He stands as if transfixed, as if not knowing where to put his body. He takes an awkward step forward. He hits Adaline's wineglass, which she has set down on the floor. The glass falls and shatters.

"Jesus," Thomas says.

Louis Wagner was arrested at eight-thirty on the night after the murders at the home of an acquaintance in Boston by both

Portsmouth and Boston police. Wagner seemed stunned by the accusation of the murders and swore that he had not been on Smuttynose since November of the previous year. He said he could not have done such a thing because the Hontvedt women had been good to him. He had heard the train whistle at nine o'clock that morning, and, since he was down on his luck in Portsmouth, he thought it might be a good thing to try Boston.

News that the police were bringing Wagner back to Portsmouth on the ten o'clock train on Friday morning swept through the town, and the train route was lined with angry, screaming mobs. Fearing for their prisoner, the police had the train stopped a quarter mile short of the station to take Wagner off, but the crowd spotted him anyway and began to pelt the prisoner — and the police — with stones and ice chunks. They called out "Lynch him" and "String him up." The Marines were summoned, and the police drew their guns. Wagner spent the night in the Portsmouth jail, but was transferred the next day to Saco, Maine, since Smuttynose is technically not in New Hampshire, but in Maine. Again police were confronted with thousands of demonstrators who once more tried to stone Wagner, who was wounded in the head. One of the men in the mob was Ephraim Downs, the fisherman who had once saved John Hontvedt's life.

The prisoner was arraigned at the South Berwick jail and then kept in the Portland jail. He was transported to Alfred, Maine, when the trial of *The State of Maine* v. *Louis H. F. Wagner* opened on June 16, 1873. Louis Wagner stood accused of delivering ten mortal wounds with an ax to the head of "Anethe M. Christenson" and thereby causing her instant death.

After Rich and I clean up the broken glass, he lifts the lobsters from the pot, and we all sit down at the dining table to eat. Thomas, who has drunk even more than he usually does, struggles clumsily with his lobster, spraying bits of white chitin around the table. Billie, as anticipated, loses her appetite for lobster when she watches me crack the shells and extract with a pick the spotted, pink meat. Adaline does not dip her meat with her fingers into melted butter as do the rest of us, but rather soaks it in a bowl of hot broth and eats it from a fork. She works her way methodically through the bright red carapace, missing not a piece of edible flesh.

Thomas goes above to the deck when he cuts his thumb on a claw. After a time, Rich, who may feel that Thomas needs company, also goes above. Billie, too, leaves us, happy to turn her back on the pile of claws and red detritus that is forming in a stainless steel bowl and is becoming vaguely repulsive. Across the table, I watch with fascination as Adaline pulls tiny bits of meat I'd have overlooked from the body of the lobster. I watch her suck and chew, one by one, each of the lobster's spindly legs, kneading the thin shells with her teeth.

"Did you grow up on a farm?" she asks. "Were your parents farmers?"

"Yes, as a matter of fact, they were," I say. "Where in Ireland did you grow up?"

"Cork," she says. "It's in the south."

"And then you went to university."

"Yes," she says. "Billie is wonderful. You're very lucky to have her."

"Thank you. I do feel lucky to have her. How did you end up in Boston?"

"I was with someone," she says. "When I was in London. He worked in Boston, and I came over to be with him. I've always liked Boston."

"How did you come to know so much about Thomas's poetry?" I ask.

She seems surprised at the question.

"I think I've always read Thomas," she says. "Even at Dublin, I thought he was extraordinary. I suppose, after the prize, everyone reads Thomas now, don't they? That's what a prize does, I should think. It makes everyone read you, surely."

"You've memorized his work."

"Oh, not really."

There is an accusing tone to my voice that seems to put her on the defensive.

"The thing about Thomas is that I think he wants to be read aloud," she says. "One almost has to, to fully understand."

"You know he killed a girl," I say.

Adaline slowly removes a lobster leg from her mouth, holds it between her thumb and finger as she rests her hands on the edge of the table. The blue-checked oilcloth is dotted with bits of flesh and yellow drips of butter that have congealed.

"Thomas killed a girl," she repeats, as though the sentence doesn't scan.

I take a sip of wine. I tear a piece of garlic bread from the loaf. I try to control my hands, which are trembling. I believe I am more shocked at what I have just said than she is. By the way I have said it. By the words I have used.

"I don't understand," she says.

She puts the spindly leg on her plate and wipes her fingers on the napkin in her lap. She holds the crumpled napkin in one hand.

"The car accident," I explain. "Thomas was driving."

She still seems not to understand.

"There was a girl with him. In the car. Thomas went off the road, caught his rear wheel in a ditch, and flipped the car."

Adaline reaches up and, with her finger, absently picks at a piece of lobster between her teeth. I look down and notice I have a spill of lobster water on my jeans.

"How old was she?"

"The same age as he was, seventeen."

"He was drunk?"

"Yes," I say.

I wait.

I see it then, the moment of recognition. I can see her processing the information, reciting lines to herself, suddenly understanding them. Her eyes move to the stove and then back to me.

"*The Magdalene Poems*," she says quietly.

I nod. "But her name wasn't Magdalene. It was Linda."

Adaline flinches slightly at the word *Linda,* as though the commonness of the girl's name makes it real.

"He loved her," she says.

"Yes," I answer. "Very much. I don't think he's really ever gotten over it. In a way, all of his poems are about the accident, even when they seem not to be."

"But he married you," she says.

"So he did," I say.

Adaline puts her napkin on the table and stands up. She walks a few steps to the doorway of the forward cabin. She has her back to me, her arms crossed over her chest.

Rich bends his head into the cabin. "Jean, you should come out here," he calls. "The light is perfect."

He stops. Adaline is still standing in the doorway with her back to me. She doesn't turn around. Rich glances at me.

"What's up?" he asks.

I uncross my legs under the table. "Not much," I say.

I fold my hands in my lap, stunned by my betrayal. In all the years that I have been with Thomas, I have never told a single person. Nor, to my knowledge, has he. Despite our fears when he won the prize, no one discovered this fact about Thomas's youth, as the records were well sealed. Now, however, I know that Adaline will tell others. She won't be able to keep this information to herself.

I can't have done this, I am thinking.

"Rich, leave this," I say quickly, gesturing toward the mess on the table. "I want to go up. With Thomas. With the light still good. I'll do the dishes later." I push away from the table. Rich comes down the ladder and stands a moment with his hands over his head, holding on to the hatch. He seems puzzled.

Behind me, Adaline goes into the forward cabin. She shuts the door.

The Honorable R. P. Tapley of Saco, Maine, was the lawyer for the defense of Louis H. F. Wagner. George C. Yeaton, Esq. was the county attorney. The Honorable William G. Barrows was the presiding judge. The members of the jury were Isaac Easton of North Berwick, George A. Twambly of Shapleigh, Ivory C. Hatch of Wells, Horace Piper of Newfield, Levi G. Hanson of Biddeford, Nahum Tarbox of Biddeford, Benajah Hall of North Berwick, Charles Whitney of Biddeford, William Bean of Limington, Robert Littlefield of Kennebunk, Isaac Libbey of Parsonfield, and Calvin Stevens of Wells.

Although all of the jury, the lawyers, and the judge were white men of early American — that is to say, English — stock, neither the accused nor the victim, nor the woman who survived, nor even most of the witnesses, was an American citizen.

In the cockpit, Thomas comes to sit beside me. Billie leans against Thomas's legs. My hands begin to shake. I feel an urge to bend forward, to put my head between my knees.

The three of us watch the sun set over Newcastle and Portsmouth, watch the coral light move evenly across Appledore and Star, leaving in its wake a colorless tableau. From below, Rich switches on the running lights.

I want to tell Thomas that I have done something terrible, that I don't know why I did it except that I couldn't, for just that moment, bear Adaline's certainty that she knew Thomas well — perhaps, in a way, even better than myself.

On Star, windows are illuminated, and people walk through pools of deep yellow light.

"You're trembling," Thomas says.

The Magdalene Poems are an examination of the life of a seventeen-year-old girl in the last four seconds of her life, written in the voice of a seventeen-year-old boy who was clearly her lover and who was with her when she died. The poems speak to the unfulfilled promise of love, to the absolute inevitability of that promise remaining unfulfilled. The reader is allowed to imagine the girl as a middle-aged woman married to the man who was the boy, as an elderly widow, and as a promiscuous sixteen-year-old. The girl, whose name is Magdalene, is — as seen from the eyes of the boy — extraordinarily beautiful. She has the long slender body of a dancer, abundant multihued hair that winds into intricate coils at the nape of her neck, and full curved lips of even dimensions with barely any bow at all.

According to the State of Maine, on March 5, 1873, six people lived in the one-and-one-half-story red cottage on Smuttynose, and there were no other inhabitants on the entire island that winter. John and Maren Hontvedt had come in 1868. Karen, Maren's sister, and Matthew, John's brother, had each come separately in 1871. Karen almost immediately entered service at the Laighton's Hotel on Appledore Island, while Matthew joined John on the *Clara Bella,* the latter's fishing schooner. Evan, Maren's brother, and his wife, Anethe, had arrived on the island in October of 1872, five months before the murders.

At daybreak on March 5, Matthew, Evan, and John left Smuttynose and sailed northeast in the schooner to draw their trawls.

The Ingerbretson men from Appledore joined them in their own schooner. The plan for the day was to fish in the morning, return for lunch, and then head for Portsmouth to sell their catch and purchase bait. But just before noon, an unexpected and swift-rising wind prevented them from making an easy sail home to Smuttynose. Because they knew they had to have bait, they called over to Emil Ingerbretson and asked him to stop at the island and tell the women that they would not be home until evening. The three women — Maren, Karen, and Anethe — cooked a stew and made bread for the men in preparation for their return after dark.

Louis Wagner, standing at Rollins Wharf in Portsmouth, watched the *Clara Bella* come into the dock. Wagner, who was wearing that day two sweaters, a white dress shirt, and overalls, helped John and Matthew and Evan tie up their boat. Louis told the men that the bait they wanted, which was coming by train from Boston, would be delayed and wouldn't be in until nearly midnight. Louis then asked John for money for something to eat, and John laughed and said that none of the men had brought any money because they had thought they would go home first, and that they would have to eat on credit with Mrs. Johnson, to whose house the bait was to be delivered. Wagner then asked John if he had had any luck with his fishing, and John answered that he had been able to save up six hundred dollars. The three men of Smuttynose said goodbye to Louis, leaving him on the dock, while they went to fetch their dinner.

Baiting the trawls was a time-consuming and slimy business. Each of a thousand hooks had to have its piece of baitfish, a stinking sliver of herring that would have come in barrels from Boston by train, and did in fact arrive much later than expected in Portsmouth that night, preventing the men from returning to Smuttynose at all. Each individual hook had to be separated from the tangle, baited, then coiled into a tub so that the lot could be thrown overboard when the schooner, the next day, had made it to the fishing grounds. To bait the trawls took three men six hours. When the work was finished, it was not uncommon for one or more of the men to have stabbed himself with fishhooks.

Louis Wagner had emigrated from Prussia to the United States seven years earlier. He was twenty-eight years old and was described by those who knew him as being tall and extremely strong, light-haired, and having "steel blue" eyes. Other descriptions of him depict his eyes as soft and mild. Many women thought him handsome. He had worked at the Isles of Shoals off and on, loading and unloading goods, and with John Hontvedt on the *Clara Bella* for two months, September to November of 1872. For seven months of that year (from April to November), Wagner had boarded with the Hontvedts, but he had been crippled much of the time with rheumatism. After leaving the Hontvedts, he signed on as a hand with the *Addison Gilbert,* which subsequently sank, leaving Wagner once again without a job. Just prior to the murders, he had been wandering in and among the boardinghouses, wharves, docks, and taverns of Portsmouth, looking for work. He is quoted as having said, to four different men, on four different occasions, "This won't do anymore. I am bound to have money in three months' time if I have to murder for it." While in Portsmouth, he resided at a boardinghouse for men that belonged to Matthew Johnson and his wife. He owed his landlord money.

According to the prosecution, at seven-thirty on the evening of March 5, Louis Wagner stole a dory, owned by James Burke, that had been left at the end of Pickering Street. Just that day, Burke had replaced the dory's thole pins with new, expensive ones. Wagner intended to row out to the Isles of Shoals, steal the six hundred dollars that John had spoken of, and to row immediately back. This would be a twenty-five-mile row, which, even in the best of circumstances, would be extremely taxing for any man. That day it was high tide at six P.M., low at midnight. There was a three-quarters moon, which set at one A.M. On a favorable tide, it took one hour and forty minutes to row from Pickering Street to the mouth of the Piscataqua River (which flowed through Portsmouth), and one hour and fifteen minutes to row from there to Smuttynose. This is a round-trip, in favorable conditions, of just under six hours. If a man tired, or encountered any obstacles, or if he did not have completely favorable conditions, the row to and from the Isles of Shoals could take as long as nine or ten hours.

County Attorney Yeaton reconstructed Wagner's plan as follows: Maren would be asleep in the southwest bedroom, and Anethe would be upstairs. Wagner would fasten the door that linked Maren's bedroom to the kitchen by sliding a slat from a lobster trap through the latch. Since the money would be in the kitchen in a trunk, he felt there would be no difficulty. Wagner mistakenly assumed that Karen would still be on Appledore. He brought no murder weapon with him.

Wagner, who had the current with him, moved quickly down the river and past Portsmouth. When he reached the Shoals, he circled the island silently to see if, by some chance, the *Clara Bella* had returned. When he was certain there were no men on the island, he rowed himself into Haley's Cove. This was at approximately eleven P.M. He waited until all of the lights in the houses on Appledore and Star had been extinguished.

When the islands were dark, he walked in his rubber boots up to the front door of the cottage, where an ax leaned against the stone step. He entered the kitchen and fastened the door to the bedroom.

The dog, Ringe, began to bark.

Louis turned abruptly. A woman rose from her bed in the darkness and called out, "John, is that you?"

I take Billie below to get her ready for bed. She still finds the head a novelty, particularly the complicated flushing of the toilet. She brushes her teeth and then puts on her pajamas. I settle her into her berth and sit next to her. She has asked for a story, so I read her a picture-book tale of a mother and her daughter gathering blueberries in Maine. Billie lies in a state of rapt attention and holds in her arms a threadbare cocker spaniel she has had since birth.

"Let's say our things," I say, when I have finished the book.

When Billie was a toddler, she learned to talk, as most children do, by repeating what I said to her. As it has happened, this particular bit of repetition, a bedtime litany, has lasted for years.

"Lovely girl," I say.

"Lovely Mom."

"Sleep well."

"Sleep well."

"See you in the morning."

"See you in the morning."

"Don't let the bedbugs bite."

"Don't let the bedbugs bite."

"Sweet dreams."

"Sweet dreams."

"Love you."

"Love you."

"Goodnight."

"Goodnight."

I put my lips against her cheek. She reaches up her arms, letting go of the dog, and hugs me tightly.

"I love you, Mom," she says.

That night, on the damp mattress that serves as a bed, Thomas and I lie facing each other, just a few inches apart. There is enough light so that I can just make out his face. His hair has fallen forward onto his brow, and his eyes seem expressionless — simple dark pools. I have on a nightshirt, a white nightshirt with pink cotton piping. Thomas is still wearing the blue shirt with the thin yellow stripes, and his undershorts.

He reaches up and traces the outline of my mouth with his finger. He grazes my shoulder with the back of his hand. I move slightly toward him. He puts his arm around my waist.

We have a way of making love now, a language of our own, this movement, then that movement, signals, long-practiced, that differ only slightly each time from the times before. His hand sliding on my thigh, my hand reaching down between his legs, a small adjustment to free himself, my palm under his shirt. That night, he slides over me, so that my face is lightly smothered between his chest and his arm.

I freeze.

It is in the cloth, faint but unmistakable, a foreign scent. Not sea air, or lobster, or a sweaty child.

It takes only seconds for a message to pass between two people who have made love a thousand times, two thousand times.

He rolls away from me and lies on his back, his eyes staring at the bulkhead.

I cannot speak. Slowly, I take the air into my lungs and let it out.

Eventually, I become aware of the small twitches in Thomas's body — an arm, a knee — that tell me that he has fallen asleep.

To get a landscape photograph at night, you need a tripod and decent moonlight. Sometime after midnight, when everyone is asleep on the boat, I take the Zodiac over to Smuttynose. I use the paddle, because I do not want to wake Thomas or Rich with the motor. In the distance, the island is outlined by the moon, which casts a long cone of light onto the water. I beach the Zodiac at the place where Louis Wagner left his dory and retrace the steps he would have taken to the house. I stand in the foundation of the house and replay the murders in my mind. I look out over the harbor and try to imagine a life on the island, at night, in the quiet, and with the constant wind. I take two rolls of Velvia 220, seventy-two shots of Smuttynose in the dark.

I HAVE BEEN thinking this morning upon the subjects of story-telling and truth, and how it is with the utmost trust that we receive the tales of those who would give them to us.

Not long after our mother had died, and I had recovered from my illness, Karen became, as I have said, the mistress of the house, and Evan and I were sent out to work, me to a neighboring farm, and Evan to sea. This was not such an unusual occurrence, not in that area and in that time.

Our father, having grown older and grieving for the loss of his wife, was going to sea fewer days than he had before and not for long journeys as he had done in the past. Thus he did not have a surplus of fish to sell or to dry. All around us at this time, there were other families in failing circumstances, some far worse off than we were, families in which the father had drowned, and the mother and the eldest son had the responsibility of feeding many young children, and also families whose livelihoods had been reduced by the economic troubles of the region and, indeed, of the entire country at that time, and there were many indigent and homeless persons as a result. By contrast, I remember very few occasions when our family actually had no food in the pantry, although I do recall at least one and perhaps two winters when I had only one dress and one pair of socks to see me through to spring, and we could not get wool to spin to make another pair.

The decision to send Evan out to work was, I believe, an easy one for my father, since Evan was a tall and strong boy of sixteen, and there were many youths of the same age in the environs of Laurvig who had been working for some time. It was thought that Evan would make a better wage as a hired mate to someone else than he might by selling the herring and the cod he would catch with my father; but because there was very little fishing work in Laurvig Bay in those years, Evan had to go to Tonsberg, which was twenty kilometers north of Laurvig. There he was told about a man named John Hontvedt, who was looking for a mate and who lived in a house with six other fishermen, one of them his brother, Matthew. From that day forward, which was 12 October 1860, until such time as Evan and John entered into partnership, Evan worked with John Hontvedt on his fishing sloop, the *Malla Fladen,* and lived in that house for six days a week.

As for myself, I stayed one more year at school, and then was hired out to the Johannsen farm. This was a grave time in my father's life, and I believe the decision to send his youngest child out to work was a wrenching one for him to make. Karen could no longer go to the boarding house as she was needed at home, and since I was only fourteen and my father did not think it suitable for me to work in similar circumstances, he inquired about work for me elsewhere, where the conditions might be more gentle. As it happened, it was Karen who was advised of the position with Knud Johannsen, who was a recent widower himself, and she urged my father to send me there.

Knud Johannsen's dairy farm lay six kilometers back from the sea, an uphill climb on my way to work in the morning and, of course, a downhill slope in the evening, which was just as well, since I usually was so very tired then that I needed gravity to propel me forward to our cottage. My hours at the Johannsen farm were long and difficult, but generally, not unpleasant. During the time of my employ at that household, which lasted two years and eight months, Evan and I did not have many opportunities to see each other, and almost never alone, and this was a sorrow to me. Because of Evan's hard work and prosperity, however, our family's fortunes did gradually increase, so that I was allowed to discontinue my work for Mr. Johannsen and re-enroll in school, where I stayed for one year and seven months, entering a course of preparation for further study, though sadly I was not ever to go on to university. It was my good fortune, while in school, however, to put my whole heart and mind into my studies and thus command the attention of Professor Neils Jessen, the headmaster, who then took upon himself the bettering of my language skills so that I subsequently found pleasure in the study of rhetoric and composition. I trust that while I was lacking in certain rudimentary prerequisites for this challenging task at hand, I acquitted myself passably well, as Professor Jessen spent many hours with me after school in hopes that I might be the first female student from the Laurvig School to attend the university in Kristiania.

As it happened, however, I was not able to go on to university, owing to a lack of sufficient funds, even though my brother regularly sent to us large portions of his wages, and so I applied for and was given a position as clerk at the Fritzoe ironworks, which I held for two years. And then, in the winter of 1865, John Hontvedt and his brother, Matthew, moved to Laurvig, and shortly after that, the direction of my life changed quite dramatically.

A house in the Jorgine Road had become vacant and was to be leased at a low price, and Evan had spoken highly of the area to John these several years. Because of his hard work and cleverness, John Hontvedt had done well for himself in the fishing trade, and with him Evan had earned enough money to put some by. The two men, with Matthew Hontvedt, thus entered into a partnership aboard a sloop which they purchased and which was called the *Agnes C. Nedland*.

John Hontvedt was not a particularly tall man, not when compared to our father and to Evan, both of whom were well over six feet, but John gave the impression of strength and of size nevertheless. He had brown hair of a cinnamon tint that he wore thick and long, combed across his brow, and he had as well eyes that hinted at a gentleness of spirit. They were hazel, I believe, or possibly gray, I cannot remember now. His face was not narrow, as was Evan's, but rather square in shape, and he had a handsome jaw. I suspect he had been thin as a boy, but as a man, his body, like his face, had filled out. His chest was round and formed like a fish barrel. He had no fat on him at that time.

Hontvedt had a habit of standing with his hands hooked around his belt, and of hitching his trousers sometimes when he spoke. When he sat, he crossed his legs at the knees, as some women do, but he was never feminine in any other of his gestures. Occasionally, when he was tense or anxious, he would hold his elbow with one hand, and swing the free arm in an exaggerated manner, an odd gesture, I always thought, and one I came to think of as belonging exclusively to John. He had lost one finger of his left hand as a consequence of having severed it in a winch.

I believe our father was, at the time I met John Hontvedt, apprehensive for his two daughters. Certainly this was true as concerns his responsibilities toward Karen, who, at thirty-three, had lost her youth and seemed destined to remain a maid. It was a shame upon a father, then as now, if he could not marry off his daughters, and I shudder to think of all the young women who have been so unsuitably given away, only to live out lives of utter misery simply to assuage the public strain of their fathers.

I will not accuse our father of such base desires, however, for,

in truth, I do not think this was so, but I believe that he was, after having watched his eldest daughter turn herself into a spin-
ster, anxious to see me well married. Also, I must add here that
my father had not recently met a man in these parts who was of
so good a fisherstock and who had prospered so well as John.
And I believe my father had reason to be grateful to John
Hontvedt for his having taken on our Evan, and in that way gradually changing the fortunes of our family.

One evening, after Hontvedt had been to our table for dinner,
he suggested that he and I go out walking together.

I had not actually wanted to go walking at all, and certainly
not with John Hontvedt, but I did not see how I could refuse
such a request, particularly as it had been made in front of my father. It was a mild night in early October, with long shadows that
caused the landscape to take on a heightened clarity. We walked
in the direction of the coast road, toward town, John with his
hands in the pockets of his trousers, mine folded at my waist, as
was proper for a young woman then. John took up the burden of
the conversation, talking, as I recall, with great ease and volubil-
ity, although I cannot remember anything of what he said. I confess it was often this way between us, as I frequently allowed my
thoughts to wander whilst he spoke, and, oddly enough, he seldom seemed to notice these absences of mine. That evening,
when after a time I did begin to attend to what he was saying, I
noticed that we were quite far from the cottage. We were standing on a headland that looked out over Laurvigsfjord. The ground
was covered with gorse that had gone aflame with the setting
sun, and the blue of the water below us had reached that deep
solid sapphirine that comes only late in the evenings. We were
admiring this view, and perhaps John was addressing me, when I
noticed that he had moved closer to me than was strictly comfortable. Nearly as soon as I had this observation, he put his hand

lightly at the back of my waist. This was a gesture that could not be misunderstood. It was, I believe I am correct in saying, a somewhat possessive gesture, and I was then in no doubt as to its intent. I think I may have moved slightly away from him, but John, who was dogged in his pursuits, moved along with me, so that he had no need to remove his hand. As we stood there, I recall that his fingers began to inch even further, so that he was able to circle my waist. I thought that if I did not speak to him at that moment he might take my passivity as an invitation for further intimacies, which I did not want, so I moved abruptly away from him then.

"Maren," he said, "there are things about which I must speak to you."

"I am feeling quite tired, John. I think we should go back to the cottage."

"You know," said John, "that I have given some thought to emigrating to America. I have been much impressed with reports of the American customs and views, particularly the idea that there is no class distinction. That a man pays only a little tax on the land he actually owns, and is not filling the pockets of the idle, who do no work at all."

"But would you leave all that you know behind and go to a country in which if you do not have money you must remain where you are on the coast?" I asked. "I have heard tales of the large sums that are necessary to travel to the interior, and even there the land is already being twice-sold so that the original owners reap enormous profits, and cheap land can no longer be had by newly arrived immigrants. I have also heard that commodities are very expensive there. A barrel of salt costs nearly fifty orts! And coffee is forty skillings a pound!"

"Since I would want to remain on the coast," he answered, "I do not see the worry about having money to travel inland. But I do understand your point, Maren. One must have a stake with which to begin a new life, for a house and supplies and transportation and so on."

"Would you truly settle there, on the coast of America?" I asked.

"I might if I had found a wife," John answered.

At the word *wife,* John looked at me, and my eyes turned toward his, even before I had understood the suggestion in his declaration. It was the first time such a thought had clearly presented itself to me, and I confess I was at first quite shocked.

"I'm sorry, Maren," he said. "You seem distressed, and this was not at all my intention. Indeed, my intention was quite the opposite. In all my days on earth, I have never met a sweeter woman than you, Maren."

"Really, John, I am feeling quite faint."

"Whether I should go to America or remain in Norway, I am of an age now, and happily of sufficient means, that I may think of taking a wife. I trust that I may be worthy enough in my character to ask . . ."

I have never appreciated women who resort to histrionics or who show themselves to be so delicate in their constitutions that they cannot withstand the intense images that words may sometimes conjure forth, but I must acknowledge that at that moment, standing on the headland, I was so sorely exercised in my futile attempts to convince my companion to cease his conversation and escort me back to the cottage that I was tempted to feign a swoon and collapse in the gorse at his feet. Instead, however, I spoke to John rather sharply. "I insist that we return or I shall be ill, John," I said, and in this way I was able, for a time, to stave off what seemed to me to be an inevitable request.

It was only the next day that my father himself broached the subject. Evan had gone off to bed, and Karen was visiting the privy in the back, so that my father and I were alone. He wished, he said, to see me settled with a family. He did not want me to be dependent upon himself, as he did not think he had many years left. I cried out at this declaration, not only because I did not like to think upon my father's death, but also because I was cross at having twice in one week the necessity to fend off the prospect of marrying John Hontvedt. My father, brushing aside my protests with his hand, spoke of John's character, his healthy financial situation, and, finally, though I thought his priorities misplaced, of Hontvedt's apparent affection for me, which might, in time, he said, develop into a deep and lasting love. I was greatly vexed by having to think upon these matters, but I hasten to tell you that in Norway at that time, it was seldom the place of a young daughter to criticize her father, and so it was that I had to hear my father out at length on the subject of my eventual marriage. Dutifully, I said that I was grateful for his concerns, but that it was too soon in my life to take such a large and grave step, and that it would only be with the utmost care and consideration that I would do so.

I thought the matter at an end, or at least held in abeyance for a time, when, due to an impulsive gesture on my part, which I was later deeply to regret, I myself caused the subject to be brought up again, and finally resolved.

It was some four weeks later, in mid-November, and the weather was quite bitterly cold, but in the late afternoons a strange and wondrous phenomenon would occur on the bay. Because the water was considerably warmer than the air above it, great swirls of mist would rise from the sea, like steam lifting from a bath. These swirls, due to the light and angle of the sun at that time of year, would take on a lovely salmon color that was breathtaking to behold. So it was that the bay, which was normally thick with fisher-traffic in and out of the harbor, had that Sunday an entirely magical quality that I do not believe was reproduced anywhere else on earth. It was a natural occurrence that Evan and myself had sometimes observed on our journeys as children along the coast road, and it had never failed to halt our progress as we stood in rapt worship of such a simple, yet magnificent, accident of nature. That afternoon, I asked Evan if he would like to accompany me out to the cliffs, where we might better observe the bay. I thought this would be a good opportunity for Evan and myself to speak with each other apart from the others, which we rarely had occasion to do. Evan was at first reluctant, since I believe that he was particularly exhausted from his arduous week (for a fisherman's work is invariably made more difficult in cold temperatures), but I persisted in my invitation, and I daresay I talked him into it.

We walked for some distance without speaking. My brother seemed rather preoccupied that afternoon, and I was somewhat at a loss as to how to begin our conversation. As Evan walked beside me, I could not help myself from making a close observation of him. Already it was apparent that, at the age of twenty-two, the sun and the sea had begun to take their toll, as he had tiny lines around his eyes and mouth and on his forehead. His brow seemed to have knit itself together in a permanent manner, and I thought this the result of a constant squint on the water. His skin was weathered, with that texture seamen get that resembles nothing so much as fine paper. The blisters and rope burns on his hands had long since turned to calluses, but I could see the scars of many hook tears on his fingers. Additionally, I observed that Evan had attained, during his absence, his full growth, and I may say here that he towered over me. He was not, as I may have mentioned earlier, built broad in the shoulders, as John was, but rather was sinewy in his structure, though he gave off the appearance of great strength. I think that partly this was due as well to his character, which was extremely reserved and not given to much foolishness.

After a time, we passed a few pleasantries between us, but spoke of nothing that might be of a difficult nature, at least not immediately. I had dressed that day in my heavy woolen cloak, and my face was wrapped in a long scarf of a fine pale blue, the wool of which I had sent for from Kristiania.

"Do you remember," I asked when we had reached the cliffs and were gazing out at the bay, from which rose what appeared to be a miasmic wall of coral and rose and pink, "all the walks we used to take along this very coast road?"

He looked surprised for a minute, and then he said, "Yes, I do, Maren."

"And the day you climbed the tree, and I took off all my clothes and went up after you?"

"It seems so long ago."

"And how you saved me at Hakon's Inlet?"

"You would have saved yourself."

"No, I'd have drowned. I'm sure of it."

"It wasn't a very safe place to play," he said. "If I saw children there now, I'd chase them off."

"We never thought about safety."

"No, we didn't."

"Those were such good times," I said.

Evan was silent for a moment. I assumed that he was, like myself, contenting himself with the fond memories of our childhood, when suddenly a great sigh erupted from him, and he turned himself away from me.

"Evan, what is it?" I asked.

He didn't answer me. I was about to ask him again what the matter was, but I was silenced by the sight of tears that had, at that moment, sprung to his eyes. He shook his head violently, so that his hair swung about. Indeed, he was shaking his head in the rough manner of men who wish literally to throw out of their heads the thoughts that lodge there. I was so frightened and appalled by this sudden show of emotion and of intense hatred toward himself that I fear I cried out in the most desperate way and flung myself to my knees, for I have never been able to bear signs of grief or of sorrow on the face of my brother — and indeed, these signs triggered in me memories of the night our mother perished, a night on which Evan, and thus myself, had nearly lost our senses.

When next I was aware of my brother, he was tugging on my sleeve and trying to get me to stand up.

"Don't be so dramatic, Maren," he said curtly. "You'll freeze to death." He brushed tiny pebbles from my cloak.

And then, without any further words between us, Evan began to walk along the coast path south in the direction of the cottage. It was apparent, from his gait, that he did not intend I should follow him.

I had never been abandoned by Evan in so horrid a manner, and although I did soon recover myself and think how distraught my brother must have been to have wept in front of me and how truly sorry I was for his troubled nature, I felt bereft there on the cliffs and also, I must say, quite angry.

I walked home with a furious step and, at a critical juncture in the road, I took a turn that I have forever regretted. At the Jorgine Road, I walked east, toward John Hontvedt's cottage.

My legs and hands were trembling as I climbed the porch steps of Hontvedt's house, from the earlier disturbances on the cliffs or simply the inappropriateness of my visit I cannot say, but as you may imagine, John Hontvedt was exceedingly surprised to see me. After his initial shock, however, he could not hide his pleasure.

I allowed John Hontvedt to make me a cup of tea and to serve this to me in his front parlor, along with biscuits that he had purchased in town. He had not fully dressed, and had no collar on, and in his haste to prepare the tea, did not put one on. Perhaps it was only the absence of the collar and the sight of his braces, but I felt as though the entire encounter were an improper one. Indeed, I could not easily have explained my presence in John Hontvedt's house to anyone were someone to come upon us. What was I doing unchaperoned in a single man's living quarters on a Sunday afternoon? Possibly it was in an effort to answer that query, even to myself, that I spoke to John.

"Do you remember that on our walk of several weeks ago you were speaking of some matters?" I asked.

He put down his mug of tea. "Yes, I do." I believe I had surprised Hontvedt in the act of trimming his beard, as it had an odd, misshapen appearance.

"And I insisted that you stop speaking of them?" I asked.

"Yes."

"I have thought about the matters which you brought up, and it seems to me that these are subjects we might at some later date continue to discuss. That is, we may explore them further."

"Oh, Maren —"

"This is not to say at all that I find the idea acceptable at the moment. I am merely stating that I will allow further discussion."

"You cannot imagine —"

"You understand, of course, that it is really too soon for me to think of leaving my father's house. . . ."

To my horror, John Hontvedt left his seat altogether and placed himself at my feet. I made a motion with my hands to make him rise, but he seized both of my hands in his.

"Maren, I shall not disappoint you!" he cried. "I shall make you the happiest woman in all of Norway."

"No, John, you have misunderstood. . . ."

He reached forward to embrace me. I believe he underestimated his strength and his ardor, for when he put his arms around me, he nearly squeezed the breath out of my body. In the next minute, he was covering my face and my hands with kisses and had leaned his entire torso onto my lap. I tried to stand up, but could not move in this embrace. I became frightened then, frightened of being overtaken by someone stronger than myself, and also quite hollow with the first sensations of a decision so wrong as to threaten to poison my entire soul.

"John!" I cried out. "Please stop!"

John then stood up, and he said that he would walk me to the cottage. I protested, as I did not want Karen or my father to see Hontvedt in such an excited state, nor did I want this excitement to carry over into any possible conversation between Father and John.

"I shall make you very happy, Maren," he said.

"Thank you," I said, although I sincerely doubted that he could do this.

And thus it was that John Hontvedt and myself came to be engaged.

Hontvedt and I were married on 22 December 1867, just after the winter solstice. I wore the walnut silk I have mentioned in these pages, as well as a fringed bonnet with braided ties that fastened behind the ears and under the chin. Professor Jessen, who remained my friend, lent Hontvedt and myself his house in Laurvig for a small wedding party after the ceremony at Laurvig Church. I confess I was not so gay on this occasion as I might have been, as I was somewhat fearful of the heavy responsibilities that lay before me as the wife of John Hontvedt, and also because my brother, Evan, did not come to my wedding, owing to the fact that he was home ill with a bronchial infection, and this was a distress both to John and myself.

After the reception, at which John drank a good deal of aquavit, which Professor Jessen had been kind enough to provide for us, I was forced to leave the others, as was my duty, and to go away with John, to his house, where we were to spend our first night together. I should say here that our initial occasion as man and wife was not entirely successful, owing in part to John's state of inebriation, which I had reason, in the event, to be grateful for, and also to some confusion, when John cried out, although there was only, I am relieved to say, myself to hear, that I had deceived him. Since I had not given any thought to these technicalities, nor had I been properly educated in that aspect of marriage, having only Karen, who, of course, cannot have had any experience herself, to instruct me, I was alarmed by John's cries, but fortunately, as I have indicated, the drink then overwhelmed him, and though I anticipated some discussion on this subject the next morning, it was never again raised, and I am not certain to this day if John Hontvedt ever retained any consciousness of the particular occurrences of our wedding night, his memory having been expunged, so to speak, by the aquavit.

Torwad Holde's hateful letter came to us shortly after the wedding. All that long winter, in the darkness, newly married, I was engaged in numerous preparations for the Atlantic crossing. John wanted to set sail in the early spring as it would allow us several months of mild weather during which to establish ourselves in a fishing community, find lodgings and lay by enough food to see us through the following winter.

Though I had no inclination myself to take this voyage, I knew the value of having stores, as I had read many America letters which attested to the necessity of bringing one's own provisions, and in sufficient quantity, on the crossings. Sometimes Karen assisted me in this work, but not often, as I was no longer living in my father's house. All that long winter, in the darkness, newly married, I made clothes for John and myself of wool, and of colored gingham when I could come by it. John built for us barrels and chests, into which I put salted fish, herring, sour milk, beer, rye rusks, whey cheese, peas, cereal, potatoes and sugar. In other chests, I packed tallow candles, soap, a frying pan, a coffee burner, kettles, a flatiron, a tin funnel with matches, many linens and so on. Indeed, I believe I so occupied myself in the preparations for our journey that I was able to put from my mind, until those last moments on the dock with Evan, the nearly unthinkable fact of the voyage itself, which would mean my departure from Norway forever. To this end, I had not made any farewells, either to my family or to my few friends, believing that to do so might weaken whatever small resolve I had in regards to my duty, which was to accompany my husband on this sojourn.

Our sailing vessel, which was sloop-rigged, contained, belowdecks, forty bunks, each of which was to be sleeping quarters, as well as storage, for two persons. So that John and I, for thirty-nine days, shared a narrow pallet with many of our provisions, and owing to the fact that I dared not remove my outer garments in that crowded room, and also to the dreadful pitching and rolling of that ship, I hardly slept at all during those interminable nights. Instead I lay in the blackness of that hold listening to various persons praying and crying and being sick, with no hope of release until North America was reached, or the ship sank, and there were nights of such wretchedness that, God forgive me, I sometimes wished for the latter.

We were not treated badly by the crew, as I have heard was the case on some Atlantic crossings, particularly aboard those vessels that were owned by the English, but water was strictly rationed, and so much so that it was a trial to most of us to manage on just one quart a day, although John and I did have the beer to drink when our thirst was almost intolerable. I had the seasickness from the second day out, and I may say here that I believe there is no physical torment, which then permits recovery, greater than the seasickness, which causes one to feel ill at one's very soul. So wretched was this affliction that I was unable to eat, and might have grown seriously ill as a consequence of this. I must, however, despite the misery of those days, count myself among the lucky, for there were those on board who contracted the ship's fever and the cholera, and it is a wonder of God that these dreadful contagions did not spread to us all. During the fourth week of our voyage, which was the worst in regards to illness on board, there were many burials at sea, the most trying of which was the burial of a small boy, who had contracted the ship's fever, which is also called typhus, and who was so thin at the time of his death that, though he had boarded the ship fat enough, he had to be buried with sand in his casket, so that the poor child might sink to the depths, and not stay afloat behind the ship, which would truly have been an unendurable torment to the mother, who was already in despair. I believe this was the lowest moment of our journey, and that there was not one person on board, who was still conscious and sensible, who was not sorely affected by this tragedy.

I am told that on the voyage, those who were not ill engaged in knitting and sewing, and some playing of the flute and violin, and I think that John, as he remained in robust health the entire trip, may have participated in the music-making and singing that sometimes spontaneously erupted out of the tedium of the crossing. We lost fourteen persons to illness during the journey, and one woman from Stavern gave birth to twins. I have always thought this a grotesquely unacceptable ratio of deaths to births, and had I paid more attention to the stories of fatal diseases on board these ships, I might have been able to persuade John Hontvedt not to make the crossing at all. But this is idle speculation, as we did make the journey, did reach Quebec, where we were quarantined for two days, and did travel further south to the town of Portland in the state of Maine, and thence to Portsmouth in the state of New Hampshire, where we were met by Torwad Holde, who took us, in his schooner, to the island of Smutty Nose, where I was to reside for five years.

In having undertaken to write this document, I find I must, unhappily, revisit moments of the past, which, like the Atlantic Crossing, are dispiriting to recall. And as I am in ill health at the time of this writing, it is a twice-difficult task I have set for myself. But I believe that it is only with great perseverance that one is able to discover for oneself, and therefore set before another, a complete and truthful story.

I had been forewarned that we would be living on an island, but I do not think that anyone could adequately have prepared me for the nature of that particular island, or, indeed, of the entire archipelago, which was called the Isles of Shoals and lay 18 kilometers east of the American coast, north of Gloucester. As it was a hazy day on our first trip from Portsmouth to the islands, we did not spy the Shoals altogether until we were nearly upon them, and when we did, I became faint with disbelief. Never had I seen such a sad and desolate place! Lumps of rock that had barely managed to rise above the water line, the islands seemed to me then, and did so always after that day, an uninhabitable location for any human being. There was not one tree and only the most austere of empty, wooden-frame dwellings. Smutty Nose, in particular, looked so shallow and barren that I turned to John and implored him, "This is not it! Surely this is not it!"

John, who was, at that moment, struggling to conquer his own considerable shock, was unable to answer me. Though Torwad Holde, who was, the reader may recall, the author of the infamous letter that had brought us to America (and to whom I was perhaps not as cordial as I might have been), yelled out with some enthusiasm, "Yes, Mrs. Hontvedt, these are the Isles of Shoals. Are they not wonderful?"

After we had made anchor in the tiny harbor, and I, trembling, had been helped onto the island of Smutty Nose, I felt a deep sinking as well as the beginnings of fear in my breast. How could I live on this inhospitable ledge in the middle of the Atlantic Ocean, with nothing around me but seawater, with the nearest shore not even within sight that day? How could I accept that this was the place where I should spend the rest of my life, and upon which shortly I was to be abandoned by all human company, with the exception of John Hontvedt? I clung to my husband, which I was not in the habit of doing, and begged him, I am ashamed to say, right in the presence of Torwad Holde, to take us back to Portsmouth instantly, where we might at least find a house that was settled on the soil, and where there might be about us flowers and fruit trees such as we had known in Laurvig. John, embarrassed for me and disentangling himself from my embrace, went to help Torwad Holde carry our provisions into the cottage that stood on that island with the forlorn look of a child who has been abandoned or not ever loved. Although it was spring, there were no inhabitants in any of the other buildings on the island, and there were no blossoms in the crevices of the rocks. The soil, when I bent down to feel it, was not even three inches deep. What beautiful thing could possibly grow in such a wasteland? Around me I could hear no human sounds, apart from the grunts and sighs of John and Torwad Holde as they went to and fro with their burdens. There was, however, the steady irritating whine of the wind, for it was a cold day in early May, not at all spring-like. I walked slowly eastward, as if in a trance, as if, having committed no crime, I had been sentenced to a life in exile in the bleakest of penal colonies. I gazed out to the horizon line, imagining that my beloved Norway lay in my line of sight. We seemed to have travelled half the earth! And for what purpose?

After a time, when I could bear it, I entered the wooden-frame house that would be my home for five years. It was sided with clapboards, and was of an entirely unadorned style I was not familiar with. It had, I imagine, originally been built for at least two families, as there were two separate dwellings within the one, each with its own front door on the northwestern side of the house. The house had been painted a dull red, and there were no shutters on the windows. A single chimney, such as might accommodate a stove, had been put into the house. Inside of each apartment, there were three small rooms downstairs and one small room up a short stairway. The stove was put into the largest room of the first apartment, and henceforth we used that room as our kitchen and living room, and, in winter, as our bedroom as well. As it was then 9 May, however, John put our bed in the southwestern corner of that apartment. I believe that the previous tenants, doubtless a fisher-family such as we, had been in rather poor financial circumstances, as the walls were papered with newsprint that had yellowed, and, in some places, torn. No curtains hung on the windows, and there was no evidence of any painting or of any effort to make a cheerful abode. The entire interior was bleak, and, if I may say so, quite gloomy, as there was, in the kitchen, only one small window at the end of the room. As the house held the smell of mildew as well, I thought it could not have been occupied for some time.

John brought a chair into the house, and I sat on it. He touched me on the shoulder, but did not speak, and then he went out again.

I sat, in an attitude of prayer, with my hands folded in my lap, though I could not pray, as I thought then that God had abandoned me. I knew that I would not be able to leave the island, that our arrival at this place was irrevocable, as was my marriage to Hontvedt, and I had, I remember, to bite my cheek to keep from breaking into tears that once started might continue forever.

But perhaps God did not abandon me after all on that day, for as I sat there, paralyzed with the weakest of sins, which is despair, I believe it was God's hand that caused me then to realize that I must somehow survive my ordeal so that I would one day be reunited with my brother. I stood up and walked to the window and looked out over the rock. I vowed then to keep as still and as silent as possible so that the strong emotions that threatened to consume me might come under my control, in much the same way that a drowning man, clinging to a life raft, will know that he cannot afford to wail or cry out or beat his breast, and that it is only with the utmost reserve and care and patience that he will be able to remain afloat until he is saved. It would not do, I also knew, to bemoan constantly my great loss to my husband, for John would quickly tire of that lament, and would feel, in addition, a personal sorrow that would inhibit his own ability to embrace the life he had chosen. I turned away from the window and examined again the interior of the cottage. I would make a home here, I told myself. I would not look eastward again.

IN AFRICA, WHEN I was on assignment there, some Masai whom I met thought that if I took a photograph of them, and if I went away with that photograph, I would have stolen their soul. I have sometimes wondered if this can be done with a place, and when I look now at the pictures of Smuttynose, I ask myself if I have captured the soul of the island. For I believe that Smuttynose has a soul, distinct from that of Appledore or Londoner's, or any other place on earth. That soul is, of course, composed of the stories we have attached to a particular piece of geography, as well as of the cumulative moments of those who have lived on and visited the small island. And I believe the soul of Smuttynose is also to be found in its rock and tufted vetch, its beggar's-ticks and pilewort, its cinquefoil brought from Norway. It lives as well in the petrels that float on the air and the skate that beach themselves — white and slimy and bloated — on the island's dark beach.

In 1846, Thomas Laighton built a hotel on Smuttynose known as the Mid-Ocean House. This hotel was a thin, wooden-frame, clapboard structure, not much bigger than a simple house. It was built on pilings and had a wraparound porch on three sides. Over the tin roof of the porch hung a hand-painted sign from a third-story window. The sign was imperfectly lettered and read, simply, MID-OCEAN HOUSE.

From photos of the hotel, there is little evidence of landscaping around the building; sand and rock and seagrass border the pilings under the porch. But history tells us that the hotel, in its heyday, boasted a garden, several fruit trees, and a bowling green. Nathaniel Hawthorne, Henry David Thoreau, Edward

Everett Hale, and Richard Henry Dana were guests at the Mid-Ocean. In one archival photograph, three unidentified people are relaxing on the porch. One man is wearing a suit with a white straw hat; a woman has on a high-necked, long-sleeved black dress, with a black silk bonnet, a costume that seems better suited for a Victorian funeral than for a holiday on Smuttynose. A second woman, who appears to be stout, and who has her hair rolled at the back, has on a white blouse, a long black skirt, and over it an apron. One imagines her to have been the cook. The Mid-Ocean House burned in 1911. In March of 1873, the hotel was unoccupied because the season didn't begin until June.

I wonder now: Did Maren ever go to the Mid-Ocean Hotel? Might John, on a pleasant summer evening, have walked his wife the hundred yards, across the rocks with the wildflowers snagged and blowing, to the hotel porch, and had a cup of tea and a piece of American cake — a bowl of quaking pudding? Whitpot? Would they have sat, straight-backed, in the old woven rockers, damp and loosened already from the sea air, and looked out to a view they knew already by heart? Might this view — this panorama of rocky islands and spray and some pleasure boats coming now from the mainland — have looked different to them than it did from the windows of the red house? Did Maren wear a dress brought from Norway, and were they, as they sat on the wooden porch in the slight breeze from the water, objects of curiosity? Their shoes, their speech, their not-perfect manners giving them away? Might they have sat beside Childe Hassam at his easel or Celia Thaxter with her notebook and passed a pleasantry, a nod, a slight bow? Might John once have reached over to the armrest of his wife's chair and touched her hand? Did he love her?

Or was the hotel a building they could not enter except as servants — John, in his oilskins, bringing lobsters to the cook? Maren, in her homespun, her boots and hands cracked, washing linens, sweeping floorboards? Did they, in their turn, regard the guests as curiosities, American rich who provided Shoalers with extra monies in the summer season? Pale natives who were often seasick out from Portsmouth?

I like to think of Hawthorne on Smuttynose, taking the sea air, as had been prescribed. Would he have come by steamer from Boston, have brought a boater and a white suit for the sun? Would he have been inspired by the desolation of the Shoals, tempted to bathe in the extraordinarily deep waters that separated Smuttynose from Appledore or Star? Might he have been invigorated by the conversation of the intellectuals and artists Celia Thaxter had gathered around her — Charles Dickens and John Greenleaf Whittier, William Morris Hunt, a kind of colony, a salon. Did he eat the blueberry grunt, the fish soup, the pluck that was put before him? And who put it there? Is it possible that a Norwegian immigrant hovered over him? Did this woman ask a question of Nathaniel Hawthorne, a pleasant question, having no idea who he was, another guest is all, in her charming but broken English? *Tings. Togedder. Brotter.*

It is almost impossible now, looking across to Smuttynose, to imagine Hawthorne on that island. There is no trace of the Mid-Ocean Hotel. It has passed into recorded memory, historical fact, with no life except in sentences and on photographic emulsion. If all the sentences and photographs about the hotel were to be swept into the sea that surrounds Smuttynose, the Mid-Ocean — Hawthorne's stay there, an immigrant's abbreviated pleasantries — would cease to exist.

No one can know a story's precise reality.

On October 2, 1867, a boxing match was held at Smuttynose. Because gambling was illegal in the 1860s, isolated locations, without much interference from the police, were in demand. The Isles of Shoals, and Smuttynose in particular, appeared to be ideal for this purpose. Two fighters went at it for an hour and a half in the front yard of the Charles Johnson house, previously known as "the red house," and subsequently to be known as the Hontvedt house. The spectators came by boat. Another fight was planned, but was canceled when bad weather prevented any observers from reaching the island and made the contestants seasick.

At dawn on the morning of the second day at the Isles of Shoals, I am awakened by unwanted and familiar sounds. I slip out of the bed, with its damp-roughened sheets, and begin to make a pot of coffee in the galley. When I run the water, I cannot hear the movements in the forward cabin. I am waiting for the coffee to drip through the filter, my arms crossed over my chest, a sense of wet seeping through my socks, when I reach up and pop open the hatch for just a sliver of fresh air. I see immediately that the sky is a darkened red, as though there has been a fire on the shore. I open the hatch fully and climb up through the companionway in my robe. A band of smoky crimson arches over all the islands, a north-south ribbon that seems to stretch from Portland all the way to Boston. The red is deep in the center, becoming dustier toward the edges. Beneath the swath of red, gulls catch the light of the slanted sun and seem momentarily imbued with a glow of color all their own. I am somewhat concerned — the way you are when nature goes off her routines — yet I want to go below, to wake Billie, to show her this phenomenon of sunlight on water particles in the air. But Billie is already there, behind me.

"I've cut my foot, Mommy" is what she says.

I turn in the cockpit. Her face is sticky and puffed with sleep, her mouth beginning to twist with the first messages of pain. She has on her summer baseball pajamas, shorts and a T-shirt — *Red Sox,* they say. Her feet are white and tiny and bare, and from her right foot the blood is spreading. She moves slightly toward me and makes a smudge on the white abraded surface of the cockpit floor. A small stray shard from last night's broken glass must have fallen below the ladder of the companionway. My opening the hatch this morning has woken Billie, who then walked into the small triangle under the ladder to retrieve one of Blackbeard's treasures, the key chain.

I go below to get towels and hydrogen peroxide and bandages from the first-aid kit, and after I have washed and dressed the cut and am holding Billie in my arms, I look up and realize there is no trace, nothing left at all, of the red band in the sky.

Rich comes up onto the deck, puts his hands to his waist, and examines the color and texture of the sky, which is not altogether clear, not as it was the day before. To the east, just below the morning sun, a thin layer of cloud sits on the horizon like an unraveling roll of discolored cotton wool. Rich, who looks mildly concerned, goes below to listen to the radio. When he returns to the deck, he brings with him a mug of coffee. He sits opposite Billie and me in the cockpit.

"How did it happen?"

"She cut it on a piece of glass."

"She's all right?"

"I think so. The bleeding seems to have stopped."

"NOAA says there's a cold front coming through later today. But NOAA is not to be entirely trusted."

Rich moves his head so that he can see beyond me. There is a gentle chop, but the harbor still seems well protected. Across the way, there is activity aboard a ketch anchored near us. Rich nods at a woman in a white polo shirt and khaki shorts.

"Looks like they're leaving," he says.

"So soon? They just got in last night."

A sudden breeze blows the skirt of my robe open, and I fold it closed over my knees. I do not really like to be seen in the morning. I have a sense of not being entirely covered, not yet protected. Rich has on a clean white T-shirt and a faded navy-blue bathing suit. He is barefoot and has recently showered. The top of his head is wet, and he doesn't have a beard. I wonder where Adaline is.

"I don't know," he says, speculating out loud about the storm.

"It isn't clear how bad it will be, or even if it will definitely be here by tonight."

I shift Billie on my lap. I look over toward Smuttynose. Rich must see the hesitation on my face.

"You need to go over to the island again," he says.

"I should."

"I'll take you."

"I can take myself," I say quickly. "I did it last night."

This surprises him.

"After everyone was asleep. I wanted night shots."

Rich studies me over the rim of his coffee. "You should have woken me," he says. "It isn't safe to go off like that by yourself. At night, especially."

"Was it scary, Mommy?"

"No. Actually, it was very beautiful. The moon was out and was so bright I could see my way without a flashlight."

Rich is silent. I pick up my own mug from the deck. The coffee is cold. Billie sits up suddenly, jogging my arm. The coffee spills onto the sleeve of my white robe.

"Mommy, can I go over with you tonight? To the island when it's dark? Maybe there will be ghosts there."

"Not tonight," says Rich. "No one's going over there tonight. We may be having a storm later. It wouldn't be safe."

"Oh," she says, dropping her shoulders in disappointment.

"I've got landscape shots from the water," I say, tallying up my meager inventory. "And night shots, and I've done Maren's Rock. But I need shots from the island itself, looking out to Appledore and Star, and to the east, out to sea. And also some detail shots."

"Like what?"

"Scrub pine. Rose hips. A window of the Haley house, the footprint of the Hontvedt house. I should have done this yesterday when I had the chance. I'm sorry."

"It's all right," he says. "We have time."

"Me too!" says Billie excitedly.

Rich shakes his head. "You stay here with your dad and Adaline." He reaches over and pulls my daughter from my lap. He whirls her around and tickles her at her waist. She begins to laugh with that unique helplessness that borders on hysteria. She tries to wriggle away from his grasp and screams to me to help her. "Mommy, save me! Save me!" But when Rich suddenly stops, she turns to him with an appreciative sigh and folds herself into his lap.

"Whew," she says. "That was a good tickle."

George E. Ingerbretson, a Norwegian immigrant who lived at Hog Island Point on Appledore Island, was called to the stand. He, like many who were summoned, spoke in a halting and imperfect English that was not always easy to transcribe. He was asked by the county attorney what he observed between seven and eight o'clock on the morning of March 6, 1873. He replied that he had two small boys and that they had come into his house and said, "They are halooing over to Smutty Nose." He was then asked what he saw when he got to the island.

"I saw one bloody axe; it was lying on a stone in front of the door, John Hontvet's kitchen door. The handle was broken. I went around the house. I saw a piece knocked off the window. Then I stopped. I saw John was coming. I did not look into the window. I only saw the bloody axe and blood around."

After John Hontvedt arrived, along with several other men, Ingerbretson went inside the house.

"Evan Christensen went just ahead of me; he opened the door. Evan is the husband of Anethe."

"Who else went with you at that time?" Yeaton asked.

"John Hontvet and Louis Nelson and James Lee, no one else. John's brother, Matthew, was with us. I do not know whether he went into the house or not."

"State what you saw."

"It was Anethe, lying on her back, head to the door. It looked to me as though she was hauled into the house by the feet. I saw the marks."

"Of what?"

"From the south-east corner of the house into the door."

"Traces of what?"

"Of blood."

"Was there any other body there?"

"Yes. Then we went out and went into another room in the northward side, north-east of the house. We came in and there was some blood around, and in the bed-room we found another dead body."

"Whose body was that?"

"That was Karen Christensen."

"Did you notice any wounds upon the body of Anethe?"

"Yes; there are some scars on the head."

"What part of the head were they?"

"In the ear most, just about the right ear. She had some scar in her face there."

"Scar on top of the head?"

"We did not look much after that time."

Yeaton then asked Ingerbretson some questions about the well that belonged to the house and its distance from the house, and whether he had disturbed any of the bodies. Ingerbretson said that he had not. Yeaton asked the fisherman if he had seen any tracks, and Ingerbretson said no, he had not seen any tracks. Before Yeaton dismissed the witness, he asked if, when he had arrived on Smuttynose that morning, there was any living person on that island.

"Yes," the fisherman replied.

"Who was it?"

"Mrs. Hontvet and a little dog."

"State condition in which you found her."

"In an overbad condition. She was in her night-dress crying and halooing, and blood all over her clothes, Mrs. Hontvet's clothes. I got her into the boat."

"Do you know whether her feet were frozen?"

"Yes. I searched her feet right off and they were stiff. I carried her over to my house."

Before a shoot, I will prepare the cameras — check my film and the batteries, clean the lenses — and I begin these tasks in the cockpit. Billie has gone below to wake Thomas. I can hear them talking and laughing, playing on the bed, although the wind, with its constant white noise, steals their words.

Adaline emerges from the companionway. She smiles and says, "Good morning." Her legs are bare, and she is holding a towel around her, as if she had just stepped from the shower, although she is not wet. Her hair is spread all along her back in knots and tangles. I can see a small bit of red beneath the towel, so I know that she has on her bathing suit, and I wonder for a moment why she has the towel around her. How strange we women are in the mornings, I am thinking, this modesty, this not wanting to be seen. Adaline turns her back to me and puts her foot up on the cockpit bench, inspecting her toes.

"I hear Billie got a cut," she says.

"Yes. She did."

"Bad?"

"Not too."

"I'm going for a swim."

She lets the towel drop to the cockpit floor. She keeps her back to me, and I notice things I have not before. The plate-shallow curve of her inner thigh. The elongated waist. The patch of hair she has missed just above the inside of her right knee. I think about what her skin would feel like. This is painful curiosity. She steps up to the back of the stern, positions herself for a dive. She skims the water like a gull.

She does not come up sputtering or exclaiming from the cold, as I might have done, but rather spins in a lovely barrel roll and swims with an economy of strokes, her feet barely moving at all. I see wisps of red amid the chop. She swims for about ten minutes, away from the boat and back. When she is done, she climbs up over the stern with ease, refusing my outstretched hand. She sits opposite me in the cockpit and picks up the towel to dry herself. She is slightly winded, which is somehow reassuring.

"You kept your maiden name," she says.

"Jean Janes had an infelicitous ring to it," I explain.

I notice that the water beads up on her skin.

"It wasn't for professional reasons then?"

"Not exactly."

She sets the towel down beside her and begins to brush out her hair.

"Did I hear Rich say there might be a storm?" she asks.

"We may have to leave before this afternoon." The thought of leaving the harbor fills me with swift, sharp regret, as if I had left something significant unfinished.

"Where are we going?"

"I don't know. Portsmouth possibly. Or Annisquam."

She bends her head to her knees, letting her hair fall forward to the floor. She brushes upward from the nape of her neck. She throws her head back and begins to brush from the sides of her face. In my camera bag is a Polaroid camera I use in test shots. Often, when I have a scene I like, I take a Polaroid first, so that I can examine the composition and the light and make adjustments if necessary before shooting the real thing. I take the Polaroid out of my camera bag and aim it at Adaline. I quickly snap a picture. She blinks at the click. I rip the film out and hold it in my hand, waiting for the image to appear. In the photograph, Adaline is holding a brush to her head. Her hair, which has dried in the sun, has streaked itself a light blond, or perhaps it is a photographic deception. Her skin looks dark by contrast, deeply tanned. I hold the picture out to her.

She takes it in her hand and examines it.

"A mere negative of my former self," she says and smiles.

In Haley's Cove, a pier supported a long warehouse and fish processing plant. The men of Smuttynose invented the process of drying fish called dunning. Large vessels would tie up inside the pier to load and offload goods and fish, which were then stored in the building known as the Long House. The area that comprises the pier, the Long House, Captain Haley's House, and the footprint of the Hontvedt cottage is not much bigger than a modest suburban backyard.

Dunfish sold for three or four times the price of regularly prepared fish. So many fish were harvested by Shoalers that in 1822 the national price of fish was quoted not from Boston but from the Isles of Shoals.

When Thomas comes up the ladder, he brings with him the smell of bacon and pancakes.

"Billie and I made breakfast," he says. "Adaline's setting the table."

I am rereading one of the guidebooks to see if I have overlooked a landmark, an artifact that I should not miss when I go across to Smuttynose to finish the shoot. In my lap is Maren Hontvedt's document and its translation, as well as a thin pamphlet, one of the accounts of the murders.

"What's that?" he asks. A conciliatory gesture. Interest in my work.

"This?" I ask, holding up the guidebook.

"No, that."

I lay my hand on the papers with the brown ink, as if protecting them. "It's the thing I got from the Athenaeum."

"Really. Can I see it?"

Without looking precisely at him, I hand the papers to Thomas. I can feel the color and the heat coming into the back of my neck.

"It's not in English," he says.

"There's a translation."

"This is an original document," he says with some surprise. "I'm amazed they let you have it."

There is a silence.

"They didn't," I say. I push my hair behind my ears.

"They didn't," he repeats.

"I knew they wouldn't give it to me, so I took it. I'll give it back."

"What is it?"

"It's a memoir. By Maren Hontvedt."

"Who is?"

"The woman who survived the murders."

"It's dated 1899."

"I know."

He hands the papers back to me, and I look up at him for the first time. His hair has been combed off his forehead with his fingers and lies in thinning rows, an already harvested crop. His eyes are bloodshot, and his skin, in the harsh, flat light, looks blotchy.

"You don't need this stuff for your assignment," he says.

"No."

He is about to turn and go back down to the galley, but he hesitates a moment on the steps. "What's going on with you?" he asks.

I shade my brow with my hand. "What's going on with you?" I ask.

At the Shoals, men have always fished for haddock and for hake, for porgies and for shad. In 1614, Captain John Smith first mapped the islands and called them Smythe's Isles, and he wrote that they were "a heape together."

Halyards slap against the mast, an insistent beat we can hear at the double bed—cum—dining table in the center of the cabin. Thomas and Billie have made pancakes — kidney shaped, oil glistened, and piled high upon a white platter. There is also bacon, which Adaline declines. She chooses toast and orange juice instead. I watch her, nearly naked, lift her mug of decaffeinated coffee to her lips and blow across the rim. I am not sure that I could now sit at a breakfast table in my bathing suit, though I must have done so as a younger woman.

Are we, as we age, I wonder, repaid for all our thoughtless gestures?

Billie, next to me, still has on her Red Sox pajamas. She smells of sleep. She is proud of her misshapen pancakes, and eats six of them. I think it is the one certain way to get Billie — any child? — to eat a meal. Have her cook it herself.

I have on my robe. Rich his bathing suit. Thomas the shirt he slept in. Is it our dishabille that creates the tension — a tension so pronounced I find it hard to swallow? Rich wears the weather report on his face, and we seem excessively focused on the food and on Billie, in the manner of adults who have not found an easy entrée into the conversation. Or who are suddenly wary of conversation: "These are wonderful, Billie. I can see the bear now." "What kind of coffee is this? It has an almond flavor." "I love bacon. Honestly, is there anything better on a camping trip than a bacon sandwich?"

Sometimes I watch the way that Thomas watches me. And if he catches me at this, he slips his eyes away so gracefully that I am not sure he has seen me. Is this simply the familiarity of bodies? I wonder. I no longer know with any certainty what he is thinking.

"Do you keep a journal?" Adaline asks Thomas.

I am surprised by the question. Will she dare a reprise of Pearse?

Thomas shakes his head. "Who has so many words that he can afford to spend them on letters and journals?" he asks.

Rich nods. "Tom's a terrible letter writer."

I haven't heard the nickname in years.

"His literary executor will have it easy," Rich adds. "There won't be anything there."

"Except the work," I say quietly. "There's a lot of the work."

"A lot of false starts," says Thomas. "Especially lately."

I look over at Thomas, and I wonder if what I see is the same face I knew fifteen years ago. Does it seem the same to me? Is the skin the same? Or is the expression now so different than it was then that the muscles have become realigned, the face itself un-recognizable?

"Is it definite that man did it?"

Adaline's question startles all of us. It takes me a second to catch up. "Louis Wagner?" I ask.

"Do they know for sure?"

"Some think yes," I answer slowly, "and some think no. At the time, Wagner protested his innocence. But the crime created a tremendous amount of hysteria. There were riots and lynch mobs, and they had to hurry the trial."

Adaline nods.

"Even now, there are doubts," I add. "He hadn't much of a mo-tive for the murders themselves, for example, and that row from Portsmouth to Smuttynose would have been brutal. He'd have had to row almost thirty miles in the dark. And it was the first week in March."

"It doesn't seem possible," says Rich. "I couldn't do it. I'm not even sure I could do it on a flat surface."

"Also, I've read parts of the trial transcript," I say, "and I can't figure out why the prosecution didn't do a better job. Maren Hontvedt's clothes were blood-soaked, but the defense didn't really pursue this. And the coroner was very careless with the murder weapon — they let the sea spray wash off all the finger-prints and blood on the journey back to Portsmouth."

"Surely, they had fingerprinting techniques then," says Rich.

"On the other hand," I say, "Wagner seems to have no alibi for that night, and the next morning he's reported to have told people he committed murder."

"Jean doesn't always get to pick her assignments," Thomas says. He sounds apologetic.

"A crime of passion," says Rich.

"A crime of passion?" Adaline narrows her eyes. "In the end, a crime of passion is just sordid, isn't it? At heart. We think a crime of passion has a morality all its own — people have thought so for years. History is full of judgments that forgive crimes of passion. But it doesn't have a morality, not really. It's pure selfishness. Simply having what you want."

"I think it's the knife that makes it seem like a crime of passion," says Thomas. "It was a knife, wasn't it?"

"An ax."

"Same thing. It's the intimacy. With a gun, you can kill a person at a distance. But with a knife, you have to touch the victim — more than touch. Manhandle. Subdue. It would seem to require, at least for the several seconds it takes to complete the deed, a sustained frenzy or passion."

"Or a lucrative contract," says Rich.

"But even then," argues Thomas, "there would have to be something in the act — the handling of the victim, the feel of the knife against the flesh — that attracted the killer to that particular method."

"Thomas," I say, nodding at Billie.

"Mommy, take a picture of the pancakes," she says. "Before they're all gone?"

I reach behind me into my camera bag and bring out the Polaroid. I shoot the platter with the pancakes that are left, and then rip the film out and give it to Billie to hold. She's a pro at this, and holds the corner casually.

"The Masai," I say idly, "believe that if you take a photograph of a person, you have stolen his soul. You have to pay them for the picture."

"The soul is for sale then?" asks Adaline.

"Oh, I think the Masai are shrewder than that."

"See, Adaline? Look!" Billie stands on the bench to hand Adaline the Polaroid. As she does, she cracks her head on the sharp corner of an overhanging cabinet. The color leaves Billie's face, and her mouth falls open, but I can see that in this company my daughter is determined not to cry.

I reach over and fold her into me. The photograph flutters onto the table. She presses her face into my chest, and I feel her breath through the opening of my robe. Adaline picks up the Polaroid. "Lovely picture, Billie," she says.

I kiss Billie's forehead, and she pulls away from me, turning in her seat, trying bravely to smile. Adaline hands the picture to Billie.

"Very game," says Adaline to me.

"Thanks."

"I envy you."

I look quickly up at her and catch her eyes. Does she mean Billie? Or does she mean having my daughter with me? Or does she mean Billie and Thomas — the whole package?

"Sometimes I imagine I have caught a likeness of a person's soul," I say carefully. "Occasionally, you can see it. Or what you imagine is the true character of that person. But of course, it's only a likeness, and that likeness is only an image, on the paper."

"But you can fool with images," she says. "Didn't I read that somewhere? Can't you change the image?"

"You can now," I say. "You can do it almost flawlessly with computers."

"So you could, theoretically, create another character, another soul."

"This is assuming that you believed the camera could capture the soul in the first place," I say.

"This is assuming that you believed in the soul at all," says Thomas. "That what you saw was not simply an arrangement of organic particles."

"But surely you believe in the soul," Adaline says quickly, almost defensively. "You of all people."

Thomas is silent.

"It's in the poems," she says.

I have a series of photographs of Billie and Thomas together, taken shortly after we have eaten the pancakes. I have dressed and am getting my gear together in preparation for the boat ride over to Smuttynose. I take out the Hasselblad, which I have loaded with black-and-white. I do four quick shots — click, click, click, click — of Thomas and Billie, who have lingered at the table. In the first, Billie is standing on the padded bench, inspecting Thomas's teeth, counting them, I think. In the second, she has bent her body so that she is butting her head into Thomas's stomach; Thomas, too, is slightly bent, and has wrapped his arms over her back. In the third picture, they both have their elbows propped upon the table and are facing each other, talking. The conversation must be serious; you can see that in the tilt of Billie's head, the pursing of her mouth. In the fourth picture, Thomas has one hand tucked inside the open collar of his shirt, scratching his shoulder. He is facing me, but he won't look at me or at the camera. Billie has turned her head away from Thomas, as though someone has just called to her from the forward cabin.

The head sea is apparent the moment we round the breakwater. Small waves hit the Zodiac and send their spray into and over the inflatable boat. With one hand on the tiller, Rich tosses me a poncho, which I use to protect my camera bags from the salt water. When I look up again, I find I can hardly see for the spray. My face and hair and glasses are soaked, as in a rain, and foolishly, I have worn shorts, so that my legs are wet and cold and covered with goosebumps.

Rich turns the Zodiac around. He has wanted to observe the ocean on the unprotected side of the island, and he has seen enough. He maneuvers back into the harbor and puts the Zodiac up onto the narrow dark beach of Smuttynose, a beach I left only the night before. I dry my glasses on the inside of my sweatshirt and inspect my camera bags for any signs of wet.

"How do you want to work this?" he asks as he is tying up the boat. His T-shirt has turned a translucent peach. "You want me to go with you and hold things? Or do you want me to wait here."

"Wait here," I say. "Sit in the sun and get dry. Rich, I'm really sorry about this. You must be freezing."

"I'm fine," he says. "I've been wet before. You do what you have to do." He smiles. "I know this is hard to believe," he says, "but I'm actually having a good time. The truth is" — he gestures to indicate the expanse of the ocean and seems to laugh at himself — "I usually have to go to a lot of trouble to be able to do this on my days off."

"I'll try not to be long. Thirty, forty minutes at the most. And if you do get cold," I say, "give a shout, and we'll get out of here. This isn't worth getting sick over."

I bend to collect my camera bags. When I stand up, Rich is wrestling with his wet T-shirt. He takes it off and wipes the top of his head with it, and then squeezes it out. I watch him walk over to a rock that is in the sun, or what is left of the sun, and lay the T-shirt carefully out to dry. When I was in Africa, I observed the women there drying their clothes in a similar manner — by laying them flat on top of long grasses over a wide field, so that often you would come upon a landscape of bright cloth. Rich glances over at me. Perhaps because he has almost no hair on his head, the thick dark chest hair that spreads across his breast draws the eye. I turn around and walk to the interior of Smuttynose.

The defense waived its right to cross-examine Ingerbretson, at which point the prosecution then called Evan Christensen to the stand. Christensen was asked to identify himself and to talk about his relationship to Smuttynose.

"In March last, I lived at the Shoals, Smutty Nose, in John Hontvet's family; I had lived there about five months. Anethe Christensen was my wife. I was born in Norway. Anethe was born in Norway. I came to this country with her after I married her."

Yeaton asked Christensen what he was doing the day of the murders. Christensen answered: "During the night my wife was killed I was in Portsmouth. I arrived at Portsmouth about four o'clock the night before."

"Who was with you when you arrived at Portsmouth about four o'clock that night?"

"John Hontvet and Matthew Hontvet. I was at work for John in the fishing business."

"Was anyone else with you that night?"

"No, sir."

"Where did you spend the night at Portsmouth?"

"I was on board till twelve o'clock; after that went up to Johnson's house and baited trolls."

"Baited trolls the rest of the night?"

"Yes, till six or seven o'clock in the morning. John Hontvet was with me when I baited trolls."

"When did you first hear of this matter at Smutty Nose?"

"Heard it from Appledore Island."

"Where were you then?"

"On board Hontvet's schooner."

"Who were with you at that time?"

"Matthew Hontvet and John Hontvet; it was between eight and nine o'clock in the morning."

"Did you go ashore?"

"Yes; got a boat and went ashore on Appledore Island."

"Where did you go from Appledore Island?"

"I went first up to Ingerbretson's house. After I left there I went to Smutty Nose. When I got to Smutty Nose, I went right up to the house and right in."

"What did you see there?"

"I saw my wife lying on the floor."

"Dead or alive?"

"Dead."

"What did you do?"

"Went right back out again."

The light is flat and muffled, colors indistinct. Thin, dull cloud has slipped over the sun, still rising in the east. I am annoyed with myself for having wasted too much time the day before shooting Maren's Rock. I walk to the spot where the Hontvedt house once stood. The air has a chill in it, or perhaps it is only that I am chilled because my sweatshirt and shorts are wet. I am grateful that Rich knew not to bring Billie.

I stand in the footprint of the house, surveying its markers. There is little here that will make an outstanding photograph; its purpose will be merely documentary. Unless, that is, I can convey the foundation's claustrophobia.

I know that it is always true that the dimensions of a house, seen from above, will look deceptively small. Space appears to increase in size with walls and furniture and windows. Yet even so, I am having difficulty imagining six grown men and women — Maren, John, Evan, Anethe, Matthew, and, for seven months, Louis Wagner — living in a space not much bigger than the single room Thomas had in Cambridge when I met him. All those passions, I think, on such a small piece of land.

I find what I think must have been one of the two front doors of the house and stand at its threshold, looking out toward Appledore, as Maren must have done a thousand times in the five years she lived on the island. I take my cameras and lenses from their separate pouches, check the light meter, and shoot a series of black-and-white stills to make a panorama of that view. Directly west of me is Gosport Harbor and, beyond that, ten miles of water to the New Hampshire coast. To my north is Appledore; to my south is Star. Behind me, that is to say east of me, is the Atlantic. I back away from the threshold and stand in the foundation's center. Beneath me, the floor of that old house has long given way to thistle and wood sage. I find a small patch of bare ground and sit down. Above me, the clouds are growing oilier, as though a film were being washed across the sky. My sweatshirt sticks to my back, and I shiver.

I dig under the brush to feel the dirt. I bring the soil up and massage it with my fingers. In the place where I am sitting, two women died. One was young, one was not. One was beautiful, the other not. I imagine I can hear Maren's voice.

22 September 1899

THE MORNING AFTER we arrived on the island of Smutty Nose, John went off with a man named Ingerbretson to Portsmouth to secure more provisions and also to see about a schooner that might be for sale. In order to make a living on Smutty Nose, around which we were told was an abundance of mackerel, cod, flounder, haddock, and menhaden, John would have to have his own boat plus full gear for fishing. This would be a great expense, and would largely exhaust John's savings, but it was clear to him that no profit, nor even a livelihood, could be earned without such expenditures.

While John was gone, I stripped the walls of the yellowed and ugly newsprint, rolling the papers into logs and burning them on the stove for warmth. At first, the house was colder than it had been, but I knew that shortly John would begin to build wooden walls, behind which he would place goat's tick for insulation. I also found a roll of blue gingham in my stores, which I hastily fashioned into curtains. When these efforts were completed, I examined our remaining provisions for foodstuffs that might make a meal, as I knew that John would be hungry when he returned. All that day I busied myself so that I did not have time for any thoughts about people or a home left behind. I have found, in the course of my adult life, that the best cure for melancholy is industry, and it was only when John and I were imprisoned in the cottage for long weeks at a time during the winter months that I fell victim to that malady and could not control myself or my thoughts and words, so that I was a worry not only to John Hontvedt but also to myself. That day, however, my first day on the island of Smutty Nose, was one of determined busy-ness, and when my husband returned from his sail into Portsmouth, I saw that the changes I had made had pleased him, and he had a smile upon his face, which, for the first time since we had left Norway, replaced the concern that he nearly always had for my well-being.

Our daily life on Smutty Nose was, for the most part, unremarkable in many of its aspects. John and I would wake early, and I would immediately remake the fire that had gone out during the night. John, who would have baited his trawls the evening before, would gather his oil pants and underclothes from the hooks that were in the kitchen, and once dressed would sit down at the table on which I would put in front of him large bowls of porridge and of coffee. We did not speak much, unless there was some unusual piece of information that needed to be imparted, or unless I was in need of some provisions, which I would inform John about. Early on, we had lost the habit of speech with each other, as I think must happen with other husbands and wives who dare not speak for fear of asking the wrong question, or of revealing a festering hurt or a love for another person which might be ruinous to the partnership they had formed.

John would then go down to the beach and from there row out in his dory to his schooner. On good drying days, when he had left the harbor, I would wash the clothes and lay them out on the rocks in the sun. I would bake the flatbrød and prepare the midday meal. I would have the task of cleaning the fish John had caught for drying or eating. I made clothes from bolts of cloth I had brought with me or John had managed in Portsmouth. I spun wool with a spinning wheel John had bought in Portsmouth, and knit various articles of clothing for both myself and for John. When I had finished these chores, and if the day were clear, I would go outside with the dog John had given me, which I had named Ringe, and walk the perimeter of the island, throwing sticks for Ringe into the water so that he might fetch them back to me. In time, John built me a hen coop and purchased in Portsmouth four hens, which were good layers, providing me with fresh eggs.

When John arrived in the evenings, I would take from him his soiled oil clothes and undergarments, and he would have a wash at the sink. I would have prepared a light meal for him. By then, he would have put on dry underclothes, and would sit near to the fire. We had both taken up the habit of smoking a pipe, as it soothed us to do so. John's face was weathering, and he was growing many lines in his skin.

Sometime during the evening, usually when I was sitting near to the fire as well, he would put a hand on my knee, and that would be a signal to me that he wished me to join him in bed. Regardless of the cold, he would remove his garments altogether, and I believe that I saw my husband in a state of undress every night of our married life, as he always lit the candle on the table by our bed. As for me, I would have preferred that our marital relations be conducted in the dark, but John would not have this. I usually kept on my nightdress, or if it were very cold, all my garments. Except for one or two occasions when I was bathing, I am not sure John Hontvedt ever saw me in my natural condition. I had, after a time, lost my physical revulsion toward my husband, and tolerated these nightly relations well enough, but I cannot say there was ever any pleasure in the event — particularly so as it became more and more obvious to me that there was something wrong with me that was preventing me from conceiving a child.

Though our daily life on Smutty Nose was one of habit and routine, I would not be correctly portraying life on the Isles of Shoals if I omitted to say that the winters there were exceedingly harsh. Of that seasonal desolation, I can barely write. I am not certain that it is possible to convey the despair that descends upon one who has been subjected to the ceaseless cold and wet, with storms out of the northeast that on occasion smashed fishing boats upon the rocks and washed away the houses of the Shoalers, causing many to die at sea and on land, and imprisoning those who survived in dark and cheerless rooms for so many days on end that it was a wonder we did not all lose our minds. It has been said that the fishermen who lived on those islands at that time were possessed of an extraordinary courage, but I think that this courage, if we would call it so, is merely the instinct to fasten one's body onto a stationary object and hold on, and have as well the luck not to have one's roof blown into the ocean. I remember weeks when John could not go to sea, nor could anyone come across to Smutty Nose, and when the weather was so dangerous that we two sat for hours huddled by the stove in the kitchen, into which we had moved our bed, and the windows and door of which we had sealed from the elements. We had no words to speak to each other, and everything around us was silent except for the wind that would not stop and made the house shudder. Also, the air inside the room became quite poisonous due to the smoke of the stove and of our pipes, and I recall that I almost always had the headache.

Many fisher-families experience lives of isolation, but ours was made all the greater because of the unique geographical properties of an island in the North Atlantic Ocean, which properties then convey themselves to the soul. There was no day, for example, that the foremost element in one's life was not the weather. There might be clear days with heavy seas, cloudy days with light seas, hazy days when one could not see the mainland, days of fog so dense that I could not find the well, nor make my way accurately to the beach, days of such ferocious storms and winds that entire houses were washed in an instant into the sea, and one could not leave one's dwelling for fear of meeting a similar fate, and days upon days of a noxious wind that made the panes of glass beat against their wooden frames and never ceased its whistle in and around the cottage. So important was the state of the elements that every morning one thought of nothing else except of how to survive what God and nature had brought forth, or, on the rare days of clear skies and no wind, of warm sun and exhilarating air, of how thankful one was for such a heady reprieve.

Because of the necessity for John to go out to sea seven days a week in season, and the equally strong necessity to remain shut in for so many weeks at a time in winter, we did not have many friends or even acquaintances on those islands. To be sure, the Ingerbretsons had befriended us, and it was with this family that we celebrated 17 May and Christmas Eve, sharing together the fattigmann, which, if I may say so, achieved a delicate and crispy texture in my hands, even with my crude implements, and also the lutefisk, a fish which was soaked in lye for several days and then poached to a delicate texture. But as the Ingerbretsons resided on Appledore and not on Smutty Nose, I had little occasion to spend time with the women in these households as I might have done were there no water barriers between us. In this way, I was often alone on the island for long stretches at a time.

At this point in my tale, I must hasten to explain to the reader that life on Smutty Nose was not entirely bereft of pleasant moments. As even the barest tree on the darkest hour in winter has a beauty all its own, I eventually came to see that Smutty Nose was not without its own peculiar charms, particularly on those days when the weather would be fine, that is to say, sharp and tingling, with silver glints in the granite, every crevice visible, the water all around us a vivid aquamarine. On those occasions, which in my mind are relatively few in number, I might sit upon a ledge and read one of the books I had been lent in Portsmouth, or I might walk about the island playing with my dog, or I might pick some of the wild growth that survived in the rocks and make a bouquet of sorts for my table.

In the five years I was on Smutty Nose, I ventured into Portsmouth four times. I had, at first, a great deal of trouble with the English language, and sometimes it was a trial to make myself understood or to comprehend what was being said to me. I have observed that such a lack of facility with a language tends to make others think of one as not very intelligent and certainly not very well educated. And this used to be a great annoyance to me, as I could converse quite well, and even, I may say, fluently and with some style, in my native tongue, but I was rendered nearly imbecilic when required to express my needs in English.

And here I must say a further word about the American inability to pronounce any Norwegian at all, even, or especially, Norwegian names that were not familiar to them. So that many of the immigrants were forced to change the spelling of their names to make them more easily understood. Thus John, over time, changed his surname to Hontvet, omitting the combination of the *dt*, which Americans found queer in the writing of it and nearly impossible to enunciate correctly. And I also acquiesced to the entering of myself on the church roll at Gosport as Mary S. Hontvet, rather than as Maren, as the Pastor wrote it that way initially, and it was some time before I discovered the mistake. In addition, I observed that after the events of 5 March 1873, the spelling of Evan's name was changed to Ivan in the American newspapers.

Putting aside the language difficulties, I did grow to have some fondness for Portsmouth. To go from the silence of Smutty Nose to the agitation and bustle of Portsmouth was always unsettling, but I could not help but be intrigued by the dresses and bonnets on the women, which I would keep in my mind when I returned to the island. We would visit the pharmacy for tonics and nostrums, and the public market for provisions, and there were always many curious sights in that city, though I confess I was appalled at the lack of cleanliness on the streets, and by the condition of the streets themselves, as they were not graded and were full of ruts and mud and so on. At that time, the main industry of Portsmouth was its ship yard, and always in the background, there was the din of the ironworks. In addition, there were many sailors on the streets, as the Port attracted ships of various nationalities. On three of my trips into Portsmouth, we spent the night with the Johnson family, Norwegians who had come before us, and with them engaged in lively conversation through the night, which was always a joy for me, as there was seldom any conversation of any duration on the island. On these occasions, I was especially pleased to receive news from Norway, and even once from the area near Laurvig, since the Norwegian families in Portsmouth were the recipients of many letters in America. More often than not, these letters were read aloud at table, and discussed at length. We always went to Portsmouth in the summer, owing to the fact that John did not like to take the risk of ferrying me during the winters and chance hitting one of the numerous ice floes that would sometimes block the passage between the mainland and the Shoals.

I did, in that time, receive three letters from Karen telling of our father (and full of vague complaints about her health and the housework), but, curiously, with few mentions of Evan, who himself did not write to us until the second year of my stay at Smutty Nose, and then to tell us of our father's death from old age. In March of 1871, we had a fourth letter from Karen, saying she would join us in America in May.

Karen's letter was a great surprise to John and me. We could not imagine what motivation my sister had for leaving Norway, as she had been quite parsimonious in her letter regarding her reasons for emigrating. She wrote only that as our father had died, she was no longer obliged to stay in that house.

To prepare for my sister's arrival, John purchased a bed in Portsmouth and put it in the upstairs bedroom. I made curtains for that room, and sewed a quilt, which was of a star pattern and took all the scraps I had from my provisions. As I did not have much time in which to finish it, I worked on the quilt all the long days and into the nights until my fingers were numb at their tips, but when the quilt was done, I was glad of the result, for the room now had a cheer which had been entirely absent before.

I remember well the morning of 4 May, when I stood on the beach at Smutty Nose and watched John bring my sister to the island in the dory. He had gone into Portsmouth the day before to wait for the arrival of Karen's ship, and I had seen them coming across from Portsmouth in John's schooner. It was a clear day but exceedingly cold, and I confess that I was apprehensive about Karen's arrival. Though it may strike the reader as odd, I was not eager to change the habits that John and I had shared for three years, nor to admit another person, or, in particular, my sister, about whom I felt somewhat ambivalent.

As Karen drew closer, I examined her appearance. Though I knew she was thirty-seven, she seemed a much older woman than when I had left her, even somewhat stooped. Her face had narrowed, and her hair had gone gray in the front, and her lips, which had thinned, had turned themselves down at the corners. She was wearing a black silk dress with a flat bodice and with high buttons to the collar, around which was a ruffle of fawn lace. She had on, I could see, her best boots, which were revealed to me as she fussed with her skirts upon emerging from the skiff.

Perhaps I should say a word here about my own appearance. I was not in the habit of wearing my best dresses on the island, as I had learned early on that the silk and the cotton were poor protection against the wind and sea air. Therefore, I had taken to wearing only the most tightly woven homespun cloth, and over that, at all times, various shawls that I had knit myself. Also I kept a woolen cap upon my head to protect myself from the fevers that so decimated the island population in the winter and even in the early spring. And, in addition, if it were very windy, I would wear a woolen muffler about my neck. I had not lost my figure altogether, but I had grown somewhat more plump in my stay on the island, which greatly pleased my husband. When I did not have to wear my woolen cap, I preferred to roll my hair on the sides and in the back, and keep some fringe in the front. The only distressing aspect of my appearance, I will say here, was that my face, as a consequence of the island sun and rain and storms, was weathering somewhat like John's, and I had lost the good complexion of my girlhood. I was twenty-five at the time.

Karen stepped from the dory and clasped her hands to her bosom. She looked wildly about her, doubtless stunned, as I had been, by the appearance of her new home. I went closer to Karen and kissed her, but she stood frozen in the sand, and her cheeks were dry and chilly. I told her that she was welcome, and she said stonily that she would never have come to such a place had she not been obliged to endure the greatest shame that ever can befall a woman. I was intensely curious as to the nature of this shame, and asked her there on the beach, but she waved me off and said that she was in need of coffee and bread, as she had been horribly sick on the boat and had not yet fully recovered.

I took her into the house, while John carried her trunk and spinning wheel and the mahogany sewing cabinet that had belonged to my mother. Karen went directly to the table and sat down and removed her bonnet and heaved a great sigh. I could see that in addition to graying, her hair was thinning at the sides and at the top, and this I attributed to the shock of having had our father die, as any death of a loved one may cause the bereaved to age suddenly.

I put on the table a bowl of coffee and a meal which I had prepared in advance. Before she ate, however, she studied the room.

"I was not given to understand from your letters, Maren, that you and John were in such unfortunate circumstances," she said with a distinct tone of disappointment.

"We have managed," I said. "John has made the walls tight and the room as warm as he can."

"But Maren!" she exclaimed. "To have no good furniture, or wallpaper, or pictures on the walls. . . ."

"It wasn't possible to bring such things on the boat," I said, "and we have had no money yet for luxuries."

She scowled. "Your curtains are hastily made," she observed. "America, I see, has not cured your bad habits. I have always said that nothing which will be done well can be done in haste. Dear Sister, they are not even lined."

I remained silent. I did not wish to quarrel with Karen so soon after her arrival.

"And you have not oiled your floorcloth. And what a curious pattern. I have never seen anything quite like it. What is this I have before me?" She had taken something up in her fork, and now put it down again and studied it.

"It is called dunfish, but it is cod," I said.

"Cod!" she exclaimed. "But it is the color of mahogany!"

"Yes," I said. "The people here have the most ingenious way of preserving and drying fish for shipping elsewhere. It is called dunning and keeps —"

"I cannot eat this," she said, pushing away the plate. "My appetite is still not keen. Do you have any honey for the bread? I might be able to get the bread down if you have honey."

"I do not," I said.

"But I see that you have grown fat nevertheless," she said, examining me intently.

I was silent and uncomfortable with such a compliment. Karen sighed again and took a sip from her bowl of coffee. Immediately she screwed up her mouth in pain, and put her hand to the side of her face.

"What is it?" I asked.

"The toothache," she said. "I have been plagued with holes in my teeth for these several years now, and have had no good dentistry for them."

"We must take you into Portsmouth," I said.

"And will you have the money for the dentist," she asked sharply, "if you have no money for wallpaper? When I was at home, I had money from Evan, though there were no decent dentists to be found near Laurvig, I am sorry to say."

Across the table from her, I picked up my own bowl and took a sip of the coffee. "And how is our brother?" I asked.

Karen lifted up her head and fastened her eyes upon mine, and as she did so I began to color and to curse myself for this weakness in my constitution. "He did not write to you?" Karen asked sweetly.

"We have had the one letter," I said. My forehead was now hot and wet. I stood and went to the stove.

"One letter? In all this time? I am quite surprised. I have always thought our brother bore you a special affection. But I suppose our Evan was never one for dwelling much in the past. . . ."

"I expect that Evan has been too busy to write," I said quickly, wishing now to put an end to the subject.

"But not too busy to be a comfort to me, you will be glad to hear," said Karen.

"A comfort?" I asked.

"Oh, most decidedly so." She opened her mouth and rubbed a back tooth. As she did, I could see that many of her teeth were blackened and rotted, and (I hope I will not offend the sensibilities of the reader by revealing this) I could as well detect a terrible smell emanating from that orifice. "Full of the most stimulating conversation in the evenings," she went on. "Do you know that we went together to Kristiania by train over the Easter holiday last year? It was tremendously exciting, Maren. Evan took me to the theater and to supper and we stayed at a hotel. And he spent one afternoon at the University, and spoke to some of the professors there quite seriously of admitting himself to a course of study."

"Evan did?"

"Oh, yes. He has prospered wonderfully and has been able to put some money by. And I do think that now I am gone, he will go to Kristiania, at least for a term, to see how he fares. And doubtless he will meet there some young woman who will turn his head. It's time he settled down, our Evan. Don't you think so, Maren?"

I tried to calm my hands by stirring the soup that was on the stove. "You don't think that Evan will come to America too?" I asked as casually as I could.

"America!" Karen exclaimed. "Whyever for? A man who prospers so well in his own country and has no need to escape will never think of emigrating to another country. No, Maren, I should think not. It was of course difficult for me to have to leave him. . . ."

"Why exactly did you leave?" I asked, turning to her sharply. I was feeling quite cross with Karen at this point.

"We may talk about that at some other time."

Karen turned her head away, and appeared once again to be examining the cottage. "You cannot keep your windows clean?"

"The sea spray," I said. "It is continual."

"At home, I like to use the vinegar."

"I would like to know what has brought you here," I said, interrupting her. "Of course, you are entirely welcome, whatever the reasons, but I do think John and I have a right to know. I hope it is not some dread illness."

"No, nothing like that."

Karen stood up and walked to the window. She folded her arms across her breast and appeared to contemplate the north-west view for some time. Then, with a sigh of, I believe, resignation, she began to tell her story. There had been a man in Laurvig by the name of Knut Eng, she said, who was a widower of fifty-four years, who had courted Karen for seven months with the implicit promise of an engagement not long in the future as they were neither of them young, and then suddenly, after a particularly silly quarrel between them, had broken off their relations, and there was no longer any talk of marriage. So abrupt and shaming was this cessation of his affections, and so widespread the gossip surrounding the affair, that Karen found she could no longer walk with any confidence into town or attend services at our church. Thus the thought of voyaging to America to join John and myself suddenly became appealing to her.

I felt sorry for her loss, though I could not help but think that Karen had most likely done her part to alienate her suitor. Nor was it altogether flattering to know that my sister had come to us only because she was embarrassed to have been spurned. But as it was our custom to welcome all visitors, and particularly those who were family, I tried to make her comfortable and showed her to the upstairs bedroom so that she might have privacy. She found the room uncheerful, and had the poor manners to say so, and, in addition, appeared not to see the star quilt at all. But I forgave her, as she was still in a state of irritation and tiredness owing to her sea-journey.

"What was the nature of the quarrel?" I asked her when she was settled and sitting on the bed.

"I had observed that he was growing more and more stout as the months progressed," she said, "and one afternoon I told him so."

"Oh," I said. I confess I had then to suppress a smile, and I turned away from my sister so that she could not see this effort. "I am sorry that this has happened to you," I said. "I trust you will be able to put all your sadness behind you now that you are in a new world."

"And do you suppose," she asked, "that there is any life for Karen Christensen here on this dreadful island?"

"I am sure there must be," I said.

"Then you, Maren, are possessed of an optimism I cannot share."

And with that, she made a fluttering motion with her hand, a motion I knew well, which dismissed me from her bedroom.

For a time, Karen was my companion during the days when John was at sea, though I cannot say that this was an easy or comfortable companionship, as Karen had grown sorry for herself, and as a result, had become somewhat tedious and dull. She would sit at her spinning wheel and sing the very saddest of tunes, whilst I went about my domestic chores in her presence. I did not like constantly to ask for information about Evan, as Karen had a curious way of regarding me when I did, which always made the blood come into my face, and so I would sometimes have to sit for hours in her company to catch one casual word of my brother, which she gave only sparingly. Sometimes I believe she deliberately withheld information about Evan, and at other times I could see that she was pleased to reveal a confidence I hadn't shared with my brother. These are harsh things to say about one's sibling, but I believe them to be true. When one night I could bear it no longer, and I blurted out to her that I believed in my heart that Evan would eventually join John and me in America, she laughed for a long time and said that Evan had barely mentioned my name in the three years I had been apart from him, and it was her opinion that though one remains attached to a family member forever, he had quite forgotten me.

I was so enraged by this utterance, which she knew wounded me deeply, I went to my room and did not emerge that day or the next day, and finally was persuaded to come into the kitchen by John, who declared that he would not tolerate discord in his house and that my sister and I must make peace between us. In truth, I was embarrassed and eager to put the entire incident, which had not shown me in my best light, behind me.

Karen and I did not have many quarrels like this, however, as she left Smutty Nose within the month. It shortly became apparent that my sister must have money for her teeth, and since there was not work on Smutty Nose, and since I did not really need any help in my domestic routine, nor did we have any extra funds to spare for her, John rowed her across to Appledore, where she was interviewed and hired as a servant to Eliza Laighton, and installed for the summer in a garret room in the hotel the Laighton family occupied and managed. In the winter, she was a personal servant to Eliza.

We were to see Karen at regular intervals during the next two years, primarily on Sundays, when John would take the dory to collect her on her afternoon off so that she might have a meal with us. I did not notice that domestic service improved her disposition much. Indeed, I would say that as the months passed, she seemed to sink further into melancholy, and it was a wonder to me how she was able to maintain her position there at all.

Despite Karen's departure, John and I were almost never to be alone again on the island, as Matthew, John's brother, came to us soon after Karen had gone into service. Matthew was quiet and undemanding and used the northeast apartment for his sleeping quarters. He was a great help to John on the boat. And on 12 April 1872, John brought home a man to board with us, as my husband needed extra monies in order to save up for a new fishing boat. This man was called Louis Wagner.

I think now, in retrospect, I was struck most by Louis Wagner's eyes, which were a metallic blue, and were as well quite canny, and it was difficult to ignore them or to turn one's head away from them, or, indeed, even to feel comfortable in their gaze. Wagner, who was an immigrant from Prussia and had about him an arrogance that I have always associated with Prussians, was large and strongly built. He had coarse hair of a sort that lightens in the elements, so that it was sometimes difficult to say whether he was fair-haired or brown-haired, but his beard was most striking, a vivid copper color under any circumstances, and shiny copper in the sun. Louis's skin was extraordinarily white, which I found surprising in a man of the sea, and his English was poor. But I will confess that he had the most contagious of smiles and quite excellent teeth, and that when he was in good humor and sat at table and told his stories, he had a kind of charm that was sometimes a relief from the silence of Matthew and John.

Louis was lodged in the northeast apartment with Matthew. In the beginning, when Louis was a mate on John's boat, I hardly saw our new boarder, as Louis ate his meals quickly and then repaired almost immediately to his bed, owing to the fatigue the long hours caused in him. But shortly after he had arrived, Mr. Wagner got the rheumatism, which he said had plagued him chronically nearly all his adult life, and he was rendered so crippled by this ailment that he was forced to stay behind and take to his bed, and in this way I got to know Louis rather better than I might have.

I had not really ever had the experience of nursing another to health, and at first I found the duties awkward and uncomfortable. As Louis could not in the beginning rise from his bed without considerable pain, I was compelled to bring him in his meals, collect his tray when he was done, and clean his room.

One morning, after Louis had been confined to his bed for several weeks, I was surprised in my lounge by a knocking at the outer door. When I opened it, Louis was standing on the stoop in a state of some disarray, his shirttails outside of his trousers and his collar missing, but still it was the first time he had been upright in many days, and I was glad to see this. I begged him to come in and sit down at the table, while I prepared some hot coffee for him.

He made his way limpingly to the chair and sat upon it with a great sigh. When he had been well, I had observed him hoisting the dory from the water as if it were a child's plaything; now he seemed barely capable of lifting his arm from the table. He had lost considerable weight, and his hair was disheveled and in need of a wash. Despite his appearance, however, he seemed that day pleased with himself, and he smiled when I brought to him the bowl of coffee.

"I am in debt to you for your kindness," he said after he had taken a swallow.

"It's nothing," I said to him in English, as I always did, since neither of us could speak the other's language. "We hope only to make you well again."

"And that I will be, if I remain in your hands."

"We are all concerned for your health," I said. "My husband and his brother."

"But you are the nurse. I am a great burden to you."

"Oh, no," I said, hastening to assure him that he was welcome. But he shook his head.

"In this country, I have been nothing but a burden. I've had no luck and have not made my mark. I owe money to everyone, and I see no real prospects of a job."

"You have work with my husband," I pointed out.

"But I'm not working now, am I? I'm sick. I can't even pay my rent to you."

"Don't be thinking of that now. You should be thinking of getting well," I said.

"Yes?" he asked, suddenly brightening. "Do you think you will make me well, Mrs. Hontvedt?"

"I will try . . . ," I said, somewhat embarrassed. "But you are hungry. Let me feed you now."

"Yes, Mrs. Hontvedt. Please feed me."

I turned to him as he said this, and he was smiling, and I thought for a moment he might be mocking me, but then I dismissed the notion. I had been waiting for the soup to come to the boil when he had knocked, and now I stirred it and poured some into a bowl. I had in addition the flatbrød that I had baked earlier in the day. The soup was a fish chowder and had, if I may say so, a wonderful aroma, so much so, in fact, that I was compelled to pour myself a bowl.

Louis sipped from his bowl with an inelegant sucking sound, and I thought that he had probably not ever been much on manners. I observed, as he drank, that his copper beard badly needed trimming, and that while I had been fairly diligent with his laundry, his lying in bed so many hours of the day had stained his shirt around the neck and under the arms. I was thinking that perhaps, if I could find some proper cloth, I would make him a new shirt while he was recovering.

"You are a good cook," he said, looking up from the soup.

"Thank you," I said, "but fish soup is easy, is it not?"

"I can't cook myself," he said. He put his spoon down. "You are lonely here?"

To my surprise, I blushed. I was so rarely ever asked questions of a personal nature.

"No," I said. "I have my dog, Ringe."

"Your dog," he said, observing me. "Is he enough?"

"Well, I have my husband . . ."

"But he is gone all the day."

"And I have work. There is always a great deal to do here. You have seen this."

"Too much work makes for a dull life," he said, and again smiled to reveal his teeth. He brushed his hair, which had grown long and somewhat greasy and overhung his forehead, with his fingers. "Do you have a pipe?" he asked.

I was, for the moment, confused by this request. I didn't know whether John would like me to share his tobacco with this boarder, but I didn't quite know how to refuse Louis Wagner.

"My husband sometimes smokes in the evenings," I said.

Louis tilted his head at me. "But he is not here during the day, is he?"

"There are pipes," I said uncertainly.

Louis simply smiled at me and waited.

After a time, uncomfortable under his scrutiny, I went to the box where John kept the pipes, handed one to Louis, and watched as he filled it with tobacco. Outside it was a fair day, with a calm sea. The sun highlighted the salt on the windows so that it looked like ice crystals.

I had never smoked a pipe without my husband, and never at such an early hour in the morning, but I confess that as I sat there observing Louis, my own yearning for a smoke grew, so that after a time, I got out my own pipe and, as Louis had just done, filled it with tobacco. I suppose I had been quite nervous altogether, for the first long draw on my pipe tasted wonderfully marvelous and calmed my hands.

Louis seemed amused that I was smoking with him. "In Prussia," he said, "women do not smoke."

"I am a married woman," I said. "My husband has taught me to smoke."

"And what other things has your husband taught you?" Louis asked quickly with a smile.

I hasten to say that I did not like this rejoinder and so did not answer him, but Louis seemed determined to tease me out of my somber demeanor, and so said to me, "You look too young to be a married woman."

"Then you have seen not too many married women," I said.

"I don't have enough money for a proper woman."

I colored at my understanding of the possible meaning of this utterance and turned my head away.

"John Hontvedt is very lucky to have such a beautiful wife," he said, persisting in this inappropriate speech.

"You are being silly," I said, "and I will not listen to such talk."

"But it's true," he said. "I've been looking at the women in this country for eleven years, and none are so beautiful as you."

I am ashamed to admit, so many years later, that at that moment I was at least partially flattered by this talk. I knew that Louis Wagner was flirting with me, and that it was improper for him to do so, but though I could scold him, I could not quite bring myself to banish him from my apartment. After all, I told myself, he meant no harm. And to be truthful, I had never in my life had a man call me beautiful. I don't believe that my husband ever said such a thing. I don't think, in fact, that he ever even called me pretty. I was not thinking at the time that any of these attentions were in any way dangerous.

"I have made some konfektkake," I said, wishing to change the subject. "Can I give you a piece?"

"What is the konfektkake?" he asked.

"It's a Norwegian sweet," I said. "I think you will like it."

I put before our boarder a plate of chocolate cake. Louis damped his pipe and laid it on the table. After he had taken his first bite of cake, I could see immediately that he had a great liking for it, and he ate steadily until nearly all of it was gone. I was thinking that I had ought to eat the remaining two pieces, as I would not be able to explain to my husband that evening what had happened to the rest, and so I did. Louis wiped the icing from his mouth with the sleeve of his shirt.

"I think that you are seducing me with all this smoke and konfektkake," he said, grinning and pronouncing the Norwegian badly.

I was shocked by his words. I stood up. "You must go now," I said quickly.

"Oh, but Mrs. Hontvedt, do not send me away. We are having such a nice time. And I am only teasing you. I can see you have not been teased much lately. Am I correct?"

"Please go now," I repeated.

He got up slowly from his chair, but in doing so, arranged himself so that he was standing even closer to me than he had been before. I did not like actually to back away from him, and besides, I would have had to press against the stove, which I could not do for fear of burning myself, and so it was that he reached out and put his fingers to my cheek, very gently, and to my everlasting shame, unbidden tears sprang quite suddenly to my eyes, tears so numerous that I was unable to hide them.

"Mrs. Hontvedt," he said in an astonished voice.

I reached up and tore his hand away from my cheek. There was no reply I could have made to him that even I myself could have understood, and as I did not think that he would leave the room, I grabbed my cloak from the hook and ran from the cottage altogether.

Once begun, the tears would not stop, and so I walked nearly blindly to the end of the island and put my hands into fists and shook them angrily at the sea.

I did not tell my husband of Louis Wagner's visit to me, as, in truth, there was not much to tell, but John shortly could see for himself that his boarder was improving in strength. I never did, after that first morning, invite Wagner into my apartment when I was alone, but I saw him often enough, as I continued to nurse him, and then later, morning and evening, when he took his meals with us. Indeed, after he was fully recovered, Wagner took to sitting by the stove in the evenings, so that there would be Wagner and myself and John and Matthew, and sometimes the men would talk, but most often, they would smoke in silence. I am happy to report that I never again lost my composure with Louis Wagner, although I must say he continued to place me under his scrutiny, and if he no longer dared to tease me with words, I did think, from time to time, that he mocked me with his eyes.

There was only one other occasion when I was seriously to wonder at Louis Wagner's intentions and, indeed, his sanity. On a late summer afternoon, while Louis was still recuperating, I heard through the wall that separated our apartment from his room the most dreadful banging about and muttering, and I suddenly became extremely frightened.

"Louis?" I called, and then again, "Louis?"

But I had no reply, and still the commotion in the next room continued. Quite concerned, I ran outside the house and looked in at the window of our boarder's room, which, I am sorry to say, I had not yet adorned with curtains. There I saw a most astounding sight. Louis Wagner, in a fit of uncommon distress, was thrashing and flailing about, upturning objects on the shelf, creating a chaos with the bedclothes, and all the time expressing a terrible rage on his face and in a series of unintelligible sounds. I was too terrified to call to him lest he turn his fury on me, but I was also apprehensive for his own well-being. And then, seemingly as suddenly as he had begun, Louis Wagner stopped his wild behavior and flopped himself back upon his bed and began that sort of hysterical laughing that is accompanied by tears, and after a time, he threw his arm across his eyes, and I think he fell asleep. Reassured that his fit, whatever its origin, had ended, I went back to my kitchen and pondered this unusual and unnatural outburst.

Gradually, as I have said, Louis Wagner recovered his health and was able to return to work for John. Several times, after Louis was up and about, John went, as accustomed, to fetch Karen from Appledore, and on these occasions, which were always on Sunday afternoons, Louis would be dressed in his best shirt, and I must say, that when his hair was washed and combed, he made a rather fine appearance. Karen, perhaps thinking that Wagner might be a possible suitor, was considerably warmer with him than she was with me, and I observed that her melancholy seemed to leave her altogether. She made some effort to fix her face, but this effort was largely unsuccessful in the way that trying to reshape a molded bit of rubber will be a futile enterprise, as the elasticity of the rubber itself will cause the object immediately to resume its original shape. One time Karen actually said to me that she thought Louis Wagner a handsome man and that he seemed to be favoring her with some attention, but as I had actually been there on every occasion they had been together, and had observed Wagner's demeanor toward my sister, which was cordial, but not overly so, I privately thought that Karen must be in the thrall of those peculiar fantasies that visit spinsters in their desperation.

On one such Sunday afternoon as I am describing, Karen came into our house with John. It was, I believe, early in September, and the weather was mild, but quite dreary, as the sun hadn't broken through the cloud in several days. Everything on the island that day was covered with a fine mist, and I fancied I could see the dew on John's hair as well when he brought my sister to us.

But my attention was most drawn to the expression on Karen's face, which seemed a mixture of secret confidence and of pleasure, and was so fixed upon me that I could not turn away from her. She came directly toward me and smiled, and I was quite at a loss as to what she meant to convey to me, and when I asked her outright what seemed to be pleasing her so, she said only that I must be patient, and that perhaps I would find out in good time. Her withholding of her secret made me, I confess, cross with her, and I vowed to put my sister and her machinations out of my mind, but so determined was Karen to whet my curiosity that it was nearly impossible to turn away from her or to avoid her glance. She then proceeded to preside, in her rather silly fashion, over the entire Sunday dinner, speaking of the personages who had been to visit Celia Thaxter, who was Eliza Laighton's sister and a poetess of some repute, of the work on the Jacob Poor Hotel, and of a small altercation she herself had had with her employer, and, in short, speaking of nearly everything but the one thing she wished me to know.

As I am not possessed of extraordinary reserves of patience, and as she meant to keep me guessing an entire week more by not revealing anything else that afternoon, I found that I could not hold my tongue when she was preparing to leave and was putting on her cloak.

"Tell me what your secret is, Karen, or I shall die of curiosity," I said, knowing that this was precisely the begging sentence my sister had wanted to hear from me.

"Oh, it is nothing, Maren," she said airily. "Simply that I have had a letter from Evan."

"Evan," I said, catching my breath. "And did you bring this letter with you?"

"I am so sorry, Maren, but I have forgotten it, and have left it back in my room."

"Then tell me what Evan has written to you."

She looked at me and smiled in a condescending manner. "Only that he is coming in October."

"Evan?"

"He is sailing in two weeks and will be here toward the middle of the month. He says he wishes to stay with you and John, here on Smutty Nose, for a time until he can settle himself."

Evan! Coming to America! I confess I must have betrayed my excitement by clutching John by the arm. "Do you hear Karen?" I asked. "Evan will be coming. And in only a month's time." I bent and picked up my dog, Ringe, who, having sensed a mood of enthusiasm in the room, was leaping about wildly.

I may truly say here that the next weeks were the most pleasant I ever had on Smutty Nose. Even Karen I was able to tolerate with some equanimity, though, irritatingly, she forgot each week to bring Evan's letter to me. I doubt I have ever been as industrious as I was in those early autumn days, scrubbing the upstairs bedroom clean, making curtains and a floorcloth, and as the time grew closer for Evan's arrival, baking many of the delicacies I knew he loved in Norway and probably thought never to have again: the rommegot, the krumcake, and the skillingsbolle. John, I believe, was quite happy to see me so content and purposeful, and I think he did not mind at all that soon we would have another mouth to feed. If the thought of my brother's arrival could cause such happiness in his wife, a happiness that was infectious and conveyed itself to all, so that there was on Smutty Nose an atmosphere of the greatest gaiety and anticipation, then my husband would accept its cause gladly. Even the weather seemed to cooperate, bestowing upon us a succession of clear days with a lively but manageable sea, so that just to walk outside that cottage and breathe in the air seemed nearly intoxicating.

Because I had taken on so many projects and had so little time in which to accomplish them, I was quite beside myself on the last day of all, and most eager to finish the floorcloth for the room that we had made up for him, so that while I might have been watching all day from the window for the first sight of Evan in the schooner and then on the dory, I was instead on my knees. Thus it was that I did not even know of my brother's arrival on Smutty Nose until I heard my husband halloo from the beach.

Actually, it was quite an evil day, with a gale from the northeast sweeping across the island so that one had to bend nearly double to make any progress. Nevertheless, I ran from the cottage down to the beach. I saw a knot of people, and in this knot, a glint of silvery-blond hair.

"Evan!" I cried, running to greet him. I went directly to my brother, seeing his face clearly in what was otherwise a blur of persons and of landscape, and with my arms caught him round the neck. I bent his head down toward me and pressed his face to my own. Evan raised an arm and shouted loudly, "Halloo to America!" and everyone about us laughed. I saw that John was standing just behind Evan, and that John was smiling broadly, as I believe he truly loved me and was glad of my good fortune.

And so it was that in the midst of these giddy salutations, my arms still clutched to my brother, I slowly turned my head and my eyes rested upon an unfamiliar face. It was the face of a woman, quite a beautiful woman, clear of complexion and green-eyed. Her hair was thick and not the silvery blond of my brother, but a color that seemed warmed by the sun, and I remember thinking how odd it was that she had not worn it pinned up upon her head, particularly as it was blowing in a wild manner all about her person, so that she, from time to time, had to clutch at it in order to see anything at all. Her face was lovely, and her skin shone, even in the dull light of the cloud. Gradually my brother loosened himself from my embrace and introduced me.

"This is Anethe," he said. "This is my wife, Anethe."

I SIT IN the foundation of the house an unreasonably long time, using up the precious minutes I have left in which to finish the assignment. When I stand up, my legs are stiff, and I am still shivering badly. I cannot take off my wet sweatshirt, since I have no other clothes with me, and I don't think there are any in the Zodiac. I gather my cameras together and begin to shoot, in the flat light, the detail shots I have described to Rich. I move methodically about the island, hunching into the wind when I am not actually shooting. I take pictures of the graves of the Spanish sailors, the ground on which the Mid-Ocean Hotel once stood, the door of the Haley house. I use six rolls of Velvia 220. I shoot with a tripod and a macro lens. I don't know exactly how much time elapses, but I am anticipating Rich's impatience when I round the island and return to the beach. So I am surprised when he isn't there.

I sit down on the sand and try to shield my legs with my arms. When that proves unsatisfactory, I roll over onto my stomach. The sand, I discover, has held the sun's warmth, and it feels good against my bare legs, even through the cotton of my shorts and sweatshirt. I take off my glasses and set them aside. Like a small sea creature, I try to burrow deeper into the sand, shielding my face with the sides of my hands. I find that by doing this, and by breathing evenly, I can almost control the shivering.

I do not hear Rich as he approaches. The first indication I have that he is near me is a thin trickle of sand, as from a sand timer, from my ankle to my knee and along the back of my thigh. First one leg, and then another.

When I do not turn over or respond, I feel the slight pressure of fingers on my back. He kneels in the sand beside me.

"Are you all right?"

"No."

"You're soaked."

I don't answer.

"What's wrong?" he asks.

I have sand on my forehead. I turn my head slightly, away from him. I can see the oily wet on the small dark rocks of the beach, a crab at eye level scurrying along the crusty surface and then disappearing into a hole. There is a constant susurrus of the wind, fainter on the ground, but ceaseless still. I think that if I had to live on the island, I would go mad from the wind.

Rich begins to rub my back to warm me, to stop the shivering. "Let me get you into the dinghy. And onto the boat. You need a hot shower."

"I can't move."

"I'll help."

"I don't want to move."

I am thinking that this is true. I do not ever want to move again. I do not want to go back to the boat, to look at the faces of Thomas and Adaline, to wonder what they have been doing, or not doing, what has been said between them. What lines of poetry might have been quoted. Or not quoted. I know that Billie is on the boat, and that because of her I will have to go back, will shortly want to go back. I will have to participate in the sail to Portsmouth or to Annisquam or find a way to survive another night in the harbor. I understand that I will have to be a participant on this cruise — a cruise for which I am responsible. I know that I will have to repack the cameras, finish the log, go home and develop the film, and hope that I have something to send into the magazine. I know that I will have to return to our house in Cambridge, that Thomas and I will go on in our marriage, as we have, in our way, and that I will continue to love him.

At this moment, it doesn't seem possible that I am capable of any of it.

I want only to dig into the sand, to feel the sand around me for warmth, to be left alone.

"You're crying," Rich says.

"No, I'm not."

I sit up and wipe my nose on the sleeve of my sweatshirt. The entire front of my body is coated with a thin layer of sand. There is sand in my hair, on my upper lip. I wrap my arms around my legs as tightly as I can. Without my glasses I cannot see the sloop or anyone on it. Even the Zodiac, only twenty feet away, is an orange blur. A shape I take to be a gull swoops down upon the beach and lurches along the pebbles. There is comfort in not being able to see the shapes of things, the details.

I bury my face in my knees. I lick my upper lip with my tongue and bring the sand into my mouth. Rich puts his hand at the back of my neck, the way you do with a child when the child is being sick to her stomach. His hand is warm.

It seems to me that we remain in that position, neither of us speaking or moving, for an unreasonably long time.

Finally I sit back and look at my brother-in-law. I can see him clearly, but not much beyond. He seems puzzled, as though he is not entirely sure what is going to happen next.

"Do you remember the wedding?" I ask.

He removes his hand from my neck with what I sense as a

complicated mixture of regret and relief. "Of course I remember the wedding."

"You were only twenty-two."

"You were only twenty-four."

"You wouldn't wear a suit, and you had a ponytail. You wouldn't kiss me after the wedding, and I thought it was because you were cross that you'd been asked to wear a suit."

"You had on a black dress. I remember thinking it was a great thing to wear to your own wedding. You had no jewelry. He didn't give you a ring."

"He didn't believe in that sort of thing," I say.

"Still."

"You and I went swimming that morning."

"With Dad. Thomas stayed home and worked. On his wedding day."

"It's his way. . . ."

"I know, I know."

"I thought at the time that Thomas was making an extraordinary commitment in marrying me. That it was almost brutally hard for him to do."

"My parents were thrilled."

"Thrilled?"

"That he'd got you. You were so solid."

"Thank you."

"No, I mean you were rooted, grounded. They were tremendously relieved he had found you."

"I wasn't going to cause him any trouble."

"You weren't going to let him cause trouble to himself."

"No one can prevent that."

"You've tried."

"Thomas isn't doing well," I say.

"You're not doing well."

"We're not doing well."

I shake my head and stretch my legs out in front of me. "Rich, I swear I think marriage is the most mysterious covenant in the universe. I'm convinced that no two are alike. More than that, I'm convinced that no marriage is like it was just the day before. Time is the significant dimension — even more significant than love. You can't ask a person what his marriage is like because it will be a different marriage tomorrow. We go in waves."

"You and Thomas."

"We have periods when I think our coming together was a kind of accident, that we're wedded because of a string of facts. And then, maybe the next day, or even that night, Thomas and I will be so close I won't be able to remember the words to a fight we had two hours earlier. The fact of the fight, the concept of an accident, will be gone — it won't even seem plausible. You called him Tom."

"Earlier. I did. I don't know why."

I look up toward the sloop I cannot see. My horizon of beach and rocks and water is a dull watercolor blur.

"What do you think is going on out there?" I ask.

Rich turns away from me. "Jean, don't do this to yourself."

"Is it that obvious?"

"It's painful to watch."

I stand up abruptly and walk away from the water. I walk fast, meaning to shake Rich, to shake them all. I want refuge — from the cold, from the island, most of all from the sight of the sloop in the harbor. I walk toward the Hontvedt house. From where I have so recently come.

But Rich is right behind me. He follows me over the rocks, through the thick brush. When I stop, he stands beside me.

"This is where the women were murdered," I say quickly.

"Jean."

"It's so small. They lived here in the winter. I don't know how they did it. I look at this island, and I try to imagine it. The confinement, the claustrophobia. I keep trying to imagine the murders."

"Listen —"

"There aren't even any trees here. Did you know that until recently children who were raised on the island never saw a tree or a car until they were teenagers?"

"Jean, stop."

"I love Thomas."

"I know you do."

"But it's been hard."

"He makes you worry."

I look at Rich, surprised at this insight. "Yes, he does. He makes me worry. Why did you shave your hair?"

He smiles and rubs his head.

"Do you love Adaline?" I ask.

Rich looks out toward the boat. I think that he, too, is wondering.

"It's a sexual thing?" I ask.

He tilts his head, considering. "She's very attractive," he says. "But it's a bit more than that. She's . . . Intriguing."

"And we're not intriguing," I say. "We're just good."

"We're not that good," he says, and he smiles. He has perfect teeth.

I put my hand on his arm.

He is stunned. I can feel that, the small jolt through the body. But he does not pull away.

"Jean," he says.

I lean forward and put my mouth on the skin of his arm. Did I misread the trickle of sand on the backs of my legs?

When I look up, I can see that Rich is bewildered. I realize this is the first time I have ever seen him lose his composure.

"Why?" he asks.

I study him. I shake my head. *Deliberately,* I could say. Or, *To do it before Thomas does it to me.* Or, *Before I have absolute proof he has done it to me.* Or, simply, *Because I want this, and it's wrong.*

Without touching me with his hands, he bends to kiss me. The kiss is frightening — both foreign and familiar.

I lift my sweatshirt up over my head. Oddly, I am no longer cold, and I have long since stopped shivering.

I can hear his breathing, controlled breathing, as if he had been running.

I feel the top of his head, that smooth map.

He kisses my neck. Around us, gulls and crabs swoop and scurry in confusion, alarmed by this disturbance in the natural order of the universe. I taste his shoulder. I put my teeth there lightly.

He holds me at my waist, and I can feel his hands trembling.

"I can't do this," he says into the side of my head. "I want to." He traces a circle on my back. "I want to," he repeats, "but I can't."

And as suddenly as it opened, a door shuts. For good. I lean my head against his chest and sigh.

"I don't know what came over me," I say.

He holds me tightly. "Shhhh," he says.

We stand in that posture, the clouds moving fast overhead. There is, I think, an intimacy between us, an intimacy I will not know again. A perfect, terrible intimacy — without guilt, without worry, without a future.

Calvin L. Hayes, a member of the coroner's jury who participated in the inquest held over the bodies of Anethe Christensen and Karen Christensen, took the stand for the prosecution and explained in some detail what he had observed: "We arrived on the island between eight and half-past eight P.M. We landed and proceeded to the house formerly occupied by John C. Hontvet.

Upon entering the house there is first a small entry from which opens a kitchen. When we entered the kitchen we found the furniture strewn all over the floor, the clock lying on the lounge face down; clock was not going. I did not look at the face of the clock; it fell evidently from a small bracket just over the lounge in the corner. The body of Anethe Christensen lay in the middle of the kitchen floor, the head towards the door through which we entered. Around the throat was tied a scarf or shawl, some colored woolen garment, and over the body some article of clothing was thrown loosely. The head was, as you might say, all battered to pieces, covered with wounds, and in the vicinity of the right ear two or three cuts broke through the skull so that the brains could be seen running through them. There was a bed-room opening from the kitchen; in that was a bed and trunk, the trunk opened, the contents scattered over the floor. The body of Anethe was placed upon a board upon a table, and an examination made by the physicians who were present. We then proceeded to the other part of the house. The arrangement of the other end of the house was similar to the end into which we first went. We went into an entry, from there into a room that corresponded to the kitchen, out of which another bed-room opened. In that bed-room, face down, we found the body of Karen Christensen. The windowsill of the first bed-room I spoke of was broken off, window in the south-west end of house. The body of Karen Christensen had a white handkerchief knotted tightly around the neck, tied at the back of the neck, so tightly that the tongue was protruding from the mouth. Upon the inside of the sill of the window on the south-west end of the house, was a mark as though made with the pole of an axe, and on the outside of the windowsill, the part that was broken off, there was another mark as though made with some round instrument, as the handle of an axe. The head of Karen Christensen was covered with wounds, but not so bad as the first one. Only one I think broke the skull. I found an axe there."

Hayes produced the murder weapon.

He continued: "I took the axe from the island. It has been in my custody since. I found the axe lying by the side of the first door we entered; it does not now resemble its condition then at all; it was besmeared with blood and covered with matter entirely. In coming from the island the sea was very rough, and the spray washed nearly all the blood off."

After Calvin Hayes testified, Dr. John W. Parsons, the physician who performed the autopsy of Anethe, took the stand.

"The examination was made on March 8," he began, "in the city of Portsmouth, at the rooms of the undertakers, Gerrish & Adams. I found upon examination one flesh wound upon the right side of the forehead upon the upper part. The left ear was cut through nearly separating it from the head, and this wound extending down behind the ear an inch or two; flesh wound merely. There was a flesh wound on the left side of the head just above and in front of the ear, under which there was a compound fracture of the skull. There was a flesh wound in front of the right ear, and another almost separating the right ear from the head, and extending down behind it. There were two flesh wounds upon the upper part of the right side of the head, above the ear. There was a small flesh wound upon the left side of the head above the large wound spoken of. There were a few other minor scratches, and wounds about the scalp, but that is all worthy of notice."

Dr. Parsons then stated that, in his opinion, a very heavy instrument had to have made the blows, and that, yes, it could have been an axe.

Rich makes me put my sweatshirt on and leads me back down to the beach. I notice that he is careful to let go of my hand at the exact point the sloop comes into view. We search in the sand for my glasses, and I clean them off. I retrieve my camera bag and lift it onto my shoulder. The sky has darkened and casts a dispiriting light.

"I've never been unfaithful," I say.

Rich scrutinizes my face. "I'd be very surprised to hear you had been."

"Thank you for —"

"Don't," he says sharply. "I'm not sure you understand. Back there I wanted to. Believe me, I wanted to. I've been angry with Thomas for a long time. Angry at his carelessness. Angry at the way he takes you for granted. But it's more than that. I've" — he searches for the word — "admired you since the day I first met you."

"Admired?" I ask, smiling.

"I don't dare use any other words," he says. "Not now."

"It's all right," I say with a small laugh. "Feel free. I can take it."

Rich crosses his arms over his chest and gazes out over the expanse of Smuttynose. I think I see, in Rich's profile, something of Thomas. The long space between the upper lip and the nose. The slant of the brow.

"Rich," I say, touching his arm lightly. "I'm only kidding."

His face, when he turns back to me, seems momentarily defeated. Sad.

"I think you're beautiful," he says.

Fat drops of rain begin to fall around us, making saucer shapes in the sand. Rich looks down at his feet, then wipes the top of his head.

"The rain is coming," he says. "We'd better go."

Early in the trial, Maren Hontvedt, the only eyewitness to the murders, took the stand. She gave her name as Mary S. Hontvet, using the name and spelling she had adopted in America. She said that she was the wife of John C. Hontvet and was the sister of Karen Christensen. Evan Christensen, she stated, was her brother.

Yeaton began to question her.

"How long before this matter at Smutty Nose did you live there?" Yeaton asked.

"Five years," Maren answered. "I was at home day before the murder."

"Was your husband there that day?"

"He left in the morning, about day-light with my brother, and his brother. Evan is husband of Anethe."

"After he had left that morning, when did you next see your husband?"

"I saw him the next morning after, cannot tell, but about ten o'clock."

"At nine o'clock that night, who were present at your house before you went to bed?"

"I, Karen, and Anethe. There were no other persons upon that island at that time."

"What time did you go to bed that night?"

"Ten o'clock. I slept in the western part of the house in the bed-room. I and Anethe slept together that night."

"About ten o'clock you went to bed."

"About ten. Karen stayed there that night; she slept on a lounge in the kitchen. The lounge upon which Karen slept was in the easterly corner of the kitchen, corner standing up that way, and my bed-room that way." Maren pointed with her hands for the benefit of the court.

Yeaton then asked her how the door between the kitchen and the bedroom had been left that night.

"Left open," Maren said.

"How were the curtains?"

"I did not haul them down, it was a pleasant night, so I left them open."

"I speak now of the curtains to the kitchen."

"Yes."

"How was the outside door to that part of the house, fastened or not?"

"No, sir, it was not fastened. The lock was broke for some time, broke last summer and we did not fix it, it was unfastened. Karen was undressed, bed made; we made a bed up."

"Was there a clock in that room?"

"Yes, clock standing right over the lounge in the corner."

"If you were disturbed that night or awoke, state the first thing that awoke you, so far as you know, what took place."

There was an objection here by Tapley for the defense, and some talk among the lawyers and the court. Finally, Maren was allowed to answer.

"'John scared me, John scared me,' she says."

"Are you able to determine in any way about what time during the night that was?"

"We woke up. I know about his going and striking her with a chair."

"About what time was it?"

"The clock has fallen down in the lounge, and stopped at seven minutes past one."

"After you heard Karen cry out, John scared me, what next took place?"

"John killed me, John killed me, she halooed out a good many times. When he commenced striking her with a chair she halooed out, John killed me, John killed me."

"What did you do?"

"As soon as I heard her haloo out, John killed me, I jumped up out of bed, and tried to open my bed-room door. I tried to get it open but could not, it was fastened."

"Go on."

"He kept on striking her there, and I tried to get the door open, but I could not, the door was fastened. She fell down on the floor underneath the table, then the door was left open for me to go in."

"What next?"

"When I got the door open I looked out and saw a fellow standing right alongside of the window. I saw it was a great tall man. He grabbed a chair with both hands, a chair standing alongside of him. I hurried up to take Karen, my sister, and held one hand on to the door, and took her with my other arm, and carried her in as quick as I could. When I was standing there, he struck me twice, and I held on to the door. I told my sister Karen to hold on to the door, when I opened the window and we were trying to get out."

"Which window was that?"

"My bed-room window, and she said no, I can't do it, I am too tired. She laid on the floor with her knees, and hanging her arms upon the bed. I told Anethe to come up and open the window, and to run out and to take some clothes on her, to run and hide herself away."

"Where was Anethe when you told her that?"

"In my bed-room."

"Well."

"She opened the window."

"Who opened the window?"

"Anethe opened the window, and left the window open and run out. I told her to run out."

"Where did she run out?"

"Out of the window, jumped out of the window."

"Go on."

"I told her to run, and she said I can't run. I said you haloo, might somebody hear from the other islands. She said, I cannot haloo. When I was standing there at the door, he was trying to get in three times, knocked at the door three times when I was standing at the door."

"What door?"

"My bed-room door. When he found he could not get in that way, he went outside, and Anethe saw him on the corner of the house. She next halooed, Louis, Louis, Louis, a good many times, and I jumped to the window and looked out, and when he got a little further I saw him out the window, and he stopped a moment out there."

"How far from the window was he when he stopped?"

"He was not far from the window; he could have laid his elbow right that way on the window." Maren then illustrated this gesture for the court.

Yeaton asked: "Who was that man?"

"Louis Wagner."

"Go on. What else took place?"

"And he turned around again, and when Anethe saw him coming from the corner of the house, back again with a big axe, she halooed out, Louis, Louis, again, good many times she halooed out, Louis, till he struck her. He struck her with a great big axe."

"Did you see that part of her person the blow took effect?"

"He hit her on the head. He struck her once, and she fell down. After she fell down, he struck her twice."

"Well."

"And back he went on the corner again, and I jumped out, and told my sister to come, but she said, I am so tired I can't go."

"Which sister was that?"

"Karen. I told Karen to come; she said, I am so tired I can't."

"You jumped out where?"

"Out through my bed-room window, and I ran down to the hen-house where I had my hens, and opened the door and thought of hiding away in the cellar. I saw the little dog coming, and I was afraid to hide away there because he would look around, and I was afraid the dog would bark, and out I went again. I thought I would run down to the landing-place, and see if he had dory there, and I would take the dory and draw to some island. I looked down the dock, but I did not find any boat there, so I went around. I got a little ways out from the house, and I saw he had a light in the house."

"Go on, and state what you saw or heard."

"He had hauled the window curtains down too. I did not haul them down, but he had them hauled down before I got into the kitchen. I forgot to state that. I went down on the island, ran a little ways, and heard my sister haloo again. I heard her so plain I thought she was outside of the house. I ran to find rocks to hid myself away underneath the rocks on the island."

"How long did you remain there among the rocks?"

"The moon was most down, and I staid till after sunrise, about half an hour after sunrise."

"What relation are you to Anethe and Karen?"

"Anethe married my brother, and Karen was my own sister."

Beyond the harbor, the sky blackens and hangs in sheets. The sun, which is still in the southeast, lights up all the boats in the harbor and the buildings on Star with a luminescence against the backdrop that is breathtaking. We can actually see the front moving.

The rain hits Rich's face and washes over his brow, his eyes, his mouth. Drops hang on the tip of his nose and then fall in rivulets down his chin. He has to narrow his eyes into slits, and, as he holds the tiller, I wonder how he can see at all. The T-shirt he has so recently dried drags on his chest from the weight of the water.

I sit with my feet anchoring the poncho over the cameras. I have taken my glasses off, and I am trying to shield my eyes with my hands. All at once, there is a green wall beside us, the hull of the boat. Rich touches my knee. I shake my head.

A figure looms above us, and a hand reaches down.

"Give me the cameras first," Thomas shouts. "I'll take them in."

23 September 1899

WHEN I FINALLY understood, on the beach, that Evan had brought a wife with him to America, I was at such a loss for words that I was unable to express anything further there on the shore, and it wasn't until some time afterwards that I had the strength to make a proper greeting to the woman, who, I must say, was possessed of such an astonishing beauty it was an effort to draw one's eyes away from her. It was a beauty the chief components of which are vibrant youth as well as lovely aesthetic form, and I could not help but observe, even in those first few moments, that my brother was most infatuated with his new bride, and that he was, except for perhaps three or four occasions in his childhood, more ebullient than I had ever seen him. He had worn that day a leather jerkin and cap, over which he had his yellow oilskin jacket, and he stood with an umbrella close to the young woman like a man servant who does not want one foul drop of rain to fall upon his mistress, with the obvious difference being that Evan was the mistress's husband and was unable to refrain from putting his hands on her in one way or another nearly all the time they remained on the beach and in my kitchen that afternoon. I had the distinct impression that Evan believed that if he did not stay near to his wife she might suddenly vanish.

Anethe was tall for a woman, perhaps only a hand's length shorter than our Evan, and after she removed her cloak in our entryway, I saw that she had an admirable figure, that is to say, she was slim-waisted but not flat-chested, and her figure was most fetchingly shown to advantage in a prettily made, high-necked, lace blouse. She had fine Nordic features (high cheekbones, clear skin, and dusty gray-green eyes with pale eyelashes), altogether an open and guileless face nearly always set in a pleasing attitude. In fact, I doubt I have ever known anyone who smiled as much as that young woman, so much so that I began to wonder if her mouth mustn't hurt from the effort, and I can hardly ever remember seeing Anethe's face in repose, except for a few occasions when she was sleeping. If her comeliness was of the sort that is lacking in enigma and mystery, qualities which I believe are necessary for true classical beauty, her mien suggested an uncommon light and, even more, a sunny disposition I have seen only in young girls. Of course, Anethe was considerably more than a girl when she came to us, being already twenty-four, but she seemed innocent, if not altogether naive. In Laurvig, she had been the youngest daughter of a shipwright and had been watched over keenly by this father, who, I was told, was loath to let her go, even at an age when young women are in serious danger of becoming spinsters if they do not marry. Also, I thought that Anethe's father must have instilled in his daughter a passionate desire to please, since her entire being, her face, her posture and her words, seemed dedicated to this effort.

My brother's wife had as well, I must add here, a remarkable head of hair, and I can attest to the fact that when she took out her combs and unbraided her plaits, this hair reached all the way to the back of her calves.

With Evan close to her side, Anethe, smiling all the while, recounted for us (with myself translating into English for our boarder, so that, in essence, for me, these tales were somewhat tediously twice-told) the particulars of their marriage vows, of their wedding trip to Kristiania, and of the crossing itself, which the newlyweds seemed to have weathered in fine fashion. In fact, so great was their enthusiasm for this adventure to America, though I trust they would have retained a desire for any sojourn so long as it allowed them to be together, that they often interrupted each other or spoke simultaneously or finished the other's sentences, a practice that began to wear upon me as the afternoon progressed, in the same way that one might come to be irritated by the overworked and frequent repetition of a once-charming trait in a young child. Also, I think it is not necessary to say that I was extremely vexed at my sister, Karen, who was not present that afternoon, but who had deliberately withheld important information from me, for what reasons I cannot think, except to cause me the most acute humiliation. At times, sitting there in my lounge, next to the stove, serving Evan and Anethe and Louis Wagner and John and Matthew the sweets I had made expressly for this occasion, thinking to please with delicacies from our Norway my brother, who, I am sorry to report, ate almost nothing that day, and observing Louis Wagner, who was, from a distance I suspect he would have breached in an instant if he thought he had so much as a chance, practically as entranced by Anethe's melodious voice and lustrous skin as was her husband, I was nearly overtaken by a rage so powerful at my sister I felt myself quiver in my very soul and had immediately to ask the Lord for forgiveness for the terrible thoughts against her person I was entertaining. I knew that shortly she would come to my house, as she did on most Sundays and certainly would this coming Sunday since it would be her first visit in America with Evan and his new wife, and I thought that I would speak to her most severely about the malign game she had played with me, and of its consequences. If I had been able to, without revealing my innermost feelings and casting some shame upon myself, I would have banished Karen altogether from Smutty Nose, or at least until such a time as she might confess her wicked machinations. Altogether, it was an afternoon of mixed emotions, and more mixed still when Evan and Anethe repaired to their sleeping quarters above the lounge. They went up to their bedroom to lay down their trunks and to change their clothes, and, ostensibly, to rest, but it was quite shamefully apparent, from the sounds emanating from that room just above my head, that resting was the furthest thing from their minds, and so difficult was it to sit there below them listening to the noise of their relations in the presence of my husband, his brother and our boarder, all of whom pretended to hear nothing and to take great interest in the cake which I had cut and served to them, that though it was an evil day outside, I put on my cloak and left that house, and had I had anywhere else on earth to go, I can assure you that I would have done so.

On Sunday, when Karen came, I said no word about my surprise at Evan's marriage, as I did not want to give my sister the satisfaction of seeing in me the very emotion she had apparently taken such pains to elicit. Indeed, I was most gracious during that particular Sunday dinner, and I like to think I confounded our Karen by openly rejoicing in Anethe's arrival to our islands, and in pointing out to Karen the comely attributes and domestic skills of the young wife, and if Karen studied me oddly and tried several times to ensnare me in my own trickery by coaxing Anethe or Evan to tell of moments the two had shared in Norway during their courtship, I trust that a certain smugness, with which Karen had entered our house that day, began to fade and dissipate as the afternoon wore on. Of course, I had had to tell some untruths, as Anethe was a most appalling seamstress and cook and was almost entirely lacking in any knowledge of housewifery whatsoever. And I think it is probably not incorrect to say that young women with beauty are seldom possessed of great domestic ability, primarily because this quality is often unnecessary in order to attract eligible men into marriage. I often wonder how many of these men, in the second or third month of their wedded life, confronted with disorder in the household and weeks of ill-prepared meals, begin to speculate about the brilliance of their choice. Our Evan, of course, was spared this disillusionment, as I remained in charge of the housekeeping and of the meals, and suffered Anethe as but a poor assistant, more in need of instruction than of praise.

For five months on that island, I lived with Evan and Anethe, and with my husband and his brother and, for part of that time, our boarder as well. In October and early November, when the men would leave for the day, Anethe would come down to the stove in her nightdress, and after she had had her bowl of coffee, she would dress and share the chores with me, but oddly I felt lonelier with her there than I had without her, and there were many days that I wished her gone or never come, and I felt badly about this, as there was nothing offensive in Anethe's disposition or in her person, certainly nothing that warranted such a desire. She was given to storytelling and even sometimes to teasing, and for hours at a stretch, while we spun or sewed or cooked, she would talk of Evan, all the while laughing, joking, and sharing the little intimate secrets that women sometimes tell each other, although I have never felt compelled to do so. I heard many times and could relate to you now the smallest details of their courtship and of their wedding, and of the long walks they took along the coast road and in the forest. Occasionally Anethe would attempt to glean from me anecdotes from my own time with Evan, but I was not so generous and could spare no stories, as they were still close to my bosom, and moreover, my poor narratives would have lacked lustre in the telling, as it was understood that in Evan's life Anethe had taken precedence, and so how could anything I relate be but a poor second cousin to the more legitimate? When the men came in the late afternoon, Anethe would run down to the cove to find Evan, and the two would play with each other as they stumbled up the path to the house. Even in the snow she did this.

It wasn't until the fourth week after Evan and Anethe had come to us that I found myself in a room alone with my brother. John and Matthew and Louis had gone into Portsmouth for provisions, but Evan had stayed behind to mend some nets. He could speak no English, and I think he was reluctant to make himself uncomfortable in that way in that city. Anethe, I recall, was still upstairs in her room. She was not an early riser and had no need to be except to bid her husband farewell in the mornings, for it was usually myself who rose before daybreak and fired up the stove and made the meal for the men, and gave them whatever clothes they might need. On this particular morning, however, Evan, too, had risen late, and had not yet had his breakfast. I was pleased to prepare it for him, although he protested and said he did not deserve it as he had been unforgivably lazy. He said this in a good-natured manner, and it was understood that he was joking. This was, as you may imagine, an altogether new side of my brother I was seeing, for before this time, he had nearly always been a pensive and thoughtful man. I began to think that his marriage had altered his very chemistry, or had, in some way, brought forth joy and hope from where they had lain buried inside him all those years.

Evan took off his jacket, as he had been down to the cove to see the men off, and he sat at the table. He was wearing a blue cotton shirt without a collar, and had exchanged that day his overalls for a pair of woolen trousers with suspenders. Over the last several years, his body had filled out some, so that I was most impressed with the length and breadth of his back, which seemed strong. Also his face, which before had shown the beginnings of the sunken cheeks which was certainly a family trait if not a national one, had filled out as well. These changes combined to give an impression of contentment and of a man who now daydreamed when once he had brooded. His hair, I noticed, had grown long in the back, and I wondered if I should offer to cut it, or if this task belonged now to Anethe. Indeed, it was difficult to know just exactly what the nature of the attachment between Evan and myself was, apart from our history, and though I wished to discuss in some oblique manner this question, I was content, for the moment, simply to be serving my brother at table.

I set before him a plate of bread and geitost, and sat down with him.

"Do you think John will be long in Portsmouth?" I asked.

"The tide is favorable, and the wind as well. They must have bait and set the trawls, and fill out the list you have given them, but I think they will be home before dark. And anyway, there is a moon tonight, so there is no danger either way."

"Why didn't you go with them? Isn't Portsmouth vastly more interesting than this poor island?"

He laughed. "This poor island has everything I need and ever wanted," he said. "My wife is here." He took a mouthful of biscuit. "And my sister," he added with a nod. "And I do not need the distraction of the city at the moment. I am content to sit here and mend the nets and think about my good fortune instead."

"You and Anethe are settling in well then?"

"Yes, Maren, you have seen this."

"She is very agreeable," I said. "And she is pleasant to look upon. But she has a lot to learn about keeping a house. I suppose she will learn that here."

"She can't fail with such a good teacher," Evan said, stabbing his spoon in my direction. I winced, for I thought sometimes that his new jocularity was overbearing and not really suited to him, however happy he had become.

"Maren, you have turned yourself into a first-rate cook," he said. "If I do not watch myself, I will grow fat from your cooking."

"You are already fat from your happiness," I said to him.

He laughed a kind of self-congratulatory laugh. "That is overweight I would not mind carrying," he said, "but you are growing fat as well, and with luck you may grow fatter still." I think my brother may actually have winked at me.

I got up at once and went to the stove.

"I mean that you will one day give us all some good news," he said amiably.

Still I said nothing.

"Maren, what is it?" he asked. "Have I said something wrong?"

I struggled for a moment over the wisdom of answering my brother, but I had waited for so long to speak with him, and I did not see when I would easily have another opportunity.

"I cannot have a child," I said, turning, and looking at him steadily.

He looked away toward the south window, through which one could see across the harbor and over to Star. I did not know if he was simply taken aback, or if he was chastising himself for so carelessly bringing up a painful subject. I saw, when he turned his head, that the silver-blond hair was thinning at the crown. He looked up. "Are you sure of this, Maren? Have you been to a doctor?"

"I have no need of doctors. Four years have been proof enough. And, truth to tell, I am not so surprised. It is something I have suspected all my life, or at least since . . ."

I hesitated.

"Since our mother died," I said quietly.

Evan put down his spoon, and brought his hand up to the lower half of his face.

"You remember," I said.

He did not answer me.

"You remember," I said, in a slightly more distinct voice.

"I remember," he replied.

"And I have thought," I said quickly, "that my illness after that time and the simultaneous onset of my womanhood . . ."

He began to rub the underside of his chin with his forefinger.

"That is to say, the beginning of my monthly curse . . ."

He suddenly took his napkin from his lap and put it on the table. "These are not matters of which we should speak, Maren," he said, interrupting me. "I am sorry to have brought up such a private subject. It is entirely my fault. But I do want to say to you that there can be no possible cause and effect between the events of that time and the state of your" — he hesitated at the word — "womb. This is a subject for doctors and for your husband at the very least. Also, I think that sometimes such difficulties may result from a state of mind as well as a state of bodily health."

"Are you saying I am barren because I have wished it so?" I asked sharply, for I was more than a little piqued at this glib remark on a matter he can have known so very little about.

"No, no, Maren," he said hastily. "No, no, I have no authority to say such things. It's just that I . . ." He paused. "Your marriage to John is a happy one?"

"We have managed," I said.

"I mean," he said, with a small, awkward flutter of his hand, "in the matter of a child . . ."

"Do you mean, does my husband put his seed into me with regularity?" I asked, shocking him, for he colored instantly and darkly.

He stood up in a state of confusion, and I was immediately remorseful and angry with myself for causing him this discomfort.

I went to him and put my arms about his neck. He separated my hands from behind his neck and held my arms by their wrists, and I leaned against his chest.

My eyes filled with tears. Perhaps it was the proximity of his familiar body and the smell of him that allowed me to weep. "You have gone on," I cried. "You have gone on, but I . . . I cannot go on, and sometimes I think I will go mad."

His smell was in the fabric of his shirt. I pressed my face into the cloth and inhaled deeply. It was a wonderful smell, the smell of ironed cotton and a man's sweat.

He pulled my wrists down so that they were at my side. Anethe came into the room. Evan let go of me. She was still in her nightdress, and her hair was braided in a single plait down her back. She was sleepy still, and her eyes were half closed. "Good morning, Maren," she said pleasantly, seemingly oblivious to her husband's posture or the tears on my cheeks, and I thought, not for the first time, that Anethe must be short-sighted, and I then recalled several other times in the past few weeks when I had seen her squinting.

Anethe went to her husband and coiled herself into his embrace so that though she was facing me, his arms were wrapped around her. Evan, unwilling to look at me any longer, bent his head into her hair.

I could not speak, and for a moment, I could not move. I felt raw, as though my flesh had torn, as though a wild dog had taken me in his teeth, sunk his teeth into me, and had pulled and tugged until the flesh and gristle had come away from the bone.

"I must go," Evan said quickly to Anethe, giving her one last quick embrace about the shoulders. "I must collect the nets."

And without a glance in my direction, he took his jacket from the chair and left the room. I knew then that Evan would take great pains never to be left alone in a room again with me.

I turned around and brought my fists close in to my breast. I squeezed my eyes shut and tried to contain the rage and longing within me so that no unwanted sound would slip through my lips. I heard Anethe walk her husband to the door. Evan would take the nets, I knew, to Louis Wagner's room to mend them, even though it was colder in there. When I heard Anethe come back to where I was standing, I made myself relax my eyelids and put my hands on the back of a chair. I was trembling.

"Maren," Anethe said behind me, reaching up to tuck a stray lock of hair into my bun. The touch sent a shiver through my back and down my legs. "I am hopelessly naughty for sleeping so late, but do you think you could forgive me and let me have some of the sausage and cheese from yesterday's dinner for my breakfast?"

I stepped away from her and, with methodical movements, long practiced, long rehearsed, went to the stove, and slowly lifted the kettle up and slowly set it down again upon the fire.

For six weeks during the period that Evan and Anethe lived with John and me, Louis Wagner was with us, and for most of this time he was well and working on the *Clara Bella*. But one day, when the men were still going out, Louis remained behind. He was, he said, experiencing a sudden return of the rheumatism. I know now, of course, that this was a ruse, and I am sorry to have to report here that the inappropriate attraction Louis felt for Anethe had not abated with time, but rather had intensified. And this was due, in part, to the fact that Anethe had taken pity on Louis, fearing for his poverty and loneliness and his inability to get a wife, and had shown him some mild affection in the way of people who are so content with their lot that they have happiness in excess of their needs and thus can share the bounty with others. I believe that Louis, not having had this form of attention, and certainly not from such a lady as Anethe, mistook the young woman's kindness for flirtation and sought to make the most of that advantage. So it happened that on the day that he pretended ill and I had gone to see if he would sit up to take some porridge, he asked me if I would send Anethe forthwith into his chamber in order that she might read to him, and thus divert his attention from his "sore joints." I did see, in Anethe's face, the smallest hesitation when I suggested this, as she had never attended to a man other than her husband in the privacy of his room, and had never nursed the sick, but I imagine that she thought that if I was so willing to be alone with Louis there could be no harm in it. She took a book out of the front door of our kitchen and into the apartment in which Louis was lying.

I do not believe she was in his room for more than ten minutes before I heard a small exclamation, a sound that a woman will make when she is suddenly surprised, and then a muffled but distinctly distressed cry. As there was no noise from Louis, the first thought I had was that the man had fallen out of his bed. I had been on my knees with a dustpan, cleaning the ashes from the stove, and was halfway to my feet when there was a loud thump as though a shoulder had hit the wall that separated Louis's apartment from the kitchen of our own. There was a second bump and then another unintelligible word. I set down the dustpan on the table, wiped my hands on a cloth and called to Anethe through the wall. Before I could wonder at a lack of response, however, I heard the door of Louis's apartment open, and presently Anethe was in our kitchen.

One plait to the side of Anethe's head had pulled loose from its knot and was hanging in a long U at her shoulder. On the bodice of her blouse, a starched, white garment with narrow smocked sleeves, was a dirty smudge, as though a hand had ground itself in. The top button of her collar was missing. She was breathless and held her hand to her waist.

"Louis," she said, and put her other hand to the wall to steady herself.

The color had quite left Anethe's face, and I saw that her beauty was truly in her coloring and animation, for without both she looked gaunt and anemic. I confess I was riveted by the contrast of the dirty smudge on the white breast of her blouse, and I suppose because I am not at all a demonstrative person I found it difficult to speak some comfort to her. It was as though any word I might say to her would sound false and thus be worse than no word at all, and for some reason I cannot now articulate, I was in an odd state of paralysis. And though it shames me deeply, I must confess that I think I might actually have begun to smile in that awful inappropriate way one does when one hears terribly bad news, and the smile just seems automatically, without will, to come to one's lips. I reproach myself greatly for this behavior, of course, and think how easy it might have been to go to my sister-in-law and put my arms around her and console her, or at least help to put behind her the absurd and almost laughable advances of the man next door, but as I say, I was frozen to the spot and able only to utter her name.

"Anethe," I said.

Whereupon the blood left her head altogether, and she fell down in a wondrous sort of collapse that I am sorry to say struck me as somewhat comical in nature, the knees buckling, the arms fluttering out sideways as if she would try to fly, and it was only once she was on the ground that I was able to unlock my limbs and move toward her and raise her head up and in that way help her back to consciousness.

When I had her in her bed, and she had nearly recovered her color, we spoke finally about Louis and about the fearful rage that this incident might provoke in Evan, and it was decided then and there between us that I would not tell my brother, but rather would suggest to my husband that there had been some disappearances of beer and honey and candles in the household for which I could not account, and that without raising a fuss I thought it might be wise to terminate our boarder's lease.

Unfortunately, however, I was not present at Louis Wagner's dismissal and, as a consequence, John did not quite heed or remember my precise advice, and said to Louis that because I had missed certain household items it might be better for Louis to look elsewhere for lodgings. Louis denied these charges vigorously and demanded to see me, but John, of course believing his wife and not his boarder, stood firm and told Louis that he would be leaving the next day. The following morning, as Louis was preparing to board Emil Ingerbretson's schooner for the passage into Portsmouth, I remained in the kitchen, as I did not want an unpleasant confrontation, but just before sailing Louis came up from the cove and sought me out. I heard a noise and turned to see him standing in the open door. He did not speak a word, but merely stared at me with a look so fixed and knowing I grew warm and uncomfortable under his gaze. "Louis," I began, but could not go on, although the expression on his face seemed to dare me to speak. Truthfully, I could think of nothing I could say to him that would not make the situation worse. He smiled slowly at me then and closed the door.

Thus it was that Louis Wagner left Smutty Nose.

I THINK ABOUT the weight of water, its scientific properties. A cubic foot of water weighs 62.4 pounds. Seawater is 3.5 percent heavier than freshwater; that is, for every 1,000 pounds of seawater, 35 of those will be salt. The weight of water causes pressure to increase with depth. The pressure one mile down into the ocean is 2,300 pounds per square inch.

What moment was it that I might have altered? What point in time was it that I might have moved one way instead of another, had one thought instead of another? When I think about what happened on the boat, and it was a time that was so brief — how long? four minutes? eight? certainly not even ten — the events unfold with excruciating lethargy. In the beginning, I will need to see the scene repeatedly. I will hunt for details I have missed before, savor tiny nuances. I will want to be left alone in a dark room so that I will not be interrupted. But after a time, I will not be able to stop the loop. And each time the loop plays itself, I will see I have a chance, a choice.

Thomas pulls me by the arms up onto the deck. He tries to wipe the rain from his eyes with his sleeve. "Where have you been?" he asks.

"Where's Billie?"

"Down below."

"It was my last chance to get any pictures."

"Christ."

"We started back the minute it began to rain." My voice sounds strained and thin, even to myself.

"The wind came up half an hour ago," Thomas says accusingly. "The other boat has already left. I don't know what's going on."

"Billie's all right?"

Thomas combs his hair off his forehead with the fingers of both hands. "I can't get her to put her life jacket on."

"And Adaline?" I ask.

He massages the bridge of his nose. "She's lying down," he says.

Rich hoists himself onto the deck from the dinghy. I notice that Thomas does not extend a hand to his brother. Rich drags the dinghy line to the stern.

"Tom," Rich calls, again using the boyhood nickname. "Take this line."

Thomas makes his way to the stern, and takes the rope from Rich, and it is then that I notice that Thomas is shaking. Rich sees it, too.

"Go inside," Rich says to Thomas quietly. "Put on dry clothes and a sweater. The foul-weather gear is under the bunks in the forward cabin. You, too," he adds, looking at me quickly and then away. He ties the line in his hand to a cleat. "I'll go down and listen to what NOAA has to say. How long ago did the other boat leave?"

"About fifteen minutes," Thomas answers.

"Did she say where she was headed?"

"Little Harbor."

As if in answer to Rich's doubts, the Morgan shudders deep in her hull from the hard bang of a wave. I can feel the stern skid sideways in the water, like a car on ice. The rain is dark, and I can barely make out the shape of the islands around us. The sea is lead colored, dull but boisterous.

I go below to find Billie huddled in her berth. She has her face turned away. I touch her on the shoulder, and she snaps her head around, as though she were raw all over.

I lie down beside her. Gently, I rub her shoulder and her arm. "Daddy was right," I say softly. "You have to put your life jacket on. It's a law, Billie, and there isn't anything we can do about it."

Invoking parental helplessness before a higher authority has usually worked with Billie, as when I tell her that the police will stop me if she doesn't put on her seat belt in a car. The door to the forward cabin is shut. Thomas knocks and enters simultaneously, a gesture that catches my breath. I can see a slim form lying on the left side of the V berth. A head rises. Thomas shuts the door.

My sneakers make squelching sounds on the teak floor grate. I kick them off, and they thwack against a galley cabinet. I strip off my sweatshirt and shorts and underwear and pull from my duffel bag a pair of jeans and a cotton sweater. Billie, hearing the unexpected bumps of the sneakers, rolls over in her berth and looks up at her naked and shivering mother.

"Can't I wear an orange one?" she asks.

"No, those are for adults. Only yours will fit you." I peer down at the life vest, with its Sesame Street motif, on the table.

Thomas opens the door of the forward cabin. I am struggling awkwardly with jeans on wet skin. Rich swings down from the deck. Instinctively, I turn my back.

Thomas drops a muddle of navy and yellow foul-weather gear onto the teak table. "There's a small one here," he says and holds it up. "I think it will fit Billie."

"Oh, Daddy, can I have it?" Billie asks, holding out her arms.

I wrestle with my sweater. I bend to Thomas's duffel bag and take out a dry shirt, a sweater, and a pair of khakis. I hold them out to him. I look at Thomas's face, which has gone white and looks old.

At the trial, Mr. Yeaton for the prosecution asked "Mary S. Hontvet" how long she had known Louis Wagner. She answered that he had boarded with her for seven months the previous year, beginning in the spring.

"When did he leave, get through boarding with you?" Mr. Yeaton asked.

"He went into Portsmouth about November," Maren answered.

"What room did he occupy in your house?"

"He had the easterly end of the house, he had a big room there."

"Where did he keep his clothes?"

"He kept his clothes in a little bed-room there hanging up. He had oil skin hanging up in my entry, when he had been out fishing, he took his oil skin off and hung it up in the entry, entry coming into my kitchen."

"Entry in your part?"

"Yes."

Mr. Yeaton then asked what was in Louis Wagner's room.

Maren answered: "He had his bed there, and one big trunk, which belonged to my sister Karen."

"Do you know what was in that trunk?"

"She had clothes, some she wore in the winter time, and she put them in the trunk in the summer, and summer clothes she did not use she put in the trunk, and she had a feather-bed that she had at the time she came over in the steamer."

"Was that in the trunk?"

"Yes, the bed was in the trunk, the big chest."

"While he boarded with you, was Karen a member of the family?"

"She came out visiting me some days."

"Did she sleep there?"

"No, sir."

Mr. Yeaton then asked Maren whether she knew if Karen had

a piece of silver money. Maren answered that yes, she had seen the piece of silver money in October or November, and that Karen had said she had gotten the money from boarders at Appledore, and that it was kept in her purse. Mr. Tapley then asked her if she knew if Karen kept anything else in that purse or if Maren had seen Karen on the day of the murders put something in the purse.

"Yes," Maren answered.

"What was it?"

"A button, white button-like."

"Have you any articles of clothing, with similar buttons upon?"

"Yes, have got some."

"Where was the button taken from, if you know?"

"From my sewing basket."

"State what was done with the button, how did it come there."

"She took the sewing basket and looked for a button, and took a button there and handed it to Karen."

"Who took it from the basket?"

"Anethe, and handed it to Karen, and Karen put it in her purse."

"Have you any buttons similar to that?"

"Yes, have them with me."

Maren then produced the buttons.

"Where did you get these buttons?" Mr. Yeaton asked.

"Got them in my sewing basket, found one in the basket and two in my box that I have always kept in my sewing basket. I have a nightdress with similar buttons upon it."

Maren produced the nightdress, and the Court said to Mr. Yeaton that it did not see how the buttons and the nightdress were relevant.

"We will connect them hereafter and offer them again," Yeaton answered.

Rich stands at the chart table, a microphone uncoiled and in his hand. Staticky sounds — a man's even, unemotional voice — drone from the radio over the quarter berth, but I cannot understand what the man is saying. Rich seems to, however, and I watch as he bends closer to the charts, sweeping one away onto the floor altogether and examining another. I am looking for a sweater for Billie.

Rich puts the microphone back into its holder and makes markings on a chart with a ruler and a pencil. "We've got a front coming in faster than they thought," he says with his back to Thomas and me. "They're reporting gusts of up to fifty miles an hour. Thunderstorms and lightning as well." A wave hits the sailboat side-to and floods the deck. Seawater sprays into the cabin through the open companionway. Rich reaches up with one hand and snaps the hatch shut.

"The wind alone could put us up on the rocks," he says. "I'm going to motor in towards Little Harbor, the same as the other boat, but even if we get caught out in the open, we'll be better off than we'd be here. There's not enough swinging room." He turns and looks from Thomas to me and back to Thomas, and seems to be making lists in his mind. He is still in his wet T-shirt and shorts, though this is a different Rich from the one I saw earlier, organized and in charge. Alarmed, but not panicked.

"Thomas, I need you to put sail ties on the main. Jean, I want you to heat some soup and hot coffee and put it into thermoses, and put dry matches, bread, toilet paper, socks, and so on — you decide — into Ziploc bags. We need to lock down everything in the cabin — drawers, your cameras, the binoculars, anything in the galley that could shift. There are cargo straps in that drawer over there if you need them. Get Adaline to help you. We want all the hatches tightly closed." Rich turns around to the chart table. "And you'll need these."

He opens the slanted desk top and pulls out a vial of pills, which he tosses to Thomas. "Seasickness pills," he says. "Each of you take one — even you, Thomas — and give a half of one to Billie. It could be a little uncomfortable today. And Thomas, there are diving masks under the cushions in the cockpit. Those are sometimes useful in the rain for visibility. Where *is* Adaline?"

Thomas gestures toward the forward cabin.

"She's sick?"

Thomas nods.

I look at my daughter, struggling with the jacket of the foul-weather gear. I open a drawer to retrieve the plastic bags. Beside the drawer, the stove is swinging. I realize that it is not the stove that is swinging, but rather the sloop itself. Seeing this, I feel, for the first time, an almost instantaneous queasiness. Is seasickness in the mind? I wonder. Or have I simply been too busy to notice it before?

Rich goes to the forward cabin and leaves the door open. Adaline is still lying motionless on the berth; she has thrown her arm across her eyes. I watch Rich peel off his wet clothes. How casual we are being with our nakedness, I think.

Rich dresses quickly in jeans and a sweatshirt. I can hear his voice, murmuring to Adaline, but I cannot hear the precise words. I want to know the precise words. He comes out and pulls on a pair of foul-weather pants and a jacket. He slips his feet back into his wet boat shoes. I can see that he is still thinking about the storm, making mental lists, but when he walks past me to go up on deck, he stops at the bottom of the ladder and looks at me.

It is strange enough that just a half hour before I was willing — no, trying — to make love with my brother-in-law. But it seems almost impossibly strange with my daughter in the berth and my husband at the sink. I feel an odd dissonance, a vibration, as though my foot had hit a loose board, set something in motion.

Thomas turns just then from the faucet, where he has been pouring water into a paper cup. In one hand, he holds the cup; in the other, a pill. I believe he is about to say to me, "Drink this," when he sees his brother's face, and then before I can pull away, my own.

Thomas's eyes move briefly from Rich's face to mine. Rich glances away, over toward the radio. I can see images forming in Thomas's mind. He still holds the cup of water with his hand. The other hand with the pill floats in front of me.

"What?" he asks then, almost inaudibly, as if he cannot formulate a whole question. I take the pill and the cup of water. I shake my head quickly, back and forth, small motions.

I hand the cup to Thomas. Rich goes immediately up to the cockpit. Billie calls to me: "Mommy, help me, please. I can't do the snaps."

With the exception of Maren Hontvedt's testimony as an eyewitness to the murders, the prosecution's case was based on circumstantial evidence and a lack of an alibi. It had been a bloody murder, and blood was found on clothing (left in the privy behind his landlady's house) belonging to Louis Wagner. Mrs. Johnson, the landlady in question, identified a shirt as belonging to Wagner by the buttonhole she had once mended. Money had been stolen from the Hontvedt house, and the next morning Wagner had enough money to go to Boston and to buy a suit of clothes. Any man who made the row to Smuttynose and back would have put a lot of wear and tear on a dory; the brand new thole pins in James Burke's dory were worn down. Wagner had talked to John Hontvedt and knew that the women would be alone on Smuttynose. In the weeks prior to the murders, Wagner had said repeatedly that he would have money if he had to murder for it. Wagner could not produce a single witness who had seen him in the city of Portsmouth from seven P.M. on the night of the murders until after seven o'clock the next morning. His landlady testified that Wagner did not sleep in his room that night.

The chief bit of evidence for the prosecution, however, was the white button that was found in Wagner's pocket when he was arrested. The button, the prosecution claimed, had been stolen, along with several coins, from a pocketbook belonging to Karen Christensen the night of the murders. The button matched those of Mary S. Hontvet's nightdress — the one she produced in court.

I slip Maren Hontvedt's document and its translation into a plastic bag and seal it. Into other plastic bags, I put my film and my cameras, my log, Thomas's notebooks, other books, and the provisions Rich has asked for. Rich and Thomas are above; Billie is beside me. I keep her close, throwing my arm in front of her or behind her like a railroad barrier whenever I feel the boat tip or catch a gust of wind. Rich and Thomas have unfastened the boat from the mooring and have turned on the motor. I can hear the cough and kick of the engine, and then a reassuring hum. We leave the Isles of Shoals and head for open water.

"Mommy, is Adaline coming to live with us?"

Billie and I are folding charts and sliding them into Ziploc bags. My daughter likes running her fingers along the seal, the satisfaction of feeling it snap shut.

I crouch down in front of her and sit back on my heels.

"She's not coming to live with us," I say. It is meant to be an answer, but it sounds like a question.

"Oh," Billie says. She looks down at the floor. I notice that water is sloshing over the teak planking.

"Why do you ask?" I put my finger under her chin and lift it just a fraction. There is a note that isn't entirely parental in my voice, and I think she must hear it. She sticks her tongue out the gap made by her two missing front teeth and stares up at the ceiling.

"I forget," she says.

"*Billie.*"

"Um." She stretches her arms high above her head. Her toes are pointed inward. "Well . . . ," she says, drawing out the words. "I think Daddy said."

"Said what?"

She flaps her arms at her sides. "I don't know, do I?"

Shockingly, tears appear at the lower lids of her eyes.

"Billie, what's the matter?" I pull her to me and hold her close. I can feel the oilskin, the damp curl of her hair, the plumpness of her legs.

"Why is the boat moving around like this?" she asks. "It doesn't feel good."

Louis Wagner's defense consisted primarily of attempts to answer prosecution questions in order to convince the jury of a reasonable doubt. Why were his hands blistered and the knuckles bruised the day after the murders? He had helped a man lay crates on a fish cart. Where had he been all night? He had had a glass of ale, then had baited nine hundred hooks for a fisherman whose name he didn't know and who could not be produced at the trial. After that, he had two more mugs of ale and then began to feel poorly. He was sick to his stomach in the street and fell down near a pump. He went back to the Johnsons' at three o'clock to go to sleep, but went in the back door instead of the front, and did not go up to his bed, but slept in the lounge. Later in the morning, he decided to have his beard shaved, then heard the train whistle and thought to go to Boston. There he bought a new suit of clothes and went to stay at his old boardinghouse in North Street, a place he had lived at several times before. How did he happen to have blood on articles of clothing that he had on the night of the murders? It was fish blood, he said, and also he had stabbed himself with a fish-net needle several days earlier. How did he come by the money to go to Boston and to buy a suit of clothes? He had earned twelve dollars earlier in the week baiting trawls for a fisherman, whose name he did not remember, and the night of the murders had earned a further dollar.

Wagner took the stand in his own defense. Mr. Tapley, counsel for the defense, asked Louis Wagner what had happened to him when he was arrested in Boston.

"When I was standing in the door of the boarding master where I boarded five years," Wagner answered, "he came along, shook hands with me and said, halloo, where did you come from. Before I had time to answer him, policeman stepped along to the door. He dropped me by the arm. I ask them what they want. They answered me they want me. I asked him what for. I told him to let me go up-stairs and put my boots on. They answered me the slippers are good enough. They then dragged me along the streets and asked me how long I had been in Boston. I was so scared I understand they asked me how long I had been in Boston altogether. I answered him five days, making a mistake to say five years."

"Did you intend to say five years?"

"Yes, sir. Then they asked me if I could read the English newspapers. I told them no. Well, he says, if you could you would have seen what was in it. You would have been in New York at this time."

"Would what?"

"I would have been in New York at this time if I knowed what was in the newspapers. I asked him what was in the newspapers. He asked me if I was not on the Isle of Shoals and killed two women; I answered him that I had not done such a thing. He brought me into station-house, Number One. I found there a man named Johnson, city marshal at Portsmouth."

Mr. Tapley then asked him what happened to him when he was brought to the station house.

Wagner said that City Marshall Johnson had asked him the

whereabouts of the tall hat he was supposed to have worn the night before on the Isles of Shoals.

Wagner continued. "I told him I had not been on the Isle of Shoals; had not wore no tall hat in my life. He says the woman on the Isle of Shoals has seen you with a tall hat that night. I asked him what woman. He told me Mrs. Hontvet. He told me that he had the whiskers, that was shaved off my face, in his pocket, that it was shaved off in Portsmouth by such a barber. I told him to show me them whiskers. He told me that he had found the baker where I had been that night and bought bread; that I told the baker that I was going to the Isle of Shoals that night. I asked him to put me before the baker, or put the baker before me that said so. He answered that I soon would see him. When the new clothes was taken from my body I was taken into another room. The city marshal Johnson stripped me bare naked; asked me where I changed them underclothes. I told him that I had them underclothes on my body nearly eight days. He says you changed them this morning when you went to Boston; he says there was no gentleman in the city of Boston could wear underclothes for eight days so clean as them was. I told him I was poor, but I was a gentleman and I could wear clean underclothes just as well as any gentleman in the city of Boston. After my underclothes was overhauled they was put on me and I was brought into the cell; stayed in the cell until the next morning; when I was taken out again from two policemen, and dragged along the street."

"Do you mean from two men?"

"They took me along the street; walked me along the street."

"What do you mean by dragged?"

"They dragged me on my hands; took me into some kind of a house; don't know what it was. I was put on a seat; was kept about ten minutes; all the people had to look at me; was taken then away out of that house where they took my picture; and was brought again to station-house."

"After that, what took place?"

"After that I was closed up again. After a spell I was taken out and brought to the depot. When they took me down to the depot, I asked them where they were going to put me to. They answered me, they were sending me back to Portsmouth, asked me if I did not like to go there. I told them yes."

"Who asked you that?"

"The policeman who took me down there."

"Do you know his name?"

"Yes, one that was here."

"Go on."

"Well, I was brought to Portsmouth. I came to Portsmouth, the street was crowded with peoples, and was hallooing, 'Kill him, kill him.' I was put into station-house. I was closed in about three-quarters of an hour when Mr. Hontvet came there. . . . Mr. Hontvet came to side door and said, Oh! damn you murderer. I said, Johnny, you are mistaken. He says, damn you, you kill my wife's sister and her brother's wife. I told John, I hope you will find the right man who done it. He says, I got him. He says, hanging is too good for you, and hell is too good for you. He says I ought to be cut to pieces and put on to fish-hooks. I told him, that the net that he had spread out for me to drop in he might drop in himself. He says, where is that tall hat that you had on that night when you was on the Shoals. I told him I had no tall hat. He says, what have you been doing with the fish that you bought last night from the schooner, or was going to buy. I told him that I had not bought any fish, and was not out of Portsmouth that night. He told me that the dory was seen that night, between twelve and two o'clock, going on board a vessel that was lying at anchor on Smutty Nose Island."

"What do you mean by dory?"

"Dory pulled on board that schooner and asked that skipper if he had any fish to sell."

"Did he say where the schooner was?"

"Yes, he said that she was lying at anchor on Smutty Nose Island. He said that this dory was seen crossing over to the westward of the island and had hailed another vessel there. I then told him, Johnny, better look after that man that has been pulling that night in the dory. Then he and his brother-in-law answered me, that I was the man. His brother-in-law told Mr. Hontvet to ask me if I could not get the money without killing the vimen."

"Who do you mean by brother-in-law?"

"Evan Christensen. I told him that I never tried to steal money, but if I was a thief I thought I could get money without killing people. He says, you stole thirteen dollars. He says, you took ten-dollar bill out of that pocket-book."

"Who said that?"

"Mr. Hontvet. His brother, Mattheas Hontvet, showed me another pocket-book and said I stole out five dollars out of that. I told him that he was mistaken. They then left me, and some more people was coming to see me."

Blood evidence was introduced into the trial. Horace Chase, a physician who resided at 22 Newbury Street in Boston, testified that he had made a study of the analysis of blood and had examined the blood found on Louis Wagner's clothing. Dr. Chase explained that the red corpuscles of fish blood differ in shape from those of human or mammalian blood. Moreover, he said, it was possible to distinguish human blood from horse blood because of the size of the blood corpuscles. "The average blood corpuscle of man measures 1-3200 of an inch; that is, 3200 laid down in a line would cover one side of a square inch; it would take about 4600 of the corpuscles of a horse; the difference is quite perceptible," he said.

Various articles of clothing had been taken to Dr. Chase in Boston for blood analysis by Mr. Yeaton of the prosecution — overalls, a jacket, and a shirt. Dr. Chase testified that he found human blood on the overalls, human blood on the shirt, and simply mammalian blood on the jacket. During cross-examination, Dr. Chase said that he had not made more than "two or three" blood analysis examinations in criminal cases.

The defense introduced its own blood expert. James F. Babcock, a professor of chemistry at the Massachusetts College of Pharmacy in Boston, testified that it was not possible to distinguish with absolute certainty human blood from other mammalian blood, and that it was not possible to say, after blood had dried on an article of clothing, how old the stain was or whether it had appeared before or after another stain. Nor were there any tests available to determine whether the blood was male or female. Mr. Babcock said that he had examined blood stains in "several" capital cases.

The defense then called Asa Bourne, a fisherman, who testified that he and his sons had been out fishing on the night of the murders, and that the wind was so strong they could not make any headway against it. In his opinion, said Bourne, Wagner could not have rowed to the islands and back.

Dr. John D. Parsons, the physician who had examined the body of Anethe at the undertaker's room at Gerrish & Adams, was recalled to the stand by the defense. He was asked whether or not it was reasonable to suppose that the wounds upon Anethe, from their appearance, were made by a person not very muscular. He replied, "I think the flesh wounds might have been made by a person of not great muscular force."

Finally, the defense made an attempt to dismiss the entire case. In the state of Maine, at that time, a person could not be convicted of murder in the first degree of another person if the victim was not accurately named and that name not accurately spelled in the indictment. When Evan Christensen first testified, he said, "Anethe Christensen was my wife." The indictment, however, reports the victim as Anethe M. Christenson, with the slightly different spelling and the middle initial. Evan was re-called to the stand, whereupon Tapley questioned him.

"What time of day did you say that you went down to that house where your wife was dead?"

No response.

"What time was it?"

No response.

"Do you understand me?"

No response.

"What time of the clock was it, after you heard of your wife's death, that you went to the house the first time, the first morning after the murder?"

No response.

"Did you go inside?"

"Yes, sir."

"Did you go around in the different rooms?"

"I went into other rooms."

"Didn't you find a good deal of blood in those rooms?"

"Yes, sir."

"On the floor?"

"Yes, sir."

"Were you asked, since you were here day before yesterday, what your wife's name was?"

No response.

"Did anybody ask you before you came in this morning what your wife's name was? Didn't somebody ask you?"

No response.

"When did anybody say anything to you about your wife's name since day before yesterday, do you understand?"

No response.

"Are you a Norwegian?"

No response.

"You do not understand, do you?"

"No, sir."

"Did you speak with any one about your wife?"

No response.

"Did you tell anybody your wife's name, before you came here this morning?"

No response.

"What is Karen's full name?"

"Karen Alma Christensen."

"Was your wife's name Matea Annette?"

"Anetha Matea Christensen."

"Was she not sometimes called Matea Annette?"

No response.

"Do you understand my question?"

No response.

"When were you married?"

No response.

"When did you marry your wife?"

No response.

Tapley finally gave up this odd appeal, and the court declared that Anethe M. Christenson, as written, was the victim in the case.

Billie is doubled over at the waist, as if she will be sick. She coughs several times. Her skin has gone a shadowy white, and there is perspiration on her forehead. She cries. She does not understand what is happening to her. "Mom," she says. "Mom."

The boat catches a gust, and it feels as though we have been hit by a train. We heel over, and I bang my head hard on the chart table. I hear the crash of dishes in the cabinets. A thermos on the counter slides the length of the Formica counter and topples onto its plastic cap. I kneel on the teak planking and hold Billie as best I can. I fight a sense of panic.

"Rich," I call up the ladder. I wait for an answer. I call again. "There's water on the floor," I shout.

It is hard to hear his response. Before the storm, the sounds from the water were soothing. The gentle slap of waves upon the hull. But now there is a kind of churning roar that is not just the engine. It is as though the ocean has become more difficult to slice through, as though the sea were causing resistance. Above this noise, I hear Rich call to Thomas, but I cannot make out the words.

Thomas slides down the ladder. He is soaked despite his slicker. He seems not to have the metal clasps fastened correctly. He sees me with Billie, with Billie bent over and crying. "What's wrong?" he asks.

"I think she's seasick."

He squats down beside us.

"She's frightened," I say. "She doesn't understand."

"Did you give her the half pill?"

"Yes. But it was probably too late."

Thomas reaches for a dishtowel and uses it to wipe Billie's forehead. Then he blots his own face. He is breathing hard, and there is an angry swelling to one side of his cheekbone.

"What happened?" I ask, pointing to the bump.

"It's rough out there," he says. He flips off the hood of the slicker, wipes the top of his head. His hair is mussed in an odd kind of sculpture that would make Billie laugh if she felt better.

He puts his hand down to the teak planking to balance himself. He is still breathing hard. Trying to catch his breath. Our faces aren't a foot apart. I think, looking at him, He's frightened, too.

Thomas yells up the companionway. "There's water over the teak, Rich. I can't tell how much."

We can hear Rich's voice, but again I cannot make out the words. Thomas stands up and leans against the ladder. "OK," he says in answer to something Rich has asked.

I watch Thomas take a tool from a galley drawer and then re-move a cushion from the dinette. In the bulkhead is a socket.

Thomas puts the metal tool into the socket and begins to ratchet it back and forth. He is awkwardly bent on the bench, and the table is in his way. I have hardly ever seen Thomas perform manual labor before.

"It's the bilge," Thomas says to me. "Rich says the electric is gone."

Thomas works intensely, silently, as if he wishes to exhaust himself.

I hear another sound then, or rather it is the cessation of sound.

"Shit," I hear Rich say loudly.

He comes down the ladder. He lifts a diving mask off his face, and I can see the crazy 8 the rubber has made. The skin around the 8 looks red and raw. "We've lost the engine," he says quickly. He looks at Billie. "What's wrong?" he asks.

"She's seasick," I say.

He sighs heavily and rubs his left eye with his finger. "Can you take the wheel for a minute?" he asks me. "I have to go into the engine compartment."

I look at Billie, who is lost in the isolation of her misery. She has her hands neatly folded at her stomach. "I could put her in with Adaline," I say. I know that Rich would not ask for help unless he really needed it.

"Get her settled," he says, "and come on up, and I'll show you what to do. The sooner the better."

I take Billie to the forward cabin and open the door. The berths make an upside-down V that joins in the middle, so that they form a partial double bed. Below this arrangement, there are large drawers, and to the end of each leg of the V, a hanging locker. Adaline is lying on her side in the berth to my left. She has a hand to her forehead. She glances up as I enter and raises her head an inch.

I hold Billie on my hip. I do not want to give my daughter up. I do not want her to be with Adaline. Billie retches again.

"She hasn't thrown up yet," I say, "but she feels awful. Rich needs me to take the wheel for a minute. Thomas is right here if you need him."

"I'm sorry, Jean," she says.

I turn to Billie. "I have to help Uncle Rich for a minute," I say. "Adaline is going to take care of you. You're going to be all right." Billie has stopped crying, as if she were too sick to expend even the effort to weep.

"Seasickness is awful," I say to Adaline. "Rich and Thomas pride themselves on never getting sick. It's supposed to be in the genes. I guess Billie didn't get them."

"It's one of the first things he told me about himself when I met him," says Adaline.

"Rich," I say, wiping the sweat off Billie's brow.

"No, Thomas."

I feel it then. A billowing in of the available air.

"When did you meet Thomas?" I ask as casually as I can.

There are moments in your life when you know that the sentence that will come next will change your life forever, although you realize, even as you are anticipating this sentence, that your life has already changed. Changed some time ago, and you simply didn't know it.

I can see a momentary confusion in Adaline's face.

"Five months ago?" she says, trying for an offhand manner. "Actually, it was Thomas who introduced me to Rich."

A shout makes its way from the cockpit to the forward cabin.

"Jean!" Rich yells. "I need you!"

"Put Billie down here with me," Adaline says quickly. "She'll be fine."

I think about Thomas's suggestion that we use Rich's boat.

I set Billie beside Adaline, between Adaline and the bulkhead, and as I do, the boat slides again. Billie whacks her head against the wall. "Ow," she says.

I am thinking I just want it to be all over.

I could not have anticipated what it is like above deck, how sheltered we have been below. I did not know that a storm could be so dark, that water could appear to be so black.

There is almost no visibility. Rich takes my arm and turns me around to face the stern and yells into the side of my hood. "This is simple," he shouts. "Keep the seas behind you just like they are now. Whatever you have to do. I'm running with a piece of sail, but don't bother about that right now. The main thing is that we don't want the boat to put its side to the waves. OK?"

"Rich, when did you meet Adaline?"

"What?" He leans closer to me to hear.

"When did you meet Adaline?" I shout.

He shakes his head.

I turn away from him. "How high are those waves?" I ask, pointing.

"High," he says. "You don't want to know. OK, now, take the wheel."

I turn and put my hands on wooden spokes at ten and two o'clock. Immediately the wheel spins out of my control, flapping against the palms of my hands.

"You have to hang on, Jean."

"I can't do this," I say.

"Yes, you can."

I take hold of the wheel again and brace my legs against the cockpit floor. The rain bites my cheeks and eyelids.

"Here, put this on," he says.

He bends toward me with a diving mask, and in the small shelter of our hoods I realize we do not have to shout. "Rich, where did you meet Adaline?" I ask.

He looks confused. "The Poets and Prose dinner," he says. "I thought you knew that. Thomas was there. You couldn't go."

"I couldn't get a babysitter. Why was Adaline there?"

"Bank of Boston was a sponsor. She went as a representative."

Rich slips my hood from my hair, and I think it must be that gesture, the odd tenderness of that gesture, or perhaps it is the fitting of the mask, as you might do for a child, but he bends and kisses my wet mouth. Once, quickly. There is a sudden hard ache inside me.

He lowers the mask onto my face. When I have adjusted it and opened my eyes, he already has his back to me and is headed for the cabin.

I think it will be impossible to do as Rich has asked. I cannot control the wheel without using both hands, so I have to steer with my neck craned to see behind the stern. The boat falls into a trough, and I think the wall of water will spill upon me and swamp the boat. The swell crests at the top, then pushes the boat along with a forward zip. The boat zigzags in my inexpert hands. Several times, I mistake the direction I should turn the wheel, and overcorrect. I do not see how I will be able to keep the waves behind me. My hands become stiff with the wet and cold. The wheel shakes, and I put all my weight into my hands to keep it from spinning away from me. Less than an hour earlier I was on the beach at Smuttynose.

A wave breaks over the railing to my left. The water sloshes into the cockpit, rises to my ankles, and quickly drains away. The water is a shock on the ankles, like ice. The boat, I see, is turning into the swells. I fight the wheel, and then, oddly, there is no resistance at all, just a spinning as if in air. To my right, lightning rises from the water. Then we are lost again in a trough, and I am once more struggling with the steering apparatus. Rich has been gone only a minute, two minutes. There is another lightning skewer, closer this time, and I begin to have a new worry.

The jib snaps hard near the bow. It collapses and snaps again. I turn the wheel so as to head into the wind. The jib grows taut and steadies.

Adaline emerges from the forward hatch.

I rub the surface of the diving mask with my sleeve. The wheel gives, and I take hold of it again. I am not sure what I am seeing. There is the smoky blur of the Plexiglas hatch rising. I take the diving mask off and feel for my glasses in the pocket of my oil-skin. There is a half inch of water in the pocket. I put the glasses on, and it is as though I am looking through a prism. Objects bend and waver.

Adaline sits on the rim of the hatch and lifts her face to the sky, as if she were in a shower. The rain darkens and flattens her hair almost at once. She slips out of the hatch entirely and closes it. She slides off the cabin roof and onto the deck. She holds herself upright with a hand on a metal stay. She comes to the rail and peers out. I yell to her.

She has on a white blouse and a long dark skirt that soaks through immediately. I cannot see her face, but I can see the out-line of her breasts and legs. I yell again. She doesn't have a life vest on.

I shout down to Rich, but he doesn't hear me. Even Thomas cannot hear with all the roar.

What is she doing out there? Is she crazy?

I feel then an anger, a sudden and irrational fury, for her care-lessness, this drama. I do not want this woman to have entered our lives, to have touched Thomas or Billie, to have drawn them to her, to have distracted them. I do not want this woman to be up on deck. And most of all, I do not want to have to go to her. Instead, I want to shake her for her foolishness, for the theatrical way she carries herself, for her gold cross.

I let the wheel go, bend forward at the waist, and clutch at a stay. The wind flattens the oilskin against my body. I reach for a winch, the handholds in the teak railing. I pull myself forward. She is perhaps fifteen feet from me. My hood snaps off my head.

Adaline leans over the teak rail. Her hair falls in sheets, then blows upward from her head. I see then that she is sick.

I am three, four feet from where she is huddled at the railing. I shout her name.

The boat turns itself into the swells and heels. Adaline straightens and looks at me, an expression of surprise on her face. The jib swings hard, and makes a sharp report, like a shot. She holds out her hand. It seems to float in the air, suspended between the two of us.

I have since thought a great deal about one time when I shut a car door, gave it a push, and in the split second before it closed, I saw that Billie's fingers were in the door, and it seemed to me in the bubble of time that it took for the door to complete its swing that I might have stopped the momentum, and that I had a chance, a choice.

In Alfred, Maine, the jury took less than an hour to reach a verdict of murder in the first degree. Wagner was sentenced to be hanged. He was then taken to the state prison at Thomaston to await execution.

The hanging at Thomaston was a particularly grisly affair and is said to have almost single-handedly brought about the abolition of the death penalty in Maine. An hour before Wagner and another murderer, a man named True Gordon, who had killed three members of his brother's family with an ax, were to be hanged, Gordon attempted suicide by cutting his femoral artery and then stabbing himself in the chest with a shoemaker's knife. Gordon was bleeding out and unconscious, and the warden of Thomaston was presented with a ghastly decision: Should they hang a man who was going to die anyway before the afternoon was out? The warrant prevailed, and Wagner and Gordon were brought to an abandoned lime quarry, where the gallows had been set up. Gordon had to be held upright for the noose to be put on. Wagner stood on his own and protested his innocence. He proclaimed, "God is good. He cannot let an innocent man suffer."

At noon on June 25, 1873, Louis Wagner and True Gordon were hanged.

Adaline goes over like a young girl who has been surprised from behind by a bullying boy and pushed from the diving board, arms and legs beginning to flail before she hits the water.

The ocean closes neatly over her head. I try to keep my eye fixed on the place where she has gone in, but the surface of the water — its landscape, its geography — twitches and shifts so that what has been there before is not there a moment later.

The sea heaves and spills itself and sends the boat side-to sliding down a trough. Water cascades onto the deck, pinning my legs against the railing. Adaline breaks the surface twenty yards from the place I expected her to be. I shout her name. I can see that she is struggling. Rich comes above to see what has happened to the boat. He takes the wheel immediately.

"Jean!" he shouts. "Get away from the railing. What's going on?"

"Adaline's overboard," I shout back, but the wind is against me, and all he can make out is my lips moving soundlessly.

"What?"

"Adaline!" I yell as loudly as I can and point.

Thomas comes above just then. He has put on a black knit cap, but his oilskins are off. Rich shouts the word *Adaline* to Thomas and gestures toward the life ring. Thomas takes hold of the life ring and pulls himself toward me.

There are thundering voices then, the spooling out of a line, a life ring missed and bobbing in a trough. There is a flash of white, like a handkerchief flung upon the water. There are frantic and sharp commands, and Thomas then goes over. Rich, at the wheel, stands in a semi-crouch, like a wrestler, from the strain of trying to keep the boat upright.

I think then: If I had put out my hand, might Adaline have grabbed it? Did I put out my hand, I wonder, or did a split second of anger, of righteousness, keep my hand at my side?

I also think about this: If I hadn't shouted to Adaline just then, she would not have stood up, and the sail would have passed over her.

When Rich hauls Adaline over the stern, her skirt and underwear are missing. What he brings up doesn't seem like a person we have known, but rather a body we might study. Rich bends over Adaline and hammers at her chest, and then puts his mouth to hers again and again. In the corner of the stern, against the railing, Thomas stands doubled over from the effort to rescue Adaline and to pull himself back into the boat. He wheezes and coughs for breath.

And it isn't me, it isn't even me, it is Rich — angry, frustrated, exhausted, breathless — who lifts his head from Adaline's chest, and calls out: "Where's Billie?"

25 September 1899

I NOW ENCOUNTER my most difficult task of all, which is that of
confronting the events of 5 March 1873, and committing them to
paper, to this document, to stand as a true account made by a
witness, one who was there, who saw, and who survived to tell
the tale. Sometimes I cry to myself, here in the silence of my cottage, with only the candles to light my hand and the ink and the
paper, that I cannot write about that day, I cannot. It is not that I
do not remember the details of the events, for I do, too vividly,
the colors sharp and garish, the sounds heightened and abrasive,
as in a dream, a terrible dream that one has over and over again
and cannot escape no matter how old one grows or how many
years pass.

It was a day of blue sky and bright sun and harsh reflections
from the snow and sea and ice crystals on the rocks that hurt the
eye whenever one's gaze passed across the window panes or
when I went outside to the well or to the hen house. It was a day
of dry, unpleasant winds that whipped the hair into the face and
made the skin feel like paper. The men had left the house early in
the morning to draw their trawls, which they had set the day before, and John had said to me as he was leaving that they would
be back midday to collect Karen and to have a meal before they
set out for Portsmouth to sell the catch and purchase bait. I had
some errands I wished him to perform, and I spoke to him about
these, and it is possible I may have handed him a list on that day,

I do not remember. Evan stumbled down the stairs, unshaven, his hair mussed, and grabbed a roll on the table for his breakfast. I urged him to stay a moment and have some coffee, as it would be raw and frigid in the boat, but he waved me off and collected his jacket and his oilskins from the entryway. Matthew was already down at the boat, making it ready, as he did nearly every morning. Indeed, I hardly ever saw Matthew, as he seemed to be on a clock different from the rest of us, rising at least an hour before me, and retiring to his bed as soon as it was dark. Karen, I remember, was in the lounge that morning, and she said to John that she would be dressed and ready to go with him after the dinner meal, and John nodded to her, and I could barely look at her, since she had had all her teeth removed, and her face had a terrible sunken appearance, as one sometimes sees on the dead. Karen, who had been with us since the end of January, had been fired from her job with the Laightons when she had said one day that she would not sweep out or make the beds in a certain room belonging to four male boarders. I suspect that Eliza Laighton had been wanting to let Karen go for some time, since Karen could now speak a rudimentary English and therefore could make her complaints and opinions known, as she had not been able to do when she first arrived. As you may imagine, I was somewhat ambivalent about Karen's presence. Since Evan's arrival, we had not been overly cordial with one another, and, in addition, there were many of us under that roof, under that half-roof I should say, since we all lived in the southwest apartment, so as to be nearer to the heat source during the long winter.

Indeed, I can barely write about that dreadful winter when we were all closed in together for so many weeks in January and February. In the kitchen most hours of the day, there would be myself and John, Evan and Anethe, Matthew of course, and then Karen, and for days on end we would not be able to leave the house or to bathe properly so that there was a constant stale and foul odor in that room, a smell composed of shut-in human beings as well as the stink of fish that was on the oilskins and in the very floorboards themselves, and that no matter how hard I scrubbed with the brush was never able entirely to remove. Even Anethe, I noticed in the last weeks of February, had begun to lose her freshness, and I did observe that her hair, unwashed for so many days, took on a darker and more oily appearance and that her color, too, seemed to have faded in the winter.

It was a severe trial to keep one's temper in that fetid atmosphere. Only Evan seemed to have any enthusiasm for his lot, being content simply to remain in Anethe's presence, though I did notice signs of strain in Anethe herself, and if ever a marriage was put to the test, it was on that island, during those winters, when small tics or habits could become nearly unbearable, and the worst in a person was almost certain to emerge. John used the hours to mend nets and repair trawls, and Matthew was his partner in this work. Matthew would often hum or sing tunes from Norway, and I do remember this as a pleasant diversion. Evan had taken on the building of a wardrobe for Anethe as a project, so that the room was filled not only with nets and hooks into which one had to be careful not to become entangled, but also with wood shavings and sawdust and nails and various sharp implements with which Evan worked. I took refuge in routine, and I will say here that more than once in my life the repetition of chores has been my salvation. Of the six of us, I was the one who went outdoors the most often, to collect wood or water or eggs from the coop. It was understood that I would keep the house in order, and I have observed that while fishermen do take seasonal rests from their labors, their womenfolk do not, and do not even when the men are too weak from old age to draw a trawl and must retire from their labors. An aging wife can never retire from her work, for if she did, how would the family, or what was left of it, eat?

Karen, during this time, attended to her sewing and her spinning, and I was just as happy not to have her in my way or in constant attendance. In the beginning of Karen's stay, Anethe set out to please this sister of Evan's, rolling the wool that Karen had spun, feigning enthusiasm for the skill of embroidery and offering to braid Karen's hair, but it was not long before I noticed that even Anethe, who previously seemed to have nearly inexhaustible reserves of selflessness, began to tire of Karen's constant querulous whine and started to see as well that pleasing Karen was in itself a futile endeavor. There are some people who simply will not be pleased. After a time, I noticed that Anethe asked me more and more often for chores of her own to perform. I had more than a few to spare, and I took pity upon her, as enforced idleness in such a claustrophobic setting will almost certainly begin to erode joy, if not one's character altogether.

As for me, I had not thought about joy much, and sometimes I felt my character, if not my very soul, to be in jeopardy. I had not prayed since the day that Evan spoke harshly to me in the kitchen, as I no longer had anything compelling to pray for. Not his arrival, not his love, not even his kindness or presence. For though he was in that room all the days, though we were seldom more than a few feet from each other, it was as though we were on separate continents, for he would not acknowledge me or speak to me unless it was absolutely necessary, and even at those times, I wished that he had not had need to speak to me at all, for the indifference of his tone chilled my blood and made me colder than I had been before. It was a tone utterly devoid of warmth or forgiveness, a tone that seeks to keep another being at bay, at a distance. Once, in our bed at night, John asked me why it was that Evan and I seemed not to enjoy each other's company as much as we used to, and I answered him that there was nothing in it, only that Evan was preoccupied and blind to everyone except Anethe.

Since the first day of March, the men had been going out to sea again, and there was something of a sense of relief in this, not only because we had all survived the gruelling weeks of the hard winter, but also because now there would be some breathing room. The men, in particular, were cheered by occupation, and I suppose I was a bit more relaxed not to have so many underfoot. My work did not seem to lighten much, however, since there were the same number of meals to prepare and increased washing now that the men would come back fouled with fish goory in the afternoons.

On the morning of 5 March, I remember that Karen painstakingly dressed in her city clothes, a silver-gray dress with peacock-blue trim, and a bonnet to match, and that once outfitted in this manner, she sat straight-backed in a chair, her hands folded in her lap, and did not move much for hours. I believe she thought that being in city clothes prevented her from taking up a domestic occupation, even one so benign as sewing. It was extremely annoying to me to observe her that day, so stiff and grim, her mouth folded in upon itself, arrested in a state of anticipation, and I know that at least once I was unable to prevent my irritation from slipping out, and that I said to her that it was ludicrous to sit there in my kitchen with her hat on, when the men would not return for hours yet, but she did not respond to me and set her mouth all the tighter. Anethe, by contrast, seemed excessively buoyant that morning, and it was as though the two of us, Anethe and myself, were performing some sort of odd dance around a stationary object. Anethe had a gesture of running the backs of her hands upwards along the sides of her neck and face and gracefully bringing them together at the top of her head and then

spreading her arms wide, actually quite a lovely, sensuous movement, and she did this several times that day, and I thought it
could not just be that she was glad the men were out of the
kitchen, for, in truth, I think she was ambivalent about not being
with Evan, and so I asked her, more in jest really, what secret it
was that was making her so happy on that day, and she stunned
me by replying, "Oh, Maren, I had not thought to tell anyone. I
have not even told my husband."

Of course, I knew right away what she meant, and it hit me
with so much force that I sat down that instant as though I had
been pushed.

Anethe put her hand to her mouth. "Maren, you look
shocked. I should not have said —"

I waved my hand. "No, no . . ."

"Oh, Maren, are you not pleased?"

"How can you be sure?" I asked.

"I am late two months. January and February."

"Perhaps it is the cold," I said. It was an absurd thing to say. I
could not collect my thoughts and felt dizzy.

"Do you think I should tell him tonight? Oh, Maren, I am
amazed at myself that I have kept it from him all this time. Indeed, it is surprising that he himself did not notice, although I
think that men —"

"No, do not tell him," I said. "It is too soon. It is bad luck to
speak of this so early on. There are so many women who lose
their babies before three months. No, no, I am quite sure. We
will keep this to ourselves for now." And then I collected myself
a bit. "But, my dear, I am happy for you. Our little family will
grow bigger now, as it should do."

And then Karen said from the table, "Where will you keep it?"
and Anethe, I think somewhat taken aback by the use of the word
it rather than *the child,* composed herself and looked steadily at

her sister-in-law. "I will keep our baby with myself and Evan in our bedroom," she said.

And Karen did not say anything more at that time.

"It is why you have been looking pale," I said, suddenly comprehending the truth of what Anethe was saying. As I looked at her, I had no doubt now that she was pregnant.

"I have felt a bit faint from time to time," she said, "and sometimes there is a bad taste in the back of my mouth, a metallic taste, as if I had sucked on a nail."

"I cannot say," I said, standing up and spreading my hands along my apron skirt. "I have never had the experience."

And Anethe, silenced by the implications of that statement, picked up the broom by the table and began to sweep the floor.

The coroner missed this fact about Anethe in his examination of her body, and I did not like to tell Evan, as I thought it would make his agony all the more unendurable.

About two o'clock of that afternoon, I heard a loud hallooing from the water and looked through the window and saw Emil Ingerbretson waving to me from his schooner just off the cove, and so I ran outside quickly, thinking that perhaps there had been an accident, and I managed to make out, though the wind kept carrying off the words, that John had decided to go straight in to Portsmouth, as he could not beat against the wind. When I had got the message, I waved back to Emil, and he went off in his boat. Once inside, I told the other two women, and Anethe looked immediately disappointed, and I saw that she had meant to tell Evan that day of her news, despite my admonition not to. Karen was quite vexed, and said so, and asked now what would she do all dressed up with her city clothes on, and I replied that I had been asking myself that question all morning. She sighed dramatically, and went to a chair against the wall in the kitchen and lay back upon it.

"They will be back tonight," I said to Anethe. "Let's have a portion of the stew now, as I am hungry, and you must eat regular meals, and we will save the larger share for the men when they return. I have packed them no food, so unless they feed themselves in Portsmouth, they will be starved when they return."

I asked Karen if she would take some dinner with us, and she then asked me how she would eat a stew with no teeth, and I replied, with some exasperation, as we had had this exchange nearly every day since she had had her teeth removed, that she could sip the broth and gum the bread, and she said in a tired voice that she would eat later and turned her head to the side. I looked up to see that Anethe was gazing at me with a not unkind expression, and I trust that she was nearly as weary of my sister's complaints as I was.

We ate our meal, and I found some rubber boots in the entryway and put them on and went to the well and saw that the water had frozen over and so I went into the hen house to look for the axe, and found it lying by a barrel, and brought it to the well and heaved it up with all my strength and broke the ice with one great crack. I had been used to this chore, since the water often froze over on that island, even when the temperature of the air was not at freezing level, and this was due to the wind. I fetched up three buckets of water and took them one by one into the house and poured them into pans, and when I was done I brought the axe up to the house and laid it by the front door, so that in the morning, I would not have to go to the hen house to get it.

Dusk came early, as it was still not the equinox, and when it was thoroughly dark, and I noticed, as one will notice not the continuous sound of voices in the room but rather the cessation of those voices, that the wind had quieted, I turned to Anethe and said, "So that is that. The men will not be back this night."

She had a puzzled look on her face. "How can you be sure?" she asked.

"The wind has died," I said. "Unless they are right at the entrance to the harbor, their sails will not fill, and if they have not yet left Portsmouth, John will not go out at all."

"But we have never been alone at night before," Anethe said.

"Let us wait another half hour before we are sure," I said.

The moon was in its ascendancy, which had a lovely effect on the harbor and on the snow, outlining in a beautifully stark manner the Haley House and the Mid-Ocean Hotel, both vacant at that time. I went about the lounge lighting candles and the oil lamp. When a half hour had elapsed, I said to Anethe, "What harm can possibly come to us on this island? Who on these neighboring islands would want to hurt us? And anyway, it is not so bad that the men have not come. Without them, our chores will be lighter."

Anethe went to the window to listen for the sound of oars. Karen got up from her chair and walked to the stove and began to spoon broth and soft potatoes into a bowl. I took off my kerchief and stretched my arms.

Anethe wondered aloud where the men would stop to eat. Karen said she thought it likely they would go to a hotel and have a night for themselves. I disagreed and said I thought they would go to Ira Thaxter's on Broad Street, for they would have to beg a meal from a friend, until they sold the catch, the proceeds of which were to have gone for provisions. Karen pointed out to me that Ringe hadn't been fed yet, and I rose from the table and put some stew into his dish. All in all, I was quite amazed that Karen had not muttered something about the men having failed to take her into Portsmouth, but I imagine that even Karen could tire of her own complaints.

While Anethe washed the pots and dishes, nearly scalding her hand from the kettle water, Karen and I struggled with a mattress that we dragged downstairs to lay in the kitchen for her. Anethe asked if she could sleep in my bed to keep from being cold and lonely without Evan that night, and though I was slightly discomfited by the thought of a woman in my bed, and Anethe at that, I did reason that her body would provide some warmth, as John's did, and besides, I did not like to refuse such a personal request. After stoking up the fire for warmth, I believe that the three of us then took off our outer garments and put on our nightdresses, even Karen, who had thought to stay in her city clothes so that she would not have to dress again in the morning, but in the end was persuaded to remove them so as not to muss them unduly. And then, just as I was about to extinguish the lights, Karen took out from the cupboard bread and milk and soft cheese, and said that she was still hungry, and I will not weary the reader with the silly quarrel that ensued, although I had reason to be annoyed with her as we had just cleaned up the kitchen, and finally I said to Karen that if she would eat at this time, she could tidy up after herself and would she please extinguish the light.

Sometimes it is as though I have been transported in my entirety back to that night, for I can feel, as if I were again lying in that bed, the soft forgiveness of the feather mattress and the heavy weight of the many quilts under which Anethe and I lay. It was always startling, as the room grew colder, to experience the contrast in temperatures between one's face, which was exposed to the frigid air, and one's body, which was encased in goose down. We had both been still for some time, and I had seen, through the slit underneath the bedroom door, that the light had been put out, which meant that Karen had finally gone to bed. I was lying flat on my back with my arms at my sides, looking up at the ceiling, which I could make out only dimly in the moonlight. Anethe lay facing me, curled into a comma, holding the covers close up to her chin. I had worn a nightcap, but Anethe had not, and I suppose this was because she had a natural cap in the abundance of her hair. I had thought she was asleep, but I turned my head quickly toward her and back again and saw that she was staring at me, and I felt a sudden stiffening all through me, a response no doubt to the awkwardness of lying in my bed with a woman, and this woman my brother's wife.

"Maren," she whispered, "are you still awake?"

She knew that I was. I whispered, "Yes."

"I feel restless and cannot sleep," she said, "although all day I have felt as though I would sleep on my feet."

"You are not yourself," I said.

"I suppose." She shifted in the bed, bringing her face a little closer to my own.

"Do you think the men are all right? You don't think anything could have happened to them?"

I had thought once or twice, briefly, not liking to linger on the thought, that perhaps John and Evan had met with an accident on the way to Portsmouth, although that seemed unlikely to me, and, in any event, hours had passed since Emil had come with the message, and if some ill had befallen the men, I thought that we would have heard already.

"I believe they are safe in Portsmouth. Perhaps in a tavern even as we speak," I said. "Not minding at all their fate."

"Oh," she said quickly, "I think my Evan would mind. He would not like to sleep without me."

My Evan.

She reached out a hand from the covers and began to stroke my cheek with her fingers. "Oh, Maren," she said, "you are so watchful over us all."

I did not know what she meant by that. My breath was suddenly tight in my chest from the touch of her fingers. I wanted to throw her hand off and turn my back to her, but I was rigid with embarrassment. I was glad that it was dark, for I knew that I must be highly colored in my face. To be truthful, her touch was tender, as a mother might stroke a child, but I could not appreciate this kindness just then. Anethe began to smooth my forehead, to run her fingers through the hair just underneath my cap.

"Anethe," I whispered, meaning to tell her to stop.

She moved her body closer, and wrapped her hands around my arm, laying her forehead on my shoulder.

"Do you and John?" she asked, in a sort of muffled voice. "Is it the same?"

"Is what the same?" I asked.

"Do you not miss him at this moment? All the attentions?"

"The attentions," I repeated.

She looked up at me. "Sometimes it is so hard for me to sit in the kitchen until it is proper to go up to bed. Do you know?" and she moved herself still closer to me so that her length was all against my own. "Oooh," she said. "Your feet are freezing. Here, let me warm them," and she began, with the smooth sole of her foot, to massage the top of my own. "Do you know," she said again, "I have never told anyone this, and I hope you will not be shocked, but Evan and I were lovers before we were married. Do you think that was very wrong? Were you and John?"

I did not know what to say to her or which question to answer first, as I was distracted by the movement of her foot, which had begun to travel up and down the shin of my right leg.

"I no longer know what is right or wrong anymore," I said.

Her body was a great deal warmer than my own, and this warmth was not unpleasant, though I remained stiff with discomfort, as I had never been physically close with anyone except my brother Evan and my husband. I had certainly never been physically close with a female, and the sensation was an odd one. But, as will happen with a child who is in need of comfort and who gradually relaxes his limbs in the continuous embrace of the mother, I began to be calmed by Anethe, and to experience this peace as pleasurable, and, briefly to allow myself to breathe a bit more regularly. I cannot explain this to the reader. It is, I think, a decision the body makes before the heart or the head, the sort of decision I had known with John, when, without any mental participation, my body had seemed to respond in the proper ways to his advances. In truth, as Anethe laid her head on my chest and began to stroke the skin of my throat, I felt myself wanting to turn ever so slightly toward my brother's wife and to put my arm around her, and perhaps, in this way, return something of the affection and tenderness she was showing to me.

"Do you do it every night?" she asked, and I heard then a kind of schoolgirlish embarrassment in her own voice.

"Yes," I whispered, and I was shocked at my own admission. I wanted to add that it was not my doing, not my doing at all, but she giggled then, now very much like a girl, and said, to my surprise, "Turn over."

I hesitated, but she gently pushed my shoulder, and persisted with this urging, so that finally I did as I was told, putting my back to her, and not understanding what this was for. She lifted herself up onto her elbow and said, close to my ear, "Take up your nightgown."

I could not move.

"I want to rub your back," she explained, "and I cannot do it properly through the cloth." She pushed the covers down and began slightly to tug at the skirt of my nightgown with her hand, and I, though somewhat fearful of the consequences, began to wrestle with the gown and to pull the hem up to my shoulders. I held the bunched cloth to my bosom as I had done once at the doctor's office in Portsmouth when I had had the pleurisy. But shortly I felt the warmth of being attended to, and I surrendered myself to this attention.

Anethe began then to stroke my skin with an exquisite lightness and delicacy, from the top of my spine to my waist, from one side of my back to the other, all around in the most delightful swirls, so that I was immediately, without any reservations, put into a swoon of such all-encompassing proportions that I could not, in those moments, for any reason, have denied myself this touch. It was a sensation I had not experienced in many years. Indeed, I cannot remember, ever in my adult life, being the recipient of such pleasure, so much so that had she stopped before I had had my fill, I would have begged her to continue, would have promised her anything if only she would again touch my skin with her silken fingers. But she did not stop for some time, and I remember having the thought, during that experience, that she must be a very generous lover, and then realizing, when I was nearly in a dream state myself, that her hand had trailed off and that she had fallen asleep, for she began to snore lightly. And hearing her asleep, and not wishing to wake her, and also not wanting the trance I had fallen into to be broken, I did not move or cover myself, but drifted into a deep sleep while the moon set, for I remember being confused and struggling for sense when I heard my dog, Ringe, barking through the wall.

What a swimming up is there from the bath of a sensuous dream to the conscious world, from a dream one struggles desperately not to abandon to the frigid shock of a startled voice in the darkness. Ringe barked with loud, sudden yips. I raised my arms up from the bed before I was even fully awake. I thought that Karen was stumbling about in an attempt to go to the privy, and that she had woken Ringe, who normally slept with me. I was about to call out to her with some irritation to be quiet and go back to bed and to send my dog into the bedroom, when I heard her say, in the clearest possible voice, "My God, what have you done?"

It was all so much simpler, so much simpler, than I said.

I sat up in my bed and saw that my sister was standing at the open door of the bedroom and that to my great embarrassment, the bedclothes were still at the foot of the bed, and that most of my naked body was exposed. I hastily pulled the cloth of my nightdress down to my feet.

I can remember the awful surprise in Karen's face, and, even now, the horror of her mouth folded in upon itself, sputtering words to me in a voice that had become more metallic, more grating with the years, and the way the words issued from that black hole of a mouth.

"First our Evan and now Anethe!" she shouted. "How can you have done this? How can you have done this to such a sweet and innocent woman?"

"No, Karen . . . ," I said.

But my sister, in an instant, had progressed from shock to moral righteousness. "You are shameless and have always been so," she went on in that terrible voice, "and I shall tell our Evan and John also when they return, and you will be banished from this household as I should have done to you many years ago, when I knew from the very beginning you were an unnatural creature."

"Karen, stop," I said. "You don't know what you say."

"Oh, but I do know what I say! You have borne an unnatural love for our brother since your childhood, and he has fought to be free of you, and now that he is married, you have thought to have him by having his wife, and I have caught you out in the most heinous of sins, Maren, the most heinous of sins."

Beside me, Anethe struggled to waken. She lifted herself up upon one elbow and looked from me to Karen. "What is it?" she asked groggily.

Karen shook her head furiously back and forth, back and forth. "I have never loved you, Maren, I have never loved you. I have not even liked you, and that is the truth. And I think it is true also that our Evan has found you selfish and self-dramatic, and that he grew so tired of you he was glad when you went away. And now you are grown old, Maren, old and fat, and I see that your own husband does not really love, nor does he trust you, for you would do anything to get what you want, and now, rebuffed, you have committed the worst possible of sins, a sin of corruption, and have chosen to steal your brother's wife, and seduce her in the most shameful manner."

No one can say with any certainty, unless he has lived through such an experience, how he will react when rage overtakes the body and the mind. The anger is so swift and so piercing, an attack of all the senses, like a sudden bite on the hand, that I am not surprised that grown men may commit acts they forever regret. I sat, in a stiffened posture on the bed, seconds passing before I could move, listening to the outrageous litany against me which I knew that Anethe was being forced to hear as well, and the beating of my heart against my breastbone became so insistent and so loud that I knew I must silence Karen or surely I would die.

I pushed myself from my bed, and Karen, observing me, and coward that she was and always had been, backed away from me and into the kitchen. At first she put her hand to her mouth, as if she might actually be frightened, but then she took her hand away and began to sneer at me most scornfully.

"Look at you in your silly nightdress," she said, "grown fat and ugly in your middle age. Do you imagine you can scare me?" She turned her back to me, perhaps to further show her scorn by dismissing me. She bent over her trunk and opened it, and took up a great armful of linens. Or perhaps she was looking for something. I have never known.

I put my hands on the back of a chair and gripped that chairback so hard my knuckles whitened.

Karen staggered two or three steps under the blows from the

chair and, twisting around, turned towards me, held out her arms and dropped the linens on the floor. I am not sure if she did this in entreaty or if she meant only to protect herself. A small exclamation escaped me, as I stood there with the chair in my hands.

Karen stumbled into my bedroom and fell upon the floor, weakly scrabbling against the painted wood like a strange and grotesque insect. I think that Anethe may have gotten out of the bed and taken a step backwards toward the wall. If she spoke, I do not remember what she said. The weight of the wood caused the chair to swing from my arms so that it fell upon the bed. I took hold of Karen's feet and began to pull her back into the kitchen, as I did not want this sordid quarrel to sully Anethe. The skirt of Karen's nightgown raised itself up to her waist, and I remember being quite appalled at the white of her scrawny legs.

I write now of a moment in time that cannot be retrieved, that took me to a place from which there was never any hope of return. It all seemed at the time to happen very quickly, somewhere within a white rage in my head. To retell these events is exceedingly painful for me now, and I will doubtless horrify the reader, but because my desire is to unburden myself and to seek forgiveness before I pass on, I must, I fear, ask the reader's patience just a moment longer.

When Karen was across the threshold, I moved to the door, shut it and put a slat through the latch so that there would be only myself and my sister in the kitchen. I think that Karen may have struggled to stand upright, and then fallen or been thrown against the door, for there was a small shudder against the wood, and it must have been then that Anethe, on the other side of the door, pushed our bed against it. I heard Karen cry out my name.

I would not have harmed Anethe. I would not. But I heard, through the wall, the sound of the window being opened. Anethe would have run to the beach. Anethe would have called for help, alerted someone on Appledore or Star, and that person would have rowed across the harbor and come up to the house and found myself and Karen. And then what would I have done? And where could I go? For Karen, possibly, was dying already.

In truth, the axe was for Karen.

But when I picked up the axe on the front stoop, I found I was growing increasingly concerned about Anethe. Therefore I did not return just then to the kitchen, but stepped into the entryway and put on the rubber boots, and went outside again and kept moving, around to the side of the house, where the window was. I remember that Ringe was barking loudly at my feet, and I think that Karen was crying. I don't believe that Anethe ever said a word.

She was standing just outside the window, her feet in the snow up to the hem of her nightgown. I was thinking that her feet must be frozen. Her mouth was open, and she was looking at me, and as I say, no sound emerged from her. She held a hand out to me, one hand, as though reaching across a wide divide, as though asking for me, so that I, too, might lay my hand over that great expanse and help her to safety. And as I stood there, gazing upon her fingers, looking at the fearful expression in my brother's wife's face, I remembered the tenderness of her touch of just hours ago, and so I did extend my hand, but I did not reach her. She did not move, and neither then could I.

It is a vision I have long tried to erase, the axe in the air. Also as well the sight of blood soaking the nightgown and the snow.

On more than one occasion, I have waited for the sunrise. The sky lightens just a shade, promising an easy dawn, but then one waits interminably for the first real shadows, the first real light.

I had to leave the boots back at the house, in keeping with the first and hasty suggestions of a story, and as a consequence, I had cut my feet on the ice. I could no longer feel them, however, as they had gone numb during the night. I held my dog, Ringe, for warmth, and I think that if I had not done so, I would have frozen entirely.

During those awful hours in the sea cave, I wept and cried out and battered my head back against the rock until it bled. I bit my hand and my arm. I huddled in my hiding place and wished that the rising tide might come in to my cave and wash me out to sea. I re-lived every moment of the horrors that had occurred that night, including the worst moments of all, which were those of cold, calculated thought and of arranging facts to suit the story I must in-vent. I could not bear the sight of Karen's body, and so I dragged her into the northeast apartment and left her in the bedroom. And also, just before I fled the house, I found I did not like to think of Anethe in the snow, and so I hauled her inside the cottage.

I have discovered in my life that it is not always for us to know the nature of God, or why He may bring, in one night, pleasure and death and rage and tenderness, all intermingled, so that one can barely distinguish one from the other, and it is all that one can do to hang onto sanity. I believe that in the darkest hour, God may restore faith and offer salvation. Toward dawn, in that cave, I began to pray for the first time since Evan had spoken harshly to me. These were prayers that sprang from tears shed in the black-est moment of my wretchedness. I prayed for the souls of Karen and Anethe, and for Evan, who would walk up the path to the cottage in a few hours, wondering why his bride did not greet him at the cove, and again for Evan, who would be bewildered by the cluster of men who stood about the doorstep, and once more for Evan, who would stagger away from that cottage and that is-land and never return again.

And also I prayed for myself, who had already lost Evan to his fathomless grief. For myself, who would be inexplicably alive when John saw the bodies of Karen and Anethe. For myself, who did not understand the visions God had given me.

When the sun rose, I crawled from the rock cave, so stiff I

could barely move. The carpenters on Star Island, working on the hotel, dismissed me as I waved my skirt. Around the shore I limped on frozen feet until I saw the Ingerbretson children playing on Malaga. The children heard my cries and went to fetch their father. In a moment, Emil ran to his dory and paddled over to where I was standing on the shore of Smutty Nose. My eyes were swollen, my feet bloody, my nightgown and hair dishevelled, and, in this manner, I fell into Emil's arms and wept.

At the Ingerbretsons', I was laid upon a bed. A story came out, in bits and pieces, the pieces not necessarily in their correct order, the tale as broken as my spirit. And it was not until later that day, when I heard the story told to another in that room, that I understood for the first time all that I had said, and from that moment on, this was the precise story I held to.

I kept to my lurid story that day and the next, and throughout the trial, but there was a moment, that first morning, as I lay on a bed in the Ingerbretson house, and was speaking to John and was in the midst of my story, that my husband, who had been holding his head in his hands in a state of awful anguish, looked up at me and took his hands away from his face, and I knew he had then the first of his doubts.

And what shall I say of my meeting with Evan, who, shortly after John left, stumbled into the room, having been blasted by the scene at Smutty Nose, and who looked once at me, not even seeing me, not even knowing I was there in that room with him, and who turned and flung his arm hard against the wall, so hard he broke his bones, and who howled the most piteous wail I have ever heard from any human being?

The white button that was found in Louis Wagner's pocket was an ordinary button, quite common, and only I knew, apart from Louis, although how could he admit to the manner in which he had come by it without showing that he was capable of an attack on a woman and thus aiding in his own conviction, that the button had come loose from Anethe's blouse on the day that he had feigned illness and had made advances to her in his bedroom. Following the discovery of the button, which was widely reported, I removed the buttons from the blouse, which I subsequently destroyed, and put them on my nightgown.

I often think of the uncommon love I bore my brother and of how my life was shaped by this devotion, and also of John's patience and of his withdrawal from me, and of the beauty and the tenderness of my brother's wife. And I think also of the gathering net Evan threw into the water, and how he let it sink, and how he drew it up again, and how it showed to us the iridescent and the dark, the lustrous and the grotesque.

Last night, lying awake with the pain, I could take no nourishment except water, and I understand that this is a sign of the end, and to be truthful, I cannot mind, as the pain is greater than the ability of the girl who attends to me to mollify it with the medicine. It is in my womb, as I always knew it would be, knew it from the time I lay ill with the paralysis and my womanhood began. Or perhaps I knew it from the night my mother died, knew that I, too, would one day perish from something that would be delivered from the womb, knew that one day my blood, too, would soak the sheets, as it did that night, so long ago, that night of my mother's death, when Evan and I lay together in the bed, and occasionally I am addled and confused and think myself a young woman again and that my monthly time has come, and then I remember, each time with a shock that leaves me breathless, that I am not young but am old, and that I am dying.

In a few weeks, we will have a new century, but I will not be here to see it.

I am glad that I have finished with my story, for my hand is weak and unsteady, and the events I have had to write about are grim and hideous and without any redemption, and I ask the

Lord now, as I have for so many years, Why was the punishment so stern and unyielding? Why was the suffering so great?

The girl comes early in the morning and opens the curtains for me, and once again, as I did each day as a child, I look out onto Laurvig Bay, the bay constantly changing, each morning different from the one before or indeed any morning that has ever come before that. When the girl arrives, I am always in need of the medicine, and after she has given it to me, I watch from the chair as she changes the filthy sheets, and goes about the cottage, tidying up, making the thin soup that until recently I was able to drink, speaking to me occasionally, not happy with her lot, but not selfish either. And in this way, she very much reminds me of myself when I was at the Johannsen farm, though in this case, she will have to watch me die, will have to sit beside me in this room and watch the life leave me, unless she is fortunate enough to have me go in the night, and I hope, for her sake, that it will be an easy passage, without drama and without agony.

26 September 1899, Maren Christensen Hontvedt.

I SIT IN the small boat in the harbor and watch the light begin to fade on Smuttynose. I hold in my hand papers from the cardboard carton.

Not long ago, I had lunch with Adaline in a restaurant in Boston. I hadn't been in a restaurant since the previous summer, and I was at first disoriented by the space — the tall ceilings, the intricately carved moldings, the mauve banquettes. On each table was a marble vase filled with peonies. Adaline was waiting for me, a glass of wine by her right hand. She had cut her hair and wore it in a sleek flip. I could see more clearly now how it might be that she was an officer with Bank of Boston. She was wearing a black suit with a gray silk shell, but she still had on the cross.

Our conversation was difficult and strained. She asked me how I was, and I had trouble finding suitable words to answer her. She spoke briefly about her job. She told me she was getting married. I asked to whom, and she said it was to someone at the bank. I wished her well.

"Have you seen Thomas?" I asked her.

"Yes. I go down there . . . well, less now."

She meant Hull, Thomas's family home, where he lived with Rich, who looked after him.

"He's writing?"

"No, not that any of us can see. Rich is gone a lot. But he says that Thomas just sits at the desk, or walks along the beach."

I was privately amazed that Thomas could bear to look at water.

"He blames himself," said Adaline.

"I blame myself."

"It was an accident."

"No, it wasn't."

"He's drinking."

"I imagine."

"You haven't seen him since . . . ?"

She was unable to say the words. To define the event.

"Since the accident," I said for her. "We were together afterwards. It was excruciating. I suppose I will eventually go down to see him. In time."

"Sometimes a couple, after a tragedy, they find comfort in each other."

"I don't think that would be the case with me and Thomas," I said carefully.

During the hours following the discovery that Billie was missing, Thomas and I had said words to each other that could never be taken back, could never be forgotten. In the space of time it takes for a wave to wash over a boat deck, a once tightly knotted fisherman's net had frayed and come unraveled. I could not now imagine taking on the burden of Thomas's anguish as well as my own. I simply didn't have the strength.

"You're all right, then?" she asked. "In your place?"

"The apartment? Yes. As fine as can be."

"You're working?"

"Some."

"You know," she said, "I've always been concerned . . ." She fingered the gold cross. "Well, it doesn't seem very important now. But I've always been concerned you thought Thomas and I . . ."

"Were having an affair. No, I know you weren't. Thomas told me."

"He held me once in the cockpit when I was telling him about my daughter."

"I know. He told me that, too." I picked up a heavy silver spoon and set it down. All around me were animated women and men in suits.

"And there's another thing," she said. "Thomas indicated that you thought . . . well, Billie must have misheard a casual invitation from Thomas to me. Billie somehow thought I might be coming to live with you."

I nodded. "You were lucky," I said. "Not having a life vest."

She looked away.

"Why did you leave her?" I asked suddenly, and perhaps there was an edge of anger in my voice.

I hadn't planned to ask this of Adaline. I had promised myself I wouldn't.

Her eyes filled. "Oh, Jean, I've gone over and over this, a thousand times. I didn't want to be sick in front of Billie. I wanted fresh air. I'd been looking through the hatch all morning. I didn't think. I just opened it. I just assumed she wouldn't be able to reach it."

"I don't think she went out the hatch," I said.

Adaline blew her nose. I ordered a glass of wine. But already I knew that I would not be there long enough to drink it.

"She was a wonderful girl," I said to Adaline.

I think often of the weight of water, of the carelessness of adults.

Billie's body has never been found. Her life jacket, with its Sesame Street motif, washed up at Cape Neddick in Maine. It is my theory that Billie had the life jacket on, but not securely. That would have been like Billie, unclipping the jacket to readjust it, to wear it slightly differently, backwards possibly, so that she could satisfy herself that some part of her independence had not been lost. It is my theory that Billie came up the companionway looking for me or for Adaline to help her refasten the waist buckle. I tell myself that my daughter was surprised by the wave. That it took her fast, before thoughts or fear could form. I have convinced myself of this. But then I wonder: Might she have called out *Mom,* and then *Mom?* The wind was against her, and I wouldn't have heard her cry.

I did not return Maren Hontvedt's document or its translation to the Athenaeum. I did not send in the pictures from the photo shoot, and my editor never asked for them.

This is what I have read about John Hontvedt and Evan Christensen. John Hontvedt moved to a house on Sagamore Street in Portsmouth. He remarried and had a daughter named Honora. In 1877, Evan Christensen married Valborg Moss at St. John, New Brunswick, where he had gone from Portsmouth, and where he worked as a carpenter and cabinetmaker. After his marriage, the couple moved to Boston. They had five children, two of whom died in infancy.

I think about the accommodations Evan Christensen would have had to make to marry another woman. What did he do with his memories?

Anethe and Karen Christensen are buried side by side in Portsmouth.

I sometimes think about Maren Hontvedt and why she wrote her document. It was expiative, surely, but I don't believe she was seeking absolution. I think it was the weight of her story that compelled her — a weight she could no longer bear.

I slide the handful of papers into the water. I watch them bob and float upon the water's twitching surface, and I think they look like sodden trash tossed overboard by an inconsiderate sailor. Before morning, before they are found, the papers will have disintegrated, and the water will have blurred the ink.

I think about the hurt that stories cannot ease, not with a thousand tellings.

Acknowledgments

I could not have written this book without the aid of the various guidebooks to the Isles of Shoals as well as the several published accounts of the Smuttynose murders, in particular *Murder at Smuttynose and Other Murders* by Edmund Pearson (1938), *Moonlight Murder at Smuttynose* by Lyman Rutledge (1958), *The Isles of Shoals: A Visual History* by John Bardwell (1989), *The Isles of Shoals in Lore and Legend* by Lyman Rutledge (1976), "A Memorable Murder" by Celia Thaxter (1875), *A Stern and Lovely Scene: A Visual History of the Isles of Shoals* by the Art Galleries at the University of New Hampshire (1978), *Sprays of Salt* by John Downs (1944), and, of course, my much thumbed copy of *Ten Miles Out: Guide Book to the Isles of Shoals* by the Isles of Shoals Unitarian Association (1972). To these authors and to others who have written about this wonderful and mysterious archipelago, I am indebted.

I am also extremely grateful to my editor, Michael Pietsch, and my agent, Ginger Barber, for their incisive comments and advice.

Finally, I am most grateful to John Osborn for his tireless research and emotional intelligence.

RESISTANCE

For our fathers who flew in the war

AUTHOR'S NOTE

This novel is entirely a work of fiction, yet it would not have been possible without the help of the following individuals: Maralyse Martin Haward, Andre Lepin, and Rosa Guyaux, who shared with me details and anecdotes about Belgium during World War II; John Rising, Chief Pilot of the Collings Foundation, who checked over the flying sequences for me; George Cole, who took me up in his plane; and, in particular, Mable Osborn, who gave the seeds of a story. I would also like to thank my editor, Michael Pietsch, and my agent, Virginia Barber.

Finally, a necessary word about the Belgian surnames. I have used, for the most part, surnames that were or are prevalent in southern Belgium. Just as the novel is fictional, however, so are the names that are attached to the various characters. I mention this because the period about which I have written is a sensitive one, and my use of certain names is not meant in any way to confer honor upon, or castigate, any Belgian families.

10 November 1993

Gentlemen,

INAUGURATION OF A MONUMENT
TO YOUR FLYING FORTERESSE B 17

On Thursday next December 30, our association will inaugurate a monument in rememberance to your aeroplane fallen down on 1943 december 30th at the Heights nearly our village.

It consists in a marble block extracted out of our village quarry on which a stele with the following inscription will be fixed.

*

Homage à nos alliés

Le 30 décembre 1943 vers midi s'écrasa à 500 m d'ici la forteresse volante américaine Woman's Home Companion

Equipage

Pilote: Lt. T. Brice
Co-pilote: Lt. W. Case
Navigateur: Lt. E. Baker
Bombardier: Lt. N. Shulman
Ingénieur: J. McNulty
Ass. Ingénieur: E. Rees
Radio: G. Callahan
Ass. Radio: V. Tripp
Mitrailleur: L. Ekberg
Mitrailleur: P. Warren

Delahaut, le 30 XII 1993
*

With this letter, we would like to invite you and your wife to be present at the inauguration. It will be a pleasure for us to offer you a lodge in Delahaut.

If you are still in contact with the other members of the crew, please will you make them known they are also welcome. Send us their address so we can invite them officially.

Meanwhile, Gentlemen, please agree our best rememberance.
Jean Benoît

December 30, 1943

THE PILOT PAUSED AT THE EDGE OF THE WOOD, WHERE already it was dark, oak-dark at midday. He propped himself against a tree, believing that in the shadows he was hidden, at least for the moment. The others had fled. He was the last out of the pasture, watching until they had all disappeared, one by one, indistinct brown shapes quickly enveloped by the forest.

All, that is, except for the two on the ground, one dead, one dying. He could no longer hear the gunner's panicky questions. The cold and the wound had silenced him, or perhaps the morphine, administered by Ted's frozen fingers, had dulled the worst of it. Dragging his own wounded leg through the battered bomber, Ted had reached the gunner, drawn to him by the pitch of the man's voice. He had separated the gunner from the metal that seemed to clutch at him and pulled the man out onto the hard ground, still white with frost even at noon. The wound was to the lower abdomen, too low, Ted could see that at once. The gunner had screamed then, asked him, demanded, but Ted looked away, businesslike with the needle, and whispered something that was meant to be reassuring but was taken by the wind. The gunner felt frantically with oily fingers for the missing pieces. The pilot and the navigator had held his arms, pinned him.

Possibly the gunner was dead already, he thought at the edge of the forest. There was too much blood around the body, a hot spring that quickly pooled, froze, on the ground. The other man,

5

the rear gunner, the man who was undeniably dead, dragged also to lie beside the wounded, had not a scratch on him.

Ted slowly tilted his head back, took the air deep into his body. As a boy he had shot squirrels in the wood at home, and there were sometimes days like this, days without color, when the sky was oily and gray and his fingers froze on the .22.

The plane lay silent on the frosty field, a charred scar behind it, the forest not forty feet from its nose. A living thing shot down, crippled now forever. A screaming, vibrating giant come obscenely to rest in a pasture.

He ought to have set fire to the plane. Those were his instructions. But he could not set a fire that might consume a living man, and so they had gathered all the provisions in the plane and made a kind of catafalque near the gunner, whom they had wrapped in parachute silk, winding sheets, the white silk stained immediately with red.

Soon people would come to the pasture. The fall of the big plane from the sky could not have been missed. Ted didn't know if the ground he sat on was German or French or Belgian. It could be German, might well be German.

He had to move deeper into the wood. He hesitated, did not want to leave the plane. He felt, leaving it, that he was abandoning a living thing, an injured dog, to be dismembered by strangers. They would take the guns first, then the engines, then every serviceable piece of metal, leaving a carcass, a dog's bones.

Gunmetal bones. A plane picked clean by buzzards.

One's duty was to the living.

Ted might have aborted. He was allowed to abort. He knew the mission was not a milk run, that they were going into German territory, to Ludwigshafen, to the chemical plant. And he had felt unlucky without Mason, his navigator, whom he had found drunk in a hotel room in Cambridge with his English girlfriend. When Ted had entered, the room had been heavy with the smell of gin. A bottle was nearly empty on a side table. Mason had looked at Ted and had laughed at him. Ted had thought then, abort. A missing navigator was a bad omen. They had flown eleven missions together, had sometimes come under heavy fire, but there had been no serious injuries, no deaths. Abort, he tried to tell himself; but at dawn, when the thin, wintry light had come up over the landing field, and he'd looked at his plane, he could not make the decision to abort. Mason was replaced. A capable man but a stranger. Together they had pinned the arms of the gunner, looked into each other's eyes.

But had the missing piece of the crew fatally altered the mix, in the same way that an error in the mix of the fuel, too rich or too thin, could also be fatal? Had unease over the missing navigator made Ted hesitate even a second when he should not have hesitated, or made him act too quickly when he *should* have hesitated? Had his belief in bad omens clouded in some indefinable way his judgment? Case, his copilot, was right. They should have ditched. But he couldn't, and it was no use pretending he could.

Twigs crackled. Ted tried to stand, leaned against the rough bark. He had dragged himself out of the clearing, his right leg wounded inside his flight suit. When he stood, the pain traveled up his thigh. He embraced the tree, his forehead against the bark. A sudden sweat broke out on his face from the pain. He bent over quickly, heaved onto the frozen leaves. He might have saved a needle for himself, but he was afraid that he would crawl into the forest and freeze to death while he slept. He knew he had to move deeper into the wood.

Today was his birthday. He was twenty-two.

Where did the gunner's dick go? he wondered.

He turned to look at the plane once again, and from his full height he saw what he had not seen before: In dragging himself to the edge of the forest, he had made a path in the frost, a path as clear and distinct as a walkway shoveled in snow. He heard the first of the muffled shouts then. A foreign voice. He dropped to the ground and pulled himself away from the pasture.

———

The boy reached the Heights before Marcel. Jean dropped his bicycle, his chest burning. He gulped in the icy air and stared at the plane on the dead grass. He had never seen such a big plane, never. It was somehow terrifying, that enormous plane, unnatural here. How did a machine, all that metal, ever get up into the sky? He approached the plane cautiously, wondering if it might still explode. He heard Marcel behind him, breathing hard like a dog.

Jean walked toward the bomber and saw the bodies, the two men in leather helmets, one man wrapped in a parachute. The white silk was bloody, drenched in blood.

Jean spun and yelled at Marcel: "La Croix-Rouge, Marcel! Madame Dinant! La Croix-Rouge!"

Marcel hesitated just a moment, then did as Jean had asked, unwilling yet to see exactly what his friend had seen.

When Marcel had gone, Jean walked slowly toward the plane. For the first time since he'd seen the giant, smoking surprise drop suddenly from the cloud cover, he could breathe evenly. He was chilled, the sweat beginning to freeze inside his pullover. He hadn't thought to fetch his coat before racing out of the school to head for the Heights.

When he reached the plane, he looked down at the bodies. Both of the flyers had their eyes closed, but the man wrapped in blood was still breathing. Beside the two men was a pile of canteens and brown canvas sacks.

Jean moved away from the men and began to circle the plane. The plane was American, he was sure of that.

The bomber rested deeply on its belly, as if partially embedded in the ground, the propellers jammed and bent under the wings. The wings were extraordinarily long. The tail seemed to have been ripped apart, to have stripped itself in the air, and there were dozens of holes in the fuselage, some of them as large as windows. There were markings on the plane and a white, five-pointed star.

Jean walked to the front of the plane. Perhaps, he thought, there were men still trapped inside the cockpit, and for a moment he entertained the fantasy of rescuing them, saving their lives. The windshield had been shot away. Jean climbed onto the wing and peered into the cockpit. He looked at the debris and glass and smashed instrument casings. He tried to imagine himself behind

8

the controls. He hopped off the wing then, and walked around the nose to the other side of the plane. Below the cockpit was a drawing he couldn't quite believe and beneath the drawing were English words he couldn't read. If Marcel had been with him, Jean would have pointed to the drawing, and the two boys would have laughed. But alone, Jean did not feel like laughing.

Slowly he circled the rest of the plane and returned to the two men lying on the ground. The man in the parachute began to moan, opened his eyes. Instinctively, Jean backed away. He didn't know whether he should speak or remain silent. For a moment, his own eyes welled with tears, and he wished Madame Dinant would hurry up and get here. What could a ten-year-old boy do for the man in the pasture?

He walked backwards from the plane, his hands frozen in his pockets. And as he did so, he saw what ought to have been obvious to him, but was lost in his eagerness to inspect the plane. Fanning out from the front of the plane to the forest were footprints in the frost — large footprints, not his own. He could see distinctly where the footprints had gone: this trail, and that trail, and that trail — all into the wood, spokes from the plane.

And then there was the one path.

In the distance, Jean heard voices, the murmur of excited, breathless voices scurrying up the hill toward the pasture. Quickly Jean marked in his memory the entry points of the various trails into the forest. Without knowing quite why he was doing this, he began to scuffle over the field, erasing footprints with his shoes. The voices grew louder. His own feet would not be sufficient. He ran to the edge of the clearing, ripped down a fir branch. He whirled around the pasture, sweeping the frost from the grass.

Anthoine was ahead of him, limping with remarkable speed up the cow path. How could such a fat, ungainly man move so fast? Henri wondered. His own chest stung with the effort. He didn't want to find this plane, didn't want to see it.

Just minutes ago, in the village, he and Anthoine had been

drinking at Jauquet's. Thinking to make something of a noon break, not quite a meeting, talking about the leaflets, drinking Jauquet's beer, not as good as his own. And then the plane dropping out of the sky as they sat there in the Burghermaster's small, frozen garden. Dipping and wobbling as they watched, three of its engines trailing dark plumes, creating an eerie charcoal drawing. He wanted to cover his head; he thought the plane would fall onto the village. The bomber barely missed the steeple of St. Catherine's, and Henri could see it had no landing gear. Excitement and fear rose in him as he watched the plane lift slightly and then fall, and then lift again to disappear over the Heights. Waiting for the explosion then, watching for billows of smoke from the field. In silence they had waited seconds. Nothing had happened.

American, Anthoine had said.

How long since the plane had crashed? Nine minutes? Eleven?

The others approached the clearing just ahead of him. Thérèse Dinant was first, walking so fast she was bent forward in her wool coat, retying her kerchief under her chin against the cold. Behind her, Jauquet was puffing hard to beat her into the pasture. Léon, a thin man with steel glasses and a worker's cap, couldn't take the hill, was falling back. And schoolboys, running, as if this were an outing.

He heard exclamations of surprise, some fear. He turned the corner and took it all in at once: the broken plane, the bodies, the scarred ground. From habit, he crossed himself.

Not a crash, but a belly landing. The smell of petrol, the thought of fire. Thérèse kneeling in the frost. Taking the pulse of a man wrapped in a parachute, speaking constantly to him in a low voice. She raised the wrist of another man beside the first, but Henri could see, even from where he stood, that the man was dead. It was the color of his face.

Dinant looked up and ordered stretchers and a truck. Girard, who worked with Bastien, the undertaker, ran suddenly from the pasture.

More people arrived in the clearing. Twenty, twenty-five, thirty. The villagers surrounded the plane, climbed onto the wings. Schoolboys rubbed the metal of the engine cowling with knitted gloves as if it were burnished gold. They peered down under the wings to marvel at how the propellers had bent in the landing. A distance was kept from the wounded and the dead, with Thérèse watching over them, except that some of the men gave their coats to be piled over the wounded man to warm him.

Henri meant to give his coat. He couldn't move.

Women — farmers' wives, shopkeepers — inspected canvas sacks, exclaiming over the provisions. The chocolate, he saw, was taken immediately. Later, he thought, after the bodies had been removed, the sacks would be picked clean.

There was activity inside the plane. Paper and instruments were spilling from the cockpit. He saw Anthoine beckoning for him to come closer. Henri stood with uplifted hands to receive the salvaged goods. He didn't want to see what the instruments were, what the papers said. It was always true: The less you knew the better.

How long until the Germans came to the clearing? Minutes? An hour? If they came around the corner now, he would be shot.

Turning, he saw Jauquet with schoolbags he'd comandeered from the children. How did the Burghermaster know which children could be trusted? Anthoine climbed out of the plane and over the wing. He slid to the ground, helped to pack the sacks.

I'll wait two hours, then go to St. Laurent. Jauquet speaking, puffed up with the mission. To tell the Germans was what he meant. Standard procedure in the Resistance, Jauquet said knowingly, though privately Henri wondered how the man could be so sure, since this was the first plane ever to fall precisely in the village. Jauquet expansive now, explaining the risk: If the Germans found the plane before they were officially told, Jauquet's head would be in a noose. But more than likely, Henri thought, the Germans were eating and drinking at L'Hôtel de Ville in St. Laurent, as they did at every noon hour, and had probably had so much beer to drink already they hadn't seen or heard the plane. It was meant to be a joke: The Belgian beer was the country's best defensive weapon.

He saw a boy by the front of the plane now, gesturing to another, looking up at something on the nose. The boys' eyes widened. They whispered excitedly and pointed. "La chute obscène," Henri heard them say.

Stretchers were arriving on a truck. Thérèse would take the flyers home, tend to the wounded. Bastien would come for the dead man. If the wounded man lived, he'd be put into the network before the Germans could find him.

The village women maneuvered in toward the sacks. More people at the pasture, gathering closer to the plane, as if it were alive, a curiosity at the circus. Fifty now, maybe sixty. Schoolgirls in thick woolen socks and brown shoes stood on the wing and crawled forward to peer into the cockpit. There was nervous giggling. Their laughter seemed disrespectful to Henri, and he was irritated by the girls.

Beside him, Anthoine's voice: We'll hide the sacks with Claire, convene a meeting in the church.

Henri turned with a protest, the words dying on his tongue. Not with Claire, he wanted to say. Anthoine's face a wall.

We've got to find the pilots, Anthoine insisted quietly. Before the Germans do.

Henri, with the heavy sacks, nodded as he knew he must. It was beginning now, he thought, and who could say where it would end?

When she was alone, she sometimes stood at the window near the pump and looked across the flat fields toward France. The fields, gray since November, were indistinguishable from the color of the farm buildings, stone structures with thick walls and slate roofs. On cold days like this, she could not always tell where in the distance the fields met the sky. She liked to imagine that in France, if she could go there, there would be color — that it would be like turning the pages of a book and coming unexpectedly upon a color plate. That was the image she had in her mind of crossing the border, a drawing of color.

She drew from the pocket of her skirt a cigarette and lit it. She stood at the window, looking out, one arm across her chest, the other holding the cigarette. The smoke wafted in a lazy design around her hair in front of the glass. This was her third already, and she knew she must slow down. Henri was good about the cigarettes. He seldom failed to come by them, no matter how scarce they were in the village. And the bargain she had made with him, one bargain of many, was that she would smoke no more than the five on any given day.

They had brought her an old Jewish woman this time. The woman had escaped the Gestapo by hiding in her chimney for two days and nights. The woman's son, who was a doctor in Antwerp, had designed the hiding place for his mother in her home because her shoulders and hips were so narrow, even at seventy-five, that she could fit inside the chimney. When the Gestapo came before dawn, the old woman ran directly to the chimney and climbed to the foot braces her son had made for her. She stood in the chimney in her nightgown, her feet spread apart on the braces. She regretted that she had not embraced her husband in the bed before each of them had jumped up and fled. She listened with fear as the policemen searched her home — once, twice, three times — and finally found her husband, who had also been a doctor, in his hiding place in the basement. It was all she could do to keep from crying out to him, so that now, in her sleep, the old woman often cried out to her lost husband: *Avram . . . Avram . . .* And Claire, through the wall, lay awake at night listening to her.

When the old woman's legs could stand no more, she slid from the braces and tumbled onto the damp hearth. She was found in the dirty fireplace, blackened beyond recognition, by the tailor's son, who had come to see if anyone in the doctor's house had survived the raids. The tailor's son at first thought the old woman had been burned alive by the Gestapo, and he vomited onto the Persian rug. But then she called out her husband's name — *Avram . . . Avram . . .* — and the tailor's son carried her to his mother's house. The tailor's wife bathed the old woman and put her into the network. It was unclear to Claire how long she had been traveling. The woman's story was told to Claire by the man who had brought her to the house. The old woman herself had very little to say.

Madame Rosenthal was upstairs now, in the small attic room that was hidden behind the false back of the heavy oak armoire. The armoire had once been part of Claire's dowry. Henri had fashioned a door in its back that opened onto a small crawl space behind; and he had made a window in the slate roof, so that some light was let into the hiding place. If one day the Germans decided to climb onto the roof, the small opening, sealed with glass, would be discovered, and Claire and Henri, too, would be taken away and shot. But the window was hidden behind a chimney stack and not visible from the ground.

Madame Rosenthal was the twenty-eighth refugee to stay with them. Claire remembered each one, like beads on a rosary. Barely had she and Henri heard of the fighting in Antwerp before they learned that Belgium's small army had been no match for the Nazis. Even so, she had been unable to believe in the reality of the German occupation until the first of the refugees from the north had arrived at their village in May 1940. They stopped in the square and asked for food and beds. It seemed to her now that important lines were drawn, even in those first few weeks. Some of the residents of Delahaut had immediately come into the square and taken the displaced Belgians into their homes. Others had silently closed their doors and shutters. When, in that first month, Anthoine had come into the kitchen of their house to ask Claire and Henri to join him in the Maquis, Claire had seen at once that Henri, on his own, might have closed his shutters. But Anthoine was persistent. Claire had languages and the nursing, Anthoine had pointed out. Henri had looked at Claire then, as if the languages and the nursing might one day be a danger to them both.

Their first family was from Antwerp, the father a professor at the university. There were six of them in all, and Claire made up pallets in the second bedroom. That night, in the kitchen, she asked Henri if they should flee themselves, but Henri said no, he wouldn't leave the farm that had been his father's and his father's father's.

Then we have to make a hiding place, she said. There's going to be a flood.

Claire turned away from the window and laid out the white sausage made with milk and bread, the sausage that had no meat that she had made for her husband's noon meal. There was also a runny white cheese and a soup made from cabbages and onions.

She had grown thin from the war, but her husband, inexplicably, had grown bigger. It was the beer, she thought, the thick, dark beer Henri and the others made and kept hidden from the Germans. There were barrels of it in the barn, bottles of it in the cellar that sometimes popped or exploded. The beer was strong, heavy with alcohol, and if she drank even one glass, she felt peaceful almost immediately.

Earlier she had crawled awkwardly with her tray into the attic space and given the old woman some of the soup, holding her narrow shoulders with one arm, feeding her with a spoon. The old woman was extraordinarily frail now, and Claire did not see how she could be moved, how she could withstand a move. But the Maquis would want her out, across the border to France within the week. The network had arranged it, and there would be others who would need the attic room. More than likely, Claire thought, the doctor's wife would die in the attic.

She put her apron on again and prepared the coffee — a bitter coffee of chicory that no amount of sugar, if they had had sugar, could sweeten. At least, she thought, it was better than the coffee they'd had last month — a nearly undrinkable coffee made of malt. She moved back to the window and watched for her husband. She didn't know where he was or even if he would be back. He had left the barn more than an hour ago. He hadn't stopped to tell her why.

In the morning, he'd gone to the barn as he always did for the milking. They had had seventy cows before the war began; now they only had the twelve. The Germans had taken the rest. Henri spent most of his days tending the tiny herd and repairing simple farm machinery — a difficult task since parts were nonexistent. He had to fashion his own parts, design them, hammer them, from old pots or kettles or buckles, anything that Claire could spare from the house. Once he had taken her ladle, a pewter ladle with a long handle that she had brought with her to the marriage, and they had fought over the ladle until her anger had subsided. He had needed the ladle more than she had; it was simple.

She didn't like to think of what it must be like each day

for Henri in the barn. Perhaps he had been drinking from the barrels already, and she wouldn't blame him. The air was frozen and raw, and sometimes it was colder in the barn than it was in the fields.

Behind the barn, they had the one truck, which they never used. There was no gasoline for the Belgians, but Henri had kept the gazogene, for emergencies. Surprisingly, the Germans had not taken the truck for themselves, although the soldiers sometimes commandeered it for a week at a time. Delahaut had escaped the fate of some towns. The Germans didn't billet there. The accommodations in St. Laurent were better.

Claire removed the brick from behind the stove and retrieved her book. That December she was reading English. Sometimes she read Dutch or Italian or French, but she preferred reading in English when she could get the books. She liked the English words, and liked to say them aloud when no one was in the house: *foxglove, cellar, whisper, needle.* She could read and speak English better than she could write it, and she was trying to teach herself this skill, though she had to be careful about leaving any traces of written English or the English books themselves in the house. She wished she could read in English to the old woman upstairs, but the woman's first language was Yiddish, to which she had retreated from the Flemish. Together they could communicate only in German, which seemed to distress them both.

She sat down at the oak table and held her book open with her crossed arms. The book had been given to her by an English gunner who had had to parachute out of his plane and who had broken his collarbone when he landed near Charleroi. She remembered the gunner, a thin, spotty-faced boy who'd been at school when he'd been called up. He was ill suited to be a gunner — you could see that at once — a reed-thin boy with a delicate mouth. In his flight suit he had two books, a prayer book and a volume of English poetry, and when he left, he gave the book of poetry to Claire. He said he'd already read it too many times, but she suspected that was not quite true. She wondered where the boy was now. She was seldom told the fate of the people who passed through her house, often never knew if they made it to

France or to England or if they died en route — shot or betrayed. She knew the beginnings of many stories, but not their endings.

The world is charged with the grandeur of God.
It will flame out, like shining from shook foil. . . .

She liked the few poems by Gerard Manley Hopkins the best, even though she could not understand them very well. She took pleasure from the sound of the words, the way the poet had put the sounds together. Often she didn't even know what the words meant. She thought she knew *shook,* but she wasn't positive. But *foil?* Yet she loved the sound of *shining from shook,* liked to say this aloud.

She felt then, within her abdomen, a downward draw and pull, a signal that soon, before nightfall, she would begin to bleed. Reflexively, she crossed herself. She shut her eyes and whispered a prayer, words of relief more than of faith. Although she was careful during the time she might conceive, putting Henri off with a sequence of subtle signs — a slightly turned head, a shoulder raised — she could never be quite certain, absolutely positive. She did not want to conceive a child during the war, to bring a child into a world where one or both parents might be taken during the night, where a child could be left to freeze or burn, or might be cruelly injured by the planes overhead. The very air above them had been violated. She herself had seen the dirty smudges and the lethal clouds. She was not even sure she would have a child after the war. Sometimes she thought that the weight of the stories that had passed through her house had filled her and squeezed out that part of her that might have borne a child with hope.

She needn't have been so worried this month though, she thought to herself. She counted. It couldn't have been more than four times. Henri was often gone late into the night with the Maquis, and she sometimes thought that the war, and what Henri himself had seen and heard, had affected her husband as well.

For skies of couple-colour as a brindled cow;
For rose-moles all in stipple upon trout that swim. . . .

She had tried to imagine England, but she couldn't. Even when the English boys told her stories of home, she could not bring the landscape into focus. And the stories were often confusing: Some were of stone cottages where, in the boys' memories, the gardens always bloomed, even in the winter; and others were of city streets, narrow streets of cobblestones and darkened brick houses.

The sound of bicycles rattled on the gravel drive, startling her. Claire swept the English poetry book onto her lap under the table. Henri and Anthoine Chimay entered the kitchen. Each of them was carrying children's schoolbags. Henri was breathless.

"Claire."

"What is it?"

"A plane."

"A plane?"

"Yes, yes. A fallen plane, in Delahaut."

"English?"

"American."

"American? Any survivors?"

"One is dead. One almost dead. There might be eight others."

"Where is it?"

"On the Heights. The others are probably in the wood."

Henri and Anthoine lay the schoolbags on the table.

"We need you to hide these," Anthoine said.

Henri looked at his wife as if to say he was sorry. "The barn is best," he said instead.

Henri was flushed — from the effort of the bicycle ride or his agitation, she couldn't say. He was older than she; he would be thirty-two in the spring. The features of his face seemed to have broadened with age as they often did in the men of the village. It was as though, in face and body, Henri had finally filled out to the shape he would retain as a man throughout his lifetime — stocky like his father, barrel-chested, his shoulders round and solid. He had thick brown hair the exact color of his eyes. A *V* of hair, like a tail feather, fell forward onto his forehead. She had begun to notice that there was a tooth to one side of his mouth that was darkening. She wondered if it caused him pain; he never complained.

"I have to go now," he said. "I don't know when I'll be back."

Claire nodded. She watched as her husband and Anthoine left the house and remounted their bicycles. She hid the book of English poetry behind the brick. She put her coat on and lifted the schoolbags into her arms. Upstairs, through the floorboards, Claire thought she could hear the old woman crying.

————

Darkness between the trees, a false night. It was somebody's birthday in the kitchen. His mother was at work in the courthouse, and his father was not yet home with the stink of meat in his skin. A song from somewhere. From the children's faces leaning toward the candles. And Frances, who had made the cake, bent over him so that he could smell her warm breath at his cheek and whispered to him in the din: A wish, Teddy. Make a wish.

When he cried as a boy, it was Frances he went to.

The ground was hard marble. From time to time he heard a distant shout, a call, a branch cracking from a tree. The cold made the branches snap, like fire did.

He had dragged the leg, a dead soldier, how many feet — a hundred? a thousand? No sun to tell him his direction, the compass button smashed. He could be headed into Germany, out of Germany, no signposts on the trees to mark the way.

When he broke his arm, falling from the tree, it was Frances who sat with him, played gin endlessly at his request. Frances who was tall like himself and had his face, but misaligned. His mother sometimes whispered that Frances would never marry.

His lower leg was stiff and swollen. The knee would not bend. He wondered if a kind of rigor had set in.

He would have liked a cigarette. Wasn't that what they gave the dying?

If he wasn't found, he thought, he would die before morning.

Yet he was terrified of being found. An unfamiliar helmet. The muzzle of a gun pressed against the skin under his chin.

On Stella's porch there was a swing. It was last night or last month, and she sat beside him in a thin cotton dress. Her skin was tanned in the hollow above her breasts, and her legs were bare beneath the skirt. He thought, oddly, of a girl on a bicycle, with bare legs, falling, scraping her knees. She was a girl, still, even then, on the porch. Was that why he had hesitated? The skirt billowed out like a parachute and hid her legs.

That was his nickname when he was a boy. Teddy. Frances called him that. Stella called him Ted.

His hands had frozen into cups. He dragged himself on his elbows. Inside his flight suit, there was a photograph. He lay back, exhausted. Perhaps he would sleep or had slept. He fumbled with the zipper of the flight suit with his frozen fingers, but they did not work. Inside there was a photograph of Stella.

The sky above the trees was the color of dust. Sometimes there were pallets of oak leaves, and they helped him slide. He wondered, when he heard a distant voice, if he should shout for help. There were procedures. What was the procedure for freezing to death in the wood?

It was 1936 or 1937. He forgot the year. Matt, his younger brother, in a rage, running up to his room, Ted's room (Teddy's room then?), and destroying all the model airplanes, hung on delicate threads from the ceiling, each wooden model laboriously assembled and painted, the models bought with money Ted had earned in the fields, the planes made and collected over many years. From below, Ted heard the sound of rage, feared the worst, then went up into the devastation in his room. Splinters and tangled threads, broken wings on the bed. A thousand hours smashed. He made a vow then never to speak to Matt again, ever, and he hadn't until the morning the train came to take him off to war. He stood on the station platform, shivering with his mother and his father and with Frances, who was weeping openly, wishing the train would come, dreading the goodbyes. Then he turned, said to Frances, I'll be right back.

He sprinted the distance, easy for him, he had won the 440 at the state championships and gone off to college on the strength of his legs. He ran past the farms and the farmhouses, the sun just coming up over the fields at dawn, raced up the steps of his own house, white clapboards with a porch, once a farmhouse, now just a house like the others at the edge of the small Ohio village. He found Matt in bed still.

He shook his hand. He said goodbye.

What was the row about? He couldn't remember now. A silly row. And Matt had been just a kid.

He wondered if he would ever run again. Walk again. Would they take the leg?

Who was *they*?

He had seen the young men with the trousers folded and neatly pinned, passing through, going home. Warnings of what was out there.

But you didn't think of that. You drank gin made from grapefruit juice, 150 proof, and hoped they didn't wake you in the middle of the night while you were still drunk.

Anything to escape the fate of his father. The village butcher. His hands in the entrails of animals. Dead flesh always under his fingernails. The stink of meat never left him. Or did Teddy simply imagine that?

His father drank Seagram's. All night.

Ted came to, realized he had slept. Or had passed out. The pain came in waves. He wished his leg would freeze altogether, go totally numb like his fingers.

Where were Case and Baker and Shulman? Case had a shot-up arm, Shulman had been limping badly. Tripp had had blood on his flight suit. Were they found, lost, dead?

It was a toss-up now between a cigarette and a glass of beer.

The thirst had announced itself suddenly. Not a good sign. He propped himself up on his elbows, looked at his leg. There was blood soaking the leg of his flight suit. He couldn't move his foot or feel it.

Were there cigarettes inside his flight suit? He couldn't remember. They might as well be diamonds in a safe. With Stella's photograph.

Her photograph was like all the others he had seen. Creased, worn at the edges. The creases skimmed across her neck.

Why, on the porch the night before he left, why had he not taken her hand, led her away from her house?

Something in him had hesitated.

Foolish, he thought, lying on the frozen ground, these moral quandaries. Hadn't there been thousands of men making love that night, simply to say they were alive?

He imagined his hand sliding up Stella's bare leg, under the parachute skirt.

Was it possible there were people on the ground when he gave the order to jettison the bomb load? It looked like farmland, endless fields, but the cloud cover was so thick he couldn't really tell, except when he came in low, and saw patches of field. The bombardier said it was just field. There wouldn't be people on frozen fields in December. Couldn't be.

He should have kept one canteen.

He drifted, dreamed of parachute silk. He was unwinding a woman and she was smiling, looking at him. He was on his knees, unwinding, but there was so much silk, endless layers . . .

He came to sharply. He had heard something, he was sure of it. Footsteps. Not in the dream.

He propped himself up, lay perfectly still. The sound was faint, not a crackle, but a soft step. There. He heard it again. Coming toward him from the pasture. He could see no one through the trees.

He looked around quickly, searching for cover. If he could hide, he could see who the footsteps belonged to before revealing himself. There was a tangle of brambles twenty feet away. It was dark enough that he couldn't see inside it. He dragged himself as fast as he dared, not wanting to make any noise. The brambles were hard, thorny. He turned, went in flat on his belly.

No voices. Only one set of footsteps.

Closer now. Definitely closer.

He wondered if he should pray. They joked about it; they called it foxhole religion. Men long out of practice, straining to remember words, fragments, sentences, get it right.

He thought he saw a figure.

The Focke-Wulfs were everywhere. The fight field was exploding, smoking. A B-17, cut in half by flak, the nose spinning, tumbling out of control, the tail floating, drifting as in flight, and in the tail, the gunner was still firing . . .

Ekberg screamed. His hands were frozen to the guns. The screaming of the men and the screaming of the plane. The noise, deafening, vibrating, was in the head, in the bones.

Was it possible, going home across the Channel, nearly out of fuel, to bounce the waves and make it? Peterson had claimed it.

A German had miscalculated the clearance, collided with a bomber. The fighter cartwheeled, plummeted, away from them toward the ground.

FWs at twelve o'clock. Count the parachutes. Where did the gunner's dick go? Parachute silk stained with blood. It was Frances who raised him, and he said goodbye to Matt. He was on his knees now, unwinding a woman, and she was smiling up at him. But there were layers, endless layers . . .

When the boy returned to the clearing, there were fewer people, an impending sense that soon the Germans would be there. No one wanted to be near the plane when the Germans discovered it. Jean had gone back to the school for his coat and dinner sack and had come on foot this time, not wanting a bicycle, however well hidden, to be traced to him. If he were caught in the wood, trying to find or help the Americans who had fled the plane, he would be sent away to the camps. He was sure of that.

He slipped into the wood unnoticed, at the point that he had memorized. In the pockets of his jacket, he had hidden bread and cheese and a small bottle he filled with water. The word had gone out that all children were to return to their lessons at once; those who did not would be punished. He could imagine the round red face of Monsieur Dauvin, his teacher, his skin becoming even more blotchy with his fury when he noticed Jean's vacant desk. He had told Marcel to say that he was sick, but he knew such a lie soon would be found out and would probably compound his punishment. He ought to have said nothing to Marcel, for now Marcel, too, would be caned.

He knew the wood well. He doubted any boy in Delahaut knew it better. His own house, his father's farm, abutted the wood to the north, and even as a very young boy he knew the forest as a safe place to be. Each day after school he walked among the beeches and oaks, observing new growth in the spring, the feathery green buds, the white lilies pushing up from the ground. He fished with Marcel in the spring and in the summer, and he had respect for the forest in the winter. He knew that a man or a boy lost in the wood in December would die there.

The path was easy to follow, too easy. The body had matted the dead grass, broken small twigs from bushes. He had to find the flyer soon, or the Germans almost certainly would. The path was too exposed, and he had no time now to destroy the traces.

What he would do when he found the man he didn't know. He pictured himself giving the flyer bread and cheese and water, and then leading him to safety. His imagination was suddenly excited as he envisioned helping him to escape to the French border, shaking hands with him like a grown man. But when he thought about this hard, doubts began to cloud his mind. Where could he offer the man shelter? He thought of his own barn, and then felt the hot flush of shame on the back of his neck. At school, some of the older boys had begun to whisper, in his hearing, "le fils du collabos," the son of a collaborator.

He learned about his father at school, when the taunts began, and at first he did not understand. When he asked his father what was meant, his father was silent. He told Jean that a war was a man's business, not a boy's. Later, Jean discovered, by watching and by listening, that his father traded for profit with the Germans, that the Germans ate bread from his father's soil and meat from his father's barn. It was as bad, thought Jean, as selling machine parts or even secrets. What did the product matter? It was one thing to have your animals taken by the Germans, as had happened to many in the village; quite another to sell for money. Sometimes the shame was almost unendurable. He had thought of running away from home, running away from school — but it was winter, and where was he to go? Even if he were to make it to France, which he imagined he could easily do, what then? How would he stay alive? Who would take in an extra boy, another mouth to feed? Mightn't he be spotted by the Germans and sent to the camps? And besides, he couldn't leave his mother. The thought of his mother weeping inevitably ended these reckless reveries.

He had come nearly three hundred meters from the clearing. He knew this part of the wood especially well. Not far from here was a pool that in the summer was filled with trout. It would be frozen now, a sheet of black ice. He wondered where the trout went — deep into the mud? He thought of the comfort and safety there. He had skates when he was younger and used to skate on the black ice at the pond, but he had outgrown them. He knew there would be no more skating for some time.

He stood still in the forest. He thought he heard a sound, a sound unlike any other. The soft brush of leaves. His stomach clenched. He badly needed to urinate. He should have done it earlier — too late now; he would be heard. He stepped cautiously forward, each footfall as deliberate and as quiet as he could manage. He stopped, listened. He could not hear the swishing sound anymore. He waited. He walked forward about ten meters, and then, unbelievably, the trail seemed to end. Confused, the boy stood near a tangle of bushes. Instinctively, he looked up. Had the man climbed an oak tree? Had he seen him coming? Suddenly he was frightened, and he wanted to protect his head. He should not be here. At the very least, he should have brought Marcel.

The need to relieve himself was urgent. Where had the path gone? He investigated the area where the trail had abruptly ended, searching for its continuation. Perhaps the man had stood up, was walking now. It would be impossible to track footprints in the dim interior light of the forest, Jean thought.

And then, turning in exasperation, he saw what he had come for. The sole of a boot at the end of the brambles.

———•——

The village was just outside Cambridge, the land flat for miles, flat and wet, the soil reclaimed from the sea. All that late fall, since October when he'd arrived, he'd taken a bicycle and ridden the roads and lanes of the countryside, where one could see in the distance, if it was clear, the next village and the next, their steeples rising, an uneventful landscape, a perfect landing field.

They'd taken the village, a massive invasion, farmers' fields now lined precisely with Nissen huts, pneumonia tubes, everyone coughing in the night, from smoke or cold, it seemed to matter little. That night, the night before the twelfth mission, he and Case had lain across from each other in their bunks, each propped up on an elbow, each smoking, talking edgily, wondering, speculating, endlessly speculating on the target, the weather, how deep the penetration, how thick the cloud cover. Case was nervous, high-strung. He sometimes boasted of his pitching arm, claimed that before the war he'd been tapped by the Boston Braves, but there was something in the way he said this, the eyes a bit evasive, that made Ted doubt his story. After missions, Case would get debilitating headaches that left him nearly lifeless in his bunk. Ted thought it more difficult for Case than for himself. Less to do as copilot, more time to think about what might be headed their way. Case could not sleep, and that night neither could he. They smoked, and Case talked about his girlfriend back home, and about the Braves. Case never slept before a mission, and Ted had lost his navigator. Ted sometimes thought that if ever they had to bail out over Germany, Case might, with luck, pass for a German — with his high flat brow and his pale, almost colorless hair. In the dark the two men could hear the coughing. One man moaned, cried out in his sleep. Case looked at Ted, said, *Shulman*. The pilot nodded. In the morning, between them on the floor, there was a pile of butts a foot wide.

Earlier that evening, after word had come down about the mission, Ted had gone to look for Mason, the only member of the crew he'd been unable to locate easily. He'd looked in the aero-club, the post exchange, the mess hall, even the chapel, then given up the search, thinking the navigator would return before the briefing at three A.M.

Each night before a mission, Ted took a shower in the outdoor stall, the water brutal, ice below his feet. It was a ritual, a superstition, a down payment on thinning luck, in the same way that Tripp wore his torn scarf, and McNulty carried a deck of cards with five aces. Returning to the hut, shivering from the icy water and still wet inside his long johns, Ted heard Case say, within his hearing, almost but not quite taunting him, that Mason had gone to Cambridge. Ted dressed, then got on his bicycle and rode in the winter dark to the hotel where he knew Mason often met his English girl. The pilot's hair froze along the way and melted in the lobby. The man at the front desk deferred to the aviator's wings and, against the rules, let him up the stairs. Ted knocked on the door and opened it. In the bed, a woman was naked. He remembered thin red hair, a mottled color to her skin. There was gin on the table, the real stuff, not GI alcohol. Mason was drunk, but the pilot knew it was fatigue that had brought him to the hotel. They called it fatigue, a gentle name for blowing all your circuits, an inability to get back into your plane when your chances of coming home alive were only one in three. When Mason had heard about the impending mission, he'd left the base. In the hotel room, he told Ted he knew he'd be court-martialed, stripped of his wings, but he added drunkenly from the bed that he didn't give a flying fuck, and then he laughed. Ted began a protest, stopped. You couldn't crew with a navigator who had fatigue, who was drunk.

He'd thought then, superstitiously, *abort*. But he hadn't.

On Christmas Day he had a meal with an English family. He brought chocolate and fruit for the children. There was a girl there, a young girl, no more than twelve, with a round face, and short hair parted at the side, a bowl cut on a face that wasn't pretty but reminded him of Frances. And he had felt in the small brick cottage, with the gristled joint on the table and gaudy paper decorations hung from lamps and doorways, a pang so deep he'd nearly wept. He'd steadied himself with long swallows of hot tea from a china cup.

There had been no missions since before Christmas, and when there were no missions, there was tedium. They played cards, they went to the pub. They waited for the mail. They walked out to their planes and talked to the mechanics. Sometimes the weather grounded them for days, and the lull made the men touchy. When they went, that early morning, to the briefing, there was a tension in the room Ted hadn't felt so keenly before. He showed his pass to the MP. Later, when he dressed for the mission, he would leave the pass behind, and take only his dog tags and his escape kit with its evasion photo and a handful of foreign currency. And every man on the ship, he knew, would carry something else as well. A lucky coin. A photo of a woman. Cigarettes. A camera. Small paper books that fit inside a pocket and were made of wartime paper that sometimes crumbled, disintegrated in your hands.

The weather would be terrible. They already knew that. Walking from the hut to the briefing room, each man had searched the night sky for a star, the briefest slip of a moon, some ghostly break in the cloud cover. But the dark that early morning was impenetrable. Ted thought that if they went at all, they would have to corkscrew up, break free of the clouds. Forming up was sometimes catastrophic. He knew of planes colliding in the fog, exploding, spinning to earth when they weren't a thousand feet in the air. A lost squadron dragging through another in the thick cloud, the carnage devastating. Senseless death, as if any death made sense.

Case worked a toothpick; Shulman behind him was humming. Glenn Miller. "A String of Pearls." Shulman was from Chicago, a welder, like his father before him, he had said. He had bad skin and small, tense eyes. Mason had been a drummer with a band. He played in dance halls in New York City. Sometimes in the pub, he had entertained them with wooden sticks made from a pointer he'd stolen after a briefing, then whittled and sanded. Watching his hands fly over the barroom tables, you could imagine yourself in a supper club, at a table on the floor, listening to a solo and drinking pink gin with a woman in a red dress, although Ted had never actually done this. In the briefing room, Case was opening packs of gum and methodically putting the dry sticks into his mouth, one by one. His foot was jiggling. Despite the cold, the sweat had started already, tricking down the copilot's temples.

Ted looked at the map, shrouded in the black covering. He wondered how long the thin, red strand of yarn would be this time, where exactly it would lead them. In the room the men were coughing, and you could see your breath.

He remembered the oil-stained concrete below the plane, and the way the dawn announced itself — an almost imperceptible lightening in a field of endless gray. On the hardstand all around him were other planes, other ground crews, bomb loaders, fuel trucks. Beyond that were the barren fields and the trees, and in the distance, the lonely rhythmic chugging of a train.

He let Case take up his parachute pack and flight bag, while Aikins, the ground chief, gave him the 1A. A bolt on the landing gear had been repaired, he read, and he began his visual inspection of the outside of the plane. The B-17, which resembled a piece of hammered metal, had been repaired well enough to fly — but not cosmetically. Countless missions had taken their toll. Paint was scratched to reveal the silver of metal; bullets and shrapnel had left their imprint. The olive paint near the top of the plane was stained with oil from the engines.

At the rear of the plane, the men were putting on their Mae Wests. His crew was young — nineteen, twenty — and discouraged by the heavy losses. They called him "the old man," even though he was only twenty-two that day. If they made it back he would tell them, and he'd get drunk and stay drunk until the New Year. Warren was a farmer's son; Ekberg had worked in a bowling alley. They were strangers thrown together, men you wouldn't gravitate toward back home. Once in a while, if it worked, there were friendships.

Ludwigshafen. He rolled the name on his tongue. Synthetic fuel and chemicals a hundred and twenty miles into Germany, a plant near Mannheim. In the briefing room, the squadron commander had dimmed the lights, and they had all studied the reconnaissance photos — searching among the gray shapes for the targets they were to hit, small rectangles that looked different from the rest. Every briefing ended the same way, with the time-tick and a worn and dreary message: If they didn't do it, someone else would have to.

He walked forward past the waist to the left wing and to the engines. He looked for nicks or cracks in the propellers. One of the ground crew was polishing the Plexiglas nosepiece and saluted him. Ted hoisted himself up into the plane for the interior check. And it was with that gesture, as it always was, that he began to feel uneasy. Not because he was afraid — he was, like all the rest of them — but because he didn't want to be in command. He was a good pilot, maybe even a very good pilot. But he knew he didn't want the responsibility of all those lives behind him. He'd hoped for reconnaissance work when he'd signed up. He'd wanted to be alone.

Case was in the cockpit, his face already white and doughy. He'd be better once they were airborne, Ted knew. It was the waiting before each sortie that put him on the edge.

A pilot was supposed to love his plane, but Ted didn't really. Not love it, actually. He'd heard the other pilots speak of their planes as if they were the women they named them for — *Miss Barbara, Jeannie Bee, Reluctant Virgin* — caressing them before a mission, kissing them wildly if they made it back. But to Ted, the bomber was a machine that might malfunction and sometimes did — a machine with which it seemed he had barely made a grudging truce in the eleven missions before. He respected the plane, and the men who had to climb inside it, but when the mission was over, he was always glad to leave it behind.

The two pilots were in a five-foot cube. All around them — to the front, sides, behind them on the ceiling, and even on the floor — there were controls, switches, levers. In a B-17, flying was a purely relative concept, he thought, more an engineering operation than a defiance of gravity. In about twenty minutes he would be called upon to perform a complex series of maneuvers in heavy machinery 26,000 feet above the earth, in temperatures of sixty degrees below zero, while German pilots were shooting at him. You weren't supposed to think about it.

Shulman was in the nose; Warren would soon crawl into a fetal position in the ball turret; Ekberg was in the tail. Baker, the new navigator, was quiet with the unfamiliar crew. In the radio compartment, Callahan and Tripp were razzing Rees, who had vomited on the last mission — from fear or from the lousy food on base, the pilot hadn't known. Rees had a large nose, a slipped grin, the grin a defense against the unthinkable.

You puke again, I'm sending you to Ludwigshafen with the load.

Rees leaned toward Tripp, faked a heave.

Fuck off, Rees, Tripp said, pushing the gunner away.

Case, you got any gum?

Case was opening his third stick in as many minutes. He had another one behind his ear. Ted went over the checklist once again, to steady Case's nerves.

Intercooler. Check. Gyros. Check. Fuel shutoff switches. OK. Gear switch. Neutral. Throttle. Check. De-icer and anti-icer, wing and prop. Off. Generators. All set to fire up.

And then he heard it through the radio. The ceiling had lifted just enough over the target. They were going up.

Once, in October, he had really flown a plane. A brigadier general needed to be ferried to another base, and Ted, who had completed his third mission just the day before, was asked to take the job. The plane was a gift from God — a single-engine Tiger Moth that lifted from the runway like a bubble. He wondered who had owned it before the war. A titled playboy with a huge estate? The day was clear, no haze on the horizon, a strafe of thin white cirrus high above them. He made the ferry to Molesworth by the book, the general saying little, Ted even less. But when the man saluted him from the ground, Ted knew he had the plane to himself.

He'd bumped, like a toy, over the Molesworth airfield and hit the smoother surface of the runway. All around him were empty hardstands, waiting for planes that might or might not come back. He saw the Nissen huts, the emergency trucks, the wind sock stuttering toward the east. A mechanic on the wing of an injured B-17 stood to watch him and gave him a wave. Ted opened the throttle. As if sprung, the plane began moving fast. He bounced lightly on the runway, gathering speed. The bouncing stopped. The ride turned silky.

He banked immediately for a turn. Outside his window, the earth pulled away to reveal a stitchery of green and brown and gold, with bits of water glinting in the sun. He saw a tractor plowing, a dog running behind. He could smell the fertilizer on the ground. In another pasture there were sheep, and beyond them, the abstract shapes of hay bales. At the periphery of his vision he was aware of the Nissen huts, the hangar, the wooden control tower — tiny shapes now, of little consequence. Indeed, nothing on the ground seemed to have any consequence at all.

He flew over the village with its pub and church and narrow terraced houses. He followed a dirt lane out to a stone cottage and was rewarded by a reflection of sun from a top window. The sky was a rich navy, the sun glare almost too bright against the nose of the plane. He hit a pocket of turbulence, was buffeted, fell a hundred feet. To the south was a charcoal stain — London, he suspected.

He dove suddenly and went in low over a field of rye to gather speed. He nosed the plane straight up and was pinned against the back of his seat. He climbed into a long, high loop, and for a second, at its apex, he hung motionless, upside down, a speck suspended over the countryside. He fell then into a run out the other side that physically thrilled him. He banked, turned, cruised in an invisible figure eight. They taught you this in flight school, then put you in a thirty-five-ton bomber you were lucky to get off the ground. He was soaring in a barrel roll over the countryside on a day as fine as England had seen in weeks, and he felt, for an instant, free. Free of Case and Shulman and McNulty and the sleepless nights. Free of the pneumonia tubes and the rotten food. Free of the fear of death. Free of the war itself. He had told himself, after the hell of his first mission, that he'd never get into a plane again once the war was over. But on that day — drifting in a slow roll out toward the horizon — he felt, for a moment, the exaltation of flying. A faint whiff of exuberance passed like a mist through his chest, close to his heart.

When the plane stalled, it fluttered and fell like a fledgling that had not meant to leave the nest. He could feel the lightness of the air beneath him, the way the plane began to list. The right wing dipped, and the dip became a spin. He let it go, losing himself in the spiral. He flirted with the spin. But when he knew he had run out of altitude, he put the plane into a steep dive to pull her out and up.

He was a hundred feet from the fields. He'd be grounded if anyone had observed and reported him. He could see the spires of Cambridge in the distance. He began to climb then, as high as he could push the plane. He wanted to take himself aloft — away from the earth.

Case's cheeks were vibrating with the plane. They waited for the takeoff flares. Over the intercom, the pilot asked for position checks. Ekberg, in the tail, sounded drunk. How had he not noticed that before? They would be the second plane behind *Old Gold*, the lead ship painted garishly to identify it in the air — a gaudy duck with its dull flock behind. Twenty planes, and they were number two.

Ted looked at his mission flimsy, passed it over to Case. On it were the code words and the details of the mission. It was made of rice paper; if they went down, Ted was supposed to eat it. He saw the flares then, gave the thumbs-up sign to the chief on the ground to pull the chocks, closed the window. He taxied out of the hardstand and got into line on the perimeter track. He could not see over the nose and had to use the edge of the taxiway for a guide. Already the noise inside the plane was deafening. He thought sometimes he minded the noise the most, and that if there was a Hell, it would sound like the interior of a B-17. He ran up the engines to test them. They were loaded to the limit, with five thousand pounds of bombs and twenty-six hundred gallons of fuel; it was always a guess as to whether they'd make it off the ground. He thought of Shulman in the nose, watching the rush of the ground beneath him.

Old Gold left the runway; Ted gunned the engines. The noise, which before had seemed unbearable, now became monstrous. He knew that behind and below him the men were praying: Get this sucker off the ground. That's right, he thought, get the bomber off the ground, and then do it, if you're lucky, thirteen more times. The runway ended, and they were up into the soup.

The RAFs called it the milky goldfish bowl. Ted climbed in a

spiral over the beacon, looking out for a shadow in the mist —
another groping B-17 that might stray too near. At 10,000 feet, he
gave the order for oxygen and put on his own mask. Twenty seconds without oxygen could be fatal. Squeeze the pumps, he reminded them; don't freeze your spit. He added, as he always did,
to keep the glove liners on, no matter what. The gunners sometimes stripped them off in the heat of battle in order to better
manage the machinery, but at high altitude, fingers would freeze
on gunmetal and have to be ripped off. It would be so cold the
navigator wouldn't be able to make a note with a pencil; lead froze
at 20,000 feet. Icy air blasted through the openings in the waist
where the gunners stood. Most of the men were plugged in, their
electrical suits keeping their bodies functioning. But Ted, after
he'd burned his leg on his eighth mission because of a frayed wire,
had decided to stay with the sheepskin. They all wore their Mae
Wests, but few of them could perform their jobs with their parachutes on their backs. They kept them nearby, hanging on hooks.
When they hit the flak, he'd give the order for the flak jackets.
Rees would stand on his as he almost always did. On a mission
with another crew, Rees had seen a Luftwaffe Junker rake the
bomber's belly. The left waist gunner was shot from below. The
blast had made a hole two and a half feet wide, and the dead man,
to Rees's horror, had simply fallen out the bottom of the plane.

The engines were straining in the climb. At 14,000 feet they
broke into the clear.

From the Channel to the rally point, he rotated with Case
every fifteen minutes, a tactic he had learned to prevent Case from
seizing up on him. Fly the plane close to the others in the formation, but not too close. Scan the sky for the fighters you knew
would soon be out there.

Over the intercom, he could hear the chatter. Idle chatter
20,000 feet over the Channel. You were still alive if you could talk
to your buddies, joke around. The words played along the surface
of the tension, skittering here and there from the nose to the tail.

Those cold-storage eggs weren't any better than that pow-
dered shit. You'd think they'd give the condemned a decent break-

fast. Even prisoners get treated better. Shut up with that condemned shit, McNulty. You'll jinx the plane. Listen, Callahan, it's simple. You accept you're dead already, what's the problem? Enjoy the ride. Christ, I hope we don't have to bail out. My chute's fucked up. The wires are out in my boots. My feet are freezing. You sure? I'm positive. Hey, Warren, give me your boots. No fuckin' way, Ekberg. We go down, I'm coming back to haunt you. Man, I love comin' up over those clouds. I couldn't stand to live in this country. How do they stand it? Day after day after day, nothing but rain. What's the matter with *I'll Be Home*? Is she throttling back? No, she's caught in the turbulence. How many of us are up here? I dunno, twenty-five, thirty? Boy, am I ever going to let loose tomorrow night. They're bringing the girls all the way from Cambridge for the party. None for you, Shulman, you're married. Nineteen forty-four. Can you believe it? You think the war will end in '44? Listen, Rees, I just wanna stay alive in '44. Think we can manage that?

Ted listened to the chatter, scanned the skies. The fighting, he knew, could sometimes be a thing of such beauty it took your breath away. The graceful arc of a fighter that had put its armored back to you, even as it glided down and away, out of sight, out of range. The flashbulb pops from silver planes that came at you from the sun. The way a B-17 seemed slowly to fall to earth with great dignity, as though it had been inadvertently let go by God. The odd inkblots against the blue, floating curiosities twenty feet wide and filled with exploding steel. Long white contrails in formation, road maps for German fighters. A plane, severed at the waist, that made your heart stop. Count the chutes. And breaking radio silence, shouting wildly at the doomed crew to bail out, bail out. It was the worst thing you had ever witnessed, and when it was over there was no place to put it. No part of you that could absorb it, and so you learned to transform the event even as it was happening, a sleight of hand, a trick of magic, to turn a kill into a triumph.

Right waist to pilot. *Harriet W.* is off to the right.

Roger, right waist. Tail gunner, what have we got back there?

Tail to pilot. Our wingman is about three hundred yards back and down off the right wing. Two other 17s about a quarter mile out to your right.

Thanks, tail gunner.

Ball turret to pilot. Contrails.

Roger, ball turret.

Ted thought of Warren in the turret. Five, six, nine hours in as cramped a position as Ted could imagine. A view straight down with nothing but the earth below you. And if the turret jammed, which it sometimes did, the gunner was a prisoner then and had to endure whatever fate dealt him: the plane hit and going down with no chance to bail out; a belly landing in which he would be flattened. The worst position in the crew.

Left waist to pilot. The wing ship has peeled off. Looks like she's aborting.

Roger.

Tail gunner to pilot. We have another formation at three o'clock high.

Thanks. Keep your eye on them.

Over the Channel, he heard Shulman give the order to test fire the guns. There were bursts of fire, and Ted could smell the smoke passing through the flight deck.

Right waist to pilot. We've lost another ship. She's feathering her prop.

Navigator to pilot. Enemy coast.

Roger. Pilot to all crew. Flak jackets.

He remembered they had just rendezvoused with the escorts, and that his back was hurting from the ceaseless vibrating of the plane. He could smell, he thought, the peculiar acrid scent of the radio emanating from the compartment. And then it was Rees who yelled, or maybe it was Ekberg in the tail. No, it had to have been Rees, and they were hit, shockingly soon, the concussion so severe Ted bit his tongue, and his mouth filled with blood.

The intercom and the skies exploded.

Bandits three o'clock high. Jesus Christ. Shit. Where're the goddamn fighters? FW at twelve o'clock level. Bursts of machine-gun fire. We're in the fight field now. Fuck, my gun is jammed. I saw him, he was hit. He was smoking. Holy Christ. The plane was pummeled, buffeted. White bursts of flame. The escort fighters with them now. Beautiful — look at that. An FW made a pass in front of the cockpit, guns blasting. Knock the pilot out, disable the plane, that's the ticket. *Lady-in-Waiting*'s taken a hit, sir. Jesus Christ, they've severed the wing. She's going down. Count the chutes. Stay in formation. The sun was in his eyes. A hit, a blow that could break a spine. But he didn't know from where. Right waist, call in. Tail, call in. Where's the hit? Just above the bomb bay, sir. Four minutes to the Reich. The navigator, Baker, reporting calmly, plotting coordinates, what was he writing with, for God's sake? Ball turret to pilot. A 17 in the low squadron on fire. Left wing on fire and diving away. Fighters! Three o'clock level. Son of a bitch. There was blood splattered on the windshield. Case was screaming. He was hit in the arm. Case was scrunched down below the instrument panel. Behind him, Rees was laughing maniacally. I got one, I got one. That's only a probable, Rees. Shit no, I got him, no probable about it. Case, white-faced, was vomiting. Tripp, get up here with a tourniquet. Case has been hit. Jesus Christ. We're on fire, sir. Tripp tearing bandage cloth with his teeth. Callahan with the fire extinguisher. Shit, the little friends are turning back. Stay in formation. The sun was in his eyes. The squadron was on its own now.

Jerry, from the east, always had the advantage. Ten Me-109s out of the sun. Oh my God, look at that. Jesus, they're hitting the high squadron. We've had it now. Hail Mary, Mother of God . . . They're cutting them down like flies. B-17s — hit, exploding. Falling in front of his eyes. Ted dove suddenly and steeply. Everything loose in the plane hitting metal. The gunners pinned against the bulkheads, lips flattened back over their teeth. No one could speak. Then pulling out, leveling off, climbing again. Jesus Christ, what was that? A near miss with a falling Fortress. Bring her up. Rejoin the formation. The Me's going for the low squadron now. My gun is jammed. He couldn't identify the gunner. Left waist, call in. The German fighters pulling away. Dull whoosh of flak. He could smell the cordite. They must be near the target. Flak jackets and helmets. They didn't have to be told a second time. Panic, pounding, the shrapnel like a shower of marbles on the metal skin. Screaming in the intercom. Two of the guns had frozen.

Old Gold was dropping back.

What?

There was Baker to talk to, and Shulman in the nose. Is she hit? I don't think so. You see a fire? Nothing I can see. Losing altitude? Maybe a little. Break radio silence? I can't. Why wasn't *Old Gold* calling him? Why wasn't *Old Gold* telling him to take over the lead? The radio shot out? Possibly. His orders were to follow the lead. He had to do it, throttle back, break formation. Would the others follow? This was suicide. He broke silence then. Had to. *Old Gold*, this is *Woman's Home Companion*. Do you read me? Silence. Come in *Old Gold*. Are you hit? Silence. He was angry now, yelling. *Old Gold*, son of a bitch, what's going on? Silence. The radio was out. The lead plane was losing altitude now, but why?

Old Gold banked slightly, and they saw it.

Her fuel was pouring out, a splash of pale ink across the sky. The plane was dropping faster now. They saw the chutes. One, two, three. They waited. Four . . . five . . . They waited. Only five. The plane, a thousand feet below them, dipped its wing and lurched onto its back.

For a moment, there was silence over the intercom.

Navigator to pilot. Sir, we're sitting ducks. You've got to get us out of here.

Case was bent over at the waist. We can make it to the Channel, Brice. We can ditch. For Christ's sake, don't go down here.

Bombardier to pilot. We've got to rejoin the formation.

Ted throttled up, pushed his plane as hard as he dared. The navigator plotting coordinates, trying to calculate how long they had to rejoin. Ted fixing the mixture; they'd lost precious fuel of their own in the fuckup. Scanning the skies till his eyes burned. They were all doing it. Without the formation, they were as vulnerable as a baby. Someone over the intercom was crying. He couldn't make out who. Case still bent over, his head below the instrument panel, retching again on the floor.

Ted looked up. The sky was ablaze — theatrical and wondrous. He thought he had never seen so many fighters. They were silver, sparkling in the sun. He had in his mind the image of hunting dogs with a fox.

Ripping it to shreds.

There was screaming on the intercom. Right waist to pilot. The tail's been hit, sir. A crack, a new vibration in the controls — severe on the rudder pedals. The control cables were damaged. Losing altitude. Put the nose down to avoid a stall. Pilot to rear gunner. Check in. Silence. Rear, check in. Silence. Left waist, check on Ekberg. Callahan moving toward the tail. Left waist to pilot. We've been hit bad. Pieces are flying off the tail. And Ekberg? I dunno, sir. Not a scratch on him. I can't see any blood. Concussion? I think so, sir. OK, pull him into the waist. Get back to your gun. Another hit and another. Everything falling. Everything pummeling. The instrument casings shattered. A direct hit on number-four engine. Feather the propeller so it won't bash and tear the engine cowling. Then a terrible scream. It's Warren, sir, in the ball turret. The screaming filled the intercom.

Jockey around. Evasive acton. Bandits everywhere. So close he could see the bladders of their oxygen masks pumping in and out fast, like his own. Another engine hit. Let's get the hell out of here. Baker was yelling now. He didn't know where they were. Pieces of the fin peeling off in the slipstream. Ted dove for cloud cover, banked, turned west. They were losing altitude and fuel. Number two's on fire. Case screamed again, We can ditch in the Channel. Head for the Channel, you son of a bitch. No we can't. We have wounded. It would kill the wounded. Screw the wounded, Brice. That's only two. There's eight others of us here who will get picked up. Get Warren out of the turret. Can't see the fighters, sir. Couldn't see the ground either. The cloud was a gray protective blanket — but lethal in its way. Bombardier, drop your bomb load, but do it over a field. The bombs were armed, sir, at the IP. Get rid of them now, bombardier. This is an emergency. He waited for Shulman to push the toggle switch to Salvo. Left waist to pilot. Just seen a piece of the stabilizer come away. Ted was fighting to control the rudder, losing altitude fast, trying to keep the plane level. He heard a whoosh — the bomb bay opened. The plane was close enough to the ground that they could feel the concussion. In the breaks, it looked like farmland, but the clouds were thick, the sky gray. Who could tell? Two thousand feet. Could he make it to the Channel? One's duty was to the living. But how could he take two men to certain death? Pilot to all crew. Throw everything out you can. We're going in on our belly. He saw a village in the distance. Pilot to navigator. Where are we? Don't know, sir. Fifteen hundred feet. Beyond the village a plateau, maybe a field. A thousand feet and falling. Pilot to crew. Assume positions for crash landing. Eight hundred feet. Pilot to left waist. Is Warren out of the turret? Yes, sir, but he's hit real bad. Beside the pilot, Case was crying. You can make it to the Channel. Five hundred feet. He was over the village, dipping, rising slightly, the engines straining. Get as far west as he could. Please God, let us make it to the pasture. He could see the field now. Maybe it was enough to land. A belly landing would slow them down. If it didn't, they'd hit the trees. Baker, still reporting. Two hundred feet. They were losing fuel. Sir, do you read me? Sir, do you read me?

He heard the screaming in his ears. Vibrations threatened to disintegrate the plane, snap a wing. He fought to keep the bomber level. He saw the steeple of the church, a pasture. Cows stumbled in the unspeakable roar; a horse reared. The wing dipped, and he righted it just as they came in. He felt the sharp hit, the first bounce, the second, the skid on the belly. There was frost on the grass.

And finally there was silence.

———

Inside his jacket, the boy began to shake. It was not the fear or the cold; it was instead, this time, the brambles, the gray sky, the fallen plane. It was as though he had never been, until this moment, in the war itself. It was one thing to imagine finding an American flyer in the wood, quite another to be staring at a soldier's feet. The man must be dead, Jean decided. He sank to his knees, crawled around to the other side of the brambles. He stared at the tangle in the gray light, afraid to find what he was searching for.

Jean saw the face — scratched, with blood on it, lying on one cheek, eyes shut. The face was pink still; the American did not look like the dead man beside the plane.

"Hullo," Jean tried, his only English, his voice cracking.

The pilot opened his eyes. Even in the dim light, Jean could see their color — a translucent green, the green of the sea glass that his mother kept in a box on her bureau. He had never seen such eyes on anyone before — the only color in the dun forest.

Jean whispered urgently in Walloon, "I am Belgian. You have fallen on Belgian soil."

The American looked intently at the boy.

Jean, shaking violently inside his jacket, tried again. He spoke, but this time he accompanied his words with gestures. Pointing to himself and to the soil, then again, then once more, repeating the word *Belgique* over and over. Insisting.

The American was motionless, except for his eyes scanning Jean's face.

The boy removed the cheese and bread and the bottle of water from his pockets. He mimed taking a drink. Jean could not reach the American through the brambles, however. He had somehow to get the man out. But how? Did he dare touch the injured leg?

As if in answer, the American began a slow slide backwards, on his belly, until he had released himself from the tangle of thorns. Jean moved on his knees to meet him at the other side of the bushes. He watched as the American rolled over and lay flat on his back, staring at the treetops. The effort seemed to have exhausted him.

Jean opened the bottle of water, cradled the American's head at an angle so the man could drink. The leather at the back of the American's head was cold to the touch. Jean's hand was shaking so badly he was afraid he would spill the water down the soldier's chin and neck. The American propped himself up on his elbows then, took a long swallow. He said an English word the boy could not understand.

The American pulled himself to a nearby tree, managed with his wrists to make it to a sitting position. Careful not to touch anything that might be injured, Jean gingerly held out the bread. The American — pilot? gunner? navigator? Jean couldn't tell — took the bread in cupped hands, angled it with his wrists and bit into it. The loaf, however, was tough, and the American had no strength in his wrists, no grip, to pull it free. Jean reached in and steadied the bread for the American, feeding him. He saw that the fingers of the man's hands were stiff, unbending, the skin an unnatural and waxy white.

The American chewed, swallowed, spoke again. Jean could tell by the inflection that the words formed a question, but he could do nothing but shake his head.

"Can you speak French?" the boy asked very slowly. This time the American shook his head.

The boy asked again, though the likelihood was improbable, "Do you speak Dutch?"

The American seemed not to understand.

Fearful that the tentative link between them might now be severed, with no words left to share, Jean pointed to his own chest. "Jean," he said.

The American nodded. He pointed to himself. "Ted."

Jean wished he were smarter. As he fed the American the bread and cheese and water, he tried to figure out how to convey his plan — a plan that had to be executed quickly, or the Germans would find the American. The frustration of being unable to speak made him want to cry. Wildly he pointed to himself, to the northern edge of the forest, and then made an arrow with his fingers that returned to the brambles.

The American studied the boy. He said something in English, shook his head, indicating he did not entirely understand.

Jean tried again.

"Germans," he said, pointing to the trail the soldier had made, leading to the pasture and the plane. But the American stared blankly at him.

"Ted," Jean said urgently, pointing to inside the brambles.

The American nodded.

"Jean," Jean said. He again pointed to the north, then back. He repeated the gesture. In exasperation, the boy said in French, "Hide yourself. I will return for you." And the American seemed to catch in the sentence a word that sounded familiar.

"Return?" the aviator asked slowly.

Jean, too, heard the word in his own language. He nodded vigorously and smiled, nearly exultant.

The flyer began to smile too, then suddenly blanched with pain. Jean looked at the leg, at the flight suit, which in his attention to the man's face and eyes he had missed. One leg of the flight suit was covered with blood, dried brown blood. Jean felt lightheaded, dizzy.

"Quickly," he urged the American, pointing to the brambles. "Quickly."

The tone of the boy's voice, rather than the word itself, seemed to reach the American. Carefully, he lowered himself, used his forearms to pull his body into the hiding place.

Jean studied the hidden American. The Germans would find him, just as Jean had, he was sure. Unless he could outwit them.

He scooped up handfuls of pine needles and bark and dried leaves and buried the American's protruding feet in mulch. But that wouldn't be enough.

The extra minutes his idea would take were critical, Jean knew, yet it had to be done.

The boy retraced the matted trail, running until he was fifty meters from the pasture. He could hear voices, though he could not make out the words or even their nationality. He began to destroy, backwards toward the bramble bush, and as best he could, the existing trail. But when this proved impossible — the matted grasses would not rise up; the broken branches could not be mended — he devised another plan and was momentarily excited by his own cleverness. He made other paths, diversionary spokes, leading out from the central hub. In a kind of madness, he dragged himself on his back, bending branches and twigs, scuffling leaves with his feet. He tried to calculate the odds that the Germans would enter the forest at the correct point and then would choose the precise spoke to the American.

He surveyed his work.

Whatever else happened, he told himself, he had at least done this.

Turning north, he bent his head to protect it, put out his arms, and scrambled at a near run through the forest. It was December, and darkness came early.

———

The bicycle shuddering, the tire nearly flat. Shit, why hadn't he paid attention to the tires earlier? People in doorways, hanging out of windows. A plane in the village, fallen from the sky like an omen. Head down, keep the head down, blend into the stone, look inconspicuous. Anthoine should slow down; people would notice they were racing. Anthoine in the kitchen with Claire. Anthoine stank of pigs. He was ugly with his pink face, his small eyes, and that greasy, thin, white-blond hair.

Claire in the kitchen. Did she know he had been drinking in the barn before he'd gone into town? Her breasts in her rose sweater, the way she stood with her arms folded under them. If she died before he did, he would remember her that way. And the way she was able to make a meal out of nothing. It was a trick, a gift she had. Like her silence, the quiet of her. She was from his mother's side of the family. Sometimes too quiet. Though he'd rather have that than what Anthoine had got himself — a shrew with a high-pitched voice. That terrible whine. You could hear it all the way to Rance. How did the man stand it? Maybe it was why Anthoine had been so quick to go with the Maquis. Get away from the old woman.

The brakes squealing from lack of oil. A dull ache up the back of his neck from the beer. Heavy, flat beer; maybe it was going bad, that's why he had the headache. How many bowls had he drunk? He wished he hadn't, but who knew a plane was going to fall out of the sky?

The drink took the edge off the cold, made the hours move. The drinking was illegal, the beer contraband, all, that is, except for the weak beer that tasted like cat piss that they let you have in the cafés. All the real alcohol was supposed to go to the German front. But Henri, like Anthoine and Jauquet, made his own beer and then kept it hidden in the barn.

Every morning the same routine: the bread, the awful coffee, the fricassee that no longer had any bacon. Then the frigid air of the barn, where he pretended he had work to do. When the war was over, if it ever ended, the farm would be exposed for what it was — a ruin. Nearly sixty head of dairy cattle gone, the Germans would get the rest before the winter was out. His father's legacy — his father's father's legacy — slaughtered. He'd keep the house, get a job in the village, maybe Rance or Florennes. But what was there to do? What could he do except make repairs to nonexistent machinery?

But nothing would ever be the same again, so what was the point of worrying? Who knew what would be left when the Germans were through with them? He'd known nothing would be the same since the day Anthoine had come with the news Belgium had fallen, and then had asked him to join the Maquis. You couldn't say no. If you were asked, you had to join. He didn't like to think too long about what might have happened to him if Anthoine hadn't asked. Ride the war out is what he'd have done. And there would have been some shame in that. If he had any motivation, and it wasn't much, it was that when this goddamn war was over he wanted to have done the right thing. Not the same as wanting to do the right thing. Not like Anthoine. Not like Claire. With her nursing and her languages.

The truth was, say it, he was scared, scared shitless every day they had a Jew or an aviator in the house, scared just to be in Anthoine's presence. He'd heard the life expectancy of a Resistance fighter was three months. Then how had he and Anthoine made it so long? And didn't that mean their time was up? You knew you would be caught one day, shot. It was the only way you could get out.

When Anthoine had asked, Henri had known he couldn't say no.

Léon now. Léon had courage. Léon had nothing left to lose. His son dead in the single week of fighting when the Germans had trampled over Belgium. Léon, angry, still grieving, but too sick for heavy work. He waited at the Germans' tables at L'Hôtel de Ville and listened to the talk, sometimes brought Anthoine messages. Léon with his steel glasses and his workers' cap. It was a wonder the Germans hadn't killed him already. He looked like a Bolshevik.

Henri didn't want to find an American flyer. He didn't want to have to hide an American flyer in his attic. If the Germans caught him at this game, he would be shot, and the American would be given a beer.

Shit, it was cold. The cobblestones made his teeth hurt. The sky the color of dust. Days like this, the cold seeped in, stayed through the night. You couldn't get rid of it no matter what you did. A young girl in a doorway. Did she wave at him? Was that Beauloye's daughter? The girl in dark lipstick. How old was she, anyway? Fifteen?

Anthoine parked his bicycle behind the church. Henri did the same. Anthoine knew how to look around and see everything without moving his head. They would go in separately, Anthoine first, then a minute later, himself. Smoke a cigarette, lean against the wrought iron railing, stub it out, sigh, curse maybe, as if you were thinking of having to go home to a woman like Anthoine's wife. The heavy wooden door squeaked open. The gloom was blinding.

Shivering already. Fear or cold? He didn't know. He swore the stone was wet. High stone, a small candle flickering in the distance. He touched the water in the font, crossed himself, genuflected. He moved toward the altar, genuflected again, slipped in next to Anthoine, Léon just beyond them.

Base Ball. The words said precisely in English behind him. Emilie Boccart. It was the cigarettes, that voice. He didn't turn, but he wanted to. She was what, forty, forty-five, and still he wanted a look at her. Long, low-slung breasts; her nipples would be erect in the cold. Her coat was open, he had seen her from the back coming up the aisle. If he turned, he could look at the outline of her breasts through the cloth of her blouse. She was Jauquet's lover. Jauquet, who had a wife and five children.

It's a game. An American game, she said. Léon coughed.

Then Léon whispering to Anthoine, so that Henri could hear

too. And any minute the words could change to a prayer. Emilie would be watching, begin to pray in an audible voice. Hail Mary, Mother of God . . . A simple signal.

Lehouk found two of the Americans already. One has a wound to the arm. The other's in shock, no memory of anything, not even his name. They've already been taken to Vercheval.

And the wounded man from the plane? Anthoine speaking.

With Dinant. She's keeping him. He's too badly hurt.

Anthoine angry now. She was told . . .

Léon raising a hand. There's no persuading her, Chimay. I tried.

The other?

With Bastien.

Where's Jauquet?

St. Laurent.

Telling the Germans, Henri thought, shifting his weight.

Again the hoarse voice behind him.

He's afraid he'll never play *Base Ball*.

Who's afraid?

The man with the broken arm. He says he's a *Base Ball* player.

We don't have much daylight, Anthoine said. We've got to cover the woods.

I'll go. A thin voice from behind and the left. Dussart. The boy with the missing ear. An accident in the quarry. Pale and thin and blond, the hair grown long to cover the bad ear. He volunteered for everything. A wild streak in him that bore some watching. If it hadn't been for the war, Henri thought, the boy would have fled Belgium, gone to Marseilles, Amsterdam.

Dussart. Then Henri. Then Dolane, another dairy farmer. Van der Elst, the butcher. Van der Elst hid Jews above the shop. Once he had been raided, but his wife, Elise, had sent the refugees over the roof to Monsieur Gosset.

Any other planes? Anthoine again.

No, just the one. The pilot was trying for the Heights.

Anthoine considered. Anthoine could kneel only on the left knee, the right injured in an accident with explosives. A tiny candle in a red glass. Jesus hanging from the cross, the blood in exaggerated drops on the Saviour's side. As a kid, it made him ill. The smell was mildew, he was sure of it. Even in the summer, the place was damp.

Emilie, tell Duceour and Hainaert. Léon, go back to the hotel.

I can't.

Why not?

I sent Chimène this morning to say I was sick.

Tell them you're better.

Léon coughing and rising. His breath making small puffs on the frigid air.

Anthoine turning now to Henri. Can you take another? He meant in addition to the old woman from Antwerp. Henri nodded. The old woman was going to die anyway. Maybe even today. A scuffle of shoes behind him. Emilie, Dussart, Dolane leaving. He heard the sharp report of high heels on the stone floor; he loved that sound. It was worth the Mass on Sundays.

The candle still flickering. Who had lit it? Emilie for herself? For them all? For the children she never had? For her sins with Jauquet? Would he and Claire have children? Four years and nothing. He didn't understand it. Was there something wrong with his seed? With Claire somewhere deep inside her? There'd been nothing like that with anyone on his side of the family; his mother had reassured him. They waited in the pew. He couldn't pray. If he prayed, it would be *not* to find an American flyer. To go home and have his noon meal instead. To go to bed.

But probably he should pray, he thought. Pray to be relieved of his fear. To want to do the work he was given. To have courage like Anthoine did, and not hate this war so much. He blew on his hands to warm them. Anthoine farted quietly. Anthoine was a pig. And a hero in the Maquis. He had blown up a bridge. Killed two German soldiers with his hands.

Henri waited his turn, the last to go but for Anthoine. He wished now he could eat. He would probably not get food until late tonight. Anthoine said a word. Henri rose, slipped along the pew. His own boots caused echoes in the sanctuary. Outside, the light, though muted by thick cloud cover, hurt his eyes. He looked all around the square. The members of the Delahaut Maquis had already disappeared into the gray stone.

———•———

Sometimes, when his father slaughtered his animals, when his father sold to the Germans not just the grain, but also the meat, Jean saw, in the barn, the odd bits left on the filthy table, odd bits crawling with maggots. A sight as sickening as anything he had ever witnessed, and now, with the barrow, with the dark seemingly sinking through the tall beeches like fog or cloud, that was the image Jean had of the forest. His forest, crawling with maggots, the Germans with their high black boots and revolvers, searching for the Americans.

The route Jean decided to take was an old hunter's route, and he doubted the Germans knew of it, though they could stumble across his path and demand to know what he was doing in the wood with a barrow. And if they went to his father, to query him about his son and the forest, his father would tell them of the hunter's path — not visible from the perimeter, but not so over-grown it couldn't be used to gain access to the interior of the forest without losing one's way. Even so, Jean didn't think anyone knew the wood as well as he — not even his father. It had been, for years, his playground; now it was his home, a place to which he could escape the unhappiness and shame in the farmhouse where his parents lived.

Steering the barrow was sometimes more difficult than he had anticipated, and occasionally Jean left the trail when two straight oaks refused to let him pass. He was not at all sure he would be able to make his way back with the American, but several months ago, in the summer, he had carried a large sow from Hainaert's farm to his own. Could the American possibly weigh more than the sow? he wondered. The man had seemed lean inside the sheepskin, tall but not heavy. Jean remembered clearly the American's face — the eyes still, not afraid, nearly smiling when he and Jean had hit upon the word they shared — and changing just the once, going white from the pain. He didn't want to think about that pain, or the cold of the forest floor, or the odds that when he arrived at the bramble bush the American would still be alive. He didn't know which he feared more — to find the American dead, or to find him gone, taken by the Germans.

He heard a voice, the crack of footsteps on dead wood. He stopped, dared not even set the barrow down. In that position he tried to quiet his breathing, to control the panting from his heavy exertions and his fear. He thought he heard the footsteps move closer, though the voices were still only mumbles, and he could not make them out. The fast settling of night, which before he was cursing, now seemed a gift. In these moments between daylight and evening, the wood, he knew, became an illusory and mystifying landscape, its geography shifting even as you observed it, a tree in the near distance vanishing, then returning, shadows taken for bushes, bats flying faster than the eye could catch them. In his old gray coat, a worn and oft-patched coat he used to hate to wear to school, he might not be seen in this light, even from only ten meters. He waited until he was certain the footsteps had moved away. He knew that soon the Germans would return with torches.

He scrambled more quickly now, aware that the temperature was dropping fast. When he arrived at the place where he had left the American, he settled the barrow on the ground and knelt beside the bush. He felt more than saw the flyer's feet, his hand reaching below the mulch cover to find the heel of a boot. When he touched the boot, the man shifted his foot slightly, and Jean let out his first sigh of relief.

"Jean," he said quickly, not wanting the American to be alarmed.

At first the man did not move, but then, after a time, Jean saw in the dim light the slow slide from the brambles. The American pulled himself free, tried to make it to a sitting position. Jean reached for his shoulder, held him upright with his weight. Jean pointed immediately to the barrow. The boy had worried about the logistics of this part of his scheme. If the American himself was not able to climb into the barrow, the entire plan would collapse. Alone, Jean couldn't lift a grown man.

Slowly the American turned, dragged himself over to the barrow. On his stomach, with his forearms, he pulled his weight up and over the lip of the bed of the barrow — a fish flopped upon a deck. Jean tried to help by hooking his hands under the man's armpits and pulling. The bouncing of the leg must have been excruciating — the American bit hard on his lower lip. When the flyer had made it as far as his hips, he rolled over. He used his elbows to pull himself back an inch or two and stopped. Jean hopped out of the barrow and with all his strength lifted the long handles. There was the possibility, he knew, that the wooden poles would break free of the barrow, but miraculously the barrow lifted. With the tilt, the American slid, tried to sit up against the barrow's back. Jean, bending his head and shoulders as far to the side as he could, mimed for the American to lie down. Stray branches in the dark could tear across the American's face.

In the dark, the boy trusted to all the years that he had played there, all the times he had come along this path. Once he ran into the thick trunk of a tree, and the American, unable to stop himself, cried out in pain. Apart from that collision, and several agonizing moments when the barrow became wedged between two trees, the trip was easier than Jean had hoped for. At the edge of the forest, Jean set the barrow down. His arms trembled from the strain. He couldn't cross the open field with the American, even in the darkness, until he was certain no one was in the barn.

He didn't stop to explain to the American what he was doing. The flyer would not move or speak, Jean was certain, and would know by now that Jean intended to hide him. Running silently across the frozen field, Jean reached the barn, lifted the heavy beam that fastened the door. He winced at the squeal of the hinges, waited for the sound of footsteps. When there were none, he looked inside the barn, satisfied himself that no one was in there.

Where before in the wood the barrow seemed to make no sound of its own, the thuds across the rutted field were thunderous in the boy's ears. The journey of a hundred meters seemed to take an hour. He set the barrow down outside the barn door. Again he endured the squealing of the hinges, wheeled the American inside.

There was a soft movement and the lowing of cows — not a

sound, Jean knew, that would alert anyone in the house. He wheeled the American to a long trough that held mash for pigs in summer, potatoes in winter, and was empty now. Truly frightened by the audacity of his plan, and by the proximity of his own house, not twenty meters away, Jean moved quickly. He reached for the American's arm, tugged him slightly toward him. He took the arm, ran the large hand along the edge of the trough so that the American could feel the shape and perhaps understand the plan. The flyer seemed to, inched himself forward, rolled, hooked his good leg over the side of the trough. Holding the man as best he could, Jean helped guide him out of the barrow and into the trough. When the American finally fell inside it, the thud seemed to Jean the loudest sound he had ever heard.

Earlier in the day, Jean had emptied the trough of potatoes. He knew he would again have to fill the trough with potatoes to cover the American. He reached for the flyer's hand again, made him touch a potato, but he didn't know if the man had any feeling in his hands. He placed a potato near the American's face, on the off chance the man might be able to smell it. But there was no more time for explanations.

Carefully, Jean placed potatoes in the trough, positioning them as gently as he could around the pilot's face and legs. The man made no sound, no protest. Knowing the gaps between the potatoes would allow the man to breath, and hoping to provide some protection from the cold, the boy filled the trough to its top, hid the sack with the remaining potatoes underneath a pile of hay. He moved toward the door, anxious to be gone from the barn, but hesitated at its threshhold.

Making his way back to the trough, he bent low over the spot where the pilot's head was. Jean's lips brushed the skin of a potato.

Return, he said in English.

His father hit him such a blow he spun, knocked a chair on its back. His world, a shrinking world inside the kitchen, went momentarily black, then spotty with bright lights. His upper lip was split over his teeth, and when he put his hand to his mouth, his fingers came away with blood. He didn't dare to move or speak.

He couldn't be exactly sure what the blow was for, and he knew it was always best to wait, to keep silent. Nothing enraged his father more than a protest or a challenge.

"Monsieur Dauvin's been here. Says you weren't at school. Not from noon on," his father yelled from the sink. Artaud Benoît picked up his lit cigarette from the table, took a quick drag, held it between his thumb and forefinger. How had his father known he would come through the door at that precise moment? Jean wondered. He'd have been waiting, and in the waiting he would have become drunk. Even from across the room, Jean could smell the beer. There were unwashed bottles under the table.

"You weren't at that plane, I'm hoping. No son of mine."

No son of mine, Jean thought. He put a hand on the tabletop to steady himself. His legs felt weak. He desperately did not want to fall. The oilcloth on the table was worn, threadbare in places from his mother's scrubbing. A single bulb hung from the ceiling, illuminating the room, casting harsh shadows on the wallpaper, the stove, the marble mantel with the crucifix and the bottle of holy water. The boy's dinner, which his mother had put out for him, lay congealed on a plate on the table. The thought of his mother, who would have gone up to the bedroom, made his chest tight.

"And your mother, lying to the teacher for your sake, telling him you'd come home sick. Weeping afterwards, not knowing where you'd got to."

Jean stood as still as he could, despising his father for the show of false sympathy for his mother. He kept his breathing deliberate and measured. He dropped his eyes to the stone floor, a floor his mother swept and washed every day.

"I hope to Christ the Germans didn't catch you at that plane. I got problems enough without having to explain for my son. Next you know, they'll be thinking you're a Partisan. And you know what they do to Partisans."

It was not a question. His father took a deep pull on his cigarette. It was poorly rolled, and bits of tobacco fell onto the floor. "Don't you stand there like a stone, or I'll give you another one of these."

Jean did not look up, but he knew a fist had been made.

53

"I know you were in the wood. I can see by the sight of you. You see any of the Americans?"

Jean shook his head.

"Don't lie to me, or you'll be no son of mine. That's what you were looking for, isn't it? You think this is a game? It's a game that'll get your neck broken, that's what. You see an American, you tell me. You understand?"

Jean nodded. The blood from his lip was in his mouth. He didn't dare to spit. He swallowed it.

His father picked up the plate that contained Jean's meal, threw it at the stove. The crockery broke against the cast iron. The boy flinched. It was a casual, unnecessary gesture on his father's part, meant to frighten the son, hurt the mother when she saw the broken plate in the morning, if she had not already heard the noise from her bedroom above. Jean knew that if his father hit him again, he'd go down. He had no strength left in his legs. He wasn't even sure he could make it up the stairs.

"I'm not through with you yet, but I'm sick of looking at you."

His father made a dismissive gesture with his arm. Gratefully, Jean left the room, not even stopping to remove his coat.

On his bed, in the small room under the eave, Jean lay fully dressed, holding a sock to his lip to stanch the blood. He had not washed because he'd have had to do so at the sink in the barn, and he could not go back into the barn. Jean had imagined he'd be reported missing from the school, but he had not thought Monsieur Dauvin himself would come to the house. He wanted to go into his mother's room, to tell her he was all right, but he wasn't all right, and she would see and be alarmed — and besides there was again the risk of encountering his father.

He lay on his bed and thought about the flyer. He tried to imagine what it must be like to lie in that cramped trough with the potatoes. He thought about the dark, the smell and feel of the potatoes, the low sounds of the cows. But the more he thought about the flyer, the more worried he became. What if the American froze to death in the trough, died before the morning? And if the man didn't freeze to death, what was Jean to do with him then?

The boy had not planned beyond getting the flyer into the barn, and perhaps during the night smuggling some food and water to the man. But as Jean lay there, the enormity of what he had done began to close in around him.

Something would have to be done before daylight. There could be no stopping now. What had it all been for, if not to save the flyer? But if he waited until morning, his father would find the American and turn him over to the Germans. Was his father right? Had he, Jean, merely been playing a game? Living out an adventure that this time might end in catastrophe?

He wanted to cry. He began to think about the flyer's leg. It needed attention, a doctor or a nurse. What if it became infected and had to be amputated — all because Jean had brought the man to the barn and could not think of a way to get him out? What if the American died of the infection? Could a grown man die so quickly from a wound? And surely there was the loss of blood, too, and shock. In the darkness he saw the American's face. The man who had called himself Ted, who had no use of his hands, who had nearly smiled at their small triumph of communicating a single word.

The boy had said he would return. He had promised that. He had to get the flyer out of the barn before daybreak.

He held the sock to his lip, fighting off sleep. He stared into the absolute darkness of his tiny room. He made his eyes stay open, and he thought. After a time, he listened to the heavy tread on the stairs of his father's footsteps, heard the door to his parents' bedroom open and close.

And when he had thought a long time, he sat up on the edge of the bed, threw the sock to the floor, and pulled his coat around him.

———

She was asleep or near sleep, listening still for the familiar sounds of Henri entering the kitchen downstairs. The scuffle of his boots. Water at the pump. A glass set on the table. She had waited up as long as she felt able, but then the chilly air had driven her to bed. Underneath the thick comforter, in her nightgown, she drifted between sleep and waking, wondering what had happened to Henri. She was not especially alarmed; it was not the first time he had been gone the entire night on a mission. But still she wished he had sent word to her somehow. She was concerned for the old woman who lay just beyond her wall, breathing irregularly now, refusing to eat, even to sip broth. Claire had wanted to bring the old woman downstairs, to lay her by the fire, but alone she couldn't manage her on the stairs. Instead Claire had piled blanket upon blanket on the frail body. But it seemed to Claire that she was merely burying the old woman, making it impossible for her to move.

She didn't have much hope for the old woman. Even if Claire could help her regain her strength, the Maquis would want the woman moved through the lines, the space cleared for the next refugee or aviator. Claire didn't even have the luxury of allowing Madame Rosenthal a room in her house. If she suggested it, Henri would tell her what she already knew. Madame Rosenthal was a Jew. A Belgian could not keep a Jew in a house. The punishment would be death for Madame Rosenthal and themselves.

But she was worried for Madame Rosenthal. Even under the best of circumstances, she guessed it would be difficult to make it across the French border, even more difficult to get to Spain. She thought of one story that had filtered back to her. In April, forty men, among them two English aviators who had been sheltered in Delahaut, had made it within twenty-five kilometers of the Spanish border. Ebullient after their harrowing journey, one of the Englishmen, while bathing in a stream, had begun a song in English. A neighbor, an old woman, heard the English words over the wall of her back garden. Tipped off by this collaborator, the Gestapo arrested the two English pilots, as well as the other escapees. Just a morning's walk from freedom, all thirty-two men were machine-gunned over a ditch, into which the bodies fell and were left uncovered as a lesson to the townspeople.

Claire sat up. She thought she heard a knock at the door. A short rap, then silence. A short rap, then silence. Instantly, her skin grew hot. She pushed the comforter off, and, forgetting her robe, ran downstairs in her bare feet to the kitchen. The stone floor was a shock to her body, the cold painful on her soles. She held her arms around her, stood behind the door. The rhythmic rapping continued. What time was it? Three, four in the morning? Had something happened to Henri, and someone had come to tell?

"Who is it?" she called from behind the door.

"It's Jean Benoît," she heard in a quiet voice.

She heard the name, but it refused to register. Jean was a boy, only ten years old. She asked the question again: "Who is there?"

"Madame Daussois," came the urgent voice. "Please, open the door. It's Jean Benoît."

Claire opened the door. The boy was shivering on the doorstep. The icy air blew into the kitchen, and she beckoned to the boy to come inside. She shut the door. In the dark of the room, she could just make out his features. She drew on an old coat of Henri's that hung on a peg beside the door, and lit a candle on the mantel. The sight of the boy made her put her hand to her mouth.

His face was swollen on the side, a dark bruise beginning. His lip was split, and there was dried blood on his chin and cheeks. His coat was filthy, with bits of twigs and bark stuck to it.

"I need Monsieur Daussois," the boy said in a barely audible voice. He cleared his throat.

She studied the boy warily. Everyone knew the boy's father was *collabos*.

"Who did that to you?" she asked.

The boy looked at her, did not answer.

"Was it the Germans?"

The boy shook his head.

"Was it your father?" she asked.

The boy seemed to hesitate, as if making a decision. Then he nodded once quickly. "I must speak with Monsieur Daussois," he said. "It's urgent."

The panic in the boy's voice sounded authentic, but even so Claire knew she must be cautious.

The members of the Maquis were always at risk. Sometimes the treachery was obvious; sometimes it was subtle. The Germans fed their own airmen into the system, men who spoke perfect English and landed on Belgian soil with American or English parachutes. They'd be sheltered, put through the networks, only, at the end, to expose all those who had helped them escape. The men and women who were captured would be tortured to reveal other names. Claire knew of men who'd been blinded or burned with electric prods. And then these men — and women — would be shot, or suffocated, and buried without winding sheets in shallow graves, where animals soon picked their bones. But this method of exposure, she knew, didn't always please the Germans. Sometimes they wanted the individual Allied airmen more than they wanted the networks. The Gestapo began then to infiltrate the networks with one collaborator along the way, one link in the chain, who could deliver, selectively, the most valuable of the allied officers, so as not to cast too much suspicion upon themselves, and thus keep the networks open. After all, who could say for sure at which link an airman had been exposed? Always it was a tenet of the Resistance that each cell know only of the one directly before it.

"Why do you need him?" she asked, eyeing the boy closely.

He gave a long sigh. She could see that the boy was frightened. Frightened and hurt. His lip and the side of his face needed medical attention.

"I have the American," the boy said simply.

At first she did not understand. How could a boy have an American? And then, meeting the child's shy gaze, she understood.

"Where is he?" she asked.

"I have hidden him in my father's barn. He's injured in his leg. I need Monsieur Daussois to help me get him out before my father goes into the barn in the morning."

"Where did you find him?"

"In the wood."

"And no one else knows?"

The boy shook his head.

She stared at the boy. Could she trust him? She wondered immediately how it was that the boy knew to come to her house and not another. This fact alone was alarming — were she and

Henri known already to the Germans? Or was this a ploy, a way to identify a member of the Maquis? Yet she had believed the boy when he'd said it was his father who had hit him, split his lip.

In a small village such as Delahaut, she had learned, it was not possible always to conceal either resistance to or collaboration with the Germans. Certain collaborators were easily known — the Black Belgians, for example, men who wore black shirts and held positions of power within the occupational force, even occasionally replacing a Burghermaster. Then there were the women who went with German soldiers, accepted presents and money for their favors. In Delahaut, there were several, and they were regarded as worse than whores. Claire had seen these women spat upon in the village streets by men and women, and she didn't want to think about what might happen to these women after the war.

But the members of the Resistance, unlike some of the collaborators, had to be extremely careful about inadvertently revealing their identity to anyone. Claire knew Henri and Anthoine had taken a risk in removing items from the fallen plane while schoolchildren were able to observe them. But schoolchildren, she knew, more often than not, saw the Maquis as heroic, longed to grow up to fight within its ranks. No, the danger was seldom children; it was instead the men and women who might come to your house, share a cup of ersatz coffee with you by the stove, even express their hatred for the Nazis in your presence, all the while listening for a sound in your home that might be different from all the others.

Suddenly, she understood how the boy had identified her.

The Resistance operated cautiously, trusting as few people as possible, but there were some villagers sympathetic to the Maquis one had to depend upon. Omloop, for example. In Belgium, everyone was rationed. The daily ration per person was 225 grams of bread, three lumps of sugar, two small sausages, and half a kilo of potatoes. But those in the escape lines — the Jews, the Allied airmen, the Belgian boys fleeing the German work camps, the Maquis themselves — had no ration stamps. Obtaining food and feeding this small army was full-time work in itself. The Resistance therefore had to rely on sympathetic shopkeepers who would pad rations from the black market. When Claire went to Madame Omloop's, the shopkeeper, without saying a word, always gave Claire larger portions than her ration book allowed.

"You've seen me at Omloop's," Claire said to Jean.

The boy looked down at his feet. When he looked up, she saw the confusion on his face.

"Monsieur Daussois is not here," she said slowly. "He's out." She left it at that. She looked toward the ceiling, thought of the old woman. "I can go with you," she added. "Perhaps together we can move the man."

Relief softened the boy's face. Claire put on her clogs, fastened her coat, and tied a kerchief under her chin. There was the old truck behind the barn, and the gazogene. Henri had said to use it only in an emergency. Could she get the gazogene to work? Could she and the boy crank the old Ford into life? She could see no other way. She hoped that the old woman would not call out to her while she was gone.

Jean, beside her, told her to turn off the lights and cut the engine while they were still on the lane and out of sight of his father's farmhouse. Quietly they opened their respective doors, got out of the cab. There would be snow in the morning, she was certain. She could smell it on the air.

The boy led, and she followed behind. She did not allow herself to think of the consequences of being caught at this. Occasionally, she had been asked to another house, to a terraced house in the village or to another farm, to nurse an injured airman or to translate. But on those trips, she had gone by bicycle, as almost everyone in the village traveled, so there had been minimal risk. A woman and a boy in a truck in the middle of the night after a plane had crashed in the village would be impossible to explain. Had the truck been spotted on the road from the Daussois farm to the Benoît farm? What time was it exactly, and how long did they have until daybreak? She cursed herself for not looking at the grandfather clock in the kitchen.

She sucked in her breath at the uneven squeal of the barn door opening. Beneath Henri's coat, she shivered in her nightgown. She could see nothing in the darkness of the barn, dared not move forward lest she stumble and fall. The boy touched her gently, and, holding her by the wrist, led her to the interior. She could smell and hear animals, but couldn't see them.

The boy tugged downward on her wrist and spoke to her. She knelt, put out her hands. She was kneeling on something soft, a mixture of hay and dried manure, she thought. Her hands touched the rough wood of a trough, the humpy shapes of potatoes.

She listened to the boy working quickly beside her. Once she heard him say, in a low voice, *Jean.* She was aware of the dull thud of the potatoes falling to the soft ground all around the boy. And then the boy stopped.

He reached for her again, this time for her hand. She let him draw her fingers over the trough and along the surface of the potatoes.

She felt the warmth of human skin, a man's face. And the boy beside her said a name.

December 31, 1943, to January 7, 1944

THE COURTYARD BEHIND THE SCHOOL WAS A BLUR OF movement as boys in ill-fitting jackets and old wool pullovers played hoop and boules and pitch-the-pebble in the few remaining minutes of the dinner hour. Few of the girls had ventured into the cold; most of them had remained behind in the classroom with Madame Lepin, who was teaching them to knit socks for the imprisoned Belgian soldiers in Germany. Jean stood at the top of the steps and surveyed the scene. Marcel, who had been waiting for him to emerge from the school, spotted him first and called to him. At the mention of Jean's name, the other boys halted in their play, watched as he descended the stone stairs. An officially designated punishment, no matter what the offense, never failed to produce curiosity in the boys. Jean walked toward his friend.

"Jean," Marcel whispered frantically. "What happened? What did Monsieur Dauvin do to you?"

Jean held out his hands, where the evidence was obvious. With an effort of will he made his hands remain still. The knuckles were swollen. On the middle fingers the skin had split, and there were slits of blood.

"The stick?"

Jean nodded.

"Better than the caning."

Jean nodded again.

Marcel shook his head. "I didn't tell them," he said, again

whispering. "I know you said to tell them you were sick, but Monsieur Dauvin was so angry, I didn't dare speak."

"That's just as well," said Jean. "Then you, too, would have gotten the stick."

"What happened to you, anyway?" Marcel asked. "Where were you all afternoon? Did you find any of the Americans?"

Jean looked beyond his friend to the place where a group of boys were playing boules. They played with a hand-whittled and sanded ball that wasn't perfectly spherical and wobbled in the dirt just beyond the courtyard. No one had asked him why his mouth was swollen or his lip was split when he arrived at school that morning. It wasn't the first time he had come to school in such a state; they knew his father often beat him.

"Jean, what happened to you? What did you find?"

Jean slowly turned his gaze back to his friend. Marcel badly needed a haircut. Tufts of hair grew over his ears. Like his own, the boy's trousers were too short. "Nothing happened," he said to Marcel. "I went back into the woods, but I couldn't find anything. When I got home, Monsieur Dauvin had been to see my father, and so he hit me."

"Oh," Marcel said. He looked disappointed.

Jean tried to put his hands into the pockets of his trousers, but his knuckles wouldn't easily bend. He knew that his fingers wouldn't work properly until tomorrow at the earliest. This was not the first time he had been rapped.

It was, however, the first time he had lied to his friend. But the lie had come immediately, before he had had time even to think about what he might say. Instinctively he'd known somehow that what had happened in the night was not to be shared with anyone. Not just for his own safety, but for Madame Daussois's as well. He could not forget the sight of her standing in her nightgown in her kitchen, nor the strength of her later in the night. She was beautiful. He was sure he had never seen a woman so beautiful, not even Marie-Louise, who was regarded as the village beauty, the village flirt. Marie-Louise stained her legs with walnut and painted a seam up the back in order to fool everyone into thinking she wore silk stockings. Jean was sure that Madame Daussois would never do such a thing. He would suffer a dozen canings for her if he had to.

In the darkness, he and Madame Daussois had together emptied the trough of potatoes, helped the airman to his feet. The American was dazed and weak — barely able to stand. Madame Daussois spoke constantly to the man, whispering English words, so that she might calm him, help him to understand that she and the boy were friends. Jean replaced the potatoes in the trough. When he stood, he could not clearly see the flyer's face, but he could feel the weight of the man, feel the leather and then the fleece of the large open collar of his flight suit. The aviator weighed even more in his heavy flight suit than he would have without it, but Jean knew that it was only the flight suit that had allowed him to survive. He had heard the stories of the flyers who had bailed out of their planes with electric suits, and who had frozen on the fields and in the woods before they could be rescued.

Madame Daussois in her nightgown and her husband's heavy coat, and Jean in his old jacket and hat, had wheeled the airman from the barn to the truck. Together they had lifted and pushed and heaved the man onto the truck bed, as if they were taking a dead animal to market. It was impossible to be silent in this effort, and with each grunt from himself or muffled cry of pain from the injured man, Madame Daussois, and then Jean, had looked instinctively for movement at the farmhouse. When they had the flyer finally in the truck, Jean had walked to the cab. He was about to hoist himself into the passenger seat for the ride back to Madame Daussois's house. It had not occurred to him that he would not go. How else was Madame Daussois to get the airman into her house if not with his help? But Madame Daussois had caught up to him, put a hand on his shoulder. He argued then, whispering as fiercely as he dared, trying to persuade her of his usefulness, but Madame Daussois would not be moved. She didn't look hard, not like Marcel's mother, for example, but she was. Of that he had no doubt now. Not like his own mother, who did not look tough and wasn't. He cringed when he thought about his mother, about the way she was afraid of her own husband.

Madame Daussois had insisted he return quickly to his bedroom. She said that if he was captured, he would not be able to withstand the torture, and in the event, would put them all at risk. For a moment, Jean had hesitated, thinking to defy her, unwilling to relinquish the airman. After all, if it hadn't been for Jean, the aviator would not have been found, might even have died in the night. In fact, Jean thought, he almost certainly would have died, or would have been found by the Germans. He remembered that his nose and eyes were running in the cold as he struggled with his own desires and fears. Finally, he shrugged and pulled away from Madame Daussois, saying not a word. He felt bad about that now. He had walked away from her in a sulk, when he had every reason to be grateful to her for having come to his aid when he had asked her. He wished now that he could go to her farmhouse and tell her that he was sorry for his behavior. He badly wanted to know how the flyer was, if he was still with her, if he had been transferred elsewhere. He had seen the alarm on Madame Daussois's face when she realized that Jean had guessed she was with the Resistance. He wanted to reassure her that her secret was safe with him, that no matter what happened he would tell no one of last night.

He had stood off to one side in the shadows, watching as she turned the truck around in the dark. He remembered the trip from her house to his, when her body had shaken so violently she was barely able to manage the gears or the clutch. The back road they had taken was badly rutted, the ruts frozen into ridges and heaves, and he knew the truck bed, thrusting and shaking over the uneven surface, had to have been an agony for the American. Driving away from Jean last night, Madame Daussois had turned on the lights only when she was a good hundred meters from the place where they had parked. They shocked Jean, their sudden brightness, illuminating each tree, casting harsh shadows that moved, and he felt anxious, as though a search beam had fallen suddenly upon her. He bit the inside of his cheek. He waited until he could no longer hear the motor of the truck before he started up the long dirt drive to his own house.

"Benoît."

Jean turned at the voice. Pierre Albert, a year older than Jean, stood close to him, tossing a wooden ball from one hand to the other. His eyes were narrowed. Pierre's cousin, Jan, had been a saboteur with the Maquis in Charleroi and had been shot by the Belgian SS when caught in the basement of his flat with explosives. Pierre never tired of telling the story, as though the heroism of his cousin conferred upon Pierre an honor he himself had earned.

"You got the stick."

Jean said nothing. Marcel looked anxious. Pierre was a bully, and Jean knew that Marcel was afraid of him.

"For what?"

"You know for what," Jean said, now painfully forcing his rigid fingers into the pockets of his trousers.

"So why weren't you at school?"

"I was sick."

Pierre sucked his teeth. He closed one eye.

"My father says he knows where the Americans are."

Jean said nothing. He doubted that Pierre's father knew where any of the Americans were. Or if he did, that he'd have told his son.

"I saw the plane myself," Pierre boasted.

Again, Jean was silent. He did not remember seeing Pierre in the pasture. Telling Pierre Albert he was a liar, however, would only make things worse.

Marcel shifted his feet, looked as though he would like to join the other boys at pitch-the-pebble. "Come on, Jean," he said.

Pierre turned and sneered. "Where are *you* going?"

Marcel stopped his retreating movement. Pierre looked back at Jean.

"So you were sick," Pierre said.

Jean stood still, didn't answer him.

"You know where I think you were?" Pierre asked, tossing the ball so that, as it descended, it barely skimmed Jean's face. Jean refused to move.

"I think you were sneaking off to St. Laurent to tell the Germans, that's where I think you were."

Jean opened his mouth to protest — this he would not allow! But before he could speak, the bell rang loudly in the courtyard, momentarily surprising him. He heard Marcel's sigh of relief.

Pierre thrust the wooden ball inches in front of Jean's face. Jean heard the hated words as the older boy turned his back and ran. *Fils du collabos*.

———

Claire knelt beside the airman. She took her scarf from her head, opened her coat. In the candlelight she could see the man's face for the first time. He looked oddly peaceful, as though he were merely sleeping. He was twenty-one or -two, she guessed. The light made shadows of the bones of his face, the shape of his mouth. There were cuts on his forehead and cheeks, and his mouth was badly swollen. Briefly, she ran the back of her fingers along the side of his cheek. As she sometimes had for the others, she wondered who might be dreaming of this man even then, which mother, which woman loved him, prayed for him, received his letters, counted the days until he might come home. If he did not regain consciousness — and she felt no certainty that he would — she would never know. She unzipped the flight suit to the middle of his chest, felt with her fingers for the chain. She held his identification disc in her hand, the metal slightly warm from his skin. She dropped the tags to the stone floor. She wanted to scream. The magnitude of the carnage was stupefying. She thought of the boys barely men who died unthinkable deaths far from home; of the men and women of her own country tortured to death simply because of the accident of their birth. No matter how long she thought about it, how deeply it had entered her life, how long it lay in her house, she did not understand how this thing had swept over them, how their lives had been forever altered. And if there ever came a time when she might understand what had happened to the Belgians, to the people of her own village, she would never be able to fathom why young men came from so far away to defend a country about which they knew nothing. Some of the soldiers she had tended had not known before the war that Belgium even existed. They could not accurately locate her country on a map. Belgium meant nothing to them — nothing real, nothing substantial — and yet they continued to come. And continued to die.

Henri returned from parking the truck behind the barn, bringing with him the sharp chill of the frigid night. Claire looked up at her husband from the stone floor on which she was kneeling. Henri's face was drawn, gray, exhausted. There was grime in the creases of his skin. He'd been stunned when, just minutes earlier, he'd bicycled into the gravel drive and found his wife in the truck bed with an injured airman. She knew that he was afraid of this work, that he was afraid of the presence of the foreign airman in his home. And yet he had never turned a soldier or a Jew away. He had never refused a request from the Maquis.

"I'm going for Madame Dinant," he said from the doorway.

Claire nodded. She wanted to tell him to go upstairs to bed, but she knew that was impossible. The airman couldn't be left alone, and Henri would be able to bicycle to Dinant's much more quickly than she could.

"Tell her to bring plaster and morphine," she said. "And tell her . . ." Claire looked toward the ceiling of the kitchen. "Tell her that the old woman is dying."

When Henri left, the room was still. She could hear the clock tick and looked up at it; it read one-fifteen. She removed the pilot's leather helmet and put a pillow under his head. His hair was the color of sand, and matted flat. She examined the rest of the flight suit. One trouser leg, the right one, was soaked in blood near the foot.

Claire stood and removed a pair of long shears from her sewing drawer. She bent over the American flyer. Her hair, unrolled, fell like sheets at the sides of her face, hampering her vision. She made an impatient gesture, swinging her long hair to one side, and, tilting her head just slightly to keep it there, she began to cut the man's trousers, starting at the ankle.

The shears were dull against the leather. Bits of sheepskin, dirty with blood, came away in tufts, and began to make a pile surrounding the man's leg. When she reached the wound, she felt a sudden nausea and had to swallow hard. The skin of his calf down to the back of the ankle had burst open like an angry blossom. As delicately as she could, she picked off dried pieces of fleece from the open wound. She heard a sharp intake of air, looked quickly at the airman's face. The skin had gone gray. He was awake now and was watching her.

"I am sorry if I am hurting you," she said in English.

He shut his eyes briefly, and exhaled slowly, trying to control the pain. The wound was exposed now to the air.

"You are safe now. You are in Belgium," she said softly. She whispered the word again, and then again. *Belgium. Belgium.*

She studied him. The color was not returning to his face. Claire noticed a day's growth of beard. He shook his head slowly. She didn't know if he meant to say they were not safe, or if he did not believe he was in Belgium. His eyes closed again, and he lay back against the pillow.

Thérèse Dinant had not slept since the previous night, but, unlike Henri, she showed no signs of fatigue. She walked noisily into the house, as if all rooms in Belgium were open to her.

"We treat the aviator first," Dinant announced, as though there had never been any question. Claire knew the aviator would be a priority: Save the airmen at all costs. But it was also triage. Tend to those who had the best chance of life.

"What is the man's name?" Dinant asked.

"Lieutenant Theodore Aidan Brice," Claire answered.

"The pilot, then," Dinant said absently.

In the warmth of the farmhouse kitchen, Dinant stripped off her coat, but she kept on her kerchief. Her face was reddened and dry, with fine hairs on her cheeks. She wore a long, black cardigan and gray knit stockings that accentuated her sturdy legs. On her feet she wore a man's clogs. Dinant worked without preliminaries and with dispatch. She had been with the Croix-Rouge and subsequently with the Maquis since its inception in 1940, and lived alone in a small terraced house in the village. She was as large and as strong as a man — larger even than Henri. She was perhaps only thirty, Claire thought, but she was of a type that had looked middle-aged for years.

Dinant injected the airman with morphine, then cut away the rest of the flight suit. She wanted the pilot naked, she explained, in order to make sure there were no other wounds. A bullet wound in the back, under a shoulder blade, might go unnoticed in an unconscious patient. Claire and Henri did as they were told, together undressing the airman, rolling him over for Dinant's inspection. Claire was sweating in the heavy wool coat, but could not remove it altogether. Anthoine, Dinant had told them, was coming soon to collect the schoolbags, and there had been no time to put a dress over her nightgown.

Dinant told Claire and Henri to keep the man on his stomach and pin his wrists down, avoiding the hands if possible, but if it became necessary, to sit on the pilot's hands. In a rudimentary English she told the pilot that what she was about to do would hurt, but she would be quick.

The pilot, drifting in and out of consciousness, raised his head and shoulders when Dinant began to treat the wound. Henri held the pilot's shoulders; Claire put her hand to the airman's mouth, and he bit the soft pad at the inside of the thumb. When that moment was over, a moment even the morphine couldn't touch, the pilot's forehead fell down onto the blanket. His skin was a terrible color.

Claire helped Dinant to roll the plasters around the man's calf. The bandage stretched from the sole of the foot to the knee. Only his toes, white and waxy, were exposed.

Her hands covered with blood, Claire became aware of another presence in the room. Anthoine Chimay had entered the Daussois kitchen without a sound. Such stealth, even grace, in a large, rotund man was always a surprise, and came, she knew, in Chimay's case, from his years with the Maquis. He wore a dirty woolen coat and knitted gloves from which the ends of the fingers had been removed. Without taking off these gloves, he pulled a crumpled cigarette from his pocket, lit it in the corner. The smell of the tobacco produced in Claire a sharp and intense longing.

"Will he live?" Chimay asked Dinant.

It was a dispassionate question. Claire heard the note of weariness in Anthoine's voice. The downed pilot was, for Chimay, merely a package, valuable to be sure, but nevertheless a parcel to be sent to England as soon as possible so that he might return to combat.

Anthoine was there, Claire knew, not only to collect the school-bags, but also to interrogate the airman. He might already have obtained information from the other airmen who had been found, but he would want especially to talk to this officer. When Chimay had as much intelligence as he could gather, he would send a message, in code, back to England, via a radio he kept in a suitcase under the hay in his barn. That message, in turn, would be forwarded to the crew's base. Until the survivors had safely returned to England, however, the aviators would be listed officially as missing in action.

Dinant shrugged, flipped her hand back and forth as if to indicate a fifty-fifty chance of survival.

"The wound is deep. There's tendon damage. He's lost a great deal of blood," she said. "And there may be some infection. How he fares will depend upon how well he can fight that off."

Chimay took a long pull on his cigarette, rubbed his forehead with his free hand. "When will he be able to talk?" he asked.

Dinant looked at the pilot's face, and shrugged. "Difficult to say. He will need the morphine for a day or two, and perhaps after that — "

"We can't wait that long," Chimay interrupted. "I'll return in the morning and try again." He looked pointedly at Claire. "Where are the schoolbags?"

"In the barn, under the feed."

Anthoine turned and threw his cigarette into the sink. He leaned both of his hands on the lip of the porcelain. In the candlelight Claire could see only the man's broad back, his hunched shoulders. "The Germans have got two of them," he said with disgust. Claire wondered if Anthoine thought himself to blame, that somehow the Resistance had not acted quickly enough.

She did not like to think about what happened to the Allied airmen when the Germans had captured them. She knew they were sent to Breendonk in Brussels, or to similar Belgian prisons in Antwerp and Charleroi. Some were tortured by the Belgian as well as the German SS. Those who survived considered themselves lucky to be deported further east into Germany, to the Stalag Lufts there. Claire had heard about the English pilots at the beginning of the war who had had their eyes put out and had been buried without coffins in the cemeteries near Breendonk. There were members of the Resistance whose ghastly task it was to locate the graves of these unlucky airmen, dig them up, and give them a proper burial. All over Belgium there were graves of unknown soldiers.

Chimay left as silently as he had come. Dinant stood and walked to the sink. She washed the blood from her hands. "You can finish this," she said to Claire. "He needs water and to be bathed. No food until midday. Any sign of infection, send Henri to me at once." She dried her hands on a towel. "The old woman is upstairs?"

Claire nodded. Dinant left the room with her bag, and Henri for the first time that night sat down. Claire suspected that her husband had had nothing to eat since noon.

"I saw the wounded American," Henri said. "The one we found near the plane." His face was ghostly with the memory. He put his head into his hands. "Dinant had him on the table in the kitchen when I went to fetch her. I've never seen . . ."

"Henri, go to bed," Claire said quickly. "You have to sleep. I can manage here, and tomorrow Anthoine may come again and need you. Do you want any food?"

Henry shook his head vehemently. "I couldn't eat," he said.

"Then do as I say." Claire had seldom spoken to her husband in such a sharp tone, but she knew that if she didn't he would not move. That he had seen something terrible she did not doubt. Only sleep might put the images at a bearable remove.

Henri rose slowly from his chair. "I'll just sleep on the sofa in the sitting room," he said. "If you need me . . ."

When Henri had gone, Claire rose and washed her hands at the sink. She filled a large kettle with water, set it on the stove. The man on the floor groaned. When the water was boiling, she added it to cooler water she had already poured into a basin. She unwrapped a small bit of soap, real soap, not the black soap made from ashes. She brought it to her nose and inhaled its fragrance. She set the basin on the stone floor.

By the fire, Claire hesitated, then rolled the airman over. He did not seem to waken, but some color had returned to his skin. She cradled his head and washed his face and neck, his chest and the hollows beneath his shoulders. She wet a sponge with warm water and let it run over him, soaking into the towels she had put at his sides. He was more muscular than she had imagined, but his pelvic bones were sharp in the firelight. Gently, she rubbed away the dried blood that had matted the sworls of dark hair on his good leg. She filled and refilled the basin with clean, warm water.

Theodore Aidan Brice. She said the name aloud. A man was in her kitchen, on her floor, and she knew nothing about him except that he had flown a plane and landed in her village. The man might die in her kitchen, and she would know nothing more about him. On the floor beside him were his possessions — a photograph of a woman, his identification tags, his escape kit, a crumpled pack of cigarettes. The flight suit itself, or what was left of it, would be burned or buried. She wondered if he was married to the woman in the photograph — a pretty, dark-haired woman who looked very young. But then she thought not, because he had no wedding ring. One English airman who had thought he was dying had given his wedding ring to Claire to send back to his wife when the war was over. Claire had refused to take it, assuring the airman he would live. She learned, later, that he had died soon after leaving her home. She wondered where this pilot was from — America was so vast. She wondered, too, what he would sound like; she had not yet heard him speak.

The morphine, as always, was miraculous. She had never ceased to be moved by its power, by the way it could transform a face, remove years, give beauty to the wounded. Pain twisted a man's features, made him ugly; but the morphine erased the pain. The American's face in repose was open — not severe, not pinched. She had seen his eyes only briefly — when he was conscious and had looked at her. They were startling, a remarkable sea green with flecks of gold. His mouth was broad, even when asleep, and she had a sudden vision then of what he might look like someday, after his lips had healed. She glanced at the place on her hand where he had bitten her. There were still faint teeth marks on her skin.

"Too late."

Claire looked up from her crouch on the floor. Dinant stood in the doorway. "She's dead," she said. There was little emotion in her voice. Claire imagined that Dinant, who had seen the worst of it, who had tended the boys who had been tortured, had come to see each death as merely another failure.

"I will tell Bastien," Dinant said. "He will come and will know what to do. And when he comes, he will help you and Henri carry the American into the hiding place. Every minute the pilot is exposed here, you are at risk."

In the Daussois kitchen, Claire thought, Dinant was a field officer, clear-headed, her orders precise. The war was being fought in kitchens and attics all over Belgium.

The pilot slept for hours. In the afternoon, Claire climbed the stairs with a cup of thin broth made with marrow bones. There was just enough room in the hiding place for her to sit, her legs folded under her. For some time, she watched the American, watched his eyes move beneath his veined lids, watched his body quiver and twitch, as if in his dreams he were still flying. She watched also the snow that dusted, then accumulated upon, the small rectangle in the ceiling. As the snow thickened, the light in the crawl space diminished, so that it seemed milky in the small room, the pilot's features less distinct. She thought of the old woman, of how she had lain there and died, of what thoughts and dreams she must have taken with her. Hers was a death that must be laid at the Gestapo's feet, Claire thought, as surely as if they had shot her in that chimney.

From time to time that first day, Claire said the pilot's name aloud, to waken him, to summon him to eat. *Theodore*. And when he finally opened his eyes, the broth was nearly cold.

His hands were swollen and stiff and incapable of holding the bowl without spilling it. He was able to lift his head only slightly. She fed him with a spoon. It was an imperfect arrangement, and sometimes the broth spilled over his lower lip and onto his chin.

She used the cloth in which she had wrapped the hot bowl to wipe his face. His thirst was keen. He asked for water when he was finished, but when she returned with the water, his head again lay against the pillow, and his eyes were closed. She waited beside him.

Perhaps she dozed. A shadow moved across the opening to the crawl space.

"I might have been a German," he said harshly. Anthoine was standing in her bedroom. He meant the open armoire, the attic room clearly seen. He meant she should be careful not to stay too long inside the attic. She crawled back into her bedroom.

"He's sleeping," she said.

"We'll have to waken him," Anthoine said. Claire thought of protesting, but knew that Anthoine would ignore her.

She was not certain that Anthoine, with his pink bulk, would be able to squeeze into the small opening at the back of the armoire; nor was she sure he would find room to sit beside the pilot once he'd managed to get inside. But as Claire waited just outside, she heard two voices — the crude English of Anthoine, who often impatiently called to Claire for a translation, and the barely audible murmur of the American, who tried to answer each question. She heard the words *flak, control cables, Ludwigshafen.* Anthoine told the pilot that a man named Warren had died from his wounds, which did not seem to be news to the American, and that men named McNulty and Shulman had been captured by the Gestapo, which was. The rest of the crew, said Anthoine, were hidden by Resistance workers in the area. One man's arm had been shattered.

Anthoine, satisfied with the interview, wedged himself back through the armoire. When he stumbled to his feet, his face was scarlet with the effort. Claire stood as well. With his bulk and height, Anthoine seemed enormous in the small bedroom, his head bent under the slanted ceiling.

"We must move all the Americans through the lines as quickly as possible," Anthoine said.

"I'm not sure he — "

"It's too risky here for any of them. The Germans know the pilots are hidden."

Claire looked away.

"We'll prepare a passport. We'll need a new photograph taken."

Claire nodded. The photographs the airmen brought with them were almost always useless, though the airmen never seemed to know this. When the air crews had their evasion photos taken at base, each man borrowed a white shirt and tie for the picture, which was supposed to make a pilot look like a civilian. The difficulty was, however, that since all of the men used the same tie, the Germans could not only identify the bearer of the photograph as English or American, but could tell which bomb group the man belonged to.

Anthoine's breath, hovering over hers, stank of old garlic. For a moment Claire had the unlikely idea that he might move her toward the bed. Where was Henri? She was trying to think. She had known Anthoine for years, since primary school, but she could no longer predict with any certainty how anyone she knew might behave. It was odd, she thought, how perfectly ordinary people, people who might not have amounted to much, people one hadn't even noticed or liked, had been transformed by the war. It was as though the years since 1940, in all their misery, had drawn forth character — water from the earth where none had seemed to be before. Before the war, she had not known of Anthoine's stamina or his intelligence, yet because he had changed so during the war, she could not predict how he might act in other matters as well. She thought also, that had it not been for the war, she might never have discovered that Henri, for all his steadiness, was, in crises, physically afraid.

The American slept long into the afternoon and evening. His face seemed to possess, in his sleep, a curious detachment. Rarely had she seen such detachment on the faces of the other men and women who passed through her house. Too often, the particular horrors each had seen and witnessed, and sometimes been a part of, were reflected in their eyes, etched into the creases of their skin. Even on the faces of the young women and the boys.

The American slept so deeply that day she could not rouse him again, not even to give him the water he had asked for. She thought that perhaps he was hoarding his strength, hibernating through the worst of his ordeal. She had an image of him sleeping all the winter, like an animal, rising finally when the warmth came in late March or April.

But that night, as she lay sleeping in her bed, with Henri snoring beside her, she woke to a terrible sound behind the wall that frightened her. It was the frantic scrabbling of a man buried alive, trying to unseal his casket. She opened the back of the armoire, crawled into the darkness, felt the pilot's hands fly past her body, caught them. His skin was shockingly hot to the touch, and when she stripped off the comforters, she discovered with her own hands that his shirt and the bedding were soaked. His body shook violently next to hers, and he spoke English words and phrases she strained to follow, to understand, but couldn't.

She lit a candle, held it near his face. His eyes were open, but as incoherent and as meaningless as his speech. She called to Henri, told him to bring towels soaked in cold water or in the snow. When Henri, in his long underwear, brought them to the attic room, and Claire laid them on the American's skin — on his chest, around his head and face — the pilot tried to fight her, to peel them off, and Claire was astonished by the man's strength. Henri reached in to hold the American down. Claire spoke to the pilot constantly, in a low voice, repeating her words, a kind of incantation. Henri brought new towels when the pilot's skin had turned the cool cloths warm. The American begged for morphine. Claire put a towel between his teeth, which he bit like an epileptic until she had found the syringe and delivered the salve to his veins.

Claire fed the American cool sips of water, while Henri dressed and went for Dinant. The pilot was quieter now, but not yet sensible. Claire listened to him tell of shooting squirrels in the woods, of airplanes with threads attached falling from the ceiling. Once he seemed lucid and asked her name.

Once again, Dinant came with her medicines and her bag. Without greeting, the woman crawled into the attic and began to cut the bandages open, exposing the source of infection. The wound, a grotesque open sore, had festered. Dinant poured alcohol into the wound and cleaned it. The pilot moaned and lost consciousness. Dinant gave the American a tetanus shot, then fashioned a different sort of bandage, a partial closure held together with bits of cloth tied at strategic places. For days, it seemed, Claire sat with the pilot, who hovered between sanity and madness. The infection refused to heal, but did not travel. Dinant wanted the leg off altogether in case gangrene set in, but Claire, who knew a man with only one leg would not make it through the lines, held the woman off — just another day, she said; just another hour — a defensive line that seemed easy to breach, but proved, in the event, to be impregnable.

———

A hundred faces hovered over him, and in the crowd he searched for his brother. His brother was thirteen or fourteen and was wearing a red plaid flannel shirt. It was important to find Matt among the faces; there was something Ted had to tell him. But Matt couldn't be there, could he, because Matt had gone to war as well, and in the war had died in the water. The ship, the telegram said, sank in the Pacific when it was hit by a torpedo. The telegram didn't say if Matt was drowned in the darkness, or if pieces of him fell into the water and drifted slowly down, or if, in the ferocious heat of midday, Matt let go of a bit of wood and dove into the coolness of the dark, beautifully colored water. Water and air. They were dying in all the elements.

So Matt couldn't be in the crowd, and in truth, when he opened his eyes, there was no crowd at all, no one by his side. He seemed to be in a small portion of an attic, with the roof of the house slanting about five feet above his head. In this ceiling there was a rectangle open to the sky, through which he saw differing shades of gray, slow movement from one side to the other. Were there clues in this movement, in the color of the sky? He tried to remember where he was, what had happened to him. There had been people with him, he was certain. He remembered a woman, a large-boned woman with a coarse face, who wore a kerchief tied around her head and who treated his leg after the morphine and wrapped it in wet bandages soaked with plaster. He felt the stab of pain, but soon it passed away, and he was floating. And sometime after that he got the fever and began to shiver, and he begged for the morphine again, begged through the wall until the other woman came and put a cool cloth on his forehead and held his hand.

And with her hand clasped in his, he had drifted.

He propped himself up as best he could and lifted the comforter from his body. He saw that he was wearing a man's shirt that seemed to be too wide and yet too short for him, and a pair of trousers that lay loosely around his waist. Raising the comforter even higher, he noticed that the trousers were too short as well and exposed the skin above his left sock. Along the right leg, the cloth had been cut to the thigh to allow for a bulky bandage. He imagined that if he could stand, the trousers would drop from his waist.

When they cleaned the wound, he remembered, the younger woman had had her hair down in the candlelight, as she bent over him, pinning him down. A man's coat had fallen open, and under it was a nightgown that looked ivory in the flickering light. He remembered the shallow V of her clavicle, delineated beneath her skin. Her hair — a thick, silky, dark blond — was like a veil that hid her face, and he remembered, in his pain, his delirium, wanting to ask her to reveal her face, and not being able to form even the English words to his question.

But he had seen her face since. It was she who had been sitting by his side, he was certain. He remembered large gray eyes and a wide brow. Sometimes she seemed to be hovering over him, sometimes to be looking away. At other times she read while she thought he slept. The eyes were sad; her face was distinctly foreign. Something in the cheekbones, the shape of her mouth; the mouth, he thought, formed by the words of her own language, by their vowels, so that in repose, her lower lip thrust slightly forward. She spoke an English precisely her own, throaty with a heavy accent that drenched the words and made him think of bread soaked in wine. Interesting words and unexpected: *anguish, supple, garland*. And then words of her own, names he had never heard before: *Avram, Charleroi, Liège*.

Her scent was of yeasty bread and violets. He smelled her scent on her throat when she leaned over him, a scent like the steam of baking bread. He saw the underside of her chin, the white of her wrists when they pulled away from her blouse. She reached across him, and in doing so, she lifted her face. He imagined her skin would feel like kid, soft but with texture. There was within him the faintest stirring of desire. He allowed himself to linger on the image of her body in her nightgown, though he sensed that this lingering would make him anxious. Her hair was cut just below her shoulders, the dark blond a color that changed with the light in the attic room, although most often when she sat with him, she wore it rolled. He realized with surprise that he had not even been told her name, or if he had, he didn't now remember it.

He thought it was a kind of anesthesia, the body's natural anesthesia, forgetfulness and sleep, but now, in the vacuum, questions were forming. What of the plane, and where were the men? Someone was dead, and someone was dying, though it had been perhaps days, and the gunner would be dead by now, he was certain. Suddenly Ted was hot; a film of sweat was on his face and neck. All around him there were German pilots in their planes. Where were Case, Tripp, McNulty? Had anyone gotten away? Had he been told that some had crossed the border into France, or had he dreamed that? Where did the bombs go, and could he have made it to the Channel? Hesitation and indecision. He had to get word back to base. He was in Belgium. He remembered now the word *Belgique,* the boy's voice frantic and insistent, crowded with tears; and the word in English, the woman's voice, low and soothing, pronouncing the name of her country as if the word itself were sanctuary.

———

She came in from the milking, washed her hands at the pump. She had seen to the herd, washed out yesterday's milk cans, poured the fresh milk into clean ones and left them, as she and Henri always did, at the end of the road for Monsieur Lechat to collect in his wagon. Lechat would take the milk to the shops and to various customers in the village. Sometimes, when Lechat collected the milk cans and left off the empty ones, he would leave a small sum of money in a metal box. It was what she and Henri lived on. Since the coming of the Germans and the decimation of their herd, the box held very little.

Henri had been gone since daybreak. He would not tell her where he was going, so that if she were questioned, she truly would not know. When Henri was gone, Claire saw to the chores. Regardless of the course of the war, the cows had to be milked and fed. More important, the appearance of seeing to the chores had to be maintained at all costs. The surest way to be denounced, Claire knew, was to draw attention to oneself. Any break in routine could rouse suspicion.

In itself, the work on the farm gave her little satisfaction. She was not like Henri in this. As a girl, she had not thought that she would spend her life as a farmer's wife. Before the war, she had imagined herself at university, in Antwerp or Brussels. Though she supposed now that she had always known that marrying Henri was inevitable.

In its own way, the coupling had been foreordained since she was in grade school, the two families well known to each other, tied to each other by several marriages and by blood. She and Henri were cousins, distant enough for the church to overlook the tentative blood relation. As though they had known, even as children, that a connection of some kind would be made between them, they had drawn together at family gatherings and at festivals to test each other out, to feel what might or might not be possible. And sometimes, if they met in the street, he would take her for a coffee in the café, and she felt important, in her schoolgirl's uniform, sitting with this man, who was then already, at twenty-one, twenty-two, a presence in the village.

They married finally when she was nineteen and he was twenty-seven, when the war in Europe was beginning. He had taken over his father's farm, and it was thought that Claire was old enough to marry.

On the marble mantel, beside the crucifix and the candles, was a photograph of Henri and herself on their wedding day. Henri, who was not much taller than Claire, wore a dark suit, and his hair had been brushed off his face with oil. It was summer, and in the photograph Henri looked uncomfortably hot. The suit was wool, the only one he owned. Claire had been married in a brown suit. She had sent to Paris for the pattern and had sewn it herself. Her mother had given her the pearl earrings and made the lace collar. No one made lace anymore, Claire thought, at least no one of her own generation. Her mother was nearly seventy-three now. She'd been fifty when Claire was born, the last of eleven children. In the wedding photograph, Claire had her hair rolled at the sides and in a snood at the back, and the hat she had splurged on to match the suit had a veil that covered her eyes. She was holding a bouquet of ivory roses with a satin ribbon that trailed down the front of her suit. Her lips seemed exaggerated with a thick, dark lipstick — as if she had not yet been kissed.

The stove was putting out a good deal of warmth — a heat that was designed to rise and permeate the stone farmhouse. Even on gray days, she thought, the room had a kind of inherent cheer. Wherever she had been able, she had placed color — the green-checked tablecloth; a hand-colored photograph of the Ardennes in spring; a blue glass vase, now filled with dried flowers, on the table. She prepared the bread and coffee to take to the pilot upstairs. It was past breakfast already, and Claire was trying to wean the pilot, who had been floating in a timeless vacuum, onto a schedule.

She set the tray on the floor of her bedroom. Immediately she became aware of a sound she had not heard before behind the wall. She stood a moment and listened. She thought it was the sound of whistling. She could not identify the tune, but it was distinctly a song, not merely another set of meaningless sounds.

She crawled through the false back of the armoire. As soon as she had done so, the American turned his head to meet her eyes, stopped whistling.

"What is your name?" he asked.

Claire knelt motionless, unable, for a moment, to answer him. Though she had been waiting for this, the clarity of his question shocked her. She thought then that all the time she had

sat with this man, she had not really believed that he would recover. She had imagined instead that he would linger for months
or possibly years in a suspended state.

"My name is Claire," she said.

He nodded slowly. "Yes, I remember now."

"And you are Theodore Aidan."

He laughed. "No, just Ted." He looked at the coffee and the
bread on the tray as if observing food for the first time.

"Is that coffee?" he asked.

"It's not real."

She made her way to her usual spot beside the pilot's bedding.
She wound her legs under her as she always did, but this morning
the gesture seemed awkward, and her legs felt too long and ungainly. Before, she had sat with him with her hair down, in her
robe if necessary, giving little thought, no thought, to how she was
dressed or how she looked. The pilot, in his transcendent state,
had seemed disembodied, not a man actually, but rather a casualty,
a patient in the most objective sense, a thing to watch over, a task
that defined her days. But now that he had returned to his body,
could speak, could ask her questions, he seemed another entity
altogether.

For the first time since she had begun tending him, she became acutely aware of how crowded the attic room was, of how
difficult it was to sit without somehow touching his bedding —
with her knee, with her foot. She drew herself together more
tightly. She had dressed hastily after waking and had rolled her
hair ineptly, thinking it unlikely that today she would see anyone
from the village. She had on a gray wool skirt that stopped at her
knees, and rode above them when she sat. She was wearing a
white long-sleeved blouse with padded shoulders, and over that
her apron. She had white socks on her feet and shoes with leather
uppers and wooden soles, ugly shoes, work shoes. Her legs were
bare. She had forgotten her lipstick. Loose strands of hair hung
at the sides of her face. Impatiently, she pushed them away.

"It's ersatz coffee," she explained. "We are not having real
coffee since before the war."

She handed him the bowl. She watched as he took it, focused on the task of holding the bowl with both hands, brought it to his lips. He took a small sip.

"It's awful," he said, smiling at his success.

She gave him the dark bread from the tray. He experimented with his fingers, distant tools that were wayward and seemed not always to obey his command. Several of the fingers were bandaged still, and the skin was shedding itself from the pads of the last three digits of his right hand. He could hold the bread when the roll was large, but fumbled with it when he had only a small piece left. She caught it on the comforter, held it to his mouth.

She watched him chew the bread.

"Is this your house?" he asked.

She nodded.

"What day is it?"

"It is six, January."

"Then I've been here . . ." He seemed to be calculating.

"Seven days."

"And all that time . . ."

"You have been here, on this bed."

He sat up sharply. "I have to try to contact the crew."

She pushed him gently on his chest. "Is done," she said. "Your crew is knowing where you are."

"Some of the men in the plane died," he said.

She nodded. "Two. One is dead already when your aeroplane crashed. One is . . . died," she corrected, "in the night of the crash."

"And the others?"

"Two are taken by the Germans. We think to Breendonk first. This is a prison near Brussels. And then after Breendonk?" She held her hands open as though to say no one could be certain where in Germany they might be sent.

He looked away briefly. "Do you know their names?"

"They are called McNulty and Shulman."

The pilot closed his eyes and nodded.

"Is story of your friends McNulty and Shulman," she said.

"When they are first captured, the Germans are offering them cigarettes. But the Americans, your friends, they are turning their heads to the side and not taking them."

The American smiled briefly. "And there was a man called Case. He was shot in the arm. Do you know where he is?"

"All the other men are sent into France, and are now trying to reach Spain. The man you are speaking of, his arm is very badly broken. It is said that he is minding that he will not be able to play *base ball*. Yes?"

The American smiled again. "That's Case. He signed with the Boston Braves just before the war. Bad break."

"Yes, the break is bad," she said, agreeing with him.

"No, I meant, bad luck."

"Ah. Yes."

"We were on our way to Germany," he said.

She nodded.

"To bomb a chemical plant," he added. "I've said this before?"

She nodded. "There is a man here, from the Resistance. He is asking you questions about your plane, to send a missile back to England."

"Message," he corrected.

She smiled with embarrassment. "Message. My English is very bad."

"Your English is very good. And I told him about the mission?"

"Yes."

"Do you know where the bombs fell?" he asked quickly.

She heard the strain in his voice. She hesitated, and he saw her hesitate.

She shook her head. "No," she said, looking down. She saw that there was a light dusting of flour on her apron. She tried to brush it away.

"In the mornings, I am baking," she said.

"Where in Belgium am I?"

His voice had a clarity she had not heard in his incoherent ramblings. Its timbre was different as well — deeper, more resonant than she remembered. "Our village is called Delahaut," she said. "It is in southern Belgium, thirty kilometers from the French border."

"And other people live in this house with you."

"There is only myself and my husband, who is called Henri," she said.

The American seemed puzzled.

"There have been others. From time to time. To help you. To ask you questions."

She would not give him Anthoine's name, or Thérèse Dinant's. There was no need for him to know.

His eyes had changed as well. The green had grown clearer, more translucent, as if his eyes, too, had taken on life. His nose was large, square at the bottom, like his jawline. His face was long, much longer and narrower than the faces of the southern Belgians. She liked his mouth. The bottom lip was straight, the upper curved. He smiled often. A good color had returned to his skin. He needed to have his hair combed.

"How bad is the leg?" he asked.

Briefly, she considered how much she should tell him, and decided this time to tell him the truth.

"Is nearly lost," she said. "To the infection. But the woman who is here?" She looked at him expectantly to see if he remembered. He nodded slowly.

"She is saving your leg. There is . . ."

She thought. She was about to say "terrible," but she did not want to frighten him. ". . . a bad scar nearly to your ankle. Yes?"

She meant: Was that all right? Could he stand that?

He shrugged.

She answered his next question before he could ask it.

"And when you are standing, we will see how you are walking."

He nodded.

"But I think, not yet. Not so soon. Not today." She shook her head quickly.

He seemed about to speak, to protest. She reached into the pocket of her skirt, pulled out a photograph. She held the picture out to him. He could not manage so thin a piece of paper with his fingers, so she put the photograph into the flat of his palm. She studied his face as he looked at the picture.

"It is your friend, yes?" she asked.

He nodded. "Her name is Stella," he said quietly. "She's my fiancée. Do you know that word?"

"We have that word."

He handed her back the picture, but she stopped him.

"No, I think is good for you to keep it nearly to you." She took the photograph from his hand and laid it on the comforter. "I would write to her? Or to your mother? But . . ." Claire shrugged. "It is not safe now. You are understanding me? Perhaps not so long after you have left us, I can do that."

His eyes were fixed on hers. "Before we landed," he said slowly, "just before we belly-landed, we had to let the bombs go. I want to know where they fell."

This time she deliberately did not move her eyes from his. "No one is telling me this," she said. "Possibly you left them in Germany?"

"I don't think so. I don't see how. . . ."

"Then I will ask someone if this is known."

"What happened to the plane?" he asked.

"The Maquis, they have removed some of the guns and a machine that . . ." She struggled. ". . . finds the place where the bombs are to be dropping — "

"The Norden bombsight," he said quickly.

"And then the Germans are coming and surrounding the plane, and taking pieces of it, and are very angry because some of the guns are missing. And so they are putting all the villagers in the church and asking them about the guns, but no one is saying anything to the Germans. And now the Germans are watching your plane, but" — she made a dismissive sound — "is only three old soldiers who are watching it, so I think is nothing there of importance."

"What is the Maquis?"

"Is Resistance. Soldiers of Resistance."

"Have you seen the plane?"

She shook her head. "No. I have been here always. But I have heard it pictured to me."

A gust of wind shook the pane of glass in the rectangle, and she looked up at the window. The sky was darker, more oily; the storm would soon begin. Because of the impending storm, the light in the crawl space had taken on a yellowish cast. Oddly, she thought of the Hopkins she had begun before the American came. "For skies of couple-colour as a brindled cow . . ." She wanted to read this difficult poem to the American, to ask him if he knew the English words *couple-colour* and *brindled*. Perhaps later, when he was not so weak.

She looked around at the small space in which she sat and he lay. Layers of old wallpaper were peeling from the walls. She wondered if once, years ago, this attic room had been part of the bedroom, or of another room in the attic.

"There was a boy," the pilot said.

"Yes," she said quietly. "The boy who is saving you."

The pilot nodded.

"But you must not tell any person about him. Yes? Is very dangerous for him."

"I would like to thank him," Ted said.

She tilted her head as if to say *maybe*. "Perhaps we are arranging this."

He was looking closely at her face. She lowered her eyes, unused to such scrutiny. A sudden warmth rose along her throat and lodged behind her ears.

"You've hidden others here as well," he said.

She nodded.

"Who was here before me?"

Claire looked up at him. "There is a woman who is fleeing Antwerp. The Gestapo, they have taken away her son and her husband. When the Resistance is finding her, they are sending her to me to get well, and then I am sending her to France, as you one day will go to France, but she is very ill, and she is dying here."

"Dying? Here?"

"Yes. The night you are coming here. She is died already."

"This is dangerous work that you and your husband do."

She looked away, arranged the bowl and plate on the small tray. "It is not so dangerous as the work the others are doing. I am safe here unless I am denounced. The work my husband is doing is more dangerous."

"What does he do?"

"I do not know. He is telling me very little of his work, because is safer for me to know as little as possible. Is true for everyone. Even you."

"How old are you?"

"I am twenty-four years. Why is it you are asking me this?"

"Just curious. Have you been married long?"

She smoothed her skirt as far as it would go along her legs. "Four years."

"And you don't have any children?"

She shook her head quickly.

The American lifted the comforter a fraction and looked down at his shirt. "I noticed that these clothes . . ."

She smiled. "They are the clothes of my husband. They are fitting you — "

"Pretty badly." He grinned. "I don't suppose you have any cigarettes."

"Yes," she answered. From her pocket she produced a crumpled packet. "Forgive," she said, "but already I am smoking all your cigarettes. These are mine and are not so nice as yours."

She put the cigarette in her own mouth, lit it, then handed it to him. Gently she helped him hold it by wrapping his index finger around it and pressing it close to his thumb. He took a deep drag, exhaled through his nose. He coughed once. "Strong," he said.

The smell of the tobacco quickly filled the small space. She wanted to join him, but she knew that the room would soon become too thick with smoke. She watched him enjoy his cigarette. She brushed away an ash that fell on the comforter.

"Your hands are becoming more well," she said. "Each day I see this. You should not worry about your hands."

"Frostbite?"

She pondered this English word. "You fingers are freezing in the forest," she said. "Is the same?"

"Yes."

"Frost bite," she repeated. "Frost eats the fingers?"

"Something like that."

He reached toward her with the cigarette, held it out to her. She hesitated, then took it. She pulled on it quickly, gave it back to him.

She raised herself on her knees a fraction. She brushed her hair behind her ears. "Is too much talking for first time," she said. "I am thinking now that you should sleep. In one hour, I will bring you soup. You must return your strength, because we have little time to do very many things."

"What things?" he asked.

She maneuvered her way to the trapdoor.

"I must make you ready to leave," she said.

January 16, 17, and 18, 1944

THE DUSK A CAMOUFLAGE. HIDING IN THE TREES. OAK, beech. Bracken on the forest floor. He stood at the edge of the field and waited for his own eyes, which were sharp, to make out the shape of the fallen plane. The pneumatic jacks that had long since deflated lay discarded under the wings. In the near dark, the broken plane looked tired and sad — already a relic. On the other side of the fuselage, smoke rose.

His own mission, secret, self-ordered. A test of will, and already he was worried he would fail. His body trembled, and in his vision he saw spots at the periphery. He made himself move forward to gain a better view. Two men, one sleeping in a roll of blankets near the fire. Yes, he thought, it might work. A sleeping guard, trapped as he was, would not be able to reach his weapon quickly, even if he awakened. The other guard sat hunched by the fire. The German soldier had wrapped his greatcoat over his head and around his shoulders. To trap the heat. Like an old woman with a shawl bent over her cooking fire. The hunched German moved slightly. A flicker of a knife blade, a long sausage, a movement of the knife blade from the sausage to the mouth. Of course, there would be only the two, he thought, three to rotate at staggered hours. A lonely watch far from town. He saw now a bicycle at the other side of the field, perhaps a second — the light was fading fast. He would have to take the hunched old woman first.

He pulled his own knife from his coat pocket, held it at the ready. His hand shook so badly he was afraid the guards would see a shimmery reflection. Retracing his steps so that he was looking at the plane from behind the guards. How casual they were, he thought — how lazy, inept. He also thought: *Now. It must be now.*

He crossed the matted field until he reached the cold metal of the plane. In a shadow he stood, listening for sounds above the rush of blood in his ears. The snoring of the sleeping German, a small shuffle. To reach the squatting guard first, he would have to circle the plane by its nose.

For days now he had been imagining the quick gestures, the snap of the head, the clean cut, so that when the moment finally came he wouldn't falter, wouldn't panic. Only seconds left now. As one man against two, he could not afford to sacrifice the element of surprise.

He cleared the nose of the B-17. He was certain he had not made a sound, but the hunched German turned slightly, cocking his ear, as though he might have sensed a presence. In the firelight, the Belgian saw the wet gray bristles of the guard's mustache, the knifepoint with its morsel of sausage in the open mouth.

In one swift movement, he reached the guard's back. The German turned, and in doing so lowered his knife. The cloak slipped from his head. Before the guard could cry out, the Belgian slapped his hand over the guard's mouth, heard him choke once on the piece of sausage. He jerked the German's head and slit the bare throat above the collar of the hated uniform. The guard in the bedroll opened his eyes, fought in a panic to free himself. Kneeling quickly then over the frightened German, executing the same cut from left to right on bare skin. Blood spurting in an arc. The Belgian reared away and stood.

His body shuddered and his bowels loosened. Stunned, he watched the German in the bedroll drown. The knife and his hand were covered with a blood that seemed black in the firelight. He thought then that he would throw the knife into the fire, burn the blood from its surface, but the fingers of his hand refused to relax their grip. He stood for a moment paralyzed, as if the knife had been welded, grafted, to his body.

And then he heard the small sound of metal chafing metal. He turned and saw a third German, his face dazed and creased with sleep, a revolver in his hand, emerging from the belly of the plane. Panicky now and flailing wildly, the Belgian knocked the revolver from the old man's hand, twisted the frightened face away from him, and dispatched this guard as he had the others. The German, his feet still pinned inside the fuselage, fell backwards over the lip of the door, toward the ground.

The Belgian began to shake violently. An awful sound came from his body. He threw down the knife, as if it had a life of its own, as if it might turn itself against him. Then, thinking better of this gesture, he picked it up again. He bent and wiped the blood from the blade as best he could on the coat of the guard who had been eating sausage. How was it they had posted all three guards at once? Or had the old soldiers simply been camping out here — a kind of sorry outpost?

He had expected to feel something — if not triumph exactly, then at least success. He had done what he set out to do. So he was confused for a moment to discover that what he felt was a kind of numbness, a terrible hollowness in his bowels, perhaps even a small seed of dread. He moved away from the plane, looking at the work of seconds, the bodies of the three old Germans in the firelight. He turned and stumbled then back to the forest.

———

Madness.

Anthoine shook his head, put his head in his hands. Angrier than Henri had ever seen him. A small lantern, shrouded with a cloth and set in the center of their circle, was the only light in Chimay's barn. Each had been called from sleep. Underneath his coat, Henri still wore his nightshirt. Emilie had not undone the braid she wore to bed. At this unforgiving hour, roused abruptly as if there had been a fire, Emilie, without her lipstick or her hair framing her face, looked years older than Henri had imagined her to be — fifty possibly, perhaps fifty-five. Her face still bore the greasy traces of her night cream.

Léon Balle smoking, coughing quietly into his gloved hand. Dussart hunched, trembling inside his thin coat. Where was the boy's enthusiasm now? Dussart had forgotten his beret, and his hair had separated over the place where he had lost his ear. Henri, who had never really examined the scar, was fascinated.

Anthoine trying to control himself. Speaking in this slow, deliberate manner only when he was enraged and was trying to remain calm. He smoked fast, with short pulls and exhales, as if that, too, might contain his anger. Anthoine had waited for them all to arrive, had spoken to no one until he made his pronouncement. *Madness,* he had said.

Henri waited. Anthoine stubbed out his cigarette on the dirt floor with a sharp twist of his boot heel.

Finally, Anthoine's announcement. Someone has killed the three Germans guarding the plane.

A long silence in the barn.

Jesus God. Emilie whispering.

Léon Balle leaning back, looking at the ceiling of the barn. Bastien, a small, pinched man with pointed teeth that reminded Henri of a rodent, shaking his head in disgust. Dussart, the boy, trembling inside his coat. Henri thought he must be ill. The young man rubbing his hands along his arms as if to warm them.

They'll think it was us. Anthoine now.

Léon then. There'll be reprisals.

Reprisals. Henri bent over. He felt heat on the surface of his skin.

Emilie spoke as if from a great distance.

The reprisals will be catastrophic, Anthoine said slowly, giving weight to each word. The house searches have already begun. They've taken Madame Bossart from her bed.

Mother of God, this is not possible. Emilie shaking her head in bewilderment. Madame Bossart is nearly seventy-five. What could they possibly want with such an old woman?

Her farm is nearest to the plane. They think she may have hidden the assassin, or one of the Americans.

This is insane.

It's what they do. We knew that.

Will it be like Virelles? Bastien talking, but everyone knew the horror of Virelles. Every male in the village, including the boy children, had been rounded up and shot in the village square in front of their wives and mothers. The SS had even worked out an equation: For every German wounded, three Belgians would die; for every German killed, ten Belgians would die.

When were they killed? asked Emilie.

The bodies were found tonight by a sentry delivering the evening meal.

Silence settling upon the circle. The light flickering in the lantern.

Anthoine turning to Van der Elst. Adrien. You and Elise should get out at once. The Germans have been suspecting you for some time. Don't return to your apartment. I'm going to put you through the lines tonight.

Elise starting forward at the news. Van der Elst clenching his jaw.

Anthoine turned to Henri.

Henri felt his stomach spasm. Unlike Van der Elst and his wife, he knew, he and Claire could not leave Delahaut. They had the American. He thought suddenly of Jean Burnay of nearby Florennes. The Belgian had sheltered five British aviators in his home. One of the aviators was caught further down the line in France and talked. Burnay and his wife were beheaded by the Gestapo.

Henri, your risk is probably less than Adrien's. But if they can take Madame Bossart, they can take anyone. Emilie will go to Claire, tell her to hide herself inside the house.

Henri nodded. But he wondered why Anthoine was not sending himself, Henri, to tell Claire. His mouth felt dry. He ran his tongue over his lips. He felt another severe spasm in his gut; he needed badly to find a toilet. He thought of Claire, alone at home with the injured American. Perhaps even now the Gestapo were raiding the house, dragging Claire from her bed.

Are there always reprisals? Dussart asked in a thin voice from his seat. It was the first the young man had spoken.

Anthoine looking at Dussart. There are always reprisals, he

said slowly. And it's worse. Tonight I have received additional intelligence that the escape routes are now the primary focus of the Germans in southern Belgium.

Thérèse must be told, said Emilie.

And Dolane.

And Dolane. And Hainaert. And Duceour.

In Charleroi, at least they have the tablets. Léon talking, his head in his hands.

A stillness in the barn. Henri felt a throbbing in his right temple. They all knew what Léon meant. In the cities, where the Maquis was better organized and had more funds, more access to matériel, each Resistance fighter was given a single tablet of cyanide. To contain the damage in the event of torture. Few men or women, no matter how brave, could withstand the prolonged and creative torture of the Gestapo — he'd heard it all — the electric prods and needles to the testicles, the gouging of the eyes. Without the cyanide, every man was a traitor.

Henri put his hands against the hay bale on which he sat, to give him leverage, to help him stand. His legs felt weak, and he did not want to stumble in front of the others.

Léon Balle looking up. White-faced with anger. Who gave a shit about the three guards? Was there a reason? Was anything taken from the plane?

Anthoine answering. There was nothing on the plane of any real value. The guns had been seized long ago.

Léon shaking his head as though he could not process this unthinkable information. Coughing suddenly and violently, and reaching for a handkerchief in his pocket.

Anthoine turning to Henri, who had managed to stand. I'm sorry, Henri, Anthoine was saying. It's not safe to move the American. There's a chance it could blow the whole Eva line.

Henri nodding stiffly. If the Eva line were blown, the denunciations, like a lit fuse that ran out from Delahaut in two directions — north to Charleroi and south to France — would be massive. Dozens, maybe hundreds, might be arrested and executed.

You'll stay here with me, Anthoine was saying now. There's a lot to do.

Anthoine himself, for the first time Henri could remember, looking afraid. Despite the cold, his thinning white-blond hair lay matted with sweat against his pink scalp.

We won't meet again for a while. Anthoine speaking, looking away from Henri, then to each of the others in turn. Henri realizing then, with the shock of an absolute truth, that before they met again, some of their number would be dead.

Anthoine bending down, removing the cloth shroud and the glass from the lantern. Blowing out the light. Léon Balle asked a question in the darkness.

Did someone really imagine that killing three old impotent men would change the course of the war?

———

She awoke feeling better than she had for days, perhaps weeks. The sun, which they had not seen since before the day the plane fell on the Heights, shone through the lace at the windows, making a filigree on the polished floor. Claire turned in the bed, felt immediately its emptiness, and remembered that Anthoine, sometime in the night, had come for Henri.

She thought of the American beyond the flower-papered wall — a silent, sleeping prisoner. Or perhaps he wasn't sleeping. Possibly he was already sitting, waiting for her to greet him with his breakfast. Yes, the sunlight had doubtless wakened him as well, she decided, shining as it must be through the rectangle.

She slipped from the bed and knocked on the wall that separated them. He knocked back and said, in a voice that was surprisingly distinct, even through the wall, "Bonjour Madame."

She shook her head. His accent was atrocious.

"Bonjour Monsieur. Je pars au village pour chercher de l'eau potable à la fontaine. Je reviens tout de suite. Pouvez-vous attendre?"

She smiled and waited.

"I never had a chance," he said finally.

"I am going to the village for drinking water from the fountain. Can you wait? I am not being long."

"Sure. But hurry. I'm starved."

Claire dressed quickly, saw to the fire in the stove, and collected her bicycle. She wondered again where Henri was, when he would arrive home. His hours lately had become increasingly erratic. She seldom knew when to prepare a meal for him, or even if he would spend the night. The two of them were all right as long as it was winter, when there was less to do about the farm. But when spring came, he would be needed. Claire wondered how they would manage then.

Most of the ice along the rue St. Laurent had melted or had been scuffed with dirt so that the ride to the village was not as hazardous as it had been in days past. Before she got the drinking water, she would stop at Madame Omloop's for the flour and potatoes and sugar and salt. With each day, the American's appetite had increased. It was not even the middle of the month yet, and it was clear Claire's stamps would not extend until the thirty-first. Madame Rosenthal had barely eaten at all and had not taxed the Daussois rations.

It was exhilarating, the sun. Odd how it could lift the spirits, she thought. She passed the Marchal farm and the Mailleux. The stone was pale in the early light, and though there were no people about yet, it was just possible to imagine that there was no war, had never been, that soon the narcissus and hyacinth would pop above the soil and that the man in her attic was merely a convalescing visitor.

She reached the outskirts of the village proper, began to pedal along the rue de Florennes. And it was somewhere along that narrow street, with its uneven cobblestones, that she realized something was different, amiss. She stopped before she reached the corner, before she would then turn into the rue Cerfontaine, and then at the following corner, into the public square. She listened closely. Yes, that was it: There were no sounds. No voices, no shouting of schoolchildren, no doors opening and closing, no clatter of bicycles, no vehicles negotiating the narrow side streets, sending cyclists careening into the brick walls. No cursing from those cyclists.

Something was wrong, but she didn't know what. Had a curfew been imposed, and she and Henri, so far from the village, failed to hear of it? On foot, she pushed her bicycle, hugging the wall. The water jugs rattled in the pannier. She peered around the corner and saw nothing. She would have to advance to yet another corner to see into the village square.

Instinct warned her to retrace her steps and her ride, to pedal back to the house as quickly as she could. But she had no water! Surely there would be activity at the fountain. Or at Omloop's. The Flemish woman never closed her shop, not even on the saints' days.

She walked her bicycle to the next corner and, standing as close to the wall as she could, bent her head and looked into the village square. Now there could be no mistake. The square, with its steepled church, its village hall with the wide stone steps, and the old monastery that was now a school, was barren. Not even the pigeons, huddled in the eaves of the church, had bothered to descend to its cobblestones. The fountain bubbled unattended.

A chill settled low in her back. Fumbling with her bicycle and pannier, she turned around, intending now to return home. She hoped only that she would not be seen. There must have been a curfew imposed: No other explanation seemed plausible. She would have to wait for information, wait for Henri to return. Perhaps she could get food, enough for the three of them, from the Marchal farm, if Marie-Louise would open her door to her.

She was nearly to the corner of the rue de Florennes when she heard a faint sound. She stopped, stood astride her bicycle. It was the unmistakable hum of a motor — but from which direction? She listened again, knowing she might be wasting precious moments. The motor — a car? a truck? — was coming from the direction in which she wished to go.

Chancing a sighting, she pulled her scarf forward over her head to hide her face, bent low over her handlebars and pedaled as fast as she could past the rue de Florennes. She knew the back streets and alleys of Delahaut well. If she could make it to the rue de Canard, she knew of an alley there that permitted a bicycle, but not a four-wheeled vehicle. It wouldn't prevent a sentry from noticing her and requiring her to halt, but she would be free of the motor. For to Claire, in the eerie silence of the village, the motor suggested only one thing: Germans.

Having not dared to look up, she didn't know if she had been spotted. Surely, she thought, a lone cyclist would be observed from behind the ubiquitous lace curtains at every window. Why did no one call to her, allow her to hide herself and her bicycle in one of the stone vestibules found behind each streetfront door?

When she reached the alley, she was struggling for breath. She had not pedaled so hard since she was a girl. Still astride her bicycle, she allowed herself to rest a moment, leaning against the back brick wall of a villager's terraced house. The icy air, taken in large gulps, hurt her lungs.

Perhaps, she thought, as she rested, she could reach Omloop's via the same kind of twisting route by which she had reached the safety of the alley. Even more than food now, Claire needed information and possibly somewhere to hide. Madame Omloop could not fail to help Claire, even in the extraordinary event that the shop was not open for business.

More cautiously now, Claire proceeded, listening hard at each blind turn, sticking to the alleys and to the narrow pathway that ran behind the cemetery. Once she saw a figure, not a soldier, run from one side of the street to the other, then disappear.

Her journey took her fifteen minutes, and when she reached Madame Omloop's, she was no longer surprised to see its door shut tight. Along her way, Claire had not observed a single open shop. Looking up and down the narrow lane on which Omloop's was located, Claire quickly rapped on the glass pane of the door. In the distance she could hear again the sound of a motor.

She rapped again — short, fast taps on the stained glass.

She rapped a third time.

There was a minute movement of the door's lace panel.

Claire bent close to the glass. "Madame Omloop," she whispered as loudly as she dared, "it's Claire Daussois."

The door opened quickly. Madame Omloop tugged sharply at Claire's coat sleeve, pulled her inside, and shut the door.

"Are you crazy?" Madame Omloop asked angrily. "You cannot come here. Can you not see the shop is closed? Go home at once."

"I don't know what has happened," Claire said.

"The reprisals! My God! Do you not know about the reprisals?"

Reprisals. Claire now understood the eerie silence of the village. She thought at once of Henri.

"Reprisals for what?" Claire asked.

"Someone has killed the German guards who were by the plane. The Gestapo have taken nearly the entire village," said Madame Omloop. "They have put everyone in the school. All the men and boys, and they are even taking women and babies."

Madame Omloop's fear was electric, contagious.

"God save us," Madame Omloop said. "It was a terrible day when that plane fell on our village. You must go at once back to your house, lock yourself in. Hide if you can."

"Henri," Claire said. "Henri has not come home."

Madame Omloop looked at the younger woman. "Wait here," she said.

In less than a minute the Flemish shopkeeper returned with three rashers of bacon, a large wedge of cheese wrapped in cloth.

"I have this food, and now it cannot all be eaten. Take this and go. Quickly."

The alley past the cemetery led, Claire knew, to a footpath that soon entered the wood on its eastern side. It was a footpath she had sometimes taken as a schoolgirl — a shortcut between the village and the river, but normally a roundabout way to reach her house. It would mean that she would have to push the bicycle the entire way and that it might take as long as two hours to get home. But it would keep her off the main road. She walked briskly, trying to stifle her fear. The American would wonder what was taking her so long. She prayed that when she got back, Henri would be there to help her.

———

He waited as long as he could. He thought he might be able to manage it. He wanted to try.

He dragged himself through the attic opening and then through the armoire. Alone, on the floor of Claire's bedroom, taking in its contents for the first time, he turned and rose to the one good knee, looked for something upon which to brace himself. The footboard of the bed would work, he thought.

Not only was his right leg useless, he discovered, but his arms were also weak. He managed a standing position, holding himself against the slanted roof of the room. Gingerly, he put some weight on the bad leg, was answered immediately with a jolt of hot pain that made him dizzy. Hopping with the good leg and bracing with his hands, he made his way to the top of the stairs, and then with the aid of the bannister to the floor below. He leaned against the wall and rested. He felt momentarily light-headed. How was he supposed to plan an escape — or participate in an escape plan — if he couldn't even limp?

He made his way into the kitchen. There were details of this room he remembered. The stove, the wooden table. The cold of the tile floor. She had a radio here, he was certain. He'd heard it through the floorboards. Ought he to try to find it? Did it have a transmitter? On the table now was a loaf of bread. He was starving. What was taking her so long in the village?

He made his way to the privy and then returned to the kitchen, where he washed himself and enjoyed it, despite the cold. He wanted to linger in the kitchen, but he knew it wasn't safe. He took a slice of bread with him back to the attic room.

Whatever strength he had hoarded in all the days he had lain in the crawl space now was spent. He drifted between sleep and waking, surprised anew each time he opened his eyes and saw the sunshine in the attic garret. When he dozed, he laid his head back against the surface of the wall, almost spongy from its many layers of wallpaper. How old was the house? he wondered. A hundred years? Two hundred? He still had not got used to the idea that in Europe — in the English village where the bomb group was billeted, and now here in this tiny Belgian town — there were houses and churches, many in fact, that were centuries older than the oldest buildings in America. He thought of Mount Gilead, his hometown in Ohio, and of the farmhouse there where he once lived with his family, which was, at best, what? — a hundred years old? This building, the Daussois farmhouse, was ancient by comparison. The layers of wallpaper and paint told a story of their own. Whose stories? he wondered. What stories? Who had been hidden here?

She had left him a book, and sometimes he opened it and read a line or two of English poetry. She had asked him to explain some of the words and phrases to her, and had been perplexed when he had not known their meaning — not even in the context of the lines. "For rose-moles all in stipple . . ." He knew neither *rose-moles* nor *stipple*. He had tried to explain to her that his education had been interrupted by the war, though he privately doubted that even if he'd finished college, the words *rose-mole* and *stipple* would have come his way. His field was engineering. He had taken only one English course: a freshman composition class with a professor whose skin looked as dry as dust, and whose breath smelled of whiskey when he moved along the rows of students.

It seemed to Ted that his years in college occurred infinitely long ago — as though lived, experienced, in another lifetime, another age, or distantly in childhood.

Even Stella was fading in her detail. He could no longer summon the sound of her voice or her scent, and the image he had of her had gradually reduced itself to the single pose in the creased and worn photograph that Claire had placed in the palm of his hand. He fumbled for the picture, beside him on the floor. Dexterity had returned to his fingers; he could slide his nails under the photograph, lift it up.

Stella was sitting at a table in a restaurant. In the picture, it was always her smile he noticed first, no matter how many times he looked at the photograph. No one, he reflected, not a single person since he left America and entered the war, had had such an open and uncomplicated smile. She had her elbows resting on the table, and in front of her were several empty beer bottles — his and hers. She was wearing a white dress that was high at the neck and had short sleeves that seemed to flutter from her shoulders. Her hair was glossy, pulled back tightly at the top, with the sides long and curly. He studied the photograph and felt a sudden despair. Stella did not know where he was; whether he was alive or dead. No one back home knew. Already his mother would have received the telegram with the words *missing in action*, and she wouldn't know if her son was alive and in a German prison camp, or had been blown to bits in the air by a burst of flak. Bill Simmons, the postman, would have come with the telegram, his steps slow and deliberate, so that someone watching at the window would know even before he got to the door that he had a telegram. When the war had first begun, Ted himself, twice or three times, had watched Bill, in his uniform, make the long, slow journey to a fated front door. Curious, Ted had slowed his own steps, waiting for the reaction at the doorway. First the hand to the mouth, and then the wail the hand could not stop.

Now Ted would not slow his steps, would avoid at all costs seeing such a scene. He had witnessed enough benumbed and grief-stricken reactions to last ten lifetimes. And he now knew what was on the other side of those telegrams — events the recipients couldn't see, couldn't even imagine, for they had no vocabulary, no internal photographs, with which to perceive such horrors. A gunner, alive, shot from his ball turret, falling to the ground, the arms flailing like a windmill; another gunner, his own, fumbling with oily fingers for the flesh of his body that was no longer there.

He put the picture facedown on the floor, lay back against the wall, and closed his eyes. Once a man had seen such things, he asked himself, how did he then erase them from his memory? He thought of the men who returned from missions seemingly unscathed — their footsteps still jaunty, eager for whatever small pleasures the base or the town could provide them, wisecracks spinning around their heads. Somehow these men had done what he had failed to do: They had had the same visions and had dismissed them. Or did they, too, have visitations in the night?

His stomach felt hollow. How long had Claire been gone? He had no watch, couldn't accurately even guess the time. The light had changed in the attic room. The sun now cast a brighter rectangle on the unslanted wall. He estimated the size of his lair to be seven feet wide and about eight feet long. He could lie down fully extended, but just. When Claire came, she had to wind her long legs beneath her skirt in order to sit beside him without touching him. He remembered the first day she came to him when he was alert and fully conscious, and her surprise at that, her awkwardness. Her legs were bare and thin; she folded them under her as though to hide them. She wore white ankle socks, odd-looking men's shoes he had not seen since. Her hair, he remembered, was falling from its pins, and there was flour on her apron and on her throat, just under her chin. She brushed the flour from her apron, but was unaware of the white dusting on her skin, and he found that somehow charming, mesmerizing — as though he had caught her, unsuspecting, in the middle of a private domestic act. There was, that day, no artifice about her, and as she talked — haltingly, nervously — he could not take his eyes from that white dust.

Her visits punctuated his days. He sensed, but couldn't be certain, that she came less frequently than she had when he was still not fully alert or well. Now she came only on missions — with a meal, with medicine, and sometimes to teach him simple French phrases, which he seemed to be particularly inept at mastering. No longer did she sit by him for indefinite periods of time, knitting or reading. He wished that she would. He could not define it precisely, but he knew that when he was drifting in and out of consciousness, and she was simply there, beside him, sometimes holding his hand, he felt safe.

Certainly she was different from any woman he had ever known. It wasn't just her accent, or the strange cut of her clothes, or her mouth with its upper lip that rose to a single point and her lower lip with its natural pout. It was a kind of self-containment. Oddly, she seldom smiled, and he was quite sure he had never heard her laugh.

Once or twice, her husband, Henri, had come with the meal, and these visits had been, because of their mutual inability to communicate, awkward and sometimes comical. Henri, on his hands and knees, pushing the tray forward, wanting, out of politeness, to greet the aviator in some way, reduced finally to gestures to the obvious tray; and Ted, embarrassed and feeling faintly emasculated, reduced as well to exaggerated nodding and smiling to convey his gratitude. Henri, he guessed, was in his early thirties. He often smelled strongly of beer and tobacco. And though Henri was never unpleasant, Ted had the distinct sense that Henri did not want him there in the attic room, that the pilot's presence was a burden he'd happily have done without. Henri's visits, mercifully, were brief.

He had now learned to distinguish Claire's footsteps from Henri's on the bedroom floor outside his lair. Many nights, Ted could tell, Henri did not come to the bedroom. He had never heard the couple making love, though he had imagined it in the way one did when one first saw the two partners of a marriage. He was relieved that he had not had to listen to such an intimate act. Perhaps his own presence just beyond their bedroom wall had inhibited them. Or possibly Claire and Henri no longer came together in that way. Ted had heard that in Europe arranged marriages or marriages of convenience were not uncommon. Or maybe Henri had a lover and that explained why he sometimes didn't return home at night to sleep with his wife.

But why was this his concern? He shook it off, feeling mildly prurient. What his hosts did, or didn't do, was their affair, certainly not his. It was the idleness, he reflected, the long hours without company or activity that had led his thoughts in such an unproductive direction. He needed to get outside, to regain his strength, to set off for France and make it back to England. Others had done it, he knew; it was not impossible.

He was aware now of a door somewhere below him opening and closing. Two muffled sounds, distant but audible. His hopes rose. He listened intently for footfalls on the stairway, for the opening of the armoire and the slip of coat hangers on the rod.

She was running on the stairs. He heard the tray set down, the outer door open. He saw, briefly, after she had opened the false back of the armoire, the dropping of a coat to the floor, an impatient swirl of headscarf. When she entered, her face was reddened — flushed, but also from the cold — and her hair was disheveled.

"I am apologizing," she said quickly. "Madame Omloop was ill today, and I am having to find the sausage and the cheese in other places. And when I am returning home, the tire on my bicycle is lying down."

"Flat."

"Yes."

He knew that she was lying. Her eyes slid off his face in an evasive manner. Her hands were shaking so badly he wanted to reach out and hold them still. He picked up the bowl of milk and brought it to his lips, all the while examining her. He put the bowl down.

"What is it?" he asked.

He watched her compose her face, that effort.

She shook her head. "I am not understanding you," she said. She picked an imaginary piece of lint off her skirt. She was wearing a cotton blouse with a deep neckline, along which was a lace border. Her high color, however she had come by it, made her features particularly vivid.

"Something's wrong," he said. "I can smell it."

She looked up at him, puzzled. "Smell?"

"I can sense it."

She shook her head again. "I am only being late, and is not good to have a bicycle that will not do what you want it to do. Is hard work in the cold, no? I am having to walk the bicycle much of the way."

He reached for her hand in her lap. She snatched it away before he could touch her. She laid it at the bodice of her blouse.

"You're trembling," he said. "You've had a bad experience. Tell me what's happened. You're beginning to scare me too."

Her silence was so long he was certain he would have to repeat his demand. He hesitated, however, not wanting to drive her away. She seemed tightly wound, poised to flee, like the small animals he once captured and held in his palm. Her hand still rested on her blouse, and nervously, unaware of what she was doing, she worked one pearllike button — so much so that he wondered if she wouldn't inadvertently unbutton her blouse. Not once did she look up at him.

"You must — "

"I'm sorry — "

They spoke simultaneously. She raised her eyes to his.

"The situation in the village is very grave," she said finally. She stopped fingering the button, put both of her hands in her lap, calmer now that she had made the decision to tell him.

"For all the days since your plane is falling, there are German soldiers surrounding the village, and three of them are watching the plane. And these are old men, harmless. I think it is not very important to be watching this plane, yes? We have spoke of this already."

Ted nodded.

"But there is some person who is killing these old men. An assassin. And the Germans, they are very angry. It is their punishment in Belgium and in other countries to make the reprisals. I have heard of this."

"Reprisals," he repeated.

"The Gestapo have come into the village and they are taking people from their houses, even old men and children, and putting them in the school. And everyone is thinking that the Gestapo will kill a precise number of Belgians for the punishment. It is for the fear. To make the fear."

He nodded slowly.

"And in the village, there is no one. Everyone is hiding in his house or is taken already, and there is a silence I have never heard."

He waited. She put her hand to her temple, let her fingers comb her hair behind her ear.

"Where is Henri?" he asked.

She lowered her head. "Henri is not coming since the night. He is sent for in the night by the Maquis, and I do not know where he is."

Ted closed his eyes and laid his head back against the wall.

One moment of indecision, a single moment of indecision, and how many deaths?

If only he had not throttled back.

Two dead immediately. And who stood innocently beneath the bomb load? Then three old Germans, and now what would the total be? A precise number, she had said. Of hostages.

"Tell me where the bombs fell," he said. He instinctively doubted that now she would lie to him.

She looked away for a moment, then returned her gaze. "They are falling in Gilles, forty kilometers east."

"In Belgium?"

"Yes."

"A village?"

"Yes."

"In the village?"

She was silent.

"What if . . . ," he asked, thinking. "What if you took me to the school and offered to exchange me for the hostages. It might work. They want the pilots. It's common knowledge."

She seemed to think for a long time, as though searching for the words she wanted.

"In this war," she said slowly, "there is no bargains. They will take you and also the others. You are not living with them as I am. And then they will come for me as well, and Henri."

"No," he said, forming a plan. "You'll leave me somewhere. Somewhere exposed, and they'll find me and take me to the school, and I'll persuade them."

"You will be tortured," she said.

"I don't think so. They want the officers out of combat, but they don't kill them. They'll send me to a prison camp in Germany. Trust me. They treat officers differently."

"You will be tortured," she repeated knowingly. "And you will not be able to stand up in the torture, and you will have to tell them of me and Henri, and if we are denounced, perhaps we will have to speak of others. . . ."

He raised his hand to silence her, put a finger to his lips. Below him he could hear footsteps, a low voice calling.

Someone is here, he said silently. He mouthed the words in an exaggerated manner, hoping she would understand him.

She listened herself, heard the muffled voice. It sounded male, but not like Henri's.

She scrambled at once to the opening of the armoire. He heard footsteps on the stairs, then a tentative voice.

"Claire?"

Claire, he could tell, had crossed to the other side of the room, doubtless to draw the visitor's eyes away from the armoire.

"Bastien," Claire said with surprise.

Ted heard the rapid French of the visitor. Claire interrupted him, and spoke herself. There was another exchange, as though Bastien were giving instructions. Ted heard the opening and closing of drawers. Then he heard what seemed to be a series of questions on Claire's part, and Bastien's answers. The next sound Ted perceived was that of Bastien's footsteps moving away from Claire, out of the room and down the wooden stairs.

The bedspring creaked with weight. Either she was sitting on the bed or was lying down. He strained to discern her movements, her breathing. He wanted to call to her, but he sensed that she would come to him when she was ready. For ten minutes, perhaps more, she seemed to be motionless. Then he heard the bed creaking again, footsteps coming toward him.

She opened the armoire, spoke through the wall. He couldn't see her, but he could hear her well. Immediately he noticed that her voice was huskier. She had been crying.

"That was Bastien," she said. She cleared her throat.

"I heard his voice."

"He is telling me that there is a woman who is coming here to tell me of the reprisals, but the Germans are capturing her."

"I'm sorry."

"And Henri is not returning for some days yet."

"Claire, I — "

"And we are being very careful not to be found," she said sharply, as though intending to end any further discussion about trading him for the hostages. "You will not be leaving here. The . . ." She seemed to be searching for a word. "The threads of escaping are too dangerous now."

He smiled at the phrase, despite the import of her message. He wished he could tell her that he would take care of her, but both of them knew that he was useless — worse than useless, a burden. Were it not for him, he knew, she could flee the village. It seemed hideously ironic that her life should be in jeopardy because of him. Oughtn't he to be protecting her, rather than harming her?

"What was in the drawers?" he asked.

"Clothes for Henri. Bastien is taking them to Henri."

"What will you do now?" he asked.

She was a long time in answering him.

"We are waiting," she said finally.

———

There was a name for it, *balustrade*, Monsieur Dauvin once said, but the boy thought of it simply as a covered walkway, with stone pillars and mosaic archways and long views down into the village square. It reminded him of pictures he had seen in the rectory, drawings of balustrades in walled gardens in Italian cloisters, hushed places where hooded monks walked and thought in silence. But this covered walkway, the boy's covered walkway, was at the top of the school, once a monastery, and access could be gained only from the deserted fourth floor. It was forbidden to go up to the attic, as the fourth story was referred to, because the floor and the ceiling were in such disrepair that the teachers worried for the safety of the children. The covered walkway, which was open to the square, was thought to be even more dangerous than the attic. The stones of the pillars and the graceful arches had worked themselves loose over the centuries. Merely leaning on the railing, which reached to the middle of Jean's chest, might cause the structure to give altogether. Several years ago, some fuss had been made over whether to repair the fourth story or raze the school altogether, but then the war had come, and all the laborers in the village had been immediately otherwise engaged.

Jean thought of the balustrade as his.

He came to this place often. He had removed the crosspieces that barred the door so many times now that the nails slid effortlessly in and out of their holes. He knew the route across the attic floor as a sapper might a minefield — which boards would give way even under a boy's weight, where to avoid the crumbling plaster chunks that dangled from the ceiling. He came here as often as he could manage. It was, within the school, his sanctuary. As was the wood when he was not in school.

All forays here meant some risk. At the least, a flogging by Monsieur Dauvin should Jean be discovered; an injury or a fall should he not be careful where he stepped or rested his weight. But this journey today was, by far, the most dangerous of all.

For the building was no longer a school. Nor was the church any longer a church. The sisters, in their white-winged cornettes, had fled to the adjacent convent to pray; Father Guillaume had not appeared since the Gestapo had entered the village. The classrooms of the school were now interrogation rooms; the school was a prison. All day, from his perch, the boy watched them come and go, heard, even through the three floors that separated him from the ground-floor classrooms, the muffled screams, followed abruptly by an uncommon silence, as though silence were the only way to survive.

The boy had known this all his life.

Earlier that morning, Jean had ridden his bicycle to school as he always did, but Marcel, whose house he daily passed en route, whispered frantically to him from an open window. Marcel, who was still in his nightshirt and who had not yet combed his hair, told Jean of the assassinations and of the reprisals, and that the school had been closed indefinitely. *Go home*, Marcel had whispered fiercely. It was rumored, Marcel added, that the Germans had brought in reinforcements from Florennes. The Gestapo were everywhere, like cockroaches. Jean, who had taken all of this in, thought it must have been Marcel's father who had said that, who had made the image of the cockroaches. Marcel was loyal, but he lacked imagination.

Jean left Marcel and rode to the dark safety of an alleyway. He was considerably closer to the school than he was to home; the ride to his father's farmhouse might, in fact, be more dangerous than remaining in the village. He could, he thought, seek shelter with Marcel: Madame Delizée would not refuse him. But the thought of being trapped all day (and all night?) in Marcel's cluttered and claustrophobic three-room apartment, where the indoor toilet seemed continuously to be backed up, made Jean shake his head quickly.

He hid his bicycle behind a pair of dustbins, hugged the backs of the terraced houses, and ventured to peer into the village square, bordered on the north by the old school. The shades at the classroom windows had been drawn. Two armed and uniformed sentries stood at the door where normally Monsieur Dauvin waited to reprimand the tardiest of the students.

All the boys knew of the basement entrance. It was where the older boys went to smoke; the younger to play cards for centimes. From the basement, there was the back staircase, filthy and always smelling of stale cigarette smoke. The teachers never used the back staircase; they complained to Monsieur Chabotaux, the old caretaker, that dust caught at their trousers.

Jean crept into the darkness of the basement, heard from the floor above the occasional tread of heavy boots. Behind the boiler, the staircase began; it encountered on each level a heavy metal door. When he had climbed to the ground floor, Jean hesitated, put his ear to the door. There was behind the green-painted metal an odd sound, the low murmur of many voices, as though he were eavesdropping on the waiting room of the railway station at St. Laurent. The sound seemed benign and gave Jean the courage to continue up the stairs, but as he put his foot on the first step, he jerked his body. A scream had come at him through the door. Paralyzed, the boy listened as the terrible voice, a woman's, trailed off and was followed once again by the uncommon silence.

He reached the walkway without much trouble, but needed immediately to piss in the corner. He crouched into the opposite corner, where there was a bit of solid wall, perhaps three feet long, before the balustrade began. He pulled his coat around him. It was cold, but not as cold as it had been, and besides, Jean knew, the sun, which was bright today and unobscured, would soon warm this southern wall of the school.

He crouched or sat all day, peering around the wall only when he heard the clatter of a truck on the cobblestones of the square. First there were the Gestapo, who sprang with their machine guns from the truck. Then the back panels were opened, and one or five or twelve men and women, and sometimes children, stepped or were dragged from the interior compartment. Mostly the prisoners were silent, particularly the men, but occasionally a woman was crying, and sometimes the children were whimpering. Only Madame Gosset, who was, Jean knew, elderly and deaf, would not get out of the truck, possibly because she did not hear the commands, possibly because she refused, even in her frailty, to cooperate; and Jean was horrified to watch the Gestapo grab her by her hair, her bun uncoiling like a thin white rope as the pins popped and fell to the cobblestones. A guard jabbed her between her shoulder blades with the butt of his machine gun. Madame Gosset fell to the cobblestones on her knees and couldn't — or wouldn't — rise. She was dragged in that position by two Gestapo, who hoisted her weightless body by her armpits.

In all, he counted sixty-seven villagers who were taken into the school. In his bookbag he found a notebook and a pencil, and he recorded the names of all those he could recognize, so that he had entries that read this way: "Pierre Squevin and his family: his wife Marie, and a sister of the wife (?) don't know her name; and Georges, 17, from the pensionale."

Fourteen villagers had left the school. Ten young men (Georges among them) were marched out, their hands behind their heads, and herded into the back of a van. The van left the square with two guards, but Jean could not hear from four stories up their destination. Three women had been let go — one was a woman with a baby. He watched the woman stand, dazed, at the bottom of the schoolhouse steps, then begin to scurry, hunching her back as if she might conceal herself and her baby, across the square to her house.

It had been an hour, at least, since anyone else had been brought to the school or anyone had left. Jean estimated the time at about three P.M. He was glad that soon it would be dark and he could retrace his steps to his bicycle. He had seen enough, recorded enough. He had not eaten since breakfast — a hard roll, a cup of bitter tea — though, in truth, the scenes he had witnessed and the sounds he had heard had intermittently stolen his appetite. The sun slanted over the village hall opposite — in another hour, it would fall behind the slate roof. When the sun set, his corner would lose whatever small warmth the stones had harbored through the day, and he would want even more urgently to leave.

Idly he looked again at the names in his notebook, thinking he might be able to fill in the blank spaces, remember a name that had so far escaped him, when he heard a new sound in the square.

Six men, one with a tall ladder, the others with shorter ladders, stepladders, two apiece, entered the square. Two uniformed guards followed the men, the guards' arms weighted down not with machine guns but with coils of rope. The Belgians were workers, laborers from the village. Marcel's father (Marcel's father?) was the man carrying the longest of the ladders. He was dressed as Jean had often seen him — in a blue overall, a pair of clogs, and his navy cap. Monsieur Delizée walked with the ladder to the eastern side of the square, along which were terraced buildings, with shops on the ground floor, apartments on the first story. All along the front of these apartments were shallow, wrought-iron balconies — wide enough for a woman to hang out a wash to dry, wide enough in summer for tubs of begonias and geraniums. The ironwork of these balconies, intricate and detailed, was thought in the village to be among the town's better features.

Marcel's father stopped, his ladder horizontal. A guard gave a command in German, then in French. Reluctantly, Marcel's father slowly righted the ladder, leaned it carefully against the ironwork of the first balcony. The guard spoke to Monsieur Delizée, handed him a heavy coil of rope.

With growing comprehension and horror, Jean watched the father of his best friend climb the long ladder with the coil of rope.

———•———

We were near the signal crossing when they picked us up. We had nothing on us. Twenty minutes earlier, Anthoine had delivered a package of propaganda leaflets to . . . well, you don't need to know to who. They were after Léon, really — and he knew it. We knew it. I think they've thought for a while now that he was, you know, leaking things he heard at the hotel. They put us in a truck. We knew the guards — all of us. They were all right with Anthoine and me, you know, because we have the livestock, and they've had our meat, and perhaps they were thinking there might be, in this, a favor somewhere, but Léon, what did he have to offer? Léon was coughing badly, he does this when he gets nervous, and besides he hasn't been well, hasn't been well at all, and Anthoine and me were looking at each other over his head, and I knew we were thinking the same thing. Léon was not going to get out of this.

"So then we were driven to the school. Inside the school there was . . . it was . . . In the classrooms, there were the children's drawings and their papers up on the walls, and on the floor and on the desks there was blood, spatters of it, the way it spatters when you've hit a calf before slitting its throat. In some rooms, there were old women huddling with their husbands, Monsieur Claussin and Monsieur Clouet. I saw Risa with her baby. But I could catch only glimpses, because they hurried us to a separate classroom — even though you could hear. It made you want to shit what you were hearing.

"And then an officer introduced himself — he was known to Léon and to Anthoine, but not to myself, and while he was telling us his name, a guard, from behind, hit Léon such a blow, a whack with his truncheon, that Léon fell over sideways and one of the lenses of his glasses shattered. So I reached over to get him, and I was hit, too, but I was bending, and the stick hit me on the side of my face, but it didn't knock me down. So I stood up. And they started on Léon first; he was the weakest of the three of us and would break first, they reasoned, and they told him they knew he was with the Maquis, and they wanted to know what we were doing at the signal crossing, where we had been and were going and so on, and Léon, who was sitting at a child's desk, put on the glasses with the shattered lens and looked up. I'll never forget this. He began to read the signs that the teacher had put on the walls for the children. 'Jean is eating an apple.' 'Michelle is playing with the cat.' He spoke the words very slowly and distinctly, like a student learning to read. This made the officer furious. He yelled at Léon to stop, and Léon did, but as soon as he was asked a question, he would begin to read the signs again in the same voice. 'Jean is eating an apple.' 'Michelle is playing with the cat.'

"Anthoine, who was frightened for Léon, said *Léon*. There were ways to answer questions without making the Gestapo angry. We'd talked about this before. But Léon, you see, he knew he was going to die, he'd seen it as we'd seen it, and he hated them so

RESISTANCE

much he wouldn't even give his *own* name when, of course, they knew it.

"So the officer, his face was purple, he couldn't stand what Léon was doing. It was suicide on Léon's part, but it was beautiful in a way, too. And the officer screamed at the guards to tie our hands and take us to another room and then return, at least that's what I think he was saying, it was in German, but Anthoine thought so, too, and we knew that if we were taken out, Léon would be tortured and killed right there. The guards began tying our hands behind our backs. Léon, who was coughing badly, looked up at us briefly and shook his head, as if to say, don't worry about me, don't think of me.

"And that was the last we saw of Léon.

"We got pushed out the door and down a hallway and shoved into an empty room, a smaller classroom with bigger desks, Monsieur Parmentier's room it was when I was a student there, and they tied us to the desks and left us.

"Anthoine was on one side of the room, and I was on the other. He said, 'Léon will die,' and I said, 'Maybe they'll just scare him,' and Anthoine shook his head. Then we struggled with the ropes for a bit, but I could not get free and neither could Anthoine, but Anthoine, who barely fit into the space between the chair and the desk, discovered something while he was struggling, and that was that two of the three bolts on the desk's pedestal had loosened. Later he said it was probably the work of a bored student. So Anthoine began rocking back and forth violently and thrashing about, he knew we only had minutes at best, and after a time the third bolt popped, and he was free. So he slid and walked his desk over to where I sat — it would have been funny maybe if it hadn't been so frightening, and actually I was so close to panic I did almost laugh, Anthoine's face was bright pink and he was huffing and puffing like a pig — it has to be said — but he got himself at right angles to me, and we fumbled with each other's ropes from behind, both at once, then Anthoine said to stop, it wasn't working, he said he'd get me free first. And that's what happened.

"When we were both free, Anthoine put the desk back where

it was supposed to be and put the bolts in and we took the ropes, so there wouldn't be any obvious evidence of an escape. Anthoine was counting on the right hand not knowing what the left was doing in all the confusion, and that maybe the guards when they returned would think we'd been taken by other guards to another classroom. In any event, we opened a window and dropped out. I stood on Anthoine's shoulders and closed the window."

Henri shivered beside her in the bed in the dark. He was naked, but the shivering was from shock. He spoke nearly in a monotone, yet his voice was unsteady because of his shaking. She had put blankets on him and was holding him in the bed, but she couldn't stop his trembling. He had come into the kitchen just as the sun was beginning to set. She had put her hand to her mouth and cried out when she saw the bruise on his face. He had stripped off all his clothes and bathed himself at the pump, waving her away when she tried to tend to the bruise. Naked, he had walked up to the bedroom, drawn the curtains and climbed into the bed.

"I can only stay a few minutes," he said when he had told her his story. It was the most he had ever revealed of his experiences in the underground. "I'm going to have to go into hiding with Anthoine for a while, until this thing with the reprisals is over. I've come for my papers and some money."

She heard what he said, held him, and said nothing.

"You should know that they are taking women," he said. "They have taken Emilie and Thérèse. And even Madame Bossart."

"It's all right," she said. "They won't come for me."

"Claire . . ."

Henri began suddenly to make a deep, heaving, gutteral sound — an awful, rough sound — that frightened Claire and made her sit up in the bed. She thought her husband was about to be sick. Henri coughed into the pillow to muffle the terrible sounds of the crying. Claire, who had never heard her husband cry, lay down again and held him more tightly and thought of the pilot who was so near them, just beyond the wall. He must be hearing this, she thought.

"It's all right, Henri," she said quietly. "It's all right."

"No," he said, stopping his crying nearly as quickly as he'd begun, wiping his nose on a pillow slip. "It's not all right." His voice was thick and full of congestion.

He felt then with his hand for the hem of her skirt, raising it beneath the comforter so that he could put his fingers between her thighs. Without waiting for a sign from her, he snapped the garters of her stockings, rubbed his free hand hard along the length of her legs, rolling down the stockings to her ankles. He pulled down her underwear, so that it, too, was tangled at her feet. Raising himself onto his knees, he climbed over her. She looked for his face, but when it passed near hers, the room was so dark, she couldn't see him clearly. He bent his head into her neck, held the skin of her neck lightly with his teeth.

When she felt him coming, she shifted slightly, jerked her hips. He spilled himself onto her thigh.

He did not move or ask why.

She thought of the pilot beyond the wall. He must be hearing this, she was thinking.

———

Ten nooses hung from the balconies, ten stepladders beneath them. The boy watched Marcel's father drape the rope through the ironwork, expertly fashioning the nooses, as if this, and not carpentry, were his trade. The villagers who had been inside the school were brought out into the square to be witnesses. From corners and doorways, a few other curious villagers joined the witnesses, so that by the time the German officer entered the square, there were perhaps fifty men and women on the cobblestones. There was among the villagers a quiet and anxious murmur. It was not clear yet who would be executed — but some of the women who had been inside the school and who had been let out and who could not now find their sons or husbands began to grow panicky, moving rapidly through the crowd, asking questions, receiving small, embarrassed shakes of the head in reply. The officer, whose name Jean did not know, stepped up on the small stone wall that surrounded the fountain in the center of the square. He read, in Walloon (for what good were reprisals if the people did not understand the reason?), the names of those who would be executed as payment for the assassinations of the three German soldiers. Jean was stunned to hear the name of the village Burghermaster, Jauquet, among the condemned, as well as a woman's name, Emilie Boccart. Several women in the crowd screamed and began to claw their way forward, but were held back by their neighbors, who knew that to confront the Gestapo was to invite a certain death for oneself. Jean watched as two Belgians led an elderly woman, who seemed overcome, quickly from the square.

The ten prisoners were led out, hatless and coatless, their hands tied behind their backs. Most of the prisoners had been beaten, and some had bloodstains on their clothes. The sun, slanting into the square and into the eyes of the condemned, harshly illuminated the black and purple swellings on the faces. Monsieur Balle, who looked to Jean odd and somehow naked without his spectacles and beret, had to be carried under the arms by two guards. The mother of one of the men rushed forward, screaming, to embrace her son. A guard hastily beat her back with his machine gun. She grasped the arm of another woman, then half fell, half staggered, to the cobblestones.

Jean picked up his pencil and tried to record the names of the ten condemned prisoners in his notebook: Sylvain Jacquemart, Emilie Boccart, Philippe Jauquet, Léon Balle, Roger Doumont . . . But Jean's hand began to shake so badly his penmanship became nearly illegible. Looking down at his violently shaking hand, the boy was suddenly afraid he might drop the pencil altogether, that it would slip through the pillars of the balustrade and clatter to the cobblestones, giving away his perch and catching the eye of one of the two dozen sentries surrounding the crowd with machine guns at the ready. Carefully, he put the pencil and notebook down, then slowly rose once more to peer around the wall.

The ten condemned were led to the stepladders, ordered to climb the steps. Monsieur Balle presented a problem, however, as he could not stand on his own. He was hoisted up the stepladder by an irritated guard, who held him in place like a marionette. The boy's eyes widened in disbelief as he saw that Jacquemart, in a bizarre twist of fate, would be hanged from his own balcony.

Father Guillaume, his broad priest's hat hiding his face, the skirts of his long robes sweeping over the cobblestones, stood before each of the condemned and made the sign of the cross. Only Balle, though he could not stand, summoned the will to resist this tainted blessing and spat at the priest.

At a signal from the officer in charge, sentries mounted each stepladder to place the nooses around the necks of the prisoners. Each guard then descended the stepladder and retrieved his machine gun. Jacquemart was looking for his wife in the crowd and calling her name; Doumont and Jauquet had their heads bent. Léon Balle was held up only by the noose itself. He seemed already to have lost consciousness. Emilie Boccart, startling the crowd, called out in her raspy voice, *Vive la Belgique!* The officer gave a command. At the signal, each guard jerked away a stepladder. There were gasps and wails from the villagers. The nine men and one woman were simultaneously hanged.

Jean watched as several of the bodies twisted and twitched. Shit ran down the trouser leg of Jacquemart and soiled his sock and shoe. Jean felt light-headed; he was certain he would be sick. The men who continued to twitch were beaten with machine guns by the guards. Jauquet's guard, infuriated by the Burghermaster's refusal to die quickly, sprayed the man with a burst of bullets, nearly severing the body.

The world, which for Jean Benoît had always held its share of treachery, now spun out of control beneath him. He fainted to the cold floor of the covered walkway, bruising his face in the fall, and dislodging a small brick that clattered onto the cobblestones.

A silence had settled over the house and, perhaps, she thought, the entire village. It was the deep hush of a heavy snowfall, a snowfall such as she had sometimes experienced as a girl in the Ardennes. Once, on a holiday, her father borrowed two pairs of skis, and together she and her father made long trails in the snowy woods.

The silence seemed so profound that even the usual ghosts

were silent tonight: She could not summon the voices of the young men and the old women who had stayed in her attic, could no longer hear Madame Rosenthal calling for her lost husband.

Henri had been gone — how long? Eight, nine hours? Was it two in the morning? Three? She had no idea. There was still moonlight through the window, but it told her nothing. Was it possible, she asked herself, that she would never see Henri again? She tried to absorb that fact, feel it, but the blanket of silence had enveloped and cocooned her as well.

Earlier, after Henri had gone, Claire had gotten up from the bed, washed herself and fixed her clothes, and prepared, as she knew she must, an evening meal for the pilot. It was much the same meal as before — the bread and cheese and terrible coffee — and she found herself longing for a piece of fruit, an apple or a pear or, more exotic, an orange or a mango. When she took the tray up to the pilot, he accepted it, but for the first time since he had regained consciousness, he would not meet her eyes. He announced that he would eat the meal in the kitchen — with or without her help, with or without her permission. Normally, she'd have protested: Of all the days or nights to be outside the hiding place, surely this was the most risky. But she no longer felt the desire or the strength to resist him.

She helped the pilot to crawl out of the attic and, once in the bedroom, to stand. He used the armoire and her shoulder to brace himself, and he stood carefully, in increments, as might an old man getting up from a chair. His head grazed the slanted ceiling, and the top of her own head barely reached the collar of his shirt. His features had altered as well since she had seen him last — or rather, she thought, her perception of his features. His eyes were more deep-set than she'd thought them before, the shape of his mouth more distinct and pronounced: the straight lower lip, the full and curved upper lip. He bore the beginnings of a mustache and beard, and with his longish hair, needing a wash and combed with the fingers behind his ears, and his ill-fitting civilian clothes, he looked not like an American aviator, but rather more like a laborer. His right leg had atrophied — she had seen and bathed the pale shin — and he could barely put his weight on it. He worked his way to the top of the stairs and, using the bannister, he hopped down the first step. She realized then the distance he had already put between them: He did not want her help.

She followed him down the stairs — he hopping on the good leg, resting all his weight on the bannister. In the kitchen, she gathered a towel, Henri's razor, and a basin, and set them by the stove. She boiled water, and from the deepest recesses of a drawer in the cupboard, she collected a parcel: clean, newly tailored clothes that had been made for his escape. She put them on the table.

She left him alone then and went up to the bedroom. She removed all the bedding from the attic, swept and cleaned the tiny area, lay clean bedding on the floor, and replaced the photograph of the pilot's fiancée and the book of English poetry. Leaving the door to the attic ajar, she opened the two windows in the bedroom. The room filled immediately with cold, clean air that she hoped would wash out the stale air of the attic as well.

When all of these tasks had been accomplished, and she thought she had given the American enough time, she carried the old bedding down to the kitchen. There she found the pilot, his hair still wet, his face newly shaved, sitting at the kitchen table. The trousers that had been made for him nearly hid the bandaged calf. The cotton shirt, collarless as yet, was opened two or three buttons at the neck. He sat with one leg draped over the other, one arm resting on the table. She paused at the doorway. He no longer looked like a laborer. With his thumbnail, he was tracing the grooves on the old oak table.

He heard her and looked up. He met her eyes for the first time that evening.

"Is your husband all right?" he asked.

She dropped the bedding into the laundry basket. "He is going into the hiding," she said.

There was a long silence between them as she stood near one end of the table.

"And you'd have gone with him if it hadn't been for me," he said.

"No. Is safer for me here. If I go with him, I am a" — she searched for the word — "heavier package?"

"I doubt it," he said, turning away. "Anyway, I'll be leaving tomorrow. I'll need a warm coat if you can spare it."

"No," she said quickly. "You cannot be leaving this house until the escape is made ready. And it will not be tomorrow or the next day or the next day. Is for my safety, too, that you are remaining here."

"Well, we'll see," he said quietly.

"Your dinner is growing old on the floor upstairs."

"I'm not hungry." He turned his face back toward her. He smiled slightly. "But I'd love a cigarette."

She sighed. "My cigarettes are finished."

She thought for a minute, then took her coat from the hook.

"Where are you going?" he asked.

"I have something," she said.

The night air was frigid and hurt her chest. She was glad, however, to be beyond the American's gaze. She had felt herself to be shy in front of him and was angry with herself for succumbing to shyness. It was evident the pilot had overheard Henri in the bedroom, heard the awful coughs of the crying, perhaps even the gruff sounds of the lovemaking. Yet that was not the word, she knew, for what had passed between Henri and herself in the bedroom. It had possibly been an act of love on her part, or more precisely an act of generosity, but for Henri it was a necessary act to forget what he had seen, to move beyond what he had seen. She thought of the way an animal shook another in its teeth; the way a cat, in a sudden burst of animal frenzy, climbed the bark of a tree.

The moon was rising and luminous. Her father had said that under certain moons one could read a newspaper at midnight. When she reached the barn, she left the wide door open so that she could see her way. She found what she had come for in the wooden boxes. She took three brown glass bottles — all she could easily carry on her own.

On her way back to the kitchen, she was alarmed by the thin threads of light around the edges of the blackout curtains. Once inside, after she had taken off her coat and set the bottles down, she switched off the light, fumbled in the dark for the curtains and drew them open. A rectangle of blue light fell across the floor and the table. "We are being safer when I am turning out the light," she said. "The moon is very much bright tonight, and we will be able to see."

She handed a bottle to the pilot.

"Is beer my husband is making. Is for me" — she made a gesture with her hand — "very strong. Is better with the cheese and bread."

She went upstairs to retrieve the tray of food, and when she'd returned, the American had removed the wire fasteners and corks of two of the bottles. She placed the bread and cheese on the table, tore the bread into four pieces, cut slices from the cheese. She felt safer, more comfortable, in the relative darkness of the kitchen. It was difficult to see the American's eyes now, even more difficult to see if he was watching her. She brought two glasses to the table, but he ignored his and drank straight from the bottle. She poured herself a glass of the dark beer, waited for the foam to subside.

"Very good," he said, raising the bottle.

"Yes."

He ate from the tray of cheese and bread. The moonlight, in its way, made the American seem blue, translucent. She was hungry herself, ate from the tray as well and took a swallow of beer.

"I think you have a radio, don't you?"

The question surprised her. Perhaps he had heard the radio on other nights, through the floorboards. "Yes, I have it," she said.

"Can we listen to it?"

She thought for a while. His voice was rich and easy, and had a kind of lilt. Though the accent was different, it was not unlike that of a Welsh flyer she'd once sheltered. It would be risky to listen to the radio with the Gestapo in the village. But perhaps they could if they kept the sound low; and perhaps just for a minute or two.

She got up from the table, worked the bricks loose. She brought the large, heavy radio to the table and set it down. She unwound the thick brown cord and plugged the radio in. When she turned it on, the sudden static shocked her, and she quickly turned down the volume. Unable to read the tiny dial in the moonlight, she turned it slowly through a variety of languages: Parisian French, Walloon French, which was her own tongue, Flemish, Dutch, German, Danish. Then the BBC in English. She sat down and inclined her head toward the radio.

They listened intently. The Germans, besieged at Stalingrad, were ignoring an appeal to surrender. A busload of children, being taken to the English countryside from London in order to escape the bombs there, had overturned into a ditch just outside Oxford. Then, seemingly in a non sequitur, the BBC announcer spoke about a man who had enjoyed a rabbit, cooked in a red-wine sauce, and who would like to thank his hosts.

"There," she said. "Is the code."

"Code?"

"Sometimes I am listening and writing this down for . . . for others. When the aviators . . . mmmm . . . when the aviators are returning to England from Belgium, from falling from their planes, they are telling their . . . superiors, yes? . . . the name of their last meal with their hosts . . . and this information is being told to the BBC, who say it over the radio — 'The rabbit in the wine tasted good tonight' — and that is how the Maquis are knowing the aviator is making it home."

The pilot pondered this. "So if I were to leave tomorrow and make it back safely, you would one day hear on the radio, 'The beer was heavy and delicious.'"

She smiled.

The announcer stopped talking. A tune was played on the radio.

"Glenn Miller," the pilot said.

They listened to the music in silence. He had sat back in his chair so that his face was in darkness beyond the reach of the moonlight. He drank two bottles of the beer. She drank half of the third bottle. They listened to Aaron Copland and Irving Berlin. Each time he told her, before the announcer did, the name of the song and the composer.

"Do you like to dance?" he asked.

"Is a very long time since I am dancing," she said finally.

"Did you go to dances before the war?"

"Not so many. Once in Charleroi, my husband is taking me to a dance hall, but here in Delahaut? We have the dancing when we have the weddings or the festivals. But you? Do you have the dances?"

"In school," he said. "And there were a few in England at the base. There was one just before Christmas. There was supposed to be another the day after we crashed. New Year's Eve."

"You are missing your plane?"

"The plane? No."

"No, I am meaning, are you missing the flying?"

He took a long swallow, set the bottle on the table. "I suppose I miss flying. I enjoy that. But what we were doing up there" — he gestured toward the ceiling — "that wasn't really flying, at least not to me it wasn't. It was, I don't know, a kind of engineering job. An engineering job under pretty awful conditions."

"Yes."

"When I get back, they'll probably put me in another bomber. Perhaps one day, I'll fly right over here again."

"And not fall."

"And not fall."

"I think you should be preparing yourself for the long waiting. Is probable that the escaping will not be soon. My husband is telling me that. And now is not safe at all for any strangers in Delahaut."

"These reprisals," he said. "What will happen to the villagers who have been taken?"

"I am not knowing this. Is usual in the reprisals . . ." She stopped.

"Go on."

"Is usual in the reprisals, there are the executions."

He made small circles with the bottle on the tabletop. "Have there been reprisals here before?"

"No, not in this village, but in other villages, yes."

"Maybe there won't be executions this time," he said.

She was silent.

He lifted the bottle from the table, held it for a moment, then brought it down hard. She thought that it might break.

He saw that she was watching him. He shifted in his chair.

"You haven't wanted children?" he asked, changing the subject. "I'm sorry, that's none of my business."

"No, is all right. I am not wanting children. Not during the war."

"And after?"

"I am not knowing."

There was an awkward silence between them.

"And you?" she asked finally. "You are being married to the woman in the picture after the war?"

He leaned forward into the light. "I suppose so. That's what we planned. Seems like an awfully long time ago. It bothers me that no one back home knows what has happened. I don't like to think of them worrying."

"When is safe, I will write your fiancée."

"Yes, thank you. Actually, I'd rather you wrote my sister."

"Your sister?"

"Frances, yes. It was she who brought me up, acted as my mother, I mean. I think she'll be worrying the most."

"Then is done," she said. "I will be writing to Frances. Before you are going, you will give to me the address, yes?"

"Yes, of course."

"And when you get safely home, you must write to me to tell me that you are safe, yes? But maybe is not safe to write me here until after the war is over."

He nodded slightly.

She stood up and turned off the radio. She rewound the plug. She listened for sounds outside the house, heard nothing. She carried the heavy radio to its hiding place, carefully replaced the bricks.

"You are finished?" she asked beside him.

"I love your voice," he said. "It's very deep for a woman, but it's beautiful."

She held the bottles in her arms. It didn't matter the language, she thought; there was a line one couldn't cross, and he was straying too close to it. There could be no reply to what he had said. She took the three empty bottles to the pantry.

"The name of your plane . . . ," she said from the pantry.

"*Woman's Home Companion*," he called in to her.

"On the side of the plane," she said, "is a picture that is making the men laugh, and when I am asking, they are not telling me."

When she returned to the kitchen, the pilot was smiling to himself. "Someday I'll tell you," he said. "But not tonight."

"Before you are leaving?"

"Yes. All right."

She cleaned away all traces of the meal, put the razor and the soap in a drawer, hid the dirty clothes and the towel beneath the bedding in the basket. She scattered the remaining coals in the hearth. She took her coat from the hook, then drew the blackout curtains so that they were in total darkness.

"You do this every night?"

"I am being careful every night, but this night my husband is telling me to be the best careful."

"The coat is . . ."

"So they are thinking I am leaving."

"Have already left. That's why you don't lock the door?"

"Yes."

"And if they come?"

"They are not come."

"Then why . . .?"

"Is habit."

She stood beside him in the darkness.

"I am putting my hand here," she said, touching him lightly on the elbow. "I am seeing the house even in the dark, yes?"

She guided him through the rooms to the staircase. He felt his way up, maneuvered his way into the bedroom. The moonlight through the open windows gave them some light.

"Chilly in here," he said.

"I am having the windows open before so the air is clean."

He stood over her, a large presence in the small room. He had braced himself with one arm against the slanted ceiling.

"Claire . . ."

Instinctively, she stepped back, felt with her own hand for the post of the footboard of the bed. The bed was now painful to her. Too intimate, too reminiscent of the acts the American had overheard just hours before.

"Claire, you shouldn't put yourself at risk for me," he said.

She shook her head and turned away. She laid her coat over the footboard.

"I am doing this many times," she said as casually as she could, folding and then refolding the coat. "Is nothing."

She watched him turn, move aside the coat hangers, open the false back of the armoire.

When she was certain that the small trapdoor was shut, she walked to the armoire and leaned her head against it.

The beer had made her not sleepy, but rather restless. What sleep she had managed to get since she undressed and slid into the bed was fitful. Her dreams fled behind heavy doors before she could catch them.

Perhaps she was afraid. Alone in this house. She wondered where Henri was at this very moment. Was he cold? Had he eaten? Did he have a bed to sleep in, or was he, too, hiding on the floor of someone's attic? Ought she to have gone with Henri? she asked herself. But wouldn't he be more at risk with a woman in tow?

She pulled the comforters up around her bare shoulders. Henri gave off heat. When he was not in the bed, she needed extra blankets. She thought of Léon with his shattered glasses. Was he dead now? Beaten to death and taken away? What was it like, precisely, to be beaten to death? Which blow actually caused the death, or was it that the whole body, at one particular instant, simply gave up? And what of Thérèse and Emilie? Would they be sent to Ravensbrück, where she had heard they sent the women? No one really seemed to know for certain. If a villager was taken away, it was never officially stated where he or she had gone. And Claire personally had never heard of anyone returning from the concentration camps. Although if that were true, how then did any of them know there was a Ravensbrück, a Buchenwald, except for the stories that came down the line? There must be paperwork, of course, but the paperwork would not tell the stories she had heard — terrible stories she could barely take in. Being sent east to Germany was to be sent into a fog, a terrible, thick fog in which no one was ever recognized and from which no one ever seemed to return.

The fast crunch of tires on the gravel made her sit up quickly in the bed. She felt the tight, unnatural beat of her heart. She heard four doors open, precisely, then the slam of two.

At the first German voice, she catapulted from the bed, drew the covers over the pillow in one swoop, then frantically opened the armoire door. A small cry of panic escaped her. She swept aside the clothes, opened the trapdoor. Abruptly she stepped into the attic, startling the American, who sat up. She put a finger to her lips. His face showed his confusion, as if he thought he was still dreaming. She heard footsteps on the gravel, a knock, a shout in German. Sickeningly, she realized she had left the coat still folded at the foot of the bed. Scrambling in her nightgown, she crawled through the armoire into the bedroom, seized the coat, dragged it to the crawl space, hurled it inside. He pulled the armoire door shut, rearranged the hangers. She heard footsteps in the kitchen now — a murmur of voices, of commands.

He stepped back into the attic room, silently shut the false door. He lay down, rolled onto his back. Claire, sitting against the wall, had her fist to her mouth. She and the pilot watched each other as they listened to the raid outside their hiding place.

She closed her eyes only once — when she heard the first footsteps on the stairs. The Gestapo were making no attempt at stealth — their boots were rapid on the stairs, as if they were running. She heard one man, then another, in the bedroom. A *whomp* as something hard smacked down on the bed. The whoosh of comforters and sheets being thrown back. If they felt the sheets, she thought, they would know. A dresser drawer wrenched open. Clothes flung to the floor. She heard the clatter of her rosary beads. A man on his knees, shuffling — peering under the bed? Then another was at the armoire, his boots not two feet away through the wall from the pilot's head. Claire heard the opening of the door, the sweeping of linens and garments to the floor, the poke of metal on wood, testing it. If the man saw, in the shadows of the armoire, the demarcations of the false back, Claire and the American would be found within seconds.

A tired voice. From the other, a note of weariness and frustration. The two voices sounded surprisingly young, not boys exactly, but young men nevertheless. She heard the bed creaking as if a man had just sat on it. A joke about falling asleep. A gruff voice from below with a question. A quick submissive answer. Again, the creaking of the bed as a man stood up. The retreat of boots. She waited. Only one pair of footfalls down the stairs. Why was the other man not descending as well? Was he looking for something? Could he see, from the head of the stairs, the outline of the attic door in the sliver of space behind the wardrobe? She heard the boots return to the bedroom, bit her knuckles hard to keep from making a sound. The man picked up an item of clothing from the floor. She could hear the swish of fabric — a faint and silken sound. Perhaps it was a slip, she thought, or her dressing gown. She did not hear the garment drop to the floor. Finally, footfalls on the stairs.

The American raised his head a fraction. She put a finger to her lips, left it there. He studied her face. A chair scraped in the kitchen. Water ran at the pump. The tread of boot heels on the stone. She heard the distinctive sound of a man pissing into a metal pot. Then the rattle of the glass panel in the kitchen door as it was shut to. She counted carefully now. Two car doors opened; four closed. Unless they were trying to trick her, they had not left anyone behind.

Again, the crunch of tires on gravel.

She dropped her head and rested it on her knees. She hugged her legs.

"There were four of them?"

"Yes."

"They've gone?"

"Yes."

"You're positive?"

"No."

"They were Gestapo?"

"Yes."

"How can you tell?"

"Only the Germans have automobiles."

"What did they say?"

"I am not hearing all of it."

"Anything?"

"They are saying I might be in hiding with Henri."

"And?"

"One of them is saying he wants to climb into my bed."

"That was when they were laughing?"

"Yes."

"Will they come back?"

"Is possible."

"Should we leave? Get out of here?"

"No."

"Why not?"

"Is safer here."

"Are you all right?"

"Yes."

"You're trembling."

"Is cold."

"Here, put your coat around you."

She looked up. He was sitting, holding her coat open for her. She slid one arm into a cool sleeve, wrapped the coat around her nightgown, slipped the other arm in. She tugged her hair loose from the collar. His face was very near to hers.

"Stay inside here," he said, putting a hand on her shoulder. "Sleep here. They might come back."

"I cannot do this. Is not right."

"What's right is for you to be careful. Listen to me. You might not be so lucky next time."

She thought about that. If she hadn't already been awake, would she have heard the car as soon as she did? *Could* she have reacted as quickly?

"I am just sitting here for a while. But you sleep."

"Maybe we should sleep in shifts."

She tilted her head. "I am not understanding you."

"Taking turns. I sleep for a while. Then I wake you and you sleep for a while."

She pondered this. "Yes, all right. You are sleeping first."

He shook his head. "Claire, I've been doing nothing *but* sleeping for days. Let's exchange places. You lie down, and I'll keep watch. If I hear anything, I'll wake you."

She looked at him a long time. When he had gone to bed, he had taken his trousers off and folded them in the corner. Now he reached for them, awkwardly maneuvered each foot into the pant legs, pulled the trousers up and buttoned them. He moved away from the bedding, closer to the wall, and indicated she should lie down. When she hesitated, he put his hand on her elbow, to guide her.

Wordlessly, she lay down where he had so recently been. The pallet still held his warmth. She let him pull the comforters over her, and with her coat on as well, she no longer felt cold, and her shivering subsided. The linens smelled wonderfully fresh. From a sitting position, he reached over her and opened the attic trapdoor and then the armoire door a half inch.

"What is this?" she asked.

"I always crack the door a bit for air," he said.

She thought about this, her thoughts floating and not sequential.

"Then you are hearing me in my bedroom," she whispered.

He didn't answer her.

She fell almost at once into a dreamless sleep.

There was a stillness in her sleep, and he thought of this stillness as a kind of innocence. He had been watching her for hours. When the moon set, the outline of her face was barely discernible, lost to him. Now, with daybreak approaching, there was the slow seepage of shadowy light into the attic. Her face and mouth were again visible.

Her body was a comma, slightly curled, her hands folded into each other at the bottom of her throat. He sat against the wall, the bad leg outstretched, the good leg bent at the knee, on which he rested his forearm.

The suggestion of innocence had begun, he knew, before the sleeping. It had been there all along in her language — her throaty language with its halting phrases, its ungrammatical sentences, the poetry of her mistakes. Yet her language, he understood, was deceptive, not innocence itself, but an innocent facade. Were he to try to speak in her language, in French, he'd be taken for less than an innocent — an imbecile. And only he knew how deeply uninnocent he was.

Just as she was. He thought of what she had seen, been forced to witness. He thought of the canniness of her judgment, the necessary wisdom of survival. No one in this country, and perhaps in all of Europe — except the smallest of the children — could be counted among the innocent, he thought. Simply to have known what they had been forced to know was already loss of innocence.

He wondered about the boy. The courage of that one particular child. Could he, Ted, at ten or twelve, have accomplished such a rescue, *dared* to attempt such a rescue? He would like to know what had happened to the boy: How would his family have fared in the reprisals? She spoke the word *executions,* and there was no poetic mistake in that word. She had known things from the very beginning, had given them to him sparingly.

He studied her sleeping face. Her hair had fallen across her forehead. Her mouth was slightly open. He had desired her since the first night she brought him to her farmhouse, but he didn't completely understand this desire. Why this woman and not another? The answer couldn't simply be that she and not someone else was here, because there were other women available, in England, when his physical need was keen — and yet he had not then felt such desire, not as he was feeling it now. He knew only that it was a strong, physical attraction, not entirely sexual, a desire to be attached to her, touch her. He desired all of this woman, particularly those aspects of her he didn't even know about yet. It wasn't simply her face, though he understood already he would never tire of her mouth; nor was it merely her body, which he had seen in her nightgown in the candlelight, saw just hours ago through the cotton of a similar nightdress before he offered her the coat. Nor was it only the timbre of her voice, rich and throaty, a voice that sometimes mesmerized him, that he could hear in his mind even now. Nor, even, could it be merely a combination of these physical attributes. (Or could it be? Was it possible that one particular constellation of features produced in another an unavoidable chemistry?) But his desire was more than physical — he understood that already. It embraced what she had not given him yet. He wanted more than just the halting phrases. It was as though he had been teased by the mystery of her language, by the very fact of this barrier, and now was destined to pursue a woman who could never be fully known, and thus would remain forever desirable.

The seeping light brought to the surface, like a photographic image emerging in its emulsion, the outline of Stella and her smile in the wrinkled picture on the floor. He had betrayed his fiancée already, he knew, even though he had not touched this Belgian woman lying beside him. Simply to have admitted to his desire for this woman was to have betrayed Stella.

But he must force himself now to think of Stella — who *was* innocent — and of Henri Daussois as well. And he couldn't think of Henri without hearing the chilling sounds through the wall just hours ago — twelve hours ago? — when Henri and his wife were in the bed. He could not understand the story Henri told, but the meaning of the odd, choking sound and the coughing was unmistakable, as were the other sounds that followed, sounds that he would like to erase forever from his memory.

It was bad enough to think of betraying Stella, but the betrayal of Henri would be even worse. For all that Ted wished that Claire's husband would disappear, the inescapable truth was that Henri Daussois was someone who had helped to save his life and the lives of other airmen, who might even, at that moment, be risking his own life so as not to reveal Ted's whereabouts. To touch Claire, or even to have told her, as he did in the kitchen, that her voice was beautiful, was to have trespassed against her husband

and, indeed, against all the people who had conspired to try to save him.

He looked again at the small space in which he had been hidden for nineteen days. He heard again the German voices, the footsteps just beyond his head. At this moment, this attic was the only world that existed — a world he might be content to remain in forever. She had said *there are no bargains*. And he himself knew that the war itself had changed the rules, twisted them beyond all recognition.

He lowered his knee, shifted his weight slightly. He reached over for the photograph of Stella, tucked it between the pages of the poetry book. He closed the book. He leaned onto his side, propped up on his forearm. His face was inches from Claire's. He studied her face, the shape of her head. With his finger, he traced the unusual outline of her mouth. The touch wakened her, and she opened her eyes. He put a finger to her lips — an echo of the warning she had made to him twice before.

She looked at him, didn't move.

"Do you understand?" he asked.

She hesitated, then nodded slightly.

He bent and put his lips to the skin of her throat. He rested his face there, inhaling her. Moving his arm, he reached for her hair, her heavy, dark blond hair, and, as he had wanted to do for so long, he lost his hand inside its weight. After a time, he sensed a small movement, then felt her fingers at the back of his neck.

He sat up then and opened her coat. He lifted a strap of her nightgown away from her skin. In doing so, he felt a strange mixture of peace and excitement. He had then an image of the hallucination he had experienced in the woods. He was on his knees, and he was unwinding a woman.

February 8, 1944

HE PEERED THROUGH THE GLASS, UNFASTENED THE metal rod, and opened the window. Though the air was still cool, he could smell the earth. He remembered spring in Ohio, when farmers emerged after long winters to till the soil, transforming a rocky, gray landscape into a rich, humpy black. But this, he knew, was merely a false spring, a tease. It was still only February.

He made his fiftieth circuit — past the door, rounding the table by the stove, over by the pump, past the dresser and the coat pegs, along the other side of the table, and back to the door. He estimated the circuit at twenty-eight feet. A hundred times, roughly half a mile. If she didn't return soon, he would start on the stairs.

He had been here more than a month now, twenty days since the house had been raided by Gestapo. Twenty days since Henri left and went into hiding with the Maquis. Twenty days that Ted and Claire had made love. Stopped in his circuit, as he was stopped every time he thought of them together, he believed he could remember distinctly every single day of the twenty, every time he had touched her.

The first was the most tentative, the most chaste, neither knowing the other. All around them there was a sense of urgency, as though they might have only that one time, as though any minute they might be found in their lair. He remembered having watched her all through the night, waking her with the touch of his finger outlining her mouth. Oddly, she seemed already to know that he would touch her. She pulled his neck slightly toward her, and he knew by that small gesture that they would make love. Beneath the coat, she was wearing the ivory nightgown. He slipped the thin straps from her shoulders and looked at her breasts. She wouldn't touch his clothes (was that because they had once belonged to someone she knew?), and waited for him to half undress himself. He remembered that there was nothing coy or hesitant about her. He kissed her, and he knew he would never forget the relief the kissing brought him. Her skin was smooth — buttery was what he kept thinking — and he felt, under the nightgown, the nightgown raised now to her hips, the wonderful curve of her side, her rib cage to her legs. She never spoke. It had been a long time since he had been with a woman, and he was afraid that he might ruin it for her, but together they had found each other. He recalled the exquisite mix of fear and happiness, an odd sensation he had never experienced before. Just a few hours earlier, they had nearly been caught by the Gestapo. He was never so keenly aware of time as he was that night, of separate minutes, seconds, and all that could be felt during each. Afterward, he didn't want to sleep. He had the sensation that if he did, he might miss something important. He wrapped her again in her coat, a kind of cocoon. Her hair was tangled, and her bare feet protruded from the hem. He held her while she slept. He remembered clearly that when she opened her eyes and saw him with her, she smiled. Before he could speak, she took his hand and, unexpectedly and thrillingly, put her mouth on his fingers. It was the most sexual thing that had ever happened to him, and even now the image had power over him: He couldn't picture her mouth on his fingers without almost immediately wanting to make love to her. As he did then, again, before he himself finally slept.

He had memories now, a hundred memories in twenty days. It seemed extraordinary to him that the happiest days of his life, all twenty of them, had occurred within this house, within this war. He thought it possible these had been Claire's happiest days as well. He knew he made her happy, he was certain of that. Though she seldom spoke to him of what it was they were doing, there was now a contented gesture she made of arching her back, running her fingers up through her hair and shaking it out. Sometimes when she did this, she turned to him and smiled. He loved watching her do this when she was naked, her breasts rising with her arms.

For two days after the Gestapo came, they hid in the attic room, emerging only briefly for necessities. Most of that time he held her against him under the comforters. She seemed to have a great need to sleep. They spoke little, sensing perhaps that this interlude was fragile, and that anything, the wrong word, the wrong memory, might shatter it. On the third day, when they had not eaten in twenty-four hours, he could see that Claire was feeling light-headed, stumbling almost imperceptibly as she got up from the floor to put on her dress. He caught her by the arm. He told her he would go out to get them food and water. She shook her head and asked him, Are you mad?, and said she would go, she'd been planning it. With his leg still a handicap, he could not argue. He remembered the hours she was gone as an agony. Every new sound, every creak in the old farmhouse, made him think they had her. Using the forest route she'd relied on earlier, she had reached Madame Omloop's. She'd returned to the house, finally, with meager rations and horrifying news: Ten villagers had been hanged; thirty-seven had been deported east to prison camps. Many had been beaten, including Jean Benoît, the boy who had found Ted in the woods.

Ted held her as she wept. "I know these people they are hanging," she said quietly. "I am knowing them all my life."

He put his hand at the back of her head and pressed her face into his shoulder. His own anger made his chest tight. He had hated the Nazis, had sometimes been terrified by them in the air. But even then he had not truly understood the ugliness that was at the core of this war. Apart from a brief glimpse of a face behind a cockpit window, he had never really been forced to see the enemy. The planes provided a kind of buffer. It wasn't just the metal; it was the deceptive sense that the air war was a game — a game of skill and wits. He knew pilots who spoke almost reverently about the German aviators with whom they skirmished. In the air, it was easy to be lulled into thinking that like-minded men were fighting with one another. But here, on Belgian soil, in a village where ten innocent hostages had been hanged, there was no buffer, no illusion.

"I think we should get out of here as soon as possible," he said. "I think we should try to get across the border."

She drew away from him, averted her eyes. "No," she said, "is not possible now." She wiped her cheeks with her fingers and shook her hair out. "And also," she said, clearing her throat, "I am hearing that it is not me the Gestapo are wanting. It is Henri. Is better for us if we stay here and are quiet."

He couldn't persuade her, and with his leg still badly weakened he couldn't force her to leave. She was stronger than he was. Even so, it was five days before she dared to venture out again. This time they lay together and talked.

"Do you have other family in Delahaut?" he asked her one morning.

"They are moving just before the war to Charleroi. My mother is frail now, and I am last of eleven babies."

"Eleven children?" In his family, there had only been the three: Frances, Ted, and Matt, and at times that had seemed a lot.

"Yes, is crowded with many children when I am growing up, but some, they are already old and having children of their own and I am aunt to persons who are older than me."

"Complicated."

"In Delahaut, the family is . . . mmm . . . superior? Yes? Family is most important. Our festivals are in the family. And many of us are relations to each other. I am cousin to Henri."

Ted, who had been lying by her side, propped himself up on his elbow. "Cousin? Is that allowed?"

"Is far cousin, so is all right." She looked away from him. She was naked under the comforter. He traced her hairline to her temple, then her ear, trying to think of how to ask this next question casually. He licked the whorls in her ear. In the end, he simply asked it.

"Did you marry Henri for love? Do you love him now?" The words came out more hurried than he had hoped.

She looked back at him. They had never used the word *love*

between them. Once she had said to him that she adored his face. But not love.

"I know from very small child I am marrying Henri. It is not arranged, like in the old days, but is known. So I think that love is not so important in such a marriage, yes?"

He almost smiled. Perhaps he did smile.

"Someday, maybe, my mother is coming to my house and you are meeting her. She is *marraine de guerre*."

"What is that?"

"She is godmother of the war."

"I don't understand."

"My mother, she writes to the Belgian soldiers who are in German prisons because they do not have anyone else to write to them. And when she does, after a time, they fall in love with her, and they are sending her love letters, and she is not young woman, seventy-three. I am loving to read these letters. Very sweet, no?"

They talked about her childhood and his, about his Frances and her mother, about what it was like for him in England, about how she had hoped to go to university. They seldom spoke of the war itself except when it intruded upon them. And after the five days, she had to go out again. They had run out of food and water. That time she came back with the information that the Gestapo had retreated to St. Laurent, the extra reinforcements to Florennes. A strange kind of normalcy, she said, had settled over the village. Even the school had reopened, though she could not imagine how the teachers had managed to remove the bloodstains from the classrooms.

He rounded the corner again, looked out the open window for Claire. He had promised her he would not leave the house. Sometimes at the doorstep she found packages of food: cheese, carrots, onions, sausage, loaves of bread, and other items — a bar of soap, a pair of socks, once even a pack of cigarettes they vowed to ration and then smoked ravenously in one day. These packages, Claire had explained, were offerings from villagers who, though they themselves were not within the Maquis, were nevertheless supportive of the Resistance.

"They know I'm here?" he asked. "That you're hiding me?"

"Yes," she said. "Some."

"And aren't you worried about that? That you might be betrayed?"

"Yes," she said evenly. "I am always worrying about the denunciations. Is every day I am thinking this. But these people who are leaving the packages? I am believing that they are good people and are wanting to help us."

"Why would they do that?" he asked her.

"You don't understand," she said. "The Belgians, we think the Americans are . . . saving us. Are our saviours, no? The French" — she flip-flopped her hand — "maybe they are not so sure, but in Belgium we are sure."

He remembered being confused by this information. "But Claire," he said, "how could you or anyone else possibly think me a saviour when I've been responsible for all these deaths?"

"You are not responsible."

"Of course I am. There must be people in the village who *hate* the day the plane fell. Ten hanged? Thirty-seven deported?"

"You are again not understanding. Sometimes in Belgium we are receiving . . . sometimes the English and American bombs fall on Belgium villages by . . . mmm . . . mistake? Or villages are bombed directly because there is German military base nearly to them, but the Belgians, we are understanding this. Without the aviators, Belgium is not ever returning." Her hand fluttered and trailed away.

Sometimes, within the packages, there were references to Henri: A bridge blown in Florennes; saboteurs at the dam in St. Laurent. There was never any message *from* Henri. Ted watched Claire carefully when she read these bulletins. She translated them for him and explained what they' meant, but beyond discussing those few scraps of paper, they never spoke of her husband. Ted assumed that she had made a secret truce within herself, and he could only guess at its price. As for himself, he tried not to think of Henri at all.

In the twenty days, the leg had continued to heal. Twice she had taken him outside at night, when there was no moon, and they walked together from the house to the barn and back again, exhilarating journeys for a man who had been kept in an attic. On the second night they did this, Claire found a message (in a precious tin of cocoa) that said the escape line had been partially blown. Claire was tight-lipped and frightened, and at first Ted didn't understand the full import of the message. That the local section of the main escape route was exposed and Ted would have to wait until another was put together struck him initially and selfishly as a wonderful and miraculous thing. He would be content, he knew, to remain with this woman for months, for years even, and he sometimes allowed himself to invent this as his future. But when she explained to him the significance of a blown line — the denunciations, the arrests, the torture, the further denunciations — he immediately regretted his earlier selfishness and became fearful for Claire. If Claire and Henri were a cog in the escape line, wasn't she, too, at risk of being denounced?

For two days they had hovered near the attic, were cautious in all their movements, listened to every sound outside the house, waiting for another raid. In the subsequent days, however, he noticed that they had become less careful, talking long into the night at the kitchen table, the candle between them. Every evening, they listened to the BBC, a clandestine activity in itself, but even more dangerous since it prevented them from monitoring any unusual sounds outside the house. One night, he made her dance with him, despite his limp, in what he knew would be a comical spectacle had there been anyone to watch them. But it was enough just to hold her in that way and pretend that one day they might dance together in Paris or New York.

"I'm supposed to be teaching you French," she said.

"I'm learning other things," he said.

In the daylight hours, he sometimes read to her from the book of English poetry or told her stories of the war as he had known it in the air. He tried to make these stories amazing or funny to please her and to make her smile. He was sometimes moved by how physically difficult her life was. When they thought it was safe and that the Gestapo were not, after all, watching the farm, he went with her to the barn and helped her with her chores: the milking, feeding the small herd, mucking out after them. Just washing the clothes took her nearly a day. He marveled at the large oak tub with the flame underneath it to boil the water, the wooden T-shaped fixture in the tub with which she agitated the clothes, the way she lay the clothes full of soap on the grass to bleach them in the light, and then rinsed them and pulled them through the wooden wringers. He watched her bake bread every day and was intrigued by the way she sliced the large round loaves: cradling the bread in her arm and slicing toward herself.

And when she was not working or they were not reading or talking or listening to the radio or performing the tasks necessary for their survival, they made love. It pleased him how often they made love, and sometimes it frightened him. It was as though they both knew that what they had could not last. When he touched her, she never demurred, never pulled away from him. She seemed to have the same need as he, a need he did not now think of as physical, or purely physical. He thought of it rather as the desire to be known — the desire to know and to be known by the one person. Sometimes he was truly baffled that the one person should be a Belgian woman who was married to another man, a man critical to his own survival — and yet at other times he made himself believe that their loving was fated, as the fall of the plane itself may have been fated.

Over the pump there was a small mirror in a painted frame (Henri's mirror for shaving, he imagined), and in his circuit, he stopped now to peer into it. He had lost perhaps ten pounds, and his face was too lean, almost hollow. He looked considerably older than he used to. He saw the foreign collar of the cotton shirt and looked down at the clothes he had become accustomed to wearing. His uniform had been burned; his dog tags buried. There was now no trace of Lieutenant Theodore Aidan Brice, except for the creased photograph of Stella, still within the pages of the poetry book. A picture he had not looked at in twenty days. He wondered if there were, in Belgium or France, American aviators who, stripped of their uniforms, had decided to remain missing, who might never emerge, even when the war was over. He thought of his navigator, AWOL in a hotel room in Cambridge. Would it be possible never to return? To meld somehow into a life here, assume a new identity — Pierre, or Jacques, or even Theo? The possibility of anonymity, of assuming another identity entirely, was momentarily delicious, and he toyed with it.

But what then of Stella? Or of Frances?

He heard her bicycle on the gravel.

Her shoulder was just inside the door, and already he had his hand between her coat and her blouse, lifting the coat up and off her shoulder. Balancing on the good leg, he had another hand behind her neck. Impatiently he kissed her mouth, her ears, her hair. The packages she carried made sharp points in his ribs. He pulled away to see her face, and as he did so, he lost his precarious footing and fell with her against the kitchen door. The glass pane rattled so sharply he thought it would break.

"You are surprising me," she said breathlessly.

Her face was flushed, the right side of her lipstick smudged into the corner of her mouth. He took her heavy hair into both hands and raised it up behind her head.

"I worry for you every time you leave," he said.

Her eyes dropped, and he was instantly sorry he had said this, for he had caused the very thing he always hoped to forestall: the inevitable moment of fear or remorse that entered her thoughts and realigned the features of her face, that took away the joy he knew he briefly gave her. She made a small movement with the packages, slipped out from under the fragile hold he had on her hair.

He knew the route Claire had taken to Omloop's, could picture it clearly even though he had never been there, had never even seen the village, except fleetingly from the air. The long dirt road through the woods to the edge of the village, the high walls of the cemetery and the cobblestone alleyways, the village square with its fountain, the shop where Claire purchased food with her stamps, sometimes received messages.

He studied the back of her coat as she took her parcels from the string bag.

Something was wrong.

He could see it: an indefinable stiffness in her movements; just as he could hear, in the hum of an engine, a catch, a misfire.

"What was happening in the village?" he asked, keeping his words as casual as he could.

"Is very . . ." She seemed to be searching for a word. ". . . quiet."

"Something's wrong," he said quickly.

She was silent, methodically removing and unwrapping the parcels from the bag. He stood by the door.

"Claire . . ."

Still she didn't answer him. Turning once, avoiding his eyes, she removed her coat, hung it on its peg. She bent to put the cheese and sausage in the icebox. She lifted a pear, a single pear, from the table.

"Is *poire* . . ."

"Pear."

"Yes."

"Is very rare, from Madame Omloop."

"Claire."

"Is Friday they are taking you."

She was wearing his favorite dress — a brown silklike fabric that drew the eye to her waist. The dress had shoulder pads and narrow sleeves, and the neckline was like that of a blouse, with covered buttons. Her hair had come loose on the right side, the careful roll of dark blond hair sliding lower over her ear.

He closed his eyes.

Friday. Four days away.

"I won't go," he heard himself saying. He had not known until that moment that he would say that.

"They are coming for you in the evening," she said in reply, as if she had not heard him.

"Then you'll go with me." In his stomach, he felt the beginnings of a knot of dread.

"Is not possible."

"You have to come with me," he insisted.

He moved toward her, but she put a hand up.

"Is not possible. I have not the papers."

"Then we'll get you some. If they can — "

"No." She interrupted him. "They will not be making me the

papers. I am waiting here for my husband." She took a step backwards, felt for the table behind her with her hands. "I am waiting here, because if I am leaving, it is the same as to denounce my husband. He is not being able to come out of hiding then. Ever. Not until the war is ending."

He stood motionless by the door. In the harsh light, even from this distance, he could see the fine lines of her face. It occurred to him suddenly that he must memorize this face. The urgency that he felt with her the first time they made love now withered in comparison with the urgency he felt at this moment: four days in which to love this woman.

"I'm not going," he said.

Her face was noncommittal. She had already made her argument. Later, he knew, she would take it up again, make her quiet pronouncements.

He took a step toward her. "When the war is over, you can leave Henri. It will be all right then."

She didn't move.

"You don't love him, do you?"

She raised her head, looked away. She made a small movement with her mouth, a tightening, as if she were biting the inside of her lip, making a decision.

"Is war," she said, turning to face him.

Inexplicably he wanted to kneel.

"Please, we are not speaking of this anymore," she said.

He walked to where she was standing, looped his arms around her. Her hair gave off a rich scent — a combination, he had always thought, of animal and soap.

He closed his eyes. He ran his hands along the length of her back. He had seen the bones there, the run of her vertebrae. He had seen the white skin at the inside of her thighs. He had tasted her — the salt of the skin above her breasts. Hadn't these acts, the most intimate acts of his life, bound them together?

It was the knowing they had only four days that was the worst, he thought. It would have been better to have been taken quickly, even if there were no time for goodbyes. As in death. The worst was *to know* you were going down, he believed, not the act of going down itself. He thought of the gunner who fell out of the sky, hoped the man blacked out as soon as he hit freefall. He thought of the villagers, taken into the square to be hanged. Those moments of anguish. Only a minute, two minutes, to make it right. And the inevitable futility of ever making it right.

Just as this could not be made right.

He wondered what would happen to her after he was gone. He could not imagine now her life here without him. Would she tend to other aviators like himself? Would she return with Henri to their bed?

If only he could persuade her to escape with him.

He heard again her sentence: *I am waiting here for my husband.*

Through the old glass at the far window, he could see the sun on the matted grasses, the spongy soil.

With his right arm, he reached for her coat on the peg, wrapped it around her shoulders. She drew back; there was a look of puzzlement on her face.

She thought that he might try to walk with her all the way to France. He took her hand, led her out of the kitchen to the barn, then behind the barn into the fields. She knew they were exposed, that he had not, in all the time he had been with her, been as visible as he was now. He limped badly, but she could see that day by day his strength was returning. She suspected that he would have this limp all his life; one leg seemed to be shorter than the other.

They walked slowly without speaking. She knew that what they were doing was madness. At any moment someone might bicycle along the road and see them. With his height, his sand-colored hair, his limp, he would never be mistaken for a Belgian. Yet she could not bring herself to refuse him this walk, just as she could not withdraw her hand from his. For a moment she closed her eyes. Ever since she had seen Madame Omloop and received the message that the escape line had been repaired and that the

American was to be moved on Friday, she had felt light-headed, dizzy. She knew that it was true, that there would not be a reprieve. And it surprised her that that was how she thought of it — a death sentence. Four more days.

He would go, and she would not know what had happened to him. He would be taken across the border, and that night she would not know where he was sleeping. And within days, or even hours, another man or woman would be brought to her to occupy the hiding place. She shook her head quickly. It was not possible that another man would come and sleep where he had slept. Where they had made love.

Sometimes, when she was with him, she prayed that Henri would not come back. She knew she would be damned for such a prayer, but she could not help herself. In all her life, she had not thought that she would love a man in the way that she loved this American. Ted. Such a short, abrupt name. A boy's name. Not a name for a grown man. She thought of the contours of his face above her, his face grown thinner in the days that he had been with her. Would there come a time when she would not be able to remember that face?

She felt the dry, hard skin of his fingertips. Perhaps he *would* take her all the way to France, where she had once imagined there would be color; and if he kept walking, she was not sure now that she would be able to ask him to stop. A wind came up across the fields. It stung her eyes.

"You're shivering," he said.

His face was slightly reddened from the wind. He released her hand and, with his fingers, pushed her hair off her face. She knew that even if a lone cyclist appeared on the distant road, she would not stop him or pull away.

He slid his hands down between her coat and her shoulders. She let herself go — what was there to lose now? He caught her weight at her back and lowered her to the ground. Sharp, dead straw stalks dug into her neck and pricked the back of her head. She was aware of heavy clothes, an awkwardness, of a sharp wind on her thighs. He put his mouth against her ear, pressed her hard. She thought that possibly he was speaking to her, but she wasn't sure. He tried to shield her with Henri's long coat. It was a kind of tent, she thought. She hoped that he would bury her, that he would cover her with himself, that he would stay there with her for days while the clouds moved.

———•———

In the end, she risked the truck. They tried the bicycle, he maneuvering with the one good foot, pulling the pedal up with his toe when he lost his momentum, but the going was slow and cumbersome.

Returning to the house, they had been overtaken by a kind of recklessness. He wanted to go out, he said — just this once, to be with her, however briefly, in a public place. As if there were not a war, and they were just a normal couple. She could not refuse him — his mood was infectious — but she would not go into Delahaut, she told him. If he wanted to venture into a village, she would drive him through the woods to a neighboring town where they would not be as conspicuous as in her own.

Henri's long, threadbare coat made him feel as though he were hiding more than just his nationality; it cloaked him, he felt, in an awkward and unattractive guilt. He wished he had his khakis on. The pallor of his skin and the beret Claire gave him to cover his light hair made him look, he knew, years older than he was. He supposed this was a good thing. Claire sat forward on the torn leather seat, with its tufts of stuffing and wire coils. He liked watching the way the inside of her left knee was exposed under her skirt. A flowered kerchief was poised at the crown of her head and tied hastily around the heavy mass of her hair.

In the woods, the road was uneven and sometimes treacherous. Occasionally the ruts in the road made the cab of the truck bounce violently from side to side; reflexively, Ted put his full weight on his bad leg, and winced. The muscles and tendons were still raw. Even though the day was cold, he couldn't stop himself from rolling down the window. The fresh air was delicious.

"I had a woods like this near my home when I was growing

up," he said when they were well inside the forest. "I used to spend a lot of time there."

"Alone?" she asked. "You are playing?"

"Usually alone. Sometimes with a friend. I had a BB gun — do you know what that is? — and I used to shoot squirrels and then skin them. Pretty awful, now that I think about it. Frances hated it. She used to squeal when I brought the skins back. I was twelve, thirteen maybe."

"I am also," she said. "I am playing in these woods as small child. Very many hours I am alone here. But I am not hunting." She smiled. "I am playing in . . . old stories?"

"Fairy tales?" he asked.

"Yes, fairy tale." She smiled again. "Beautiful stories of princess and bad wolves. You know these stories?"

He loved her smile.

"These stories," she said. "I am never thinking of this before, but is not true, these stories. Yes, there are wolves, and they are eating children and women and men, but the ends are not happy. We cannot tell children these stories now. Is wrong."

"We don't know that yet," he said quietly, looking away from her and out the window.

"But, yes, we are knowing this. The old woman I am telling you they are beating and sending away? Is happy ending for this woman?"

She stopped the truck, the engine still running. "Is there," she said, pointing to her left into the woods.

"What is?" he asked.

"Is there you are found. The boy is telling me."

Ted leaned toward her window, straining to see beyond the fencelike wall of trees. There was a small clearing fifty feet away, where the light seemed slightly brighter.

"I hid underneath a bush," he said. "The boy found me there. He followed my tracks, I suppose. I was delirious. I remember opening my eyes and seeing his face. I had no idea where I was. Not even what country I was in. It's funny. When I was his age, I can remember tracking animals in the woods. Deer. I wonder if he thought it was an adventure. Tracking a soldier."

"I think he is frightened," she said.

"Yes," he said, sitting back.

They emerged from the woods. The road was better here — past fields and some farmhouses.

"Where are we?" he asked.

"The village where I am taking you is Rance. Is not Gestapo in this village now, but still is very dangerous. In Belgium we have the people who are helping the Germans, and we are not certain what persons are good and what are not. Is like the old stories, no? The animal in the sheep's skin?"

"Wolf."

"So you are being very careful and not speaking any word."

"I promise," he said, smiling slightly as if he had been scolded. He reached along the back of the seat, put his hand inside the collar of her coat. He touched the skin at the back of her neck. The gesture caused her kerchief to slip back over her hair. He leaned toward her, kissed the shoulder of her coat. Moving her arm, she gently nudged him away. She stopped the truck for the second time and turned to him.

"We are going back?" she asked.

"No."

"In one hour," she said haltingly, "the village is empty, and there are no people in the café. If we are making this journey, we are making it now, or is . . ." She stopped, searching for a word. ". . . *Fou.*"

"*Fou?*"

"Madness," she said.

He moved his body away from hers, but kept his hand on her sleeve. Anything to be touching her.

Rounding the corner of an alley, poised to enter the village square, Ted had his first misgivings. They had been walking as though Claire were on his arm, as though this were merely a midday stroll, but it was he who leaned his weight on her at each footfall of the bad leg. They were in shadow from a church, and he made her wait. He couldn't tell if she was frightened or not — nothing in her breathing or the touch of her arm betrayed her.

Across the cobblestones of this unfamiliar village was a row of shops with foreign words in beautiful script painted on the glass fronts. To the left was a school, with children's paper snowflakes still taped to paned windows. Just to the right of the shops was the café, where several green metal tables were scattered about near the door. Some of the tables were occupied with pairs of older women and pairs of men. He noticed that there were no couples, nor any young men. He tried to imagine how this café might have looked a few years ago, but this thought, inextricably woven as it was with the possibility of having known Claire before the war, before she married, caused a painful tug inside his chest. Perhaps there'd have been a table of young men and women, drinking red wine, some rowdiness, a few songs badly sung. The café owner himself might have come out and joined the crowd. Someone would be clowning, trying to attract the attention of a certain girl. And he and Claire would be with them or apart, and would be touching, sharing the noon meal.

He took a step forward and kept his face averted when a stranger crossed his path. Even so, in the short journey from the alley across the square to the café, he sensed scrutiny. What was it that gave him away? he wondered. Was it his height? At the table, Claire gestured for him to sit sideways, so that his face was not in full view. He couldn't touch her, or even look at her for very long, and she had told him not to speak. A waiter came to the table as Ted was arranging his leg beneath it. The waiter spoke in rapid French to Claire, who answered him almost curtly. Ted's chair wobbled on uneven legs.

He allowed his eyes to meet hers — that watchful, lovely gray. A gray, he realized, he had seen before: the gray of the sun breaking through a low stratus. Looking past Claire, he noticed at the next table two elderly women dressed nearly identically in black cloth coats, black scarves, and sturdy shoes. Beside them, on the cobblestones, each had a string bag of parcels. One of the women, who had a large and livid bump at the end of her nose, raised her face and caught Ted's eye. Her neck was wattled and fell in a fold above the collar of her coat. Slowly, so as not to appear to be evasive, he slid his eyes from hers and studied the shops opposite. When Ted looked back toward Claire, he observed that the old woman was still looking at him. Worse, she was also talking to her companion.

Ted looked down at the table.

The waiter brought a cup of coffee for Claire, a tall glass of thin beer for Ted. He took a thirsty swallow and set the glass down. "I think we've been seen," he said. "I'm sorry. This was a terrible idea."

She made a small surprised movement with her hand. Her eyes, however, were expressionless.

Ted watched as the two old women gathered their possessions and slowly, leaning for support on the table, rose to a standing position. To his horror, the woman with the bump at the end of her nose approached Claire.

Leaning over Claire's shoulder, the woman in black murmured a few words. Claire kept her eyes focused on Ted and nodded, but said nothing. The woman straightened her back and, with her companion, made her way slowly across the uneven cobblestones. Claire waited until she was gone.

"The woman is wishing me the luck," she said finally in an almost inaudible voice. Ted could hear the quaver in her words. "And to you, she is expressing gratitude."

She took a sip of coffee. Her hand was shaking. His glass was already empty, he realized. He wanted another drink. Badly. How could he have been spotted so quickly?

"We should go," he said urgently.

She shook her head. "No. Is important we sit here calm."

"How can it be so obvious?" he asked. "I felt it all across the square. Is it my height?"

"Yes," she said, considering him for a time. "That and other things I am seeing here and not in the house. See now, you are sitting sideways to the table, and your leg is folded over the other at your knee. Is very . . . elegant? But not so Belgian, I think. And your hands here." She drew a line along one of his fingers with her own. She let her fingertip linger on his hand. "I am loving your hands, but they are not Belgian also." She studied him. "And the sitting. Your back is bent in its chair." She made a curve with her hand. "Relaxed, yes?"

"But not Belgian."

"No, is not even the English. Just the American, I think. Even in the old coat and hat, you are looking American. And is your eyes also. Maybe now I think is your eyes first they are seeing."

"Have you known many Americans?" he asked.

"Only one," she said.

He felt a small worm of jealousy. "Was he a soldier? A pilot?"

She looked away from him. "Is two Americans the Maquis is finding with their parachutes in the north. They are being sent to me, and I am making the room ready. And then there is mistake, and the Americans coming to me are betrayed. One is shot in the head by Germans, and I have never see him. The other one I see. He is shot in leg. Not like you. Here." She pointed to her thigh. "And the bleeding is terrible. And the American is dying that night in my house."

Ted nodded slowly. He let the worm crawl back into its hole.

He turned his head and examined a row of baguettes inside the café window. What if the woman in black was a collaborator? He and Claire might even now be under arrest. The thought of Claire arrested and interrogated made him ill.

"Have you seen many people die?" he asked her.

She took a slow sip of coffee, replaced the cup in its saucer. "Some," she said.

"Three, four years ago, would you have believed this?"

"Believed . . .?"

"This." He gestured to encompass the entire square. "The deaths. The fear. The not knowing if the guy sitting next to you is a traitor or a friend. The fact that one morning you can be talking to a neighbor, and that afternoon she is hanged — for no reason other than that she lived in your village."

"We are knowing this war is coming for many years," she said.

"The unthinkable becomes the thinkable."

"Pardon?"

"One day, getting shot at in a B-17, or watching a friend die, or going without food is no longer the horror it used to be. In a way, it even becomes romantic."

"No," she said, shaking her head firmly. "Is never the romance. We are never forgetting what is for. You, perhaps, you come so far and is not war in America, is hard to know why we are wanting to fight so much."

No, he thought, there wasn't a war *in* America, but Americans were dying all the same. He thought of his gunner — that awful, gaping wound. You could spend the entire war just thinking of that wound. The man's body, the center of the man, gone. And if you were the man's wife and remembered the man's body, how did you stand it?

But of course the wife would never know how her husband had died. She'd be told only that he'd gone quickly and hadn't suffered. If Ted were back in England, he'd be writing the letter himself.

One letter out of thousands.

One story out of thousands.

"I want to ask you a question," he said. "It was a kind of test they put to us in flight training." Her face, he thought as she cocked her head slightly, was intelligent, canny even, but essentially trusting.

"You're driving along a coast road in a jeep. You've got to get your crew to another base in order to fly a mission. It's a narrow road, one lane only, not wide enough for two vehicles. On one side, it's a sheer drop over a cliff. On the other is a solid rock wall."

She nodded.

"You go around a corner, and suddenly you see that a schoolbus full of children is coming right at you. There's no time to stop, and the bus has nowhere to go except through the space where you are. One of you has to go over the cliff."

She nodded again.

"What do you do?" he asked.

She rested her chin on her hand. She seemed to be staring at a point just over his left shoulder. He didn't know if she had entirely understood the question, but just as he was about to repeat it, she answered him.

"Is terrible question," she said, shaking her head. "And is

terrible answer. But I am understanding the answer in the war. The bus is going over the cliff, no?"

"You'd let the children go over the cliff?" he asked, alarmed by her answer.

"The crew is for the war, yes? To fly the planes. And you have job to get crew to planes."

"But what's the point of getting the crew to a plane to go up in the air to theoretically save the lives of people in another country if in the process you kill twenty children?"

"Is obligation," she said. "In war is no choice."

He shook his head slowly, unwilling to concede her point — even though he knew that she, too, was part of a military operation. One with very different equipment and personnel, perhaps, but a military operation all the same.

"I didn't do it," he said. "I couldn't do it. I was supposed to ditch in the Channel, try to make it if I could. But I had two wounded on board, and I couldn't make the decision to kill them outright. As it happened, they died anyway. And a lot more besides."

"Is like the triage," she said quietly. "I am sometimes doing the triage."

As he looked at her, he saw a boy coming from the opposite side of the square on a bicycle. The figure barely registered; but then something, the hand-knit cap perhaps, made Ted turn his head. The boy, sensing this movement, looked at Ted and, with a brief expression of astonishment, recognized the tall stranger in the woolen coat. Possibly the boy's hand came up off the handlebars. The front tire hit an uneven stone. The bicycle stopped short; the boy was catapulted over the handlebars and onto the stone square.

Ted began to rise. Claire, with pressure on his arm, stopped him. Ted watched as Claire ran to the boy. When she lifted the boy's head, Ted could see a bloody scrape on the forehead — but the boy was conscious and able to speak.

Several other people were at Claire's side. With attention now focused on the boy, Ted stood, limped quickly to the side of the café, rounded the corner into a dark alleyway. He flattened his body against the side of the building, raised his head. Above him was a slit of sky, of light.

From somewhere he could hear the drone of a plane. An engine, it seemed to him, was straining. He waited for the plane to cross his narrow window. The engine was in trouble, he decided, listening to its stutter. A bomber. But the plane did not cross his vision, and he could no longer hear it. Some poor son of a bitch lost and going down? Trying to make it to the Channel?

He knew he had to leave her. Now. His presence was for her a death sentence. Twice in ten minutes he had been identified. And even if the two sightings were benign (one, the boy's, he was almost certain of), what of others in the square who might have seen him? A man, perhaps, whom Ted never even noticed?

She would have the truck, but she would search the village first. He had to try to remember the route back to the woods — then head southwest, toward France. With luck, he'd be found again by friendly French or Belgians, sent quickly across the border.

His head hurt from the knowledge that he had to leave her. There was never a future for them together, and she had understood that all along, just as she had known all along that the schoolbus had to go over the cliff. And he was certain they would both go mad if they had to listen to the clock tick away the minutes until Friday. Far better to leave now — swiftly and without words.

He found himself, after wandering alleyways and lanes, at the edge of the village, exposed. Some hundred yards away was the beginning of the wood, a small cottage in between. A dog — a short, fast, yipping terrier — came running from behind the cottage and barked at Ted's heels, creating a sudden commotion in the silence. Frozen, Ted waited for a face at a window, a door opening. But there was nothing; the mutt must be alone. More quickly now, Ted dragged the leg into the forest. He thought that he would give his other leg for another pint of that Belgian beer.

He had been using the sun as an imperfect compass, and was aware that if he didn't make better progress, he'd be spending the night in the wood. He had been avoiding the old logging road, even though the muck and brambles of the wood made the journey difficult, because he knew she would have to stick to the logging road in the truck. But when he saw the road off to the left, he told himself he'd take it for just a few minutes, give the leg a rest.

From the angle of the sun, he estimated the time now at about three o'clock. He realized he couldn't now go back to Claire's even if he wanted to. He had no idea where her house was. With his free hand, he clutched the front of his coat. He wished he'd thought to wear a sweater. As it was, he had on only an open-necked shirt and Henri's inadequate coat. He was aware of a hollow sensation in the wake of the beer without food. He wondered if it would end as it was meant to. With himself crawling under a bush for warmth and dying there.

She would know why he had gone. And if she were in his position, he knew, she'd have done the same. He was sure of that. Always, from the very beginning, she had known that what there was between them was the story of a few days and nights within a larger drama — one over which they had no control. She would go on riding to Madame Omloop's, making the white sausage with no meat, listening to the BBC at night. She would stand at the window as she did, smoking, one arm cradled under her breasts. And himself? America seemed almost incomprehensible, something experienced in a distant childhood. Six months ago he was in Texas, waiting to be sent overseas. Now it seemed that all the important events of his life were behind him.

He rounded a bend and saw the truck, with its mottle of black and rust. It was parked in the middle of the logging road. The engine was not running. There was no one in the cab. Where the hell was she?

He moved as fast as his leg would allow. He called her name once sharply, pulled himself up onto the running board of the passenger side. Startled at the sudden sound, she looked up at him through the window. She had been bent over, her head against the steering wheel. Her face was wet.

He swung open the door, climbed up onto the leather seat,

heard the door close behind him. He reached for her head and kissed her. She could not get her breath. Her hands rose to his face.

"I am so frightened. I cannot find you," she said.

He repeated her name. The Germans or the Belgians would have to shoot him — he would not leave her now. Their embrace, inside the truck, was clumsy, like that of two teenagers. He bent her head into his chest, held her tightly against him. Her hair fell in sheets at the sides of her face, and he remembered this, from the first time he ever saw her. He lifted her chin with his hand and traced the outline of her mouth with his fingertip. Her upper lip was wet. He used his thumb then to wipe away the tears under her eyes, but his hands were dirty from his trek in the woods, and he made half-moon smudges on her cheekbones.

"The boy is all right?" he asked.

She nodded.

"We'll take the truck now," he said. "To France."

She averted her eyes and kissed him. "No," she whispered, sliding off his mouth.

"You know the way. We'll stop at the border. Go on foot."

Another whisper, the same word.

"People in France will hide us. We'll make it to Spain. Gibraltar. Hundreds have done it."

She could no longer say the word to him, but she shook her head. He kissed the top of her head, her hair warm under his mouth. He leaned his head back, closed his eyes. The comfort of holding her was exquisite. He could not imagine now a life without her.

"Claire, listen to me."

She pulled away slightly and turned her head as if to speak to him, and instantly her face changed. He felt the shudder that traveled the length of her body. She was perfectly still, as if she had been shot. She was not even breathing.

He tried to focus on her face. He twisted around to discover what it was she had seen outside the back window.

At the bend in the road, not a hundred feet behind them, was a man. His face was obscured by dirt, his hair grown long over his ears. He was standing with his hands in his pockets, staring at the truck.

"Henri," Claire said.

———

Monsieur Gillian, the owner of the café, had made him put his bicycle in the back of the small van. Jean had protested. He was fine, he said; he could easily walk the bicycle home. But even he, looking at the mangled front wheel, knew that it would be a journey of hours, that it would be long past dark, long past the evening meal, perhaps even near to midnight, before he made it to the farmhouse. He'd had to accept the ride in the van then, his confusion making him nearly mute no matter how much Monsieur Gillian tried to coax him into a bit of conversation.

Everyone, it seemed, knew about the flogging by the Gestapo. Adults were no better than his friends when it came to wanting all the facts, he thought. Even when it was a terrible story, one they knew shamed you or caused you pain, they wanted the details: How had he been discovered? Had he really fainted? Had he tried to flee? How many lashes? Did he still have scars?

Oh, yes, he still had scars, he could tell them. Sometimes in the morning, when he rose from the bed under the eave, he saw thin stripes of blood on the sheets. He would remember the pain then and wonder when the wounds would heal. And then he would turn the sheet over or, if he had time, try to wash out the stains so that his mother would not see.

Madame Daussois had lifted his head from the street. His vision was blurry, and there was blood in his eye. She held his head gently with her hands and, as she was calling for help, turned his face to her chest. The gesture left a bloodstain on the front of her coat.

He was dizzy, disoriented. He tried to tell her once, just before Monsieur Gillian carried him into the café, that he wouldn't tell about the pilot. But she shook her head quickly to silence him.

How fast does such a thing happen? he wondered. He was crossing the square, thinking of beginning the long journey back to school, when the face turned toward him, and he knew at once. It wasn't possible ever to forget those eyes — the green with the light behind them. Were it not for the eyes, he might not have recognized the man. A beret that was too large for him hung over the man's ears. The coat was that of a peasant. When he'd last seen the pilot, near death though he was, he'd been in uniform, and a uniform never failed to convey authority — no matter how torn and dirty that uniform was.

Monsieur Gillian asked him what he had been doing in Rance.

"A parcel, sir. For my aunt."

Monsieur Gillian nodded. The truth was that Jean went there every day now, at the noon hour, unable to bear the sight of the center of Delahaut. He could not look at the balconies of the terraced houses without seeing the faces and twitching bodies of the hanged. He saw this even in his dreams. And he could not enter the square without his eyes being drawn, against his will, to the balconies. It was a kind of self-torture.

So he went to Rance every noon hour, and sometimes was late getting back to school for the afternoon classes. If he didn't go to Rance, he'd bicycle to the woods, or even to St. Laurent, though that was riskier since the Germans were still at L'Hôtel de Ville.

"Here, sir. If you please. I can go the rest."

They were on the road to the Benoît farm. Jean did not want to be seen emerging from the van.

"But you are injured, no? I must take you to your house."

"No, please, it's best here. Please." Jean heard the sudden begging in his voice. So be it. Better to humiliate himself now than to excite his father's anger even more than it would be.

Monsieur Gillian stopped the van. Jean quickly hopped out of the passenger side before Monsieur Gillian changed his mind. Reluctantly, the café owner walked to the back of the van and opened the paneled doors.

"You're sure you don't want me to go in with you, speak to your mother?" Monsieur Gillian offered, as he lifted the bicycle to the ground.

"I am certain. Thank you for the ride."

Monsieur Gillian hesitated, looked puzzled.

"You're all right?" he asked.

Jean nodded, tried to smile.

"You're all right at home, I meant," Monsieur Gillian added.

Jean wondered for a moment if Monsieur Gillian knew about his father. Then, to reassure Monsieur Gillian, Jean nodded eagerly, quickly. He was anxious to be gone now.

"Well then, I'll be off. But I can't say I like this."

The boy watched the café owner climb up into the driver's side, shut the door, and reverse the van into a turn. Jean waited until the van was on its way back to Rance, and then waved. A hand shot out of the window and waved back at him.

Slowly he turned in the direction of his house. It would become visible around the next corner. The wayward front wheel of the bicycle made forward progress impossible. Jean had to lift the front wheel, then guide the back wheel as if it were a unicycle. He was glad now that he'd accepted Monsieur Gillian's offer to drive him home.

She'd put the plaster on his forehead. Monsieur Gillian had given her iodine for the cut. After the forehead was tended to, she'd ordered milk for him and a roll.

"I have to go now," she'd whispered to him when Monsieur Gillian had gone to fetch the milk. "You understand?"

He understood she meant the pilot. She had to go to him. He badly wanted to ask her so many questions: How was the American? How was the wounded leg? Did the American remember the night in the forest and in the barn? When was he leaving? How were they getting him out of the country? But he asked her nothing.

Then she'd done a strange and wonderful thing. She'd bent forward and kissed him. The kiss landed somewhere between his left eye and cheek. His face flushed. She said thank you to him — twice quickly, in a whisper — when it was he, really, he thought, who ought to be thanking her.

He brought a hand up now to touch the place where she had kissed him.

He left the bicycle in the gloomy barn, out of sight. His father would go on about his carelessness when he saw it. Tentatively, he pushed open the kitchen door. His mother, at the sink, had her back to him.

She turned, her eyes widening at the sight of him. And what amazed him, even then, was how her face went from boredom, to surprise, to alarm when she saw the plaster, and then immediately to fear as her eyes darted sideways to the door of the parlor. It meant his father was home. It meant there would have to be questions and explanations — questions that would be confusing and impossible to answer; explanations that would be inadequate no matter how hard he tried, how careful he was. He took a step forward, and she looked at him again. He knew what she was thinking. If only they could hide the plaster.

The smell of cigarette smoke hung in the air. He saw his father in the doorway.

"I fell," the boy said at once. "It was an accident."

His father was unshaven. The man didn't shave but twice a week. He was wearing a grease-stained blue workshirt that opened midchest.

"What accident?"

"On my bicycle. I fell off my bicycle."

His father leaned forward to look out the window. "Where's the bicycle now?"

"In the barn."

"So why aren't you in school? School's not out yet."

"They thought I should come home," he lied.

His father's eyes narrowed. He seemed to smell the lie. He always did. Jean's mother wiped her hands on the dishtowel. She took a step toward him. "I'd better see to that plaster," she said.

"Leave him be."

His mother stopped.

"Where'd you get the plaster?"

Jean hesitated. He'd better leave the school out of this. That was shaky ground. "It was in the square. The accident. And Madame Daussois fixed it."

"Madame Daussois?"

Jean winced, cursing himself silently.

"What were you doing with Madame Daussois?"

"I wasn't exactly. It's just that she ran to me when I fell, and it was she who put the plaster on."

"Madame Daussois was in the square?"

Jean looked down. His mind raced. Where was this going? Where would he trip himself up? How could he have been so foolish as to mention Madame Daussois's name?

His father moved closer to him. Jean could smell once again the stale breath of the drinking.

"Madame Daussois was in the square?" his father repeated more loudly.

"Yes, yes," the boy stammered.

"The square of Delahaut?" His father was almost shouting.

In his thoughts, the boy panicked. He could not mention Rance — he would never be able satisfactorily to explain why he went to Rance. Oh God, why had he mentioned the name Daussois?

Always later, when Jean was alone, he tried to reconstruct the argument, tried to figure out where the trigger was, what it was that had set his father off. But it was like an endlessly repeatable science experiment that never produced the same results.

The hand to the side of his face came sooner than he'd expected. He heard his mother exclaim. He put his hands up over his head. In doing so, he fell back against the wall, couldn't keep his balance, slid to the floor. His father stood over him.

"You think this is a game? You think I don't know what you're doing sniffing around Madame Daussois? You want to be with the Maquis, maybe? The Partisans?"

Jean brought his knees up, sheltered his head with his hands. It was always the same.

His father pointed a finger and shook it. "You want to fight the Germans, do you? You want to be a hero? A Resistance fighter?"

Jean was silent. It was no good shaking his head no. That would only further enflame his father.

"Well, I'll tell you something, you sniveling little shit, you're going to get yourself killed. That's what's going to happen. I ever catch you near the Daussoises' again, I'll beat you to a bloody pulp."

Jean wanted to laugh. If you don't get killed first, I'll kill you. His father kicked him. His father's rages often ended with a kick.

But the toe of his father's boot connected only with the wooden sole of Jean's shoe, and the boy didn't feel the blow. For a minute he was afraid that, having missed, his father would kick him again.

Instead, mercifully, his father went out the kitchen door, slammed it.

Jean brought his hand to his cheek. It was the same cheek she had kissed. He felt the skin with his fingers.

———————

Claire brought her hand to her mouth. Ted didn't know if the gesture was for having been seen together, or if it was simply horror for the state Henri was in.

Ted thought of the Depression bums and the hoboes who had sometimes come to the back door of the house in Mount Gilead. He remembered how Frances would make cheese sandwiches and wrap them in wax paper and give them to the men who knocked at all hours of the day. It was seldom the same man, but the word seemed to have gone out: You can get a sandwich and a cup of hot coffee in that kitchen. Ted, barely a teenage boy, would watch in fascination, trying to imagine such a life. At the time, the thought of sleeping by the tracks and riding on railroad cars, not knowing one's destination, was a promise of infinite adventure.

Henri had grown a beard. His hair lay in greasy strands across his forehead. His eyes seemed sunken in hollows that might have been caused by grime or by lack of sleep. His trousers were frayed at the hems, and his coat no longer had buttons. His shoes had given out. Ted wondered what had happened to the man. He wondered how he could walk.

Claire got down from the truck, her kerchief untying itself and fluttering to the ground. He watched her walk toward her husband, put a hand on his arm, speak to him. He felt the touch of Claire's hand on her husband's arm like the blow of a baseball bat to his gut. Barely aware of what he was doing, he opened the passenger door of the truck and stumbled down. He walked to the other side of the truck and picked up Claire's scarf. He held it loosely in his fingers, staring at the pattern, as if he had come upon an important artifact and did not know what it meant. Then he folded the scarf and put it in his pocket.

When he looked up, Henri and Claire were approaching him. She was not touching her husband now. Henri studied Ted, then said, remarkably, "Bonjour." He removed from his pocket a crumpled pack of cigarettes, shook one loose, offered it to Ted. Ted, anxious to break the tension, to have something to do, took the proffered cigarette and bent his head as Henri lit a match. The man smelled foul, as if he had not bathed in weeks, and Ted supposed he hadn't. Cupping his hands around the flame in Henri's hand, Ted glanced up at Henri's face. Within the sunken sockets, Henri's gaze was steady — not sullen, not wounded — and yet there was an unmistakable sense of deep exhaustion, an exhaustion that puts a man beyond the range of normal feelings. Henri looked at Ted's face, then examined the length of him to his feet. Claire stood with her hands in the pockets of her coat. She bit the inside of her cheek. Her hair was loose over the shoulders of her coat. Oddly, Henri lit a cigarette for himself, but did not offer one to his wife. Ted watched as Henri put the packet away inside his buttonless coat.

Ted took a long pull, turned his face, and blew the smoke away. He caught Claire's eye as he turned. Henri, who held his cigarette between his thumb and forefinger, took a quick drag, looked again at Ted. Ted left them then and walked to the truck bed. He climbed onto the back, leaned against the metal side. He rested the hand with the cigarette on a raised knee. He smoked quietly, a kind of desperate humming in his ears. What was preventing him from taking Claire, putting her in the truck and heading for France? he asked himself. He wanted to tell Henri the truth of what had passed between himself and Claire, but he couldn't even speak to the man without forcing Claire to translate. It would have been laughable, he thought, if it hadn't been so serious.

But Henri, he realized with a sudden jolt, watching the man walk slowly around the truck bed to the passenger side, already knew. He hadn't needed a translation. It was why he'd offered Ted the cigarette, he thought now; it was the cause of the steady gaze, the cause of the prolonged scrutiny from Ted's face to his feet. It was a curious kind of knowledge on Henri's part, Ted thought, a *knowing* without precisely having been told. A knowing not just of the facts, but of what lay behind the facts. Ted had sometimes seen this on Claire's face as well.

Claire drove. The truck bounced over the ruts while Ted hung on to the side to keep from banging helplessly around the back. At the house, Henri went immediately inside. Ted stood by the rear of the truck, unsure of what to do.

Claire came to speak to him. She glanced briefly at him, looked away.

"I am to go for Dussart," she said. "My husband says you will leave this house tonight."

Ted reached forward, caught the sleeve of her coat.

She shook her head quickly.

He released the sleeve.

Ted did not enter the house. Henri was there, somewhere inside, perhaps washing at the pump, perhaps lying on the bed. The image of the latter made Ted almost ill. Or maybe the man was eating. Ted felt a gnawing at the bottom of his stomach that was distinctly not hunger. He had the sense that he had only minutes left, that something was about to happen to him over which he had no control. In the near dark, he looked down at his hands. They were raw from the cold, and shaking. He remembered the half-moon smudges on her cheekbones.

The sun was just setting across the fields. A wind was blowing, making a faint whistle. For a moment, just before it set, the sun lit up the landscape and turned everything — every tree, every matted piece of straw, the barn, the gray stone of the house — to a pink salmon that seemed to have a life of its own, to imbue the world around him with beauty. The straight furrows of the fields, only minutes ago just barren troughs, were luminous arrows pointing toward the west. A large bird overhead was a black silhouette with a golden wing. Even his hands, which had been a mottled red, seemed now to glow with the pink light. He felt exhilarated by the sudden light. It was an exhilaration he'd sometimes known before — in a Tiger Moth 2,000 feet over East Anglia; at 15,000 feet at dawn, leaving the Channel behind him. It was impossible to believe, at such moments, in the decay of war or in a world that did not contain the possibility of joy. He imagined then the search after the war for Claire, their reunion. He saw this as a certainty. He shut his eyes to contain the vision, to seal it.

When he opened them, the sun, directly west of the house and the stairs on which he sat, sank abruptly — and just as abruptly the pink light was gone. Like a swift cloud, the air around him darkened; color left the landscape. Two bicycles entered the drive, stopped in front of him. An odd-looking man, not much older than a boy, swung a leg over one of the bicycles. Claire dismounted from the other. Ted saw that the man was missing an ear. His name, said Claire, was Dussart. He and Henri were taking Ted that night to meet with two other aviators — not from his own crew, she added quickly; then the three would be transferred to the next stop further down the line. They would leave when it was fully dark, in one hour. Now she would make some food for all of them, she said. She climbed the steps beside Ted. Dussart followed her. She hesitated at the top. She asked Ted to come in to have the meal with Henri and Dussart. Ted shook his head.

For a time he heard muffled sounds emanating through the shut kitchen window. Men speaking. The chink of crockery. He wondered occasionally as he sat on the stoop — shivering badly now from the cold; the beret had been lost in the woods, and he had no gloves — if he ought to go inside, eat the meal that had been offered him. It might be some time before he'd get another. And he wondered, too, if he shouldn't allow himself to watch Claire at the pump and the stove, experience the last few minutes they would have together for some time as well. But the thought of sharing the small room with Henri and the young man with the missing ear stopped him.

He heard the door open. She had her coat on and sat on the step with him. She lay the book between them, the photograph of Stella peeking out of the top. In her hands she held some papers, which she gave to Ted. They were, he saw, his identity cards. He could not read his new name in the darkness.

"I am bringing you these," she said.

He glanced quickly at the book, looked away. He didn't pick it up.

"Has he said anything to you?"

"No."

"I'm sorry."

She nodded.

"He knows, doesn't he?"

She was silent. Again she nodded.

"I love you," he said.

She didn't answer him, and he was momentarily stung by her silence. And then he sensed that she was trying to speak, but couldn't. Was it that she didn't know the precise words, or was it something she simply couldn't say?

He rubbed the toe of his good foot against the hard dirt. She shifted so that she was facing him. He could barely see her in the darkness. She put a hand on the book, and he covered it quickly. Her hand was so warm — his must feel like ice to her, he thought. Neither of them moved. He closed his eyes, concentrated on her hand. He tried to memorize the feel of it — the skin like kid beneath his own. He felt her wedding ring, the hard gold band, left it alone. He felt the tips of her fingers, the short slices of nails.

They heard voices just beyond the door.

"*Non,*" she said quickly, with a kind of strangled cry. She pressed her forehead to his face — a frantic gesture. "I am . . . ," she began, then was stopped.

The door opened noisily, shut against its frame. Henri, after bathing, looked a different man. Claire withdrew her hand and stood up. Ted did likewise. He looked for her face in the darkness. What had she been about to say? *I am . . . loving you? I am . . . afraid?*

Henri spoke to his wife.

Claire put her hands in the pockets of her coat. She said: "They are taking you now. My husband is telling me you are walking between them, and when is time, my husband will say to you *courage. . . .*" She turned to Henri. "*Courage?*" she asked. He nodded. She looked back at Ted. "He will say *courage*, which is to you courage, and you are then walking forward alone to the automobile which will be there. They are not walking with you, because they are not wanting to see the faces of the persons in the next cell, yes?"

Dussart and Henri walked a few feet away and stood waiting for Ted.

He tried to say, "I want to thank you," which was true, and which he could say to Claire in front of Henri and Dussart, but his voice left him. He felt a hand on his arm. She kissed him once on each cheek. She said quietly into his ear, "I am remembering you." He felt her hand linger on his arm. And then the touch was gone.

Ted watched the door close behind her.

He thought then that it was the hardest thing he'd ever done — harder even than the belly landing in the pasture, which had brought him to this place. He looked toward Henri and Dussart. Henri's eyes slid away from Ted's. He realized then, with the shiver of an absolute truth, that not only had Henri known about himself and Claire, but the whole village had also known. The affair, the allowance of the affair, had been a gift to him and to Claire. To him because he was the American. To Claire because she was Resistance.

The wind blew up, and his eyes stung. He shoved the documents into his pocket and felt Claire's scarf. He left the book and the picture on the step where she had put them.

They walked for what seemed like hours, but what must have been, Ted calculated reasonably, not more than forty minutes. It was his leg that distorted time — that and the distance he was creating with each step between himself and Claire. *I am remembering you,* she said. Her throaty, low voice had lodged somewhere deep within him. He knew he would always be able to hear her.

But there was so much he would never know. A year from now, would she think of him? Would she one day have a child, two children — put the war and himself far behind her? Had she begun that process already to keep from going crazy? *Fou,* she had said. He tried to imagine her as a middle-aged woman, an old woman. Her gray eyes, he was certain, would never change. He tried to picture her with Henri — could not, would not.

They were traveling west. Southwest. Impossible to be sure. Perhaps they were walking all the way to France. The fields in the near-perfect dark were full of ruts and holes. Several times Ted stumbled, caught his balance. Occasionally, there were night sounds — the low calls of unfamiliar birds, a sense of creatures scurrying beside him. He began to imagine a small smile of satisfaction on Henri's face as the man took the American aviator farther and farther away from the Belgian farmhouse. Yet Henri too, he thought, had to be nearly comatose with exhaustion. Only Dussart, who had tried unsuccessfully to engage Henri in conversation, whistled tunes from time to time. He wondered why Henri would not chat with Dussart. Was there a kind of hierarchy within the Resistance that did not permit fraternization? Or did they simply have nothing in common except this mission?

The first signal was so brief, Ted thought it was a spot of light the eye had produced, the way straining into cloud could create tiny bright stars. But the second was unmistakable. The flash of a torch in a horizontal line, held at the height of a man's waist. A sole tree intersected the light at each pass. In the brief swathes of the signals, Ted could see finally the lay of the land — the hard furrows, the jutting pieces of straw.

Dussart murmured something to Henri, who answered him. Henri briefly put an arm in front of Ted, slowing his forward progress. They proceeded more cautiously now, inching toward the torch. Fifty feet from the source of the light, Henri called out a name or a word — Ted wasn't sure. A man answered briefly. Henri motioned for Ted to stop. The torch now swung away, cast a swift streak of light across a small, colorless car with a high roof. Dussart, in a quick anxious whisper, asked Henri a question. Henri answered curtly, dismissively. Dussart began to protest. Henri cut him off. In his ears, Ted felt again the desperate drumming. Beside him, Henri was removing an object from his pocket. The object crinkled faintly in the silence. Ted thought it must be cigarettes, and that Henri would offer him one before sending him off to

France. Instead Henri reached for Ted's wrist, placed the object in Ted's palm. The object was flat and thin, wrapped in paper.

"*Chocolat,*" Henri whispered beside him.

Confused, Ted held the bar of chocolate. What was it for?

Then Henri said distinctly the one anticipated word: "*Courage.*"

The shaft of light now made small circles on the ground, a continuous circle toward which Ted had to walk. Where would Claire be now? he wondered. Sitting at the table in the kitchen? Lying in her bed, listening to the night? Henri said again, in a low voice, the single word: "*Courage.*" Ted took a step forward, hesitated, took another. Where were the other aviators? He felt his way over the uneven terrain. Behind him, to his surprise, he heard the sound of retreating footsteps. Ted whirled around, wanted to call out to the fleeing figures. Why were they leaving him so soon? There were so many questions to ask. In the distance he could hear a dog barking. He turned back to look at the spot where the colorless car must still be. The car was his promise of freedom, wasn't it? The promise of a life as it was meant to be lived, on familiar soil? He laughed once in the dark. He looked at the steady movement of an unknown arm — the continuous circle of light on the dark ground. There was nowhere else to go.

April 5, 1944

When she pressed her hand to the stone, the palm came away wet. Sometimes she thought she could hear the water running down the walls.

A tiny rectangle, the size of a book, had been cut from the stones at the top of the outside wall. She sat on the hinged board that passed for a bed, wrapped her arms about her, and watched the dawn begin to illuminate the cell. She thought the light through the rectangle was different with each passing day — stronger, brighter — and that she could see a hint of color now: the fuzzy, yellow-pear of leaf buds. In the distance, as always, she heard the traffic of Antwerp, as people, miraculously, went about their business, unaware of or indifferent to the activities within these walls.

She heard the outer door to the corridor open noisily and then shut. There was the smart tread of boot heels, two pairs, and the slough of a body along the stone floor. At the sound of the boot heels, the women in the other cells started screaming — screams that were angry, or near madness, or simply trying to attract the attention of the guards. The metallic clatter of keys echoed throughout the block, and beyond the door a woman coughed. There was a sudden harsh light. They brought Odette into the cell.

Claire knelt, lifted the woman's head. Odette appeared to be still unconscious. She coughed once, and a quantity of blood spilled out onto her dirty shift.

Bastards, Claire whispered.

As gently as she could, for she did not know as yet what

damage might have been done, she rolled the woman onto a blanket on the stone floor. She would have preferred to lift her onto the hinged bed, but until she regained consciousness that would be impossible.

In the dim light, Claire tried to inspect Odette's body. There were bruises upon bruises now. The mouth was badly cut; Claire put her fingers inside to feel for loose teeth. The woman, who had been rounded up in the raids on Louvain, had been with her for four days now. As best as Claire could tell, Odette had been a courier within the Partisans. She was only eighteen years old.

Odette coughed again, struggled, tried to sit up. Claire put a hand on her chest, pressed her down. "You're safe now. I'm here. Just rest."

"Why are they Belgians?" the young woman from Louvain asked in a hoarse whisper.

That their torturers and interrogators were all Belgians had bewildered Claire, too. She had seen some of this in Delahaut — men who were willing collaborators; women who went with the German soldiers — but she had never seen anything like the insidious brutality that existed within these walls. Perhaps they did it for food and money, or out of fear of being beaten themselves. Many of the guards, she had discovered, were street criminals who'd been let go. Political prisoners were the maggots at the bottom of the pile — of lower status than even thieves and murderers.

Claire supposed that she herself should feel fortunate that her own beatings had not produced as much damage as was apparent on the young woman from Louvain. Claire had suffered several broken ribs, and she was now deaf in one ear, but she was still alive and had not vomited blood. The circular trap slid open. Claire lay Odette's head down on the blanket, went to collect the two cups of cold broth and the two slices of black bread from the tray. She set the food down beside her cellmate.

"Can you eat anything?" Claire asked.

The woman from Louvain shook her head. "But you take mine," she said. "Don't let it go to waste."

Claire carefully pulled her to the wall, propped her into a half-sitting position. She was afraid the woman might choke and drown if she lay on the cold floor much longer. She brought a washrag to the woman's face, wiped off the sweat and dirt there.

"What, what have they done to you?" Claire asked angrily.

Odette shook her head from side to side.

Beside her, Claire raised the tin cup to her own mouth. The broth smelled foul. As always, it was some form of cabbage soup, but other ingredients — chewy, unrecognizable items — were sometimes added. She forced herself to drink the liquid. She was afraid to give Odette anything to eat while the woman was coughing blood; yet Claire knew that if the woman did not eat even the foul rations they were given, she would lose what little strength she still had.

When Claire had finished the broth and bread, she leaned against the wall and held the woman's hand. Her own chest hurt. With her fingers, she massaged her rib cage, where the bones were knitting themselves together without having been properly set. She had not seen a doctor since entering the prison. Her thighs, beneath her thin shift, were only loose skin over bone. Her breasts still swelled slightly, and there was the small round abdomen, but the rest of her was shrinking. She wondered dispassionately — scientifically — if the body of a starving mother would die before the fetus inside her; or if the baby would die first, and then the mother later.

She felt the stiff tufts of Odette's hair. They had hacked off her own, too, and she was glad of this. In the beginning, they had yanked and dragged her by the hair so forcefully she was afraid they'd snap her neck. Now her hair stood out from her scalp in uneven, ragged bits. Bathing with the tiny square washrags and with the small ration of water they were given was difficult. She knew she smelled, as did the woman beside her. She wondered how the guards could stand it: all these foul and retching women; all these screaming women day and night. Perhaps it was a kind of punishment for the guards. She fervently hoped so.

Today they were taking her east to Ravensbrück, but they wouldn't tell her why. The interrogations and the beatings had stopped some weeks ago, and there had been no explanation for that either. Since she had been in the Old Antwerp Prison, she had heard terrible stories about Ravensbrück, but it was hard for her to imagine it could be worse than what she was living through. In any event, she reasoned, they were bound to see daylight on the journey, either en route or when they got there. She badly needed to see the light.

Odette started forward. She seemed to be trying to flee. Claire restrained her, held her arms. "It's all right. You're with me. You're safe now."

The young woman, Claire knew, was terrified of the beatings. There was no respite: When you slept, you had them in your dreams. The first days were the worst.

"Did they tie you to a chair?" the woman asked. Her voice wasn't much above a whisper.

"Yes."

"And they beat you then?"

"Yes."

"No matter how you answered the questions?"

"Yes."

"Why are they still doing this? I've given them all the names."

"I don't know."

They had come for Claire near dawn. SD officers in black coats and peaked caps. A Wehrmacht truck outside. She'd fallen asleep at the kitchen table, and when they broke the door, bellowing loudly in her ears and dragging her across the floor by her hair, there'd been no thought of escape. No thought at all, so great was her disorientation. They shouted questions at her incessantly, toppled tins from their shelves. They kicked her out the door so that she fell onto the dirt. They shoved her into a truck. A convoy to Antwerp. Inside were other villagers, their heads bent, some clutching children. Some weeping. No one dared to speak to her.

That night, when Henri and Dussart had taken Ted, she had sat at the kitchen table, wrapped her arms around herself and finally wept. The unthinkable becomes the thinkable, he'd said. She'd sent the American pilot away as she'd known she must. She did it with her silence.

She remembered walking toward Henri from the truck in a kind of stumbling trance. She'd thought, even before she reached her husband: I'll tell him now. But when she stood in front of Henri, and put her hand on his arm, she'd looked into his eyes. There was something different there. It was Henri, and yet it was not the Henri she had known. And then she'd been frightened.

It was over then, she thought.

He promised her they would get the American out at once. She was urgent, frantic. It had already been arranged, he said. He just needed Dussart. They must not find the American with them, she said to her husband, when what she really meant was: They must not find the American at all.

Ted.

She thought of the color of his eyes, that shimmery green. She thought of the way the small of his back never touched a chair. She remembered his smile and could hear his voice, but she could no longer remember what it felt like to make love with him. She wondered if, as the flesh left you, the pleasurable sensations of the flesh left you as well. Or if this inability to feel was merely protective. That if you could remember, the memory would be intolerable.

That night, they'd taken her in the truck to Antwerp, where the beatings had begun immediately. When she emerged from the convoy into the light, a guard had hit her ear so hard she spun to the ground. She'd been dragged into the prison, where the new arrivals all stood in two lines facing each other — men on one side, women on the other. An officer told them all to undress right there. The shame of that moment still haunted her, despite all that had happened since then.

The days that followed seemed to have no sequence. Fifty days, sixty days — even now she couldn't be sure. No one knew precisely the date. Some thought it March; others thought it already April. In the corridors, with the screams, Claire sometimes heard news: The Partisans in Charleroi had been decimated; the Americans were at Anzio.

At first, there was no night, no day; there were no regular

meals and no events that were at all familiar to her. All that she knew was that she was taken to a room, tied to a chair, and asked the same questions, over and over — asked about the same names, over and over. Except for Anthoine's name, and Dussart's, Claire did not truthfully know any others. But as the days wore on, as the beatings became more severe, the names blurred together, and sometimes she said yes when yes was not the correct answer, and sometimes she said no, even to her husband's name. She waited for them to say Ted's name, but they never did. She didn't like to think about what that might mean. Had he been caught? Was he dead already? Oddly, through all of this, they did not ask her about anyone she had hidden in her home. She kept the secret of the attic room.

Sometimes they hit her with a flat hand to the face; sometimes they used fists — on her arms and back and chest. Occasionally there was only one man who beat her; at other times there were three. Always, though, her interrogator was the same: a slim Belgian officer with a sharp chin and an eye that wandered. He was Flemish, from the north. He called her *Liebchen*. He gave the signal for the beatings with one raised, well-manicured finger.

On the last day of the beatings, the interrogator had her tied to the chair but the guards did not hit her. He queried her once again, but with a weariness she had not seen before. He didn't seem to care anymore about her answers.

She risked a question.

She asked where Henri was. The officer didn't answer her. She asked if she could see her husband. He refused her. She asked if Henri was well, or even still alive. He remained silent.

She didn't know if Henri had been taken to Antwerp or to Brussels. Or if he'd been shot resisting arrest. Or if, miraculously, he was free.

Odette stirred beside her. She leaned her face into Claire's chest. "They broke a chair against my head," she said.

Claire smoothed the woman's hair. "It will end soon," she said.

"Why are you here?" she asked.

"It's better for you if you don't know," Claire said.

Suddenly, Odette coughed blood onto her chin and neck. Claire held her arms.

"Am I going to die?" the young woman asked.

"No," Claire said. "Sleep if you can. Whatever is injured inside you needs to heal."

She didn't believe the woman would heal. She believed the woman beside her would die that day. Or if not today, then soon. In some ways, she thought the woman lucky.

"When the war is over, Georges and I are getting married," Odette said. "Were you very happy with your husband?"

"Yes," Claire lied quickly.

"Georges was with me in the Partisans."

"Shhhh," said Claire.

"But I've already said his name. I *had* to say his name."

The woman began to weep quietly.

"We all do it," said Claire. "No one can withstand the torture. And you didn't tell them anything they didn't know already. Your Georges will be all right. I'm sure it's not the first time his name has been given. He's probably more worried about you."

"I was supposed to meet him," she said. "At the house of Barbier. And then they came for me. They took my mother and my father and my grandmother. They dragged my grandmother by her dress. . . ."

"Shhh . . . ," Claire said again. "Try to sleep. It's best."

Sometimes, sitting in her cell, she thought of the twenty days they'd had together. Occasionally it would seem to her that it had not really happened — that such an interval could not have existed simultaneously with the events that occurred on a daily basis just inside this prison — but then a detail would come back to her, and then another, and she would know that what she remembered was true. The details were tiny, seemingly insignificant: a fragment from a tune he had whistled through the wall; his face turning away to the side when he laughed, so that she saw his smile in profile; the way he sat slouched with his hands in his pockets, as if nothing in the world were serious. She could see his skin from his cheekbone to his jawline. She could remember how he looked that first night, wounded and naked by the fire. She could not remember everything, and she could no longer *feel* much, but she knew for certain it had really happened. She tried then to imagine him at his air base, the leg healed, as he walked across a green lawn toward a silver plane, his hands in his uniform pockets. Was it at all possible that, against the odds, he'd really made it back to England?

Abruptly, she became aware of now familiar sounds: the corridor door; the boot heels; the echo of the massive ring of keys. They've come, she thought. She brought a hand up to shield her eyes from the light. A figure stood in the doorway.

In a small room, they moved away from her and asked her to strip. She let her shift fall to the floor. Instinctively she sucked her belly in as best she could.

The bright electric light illuminated the bruises. They looked like purple and yellow spills that had stained her arms and thighs. There was so little flesh on her legs that her knees stood out sharply — knobby, awkward joints. She resisted the temptation to cover herself. A nurse handed her a sliver of soap and a cloth, and pointed to the door to the showers.

"As you have been told, you are being transported to Ravensbrück today," the nurse said. "But first you will see the doctor."

Claire gripped the soap and cloth. She was unable to move. The doctor, she thought.

"What is it?" asked the nurse, turning to Claire with irritation. "Is there something wrong?"

The water was not hot, but it was not cold either. In the showers, there were other women with her. It was the first time she had bathed properly since she'd been taken from her house. She wondered if the showers were a good sign. Perhaps the sanitary conditions were better at Ravensbrück, and the Belgians didn't want to be accused of sending dirty women to the German prisons. She wondered how long they would give her in the shower. She was careful with the sliver of soap — she needed to make it last so that she could wash her hair, too.

Her hands trembled, and she had trouble keeping the soap from sliding out of her grasp and onto the tiled floor. How thorough would the doctor be? Mightn't he miss the signs? Or would he be looking for this very thing in the women he examined?

She herself had almost misinterpreted the symptoms. One month, then another. She thought it was the trauma to the body; the near starvation. Other women, long-timers, told her they hadn't menstruated in months. But then she'd tasted the strange, metallic swallow at the back of her throat, and felt that her breasts were tender in a way the bruises weren't. Tender from the inside out, and swollen. This sudden and absolute knowledge had passed through her with a shiver of unexpected pleasure. There was life inside her — proof of the twenty days.

She dried herself with a small towel. Even the rough nap was luxurious on her clean skin. She was told to comb her hair, and she was given a clean shift. Her anus and her vagina were searched. Then she was told to dress and stand along the corridor with the other women.

As she leaned against the tiles, she heard French and Walloon and Flemish, many dialects. The cleanliness had produced civility and chatter. The women talked among themselves of the upcoming transfer as if they were secretaries in a firm. Would they go by train? she heard a woman ask. No, answered an older woman, it would be the trucks like always. But would it take more than a day? Ravensbrück was deep, said the older woman, deep into Germany. Claire did not know if this was true. It must not be so bad in Ravensbrück, said another woman. They wouldn't have given us the showers.

The line moved briskly forward one woman at a time. A doctor's assistant would open a door and call a name. Claire's feet were cold and lined with blue veins. The shift was too big for her and kept slipping from her shoulders.

She hadn't prayed in nearly two months, not since the first beating. When the beatings continued with no sign of mercy —

indeed grew worse — she stopped the prayers. And even when the beatings ceased, she found she couldn't pray.

Now, leaning against the wall, moving forward in small increments, paper slippers barely covering her toes, she prayed. No matter what else happened to her, she said silently to God, no matter what she was asked to do, she would keep the baby inside her. It was a declaration, a challenge.

The woman in front of her was small and graying. Her back was hunched at the top of her spine. Claire saw the bruises on the woman's naked arms. How strange we all are, she thought. Each of us with the same awful medallions, chatting as if this were merely an outing.

The graying woman's name was called. Claire watched her disappear behind the door. She caught a glimpse of a leather gurney, metal stirrups, a sheet. Somehow, she knew, she had to avoid putting her feet into those stirrups.

She waited for her turn. She wondered what happened on the other side of the doctor's office. Where did the women go? Were they given more clothing for the journey? It was late March or early April. Perhaps there would be a calendar in the doctor's office. But whatever the date, they would all need warmer clothes. They couldn't travel in trucks in cotton shifts. They'd all be frozen before they even got to Germany.

She thought about Henri. She tried to imagine him alive. But if that was so, how had he eluded the Gestapo? He'd have had to flee to another village, perhaps even across the border into France. She did not think it likely she would ever see Henri again, even if he was alive. She fervently hoped that if he were caught he'd be shot and not hanged. She did not feel guilt for what she had done to Henri. It did not seem to her an act of betrayal. It was only twenty days out of a lifetime. She could not bring herself to believe that loving the American was wrong. And then she wondered briefly: If she did not feel guilt, was she entitled to the prayers?

"Daussois."

The doctor's assistant held the door. Claire wanted to say, I too am a nurse. Was a nurse. In a corner, she saw a tall, dark-haired man in a white coat who had his back to her. The doctor.

The room was all white and glass and chrome with the brown leather gurney. Over the movable cabinets were fixed cabinets with paned glass fronts. In some of them she recognized the contents: the instruments, the sizes and shapes of the plasters and dressings. There were two other doors to the room. One was unmarked; the other had a sign: *Contagion*.

The doctor was working with something Claire couldn't see; he seemed irritated and called to his assistant to help him. With a sigh of frustration, he told the assistant he had another syringe in the laboratory. The assistant went quickly through the door marked *Contagion*, closed it behind her.

The doctor seemed to have forgotten Claire's presence altogether. She looked quickly at the unmarked door, wondered where it led, how far she would get. She moved silently a step closer to the door. She watched the doctor raise a small vial to his face, tap it twice with his finger.

The door marked *Contagion* suddenly swung open, and the doctor's assistant walked through, holding a syringe. Through the open door, Claire could see a narrow hallway, and across that, another open door. She could see a doctor with a pince-nez and in front of the doctor, with his back to the door, a man seated at a table.

The man had his shirt off. There were no bruises or cuts on his skin. She saw the back of his neck, the line of his shoulder.

She sucked in her breath and took a step forward. How had he been taken? And when? If he was in Antwerp, didn't that mean he hadn't made it out of Belgium?

Something in her posture — a start, the hand on her abdomen — made the doctor who was examining the man glance briefly up at Claire. Mistaking her stare, he smirked, said something to his patient.

Ted turned around.

He looked at her, but he seemed not to know her. Didn't he recognize her?

She took another step forward, opened her mouth as if to speak. The doctor behind Ted turned away, removed his stethoscope from his neck.

He was thinner in the face and paler. His eyes seemed somehow larger — translucent circles in beautiful shadowy sockets. Seeing him, she could finally remember what it was like to feel the skin on his face. His hair had been badly cut.

He did not turn away, but his face remained expressionless.

She wanted to hear his voice, to have some small indication that he knew it was she. She wanted to say his name.

He sat perfectly still, his body half-turned, his bare arm braced on the back of the chair.

She put her hand to her chest. In all the time since the door had opened, she had not drawn a breath.

Briefly — so briefly it might have been a baby's kiss — she put a finger to her lips, took it away.

Casually, her back to Claire, and remembering the door, the doctor's assistant reached over with her hand and pushed the door shut.

Claire closed her eyes, swayed on her feet. She put a hand on the gurney for balance.

He was gone, and she didn't know if he had *seen* her.

———

The trick God plays so that everything won't happen at once. Frances used to say that to him in answer to his endlessly tedious questions about time: How long until my birthday? How many days until Christmas? When will we be there — a long time or a short time? A long time or a short time. Twenty days or a thousand days. Yet an entire lifetime could change in a second. A catch in an engine, the giving of a name. He was not sure he understood time any better now than when he was a kid. Not so long ago, the thought of only four days was an agony. Now the idea of four days more seemed almost intolerable.

From his position on the bed, he could watch the day begin in increments — almost imperceptible degrees of light, until soon he would be able to discern the outline of the objects in the cell. A slop bucket. A chair. A pair of boots by the wall. He shivered on the cot, drew the blanket higher on his chest. He coughed hard, breathed deliberately and slowly to stop the coughing. They had made him wear a khaki shirt and pants. They wanted him to be an American pilot. He could not imagine how Belgian prison officials in Breendonk had come by American military khakis. He didn't like to think about it much.

They called him Lieutenant and asked about his plane and crew, but always he responded the same way — with his rank and his name and his military number. They threatened to beat him, but they never did. They appeared to be holding to a code that Ted could only guess at. At Breendonk, they had kept him in solitary confinement, withheld some meals and all medical attention, and woke him at all hours of the day and night to disorient him. Yet they never touched him except to take him to and from the cell. Indeed, sometimes the Belgian officers seemed almost genial. Occasionally they offered Ted cigarettes and lit them for him and asked him questions about the B-17 or the P-38; not, Ted thought, to elicit information, but rather in the same way two men might smoke and compare the features of a Ford versus a Chevy.

Had he kept track, he would know what the date was. But in the beginning, his anger and confusion were so great that the passage of time meant nothing to him. Now a single hour was among the worst tortures he could imagine — every minute anticipated, painstakingly observed, and noted in the brain. Then that minute passing to the next.

He rolled over onto his side. He thought, as he had thought a thousand times since he had been here, that an excess of time was not the worst torture he could imagine: The worst was not knowing.

Retreating footfalls behind him, he walked forward over rough field. The circle of light spun incessantly, beckoning him. In his hand, he held the chocolate bar. The documents and her scarf were in his pocket. Would he be expected to know his false name? he wondered. Would the promised aviators already be there?

When he was five feet from the circle, the light went out. Immediately, there were two men, one at each elbow. They guided him politely to the car, opened the door to the back seat, gestured for him to get in. In the car, behind the wheel, was another man. Ted saw, just briefly, the glint of a bar on a shirt under a nondescript raincoat. He thought quickly of the boy, Dussart, with his missing ear, his tone of voice with Henri. Ted knew then, processed the information in an instant. The knowledge hit him like a shell — once, hard and deafening. He bent slightly forward, put his head in his hands. He thought he might be sick.

Henri.

And Claire as well?

The man to his right took the chocolate bar from Ted's hand. In perfect, if heavily accented, English, the Belgian said: "You won't be needing this where you're going."

"Where am I going?" Ted asked.

The man cleared his throat. He spoke as if he'd rehearsed his pronouncement.

"Lieutenant Theodore Brice, I am sorry to inform you that you are not going to France. You are being taken to Brussels."

Ted thought he saw a slight smile, as if in satisfaction at having accomplished an important task for a superior.

They rode through the night, first on bad, unpaved roads, then on a smoother highway. The man beside him broke the chocolate bar in pieces, gave some to the driver and to the man at Ted's left. Had there been a sign, a clue? He tried to remember all of it, play it through like a film. He saw Claire's face in the truck, wet from crying, and her obvious relief. But then he saw her hand on Henri's arm, the intimacy of that gesture.

What had it meant, then, her loving him?

And what had she been about to say? *I am . . . not what you think?*

His mind looped and circled, reversed itself, took off. He couldn't put his thoughts into a logical sequence. He started again, played the film through. He saw every hour, searched every gesture. Beside him the two men spoke in a rapid French and sometimes laughed. They seemed relaxed and happy. His head spun, momentarily cleared, spun again. His stomach was hollow and nauseous — the kind of nausea he sometimes had emerging from the plane after a bad mission. It was the aftermath of shock,

shock you couldn't allow yourself to experience in the air. But it always hit you when you landed. Like Case, who got the headaches when his feet touched the tarmac. Where was Case now? Home? Out of the war with a shattered arm?

Had Henri been paid? Or had he done it for a cause, for a belief? Did Henri positively know that Ted and Claire had been lovers? Did he approve? Enjoy the irony of the aviator's guilt?

Along the way to Brussels, the driver stopped the car once so that each man could get out to piss. When the two Belgians guarding him left the car, the driver turned around and pointed a revolver at Ted. It wasn't six inches from his face.

He almost said, Do it.

For weeks he didn't care about his cell or time, in the same way (and yet its opposite) that weeks earlier he'd have been content to remain in the attic room forever. He wanted only to play the film through, over and over, again and again. He minded the interrogations not because he feared them but because they distracted his focus. He tried to remember how much he was supposed to tell his captors, what he was supposed to do to escape. Once, bitterly, he flirted with Henri's name and even with Claire's, stopping himself on the threshold of revenge. Some days he was certain she'd been in on the plan. The details and nuances could be put together just so to construct a plot. At those moments, he would see her canniness and instinct for survival as traits nurtured not by resistance but by pragmatism and opportunity. Then he would remember the way she reached for his hand, put her mouth on his fingers, offered herself. Never again, he knew, would he be able to see something, taste something, and say, This is positively so.

After a time (weeks, a month?) he became ill. He had fevers and soaked the khakis. Then the damp in the cell set in and chilled him and made him shiver so violently he thought he might never get warm. He began to cough, and his chest seized up when he breathed. He felt as though there was something lodged inside his chest, an unfamiliar entity — as anger was, or bitterness.

At Breendonk they said they had no medicines for him and no doctor, but the interrogations stopped, and he was sometimes given dry blankets. He became delirious and spoke aloud to Frances and to the group captain, a man he'd barely known at base. He thought he was in Ohio, then in the air. Once he dreamed of finding Claire tangled in a parachute above the clouds. In another dream, Henri was beside him in the truck, whistling and smiling.

He drifted in and out of consciousness, recovered slightly, relapsed. He thought once he had been visited by an RAF named Bernie, an officer who still had his own uniform and seemed to swallow his vowels. This visitation had about it a quality that was unlike all the others, and so Ted thought it had probably actually happened. The RAF was solicitous and asked Ted what he needed; then he confessed he couldn't help the American much. He, too, was a prisoner. His crew had bailed out over, of all places, Brussels, and he'd been arrested immediately. He seemed fascinated by the story of Ted's crash, and, as the conversation progressed, pressed for more details about the damage to the plane, Ted's night in the woods, and his rescue by the Belgian Resistance. On the verge of confiding the tale of the boy who found him, Ted saw in the RAF's movements (the too-casual way he lit a cigarette, surveyed the cell; and why wasn't the RAF frightened or his uniform dirty?) an overeagerness that set off a faint alarm. Or was he, Ted, becoming more and more paranoid, seeing betrayal everywhere, even where it couldn't be? He feigned sleep, heard the RAF sigh with exasperation, call for a guard. Ted never saw the man again.

He slept again with the blanket up around his ears. His sleep rose to the surface, floated near a state of wakefulness, sank again to a world without dreams, then rose again and dissipated like fog. He sat up finally, remaining still a moment to get his bearings. The cell seemed somewhat lighter now — he estimated the time at near eight A.M. Over at the door, the circular trap had been opened. A mug of tea, once hot, had cooled in its tin cup; two hard rolls were beside it. He bent forward, tested his legs, stood. He collected the food from the tray and returned with it to the bed.

He held a roll in one hand, the tin mug in the other. His

hands seemed overly large on his thin wrists — the hands of a cartoon character. He wondered how much weight he'd lost since the crash — twenty, thirty pounds? He bit into the stale roll. The sun had etched a rectangle against the gray stone. Some days, from his bed in Breendonk, he watched the rectangle descend the entire length of the wall until it folded itself onto the floor.

He coughed, put a fist to his chest. If you loved a woman, and you discovered she was not what you thought she was in one particular detail — one particular important detail — did you no longer love that woman? He could never answer that question. He tried to make himself believe that she had known what Henri was about to do, and when he thought he was thoroughly convinced, he asked himself if he still loved her. And almost as soon as he thought about loving her, the entire construct collapsed, and he could not believe in her guilt. How intimately could a face lie and not, over a period of twenty days and nights, betray itself even once?

He replaced the empty tin and plate on the circular tray, picked up his boots. They were Belgian issue of indeterminate material, too small for him, but still preferable to walking the damp floor in stocking feet. His evasion clothes had been taken from him his first day in prison, and he had been wearing the same shirt and pants and socks for nearly two months. Socks. What he wouldn't give for a clean pair.

He put his hands in his pockets and tried to make a few circuits in the cell. The leg couldn't bear all his weight, and so he still limped. Several days after he arrived at Breendonk, a Belgian officer ordered the bandages removed. A laborer was sent in with industrial scissors and a small saw; Ted was certain the man would sever his foot.

After ten revolutions, he stopped at the bed, lay down flat, stared at the ceiling. He knew he tortured himself with images of Claire and Henri together. Perhaps they even talked about him. Henri must have known, must surely have guessed when he saw Ted and Claire in the truck. Had he forgiven her? Or worse, were the twenty days merely part of Henri's larger plan? He covered his eyes with his arm.

A neat click in the door made him turn his head. He waited for the circular tray to slide the mug and plate to the other side of the door, but instead the door opened. A figure beckoned to him.

He sat up, knowing he had no choice but to comply. With his limp, he left the cell, followed the guard along a series of corridors and into a room. A scrubbed green wall, a three-legged stool. Two large guards stood sentry by the door. The floor was wooden, and on it were bloodstains. An officer was sitting behind a clean metal desk. He gestured for Ted to sit.

The officer took off his peaked cap, put it on the desk. He removed a handkerchief from a trouser pocket, wiped his brow.

"You've come from Breendonk."

"Yes."

"You've been ill."

"Yes."

"You're better now."

"A little."

"You've eaten your rolls."

"Yes."

"You know you're being sent into Germany today. To a Stalag Luft."

"Nope."

"Do you mind if I ask you one or two questions?"

"Yes, I mind."

"Lieutenant Brice. Your resistance and silence in Breendonk were useless. You are not in good health, which I regret."

"Sure."

"I could make your circumstances more comfortable. I could arrange for your release."

"I doubt it."

The stool was short, and Ted felt ungainly sitting on it, with his knees raised above his waist. There was no possible way to assume a dignified position. He wondered how long it would take the guards to get to him if he suddenly lunged at the officer and tried to snap his neck.

"Lieutenant Brice, do you know a" — the officer leaned forward to examine a piece of paper — "Henri Daussois?"

He sat perfectly still, knowing that by his lack of expression and his momentary silence, he was giving himself away. He felt the heat rise to the back of his neck. He put the palms of his hands on his knees to steady himself. He tried for a tone of indifference.

"My name is Lieutenant Theodore Brice. My military identification number is AO 677292."

"Yes, yes." The officer fluttered a hand at Ted, as if having expected this reply, but disappointed even so.

Didn't they know it was Henri who betrayed him? Or did they know him only as a courier, and not as a double agent? Did they have Henri in custody, or were they searching for him?

Blood rushed to Ted's head, sloshed in his ears. He could sink Henri with one sentence — so easy, hardly any effort at all. He remembered how Henri handed him the chocolate bar in the darkness, marking him. It would be a swift and sweet revenge. Almost certainly, Henri would be shot or hanged.

"Let me ask you again, Lieutenant Brice. And bear in mind that I might be able to arrange a release for you. Regardless of what you may have heard of the relatively better conditions at the Stalag Lufts, they are not places you want to be — particularly not with your health as it is."

Ted closed his eyes. He felt his head spin as it sometimes did when he'd had too much to drink. He opened his eyes to stop the spinning, and he saw that one hand on his knee had curled itself into a fist. He extended the fingers and tried to relax the hand, but not before the officer had seen him do this.

"Lieutenant Brice, I do require an answer."

His chest hurt. He coughed, again pressed his fist against his breastbone. He looked up at the officer. Yes, he could betray Henri with a sentence, but he wouldn't be able to stop the fuse once lit.

"My name is Lieutenant Theodore Brice," he said. "My — "

"Please." The officer cut him off. He rubbed his eyes. He put his fingers to the bridge of his nose.

"There is a woman," the officer said wearily, "a Claire Dausois. Did you by chance ever meet her?"

He knew, thought Ted. He didn't want an answer because he already knew the answer. He merely wanted to see Ted's reaction.

And then Ted had another thought, simultaneously, one that made him want to vomit.

They had her.

"Claire Daussois," the officer repeated. "Did you know her?"

Ted didn't trust his voice. He hated the way her name sounded on the man's tongue. He wanted to tell him to shut his fucking mouth. Instead, he sat back, deliberately tried to cross his legs in a casual pose. He stuffed his trembling hands into his pockets. He forced himself to look toward the window and to whistle. Glenn Miller. "In the Mood."

"Let me put the question to you another way, Lieutenant Brice. I think you knew both Monsieur and Madame Daussois rather well."

For the first time since being captured, indeed for the first time in the entire war, Ted felt himself suffused with rage. The heat and the color had now come into his face. He didn't now care what Claire had done or not done. It would not be he who linked her to the escape route, or who confirmed that link.

But the rage quickly gave way to an almost paralyzing ache. He forced himself to whistle another tune. "Hot Chocolate." Duke Ellington. He jiggled his foot nervously to the beat. He sat there in his trapped nonchalance, desperate for a word of Claire, but he couldn't ask. It was possible he would never know what had happened to her. He thought suddenly of the story Claire had told him of Léon Balle — his recital of the children's reading lessons.

"For skies of couple-colour as a brindled cow," he began. "For rose-moles all in stipple upon trout that swim. . . ."

He could not go on. He folded his arms in front of his chest, pressed his lips together.

The officer looked momentarily confused. Then disgusted. He stood.

"Take him to the doctor," he said quietly to the sentry.

He vomited into the toilet, the first toilet he had seen in weeks. There was no food in his belly now; his body simply wanted to heave itself inside out. He wiped his mouth on the back of his sleeve. Outside the stall, the guard banged impatiently and mumbled something in French.

Ted stood up, opened the stall. They were in a different part of the prison, the infirmary if he had to guess. Beyond the stall, he could hear water falling. Showers. One of the guards handed him a towel, a small bar of soap, pointed in the direction of the rushing water.

Barely knowing what he was doing, he stripped off his clothes, left them on the floor. He entered the shower room, dimly aware of other men who seemed too absorbed in the pleasure of the shower to notice him. He turned on the water, warmed it up to tepid. Performing a set of motions learned long ago, he lathered his body, scrubbed his hair. His right leg, he noted from a far distance, was withered at the shin. With his mouth open and his eyes closed, he let the water cascade over him and down his throat. He stood motionless until another naked man, nudging him aside, pointed to an exit door.

He dried himself, put on the clothes folded neatly on a table. More khakis. Too small. He wondered briefly what had happened to their owner. Shot? Shot down? Escaped to England?

The moist air from the shower room momentarily cleared his chest. He breathed deeply for the first time in weeks. He was led to a long line of men sitting on a narrow bench. Thirty, maybe forty men. At the end of the bench was a door, into which the men, one by one, disappeared.

There was some talk, a ripple along the water (*cat's paws*, Frances used to say). He could not understand any of it.

How many dead now? he wondered. He tried to count. Two in the plane. Three guards. Ten hanged. And who else? Nineteen? Thirty-five? Fifty-five? In the end, didn't it come down to numbers? That was how they tallied it at base: Four planes missing. Twenty-seven dead. Twenty-four missions, one to go. He slid along the bench with the other men.

Today he was going east into Germany. Don't bail out over the Germans, they told you at briefings, you'll never get out. Well, that was all right. He hoped only that some asshole of a group

captain didn't try to get them to dig their way to France. He just
wanted the Germans to park him somewhere, leave him alone. He
needed a deck of cards. He needed a drink. He wondered if the
prisoners at the Stalag would have the means to make a home-
made booze. A hundred and fifty proof. Lethal. Didn't seem likely.
He'd heard the stories: After a while you stopped fantasizing about
sex, started fantasizing about food.

The line moved, and he moved with it. An assembly line to
Germany. He looked down the line; he was the only one in a
uniform. Who were these other men? he wondered. What had
they done? Hidden an Allied aviator? Distributed a few leaflets?
Blown up a bridge?

He heard his name as if from very far away. The accent was
like hers, and, for a second, a painful memory stirred.

He entered a room with a stretcher to one side. In the center
of the room was a desk with a chair in front. Cabinets with medical paraphernalia were attached to the walls. To the right of the
desk was a door open to a corridor.

A man in a white coat, with a stethoscope around his neck, sat
on the edge of the desk. He appeared to be making notations on a
clipboard. He looked up as Ted entered the room and, oddly, smiled.

"Lieutenant," he said in very good, if accented, English. The
doctor had a pince-nez at the bridge of his nose. It had been years,
Ted thought, since he'd seen anyone with a pince-nez.

The doctor gestured for him to sit in the chair, which had
been positioned sideways to the desk.

"This is merely routine," the doctor said amiably. "A physical
before sending you off. I see you're headed for a Stalag Luft. You'll
like it better there. More like being in a barracks than in prison.
And you'll be left alone. Pretty much. No more interrogations.
You're the first American I've had in a while. You are American,
I take it."

Ted nodded.

"Here, stick this under your tongue. I'll have a listen to your
chest."

Ted closed his mouth around the thermometer. The doctor
bent to Ted's chest, put the stethoscope against his shirt. The

doctor's mouth was a thin line of concentration. He repositioned the stethoscope. He did this repeatedly, then stopped.

He took the thermometer out of Ted's mouth.

"I think you'd better take that shirt off."

The doctor scrutinized Ted's face and eyes as Ted removed his shirt. Ted laid it on the desk.

The doctor felt his neck, behind his ears.

"You've had some coughing?"

Ted nodded.

"Congestion?"

"Yes."

The doctor bent again to listen to Ted's chest. He moved the stethoscope along the skin. He thumped Ted's back, which made him cough.

The doctor stood up, crossed his arms, studied his patient. "You should have seen a doctor sooner."

"I tried."

"It sounds like pneumonia to me. I'll prepare an injection. Normally, I wouldn't suggest moving you, but I want you out of here. You'll die if you stay here," the doctor added matter-of-factly. "I'm not promising it will be a lot better in the Stalag, but it can't be much worse. Well, look at that. Not bad, even without the hair."

Ted glanced up, followed the doctor's gaze out the door and across the corridor.

Her hair, slightly damp, fell in jagged bits around her face. Her mouth was parted, one hand flat against her stomach. The chin shift she wore outlined the shape of her breasts and nipples. He saw the purple and yellow stains on her legs and arms.

A rush of heat moved from the center of his body to his skin.

Silently, he bellowed her name.

Her face was whiter than he had ever seen it, and so thin he could see the bones beneath the skin. She opened her mouth, and he thought she would speak to him. He willed her to speak, and then instantly willed her to be silent. He hooked an arm around the chair to anchor himself, to keep himself from catapulting across the corridor.

Only two, three seconds had passed.

But in those seconds, he had understood that he could not acknowledge her. For to do so was to convict her of knowing him. A death sentence. She would not be in this infirmary, he told himself, if she had already been sentenced to death.

His decision was immediate and agonizing. He could see she did not understand.

He wanted to cry. Even after all they had done to her, she was more beautiful than any other woman he had ever seen.

She took a step forward, put a finger to her lips.

It was a gesture he would remember all his life.

The door across the corridor slammed with a shudder.

———

A steady breeze made the new leaves turn their backs. Underfoot, the green of the pasture was uneven, with the onion grass sending up tall shoots. The boy laid down his bicycle. Bright reflections from the plane hurt his eyes where the metal had been scuffed shiny. With his hands in his pockets, he walked toward the plane, examining it as he went. It seemed to him a broken animal, an old dog, that had lain down to rest. Around the belly, dug into the pasture, weeds and wildflowers grew. The skin of the tail made a rat-a-tat-tat sound as it slapped against its frame.

The rumor was that tomorrow the Germans would come to dismantle the plane. He wondered if they'd hack it to death, and what tools they'd use. Everything that could be removed from the plane had already been taken. Only the carcass — dented, pockmarked, bent — was left. They were going to turn the pasture into a landing strip, it was said. German cargo planes. Jean thought the American pilot would probably shake his head in amazement to think that his emergency landing had led to this development. There was no telling sometimes how one thing led to another.

The pilot was gone, and Jean didn't know where. He'd seen him in the square at Rance, and the next day he'd heard that Madame Daussois had been taken. It wasn't known if the American had been taken with her, or if he'd gotten away. Jean hoped passionately that the aviator, with his ill-fitting beret and peasant's coat, had made it safely to Spain and beyond. Sometimes, when the boy heard the drone of a bomber, he looked up and wondered. Surely if the aviator flew over Delahaut, he would signal them somehow.

When the boy drew closer to the plane, he touched the wing with his hand. So much had happened since the plane had fallen a little over three months ago. He remembered the scar the plane had made that day; it was now just a wide rut covered with a mat of grass. He remembered the search through the woods, the shock of seeing the foreign pilot's boots. He thought it lucky that the crash had happened in the winter. With the new foliage, the boy doubted he'd be able to find a man now.

He rounded the nose, trailing his fingers along the metal. He was worried about Madame Daussois. Where had they taken her? And when would she be back? On most days he made it a point to ride by her house. The grass was beginning to grow over the foundation, and her bicycle leaned against the gray stone. The blackout curtains had not been opened and gave the house a gloomy look. The truck, the one that everyone knew she kept behind the barn, had been taken by the Germans. Jean was surprised they hadn't taken her bicycle as well.

He thought that when the war was over, he would ask Madame Daussois if he could live with her. She didn't have any children of her own, and he could offer to work for his keep. He was a good worker, and he knew she trusted him. Maybe she'd been lonely without any children of her own.

But no matter what happened, he'd already decided, when the war was over, whatever the outcome, he was going to leave his father's home. If the Allies were defeated, living with his father would be intolerable; if they won, his father would be tried as a collaborator and probably shot. Jean couldn't bring himself to actually *hope* that his father would be shot; it was just that he thought he would be. In either case, Jean couldn't stay at home anymore. He'd see the war out, for his mother's sake, but that was all. She couldn't expect more than that from him.

He thought suddenly that the next time he passed the Daussois house he would see if he could find a scythe in the barn, cut the grass for her. Yes, that was a good idea. He'd keep the place up. On his own. She'd see then what a good worker he was. He might even begin today, after school.

He banged against the metal as he circled the plane. He wished the Germans wouldn't hack it up. It was a wonderful thing, the plane. He put his hands together in the shape of a bomber, the thumbs hooked together as a fuselage, the two sets of fingers the wings, and made his imaginary plane fly over Belgium, falter, loop low over the village, and execute a belly landing in a field. He separated his thumbs, put his hands in his pockets, and ducked around the tail. He ought to be getting back to school, he knew. Afternoon classes would begin soon.

But heading out of the pasture to fetch his bicycle, he stopped. He turned for one last look at the plane. He studied the cockpit with its smashed windshield. He thought about the waist with its exposure to the cold and to the German bullets. He tried to imagine being a gunner in that waist, or the pilot in the cockpit. Impulsively, not knowing quite why, he ran back to the plane and hoisted himself up onto the surface of the near wing. He turned, looked out over the pasture and toward the woods. The day was clear, but the young trees bent and dipped in gusts.

Jean carefully made his way to the tip of the wing, unbuttoned his jacket, and closed his eyes. His jacket filled and billowed behind him.

The boy arced his body and spread his wings. He jumped as far as he could go.

December 30, 1993

HER VOICE LINGERED LONG INTO THE NIGHT AND stopped quietly, like a candle that had been pinched out, and he thought then that he understood, or imagined, how it must have been.

Between them on the table was an empty bottle of red wine, the remains of a simple meal, and an ashtray full of cigarette debris — hers. She had more or less chain-smoked the entire time she talked, and the air around them in her kitchen was faintly tinged with blue. Once or twice she had interrupted her story to leave the room; Tom didn't know where she had gone. And once she had stopped to put together the meal — bread, cheese, sausage, a plate of fruit. On the table there was an ivory lace cloth.

Her voice was easy to listen to — deep and steady and without drama. Most often she sat with her chin resting on the heel of her hand, her fingers and the cigarette held away from her face. She had pushed her sleeves up to her elbows when they sat down; her wrists and forearms were both thin and strong.

But it was her eyes that night that Tom noticed most. Large and pale gray — a gray he thought of as calm. She had ivory skin, and it seemed as though it would be powdery to touch. There were many lines on her face, but beneath the skin, her bone structure was distinctive, and it was not hard to see, as it sometimes was in older people, the younger woman she had been. Her hair was white and drawn back behind her ears. She wore a linen blouse and a gray cardigan that matched her eyes; her skirt fell just below her knees. She wore no jewelry of any kind. Her back was straight, and her posture made her look younger than he knew she had to be.

When he had sought her out just before the ceremony began, he had seen that she was not entirely surprised to see him — even though she started a bit when she first looked into his face. The ceremony was impressive and moving, he thought, particularly the flyby by the Belgian Air Force, and the priest making the sign of the cross on his father's engraved name. After the ceremony, she asked him to come to her house for a cup of coffee. And it was then, in her kitchen, with a weak sun slanting through the windows, that she'd begun her story — with her low voice and her accent.

She'd been talking for hours.

When she finished, it was some minutes before he could speak.

"Why did Henri kill the German guards?" he asked quietly.

She turned sideways in her chair, crossed her legs. She had one elbow on the table still; in her other hand, she held a glass. "I did not know this until after the war. The war was terrible for Henri. He was afraid, as I am telling you. I think he wished to show to himself he had the courage."

She took a small sip of wine.

"After the war," she said, "I am discovering that when Anthoine is escaped from the school, Henri is stopped. He is tortured, or I think he is threatened with the torture, and when he is let go and he returns to Anthoine, he has . . . turned. Yes?"

"A spy," Tom said. "A double agent."

"Yes. He is making the bargain: His life and my life for the information."

"You said there are no bargains," he said quietly.

"Yes, and I am correct in this. The Germans, they shoot Henri before the war is over, when he has given them the pilot and helped to make the new escape line. And when he is not telling them where the pilot was hidden."

"He never gave them you."

"No."

"But you were picked up."

"Yes. For the interrogation. But I have not the execution."

"You went to Ravensbrück."

She was hard of hearing in her left ear, and when Tom spoke she turned her head so that her good ear was toward him.

"No. That day I am telling you of I am put into a truck. But this truck is last in the convoy, and is something wrong with it, and is not starting. So we are taken off and put back in the Old Antwerp Prison. I was very disappointed that day, but later I see that I am having the luck after all. I stay in Antwerp Prison for three months more, and then I am taken to Antwerp train station for the deportation, and at train station all the women I am with, we are let go. I have never know why."

Tom looked around at the room they were in. The cast-iron stove was still intact, but the cabinets and appliances were white and new and distinctly European; they fit together like an expertly designed puzzle. The stone floor, he guessed, was probably the same as had been there in his father's day, and behind the white cabinets was a wallpaper with small bouquets in a seemingly random pattern. Had that been the paper when his father was in this room? On the marble mantel were a crucifix and two silver candlesticks.

He was sitting with one hand on the lace cloth. He couldn't hide his curiosity. He lifted up the cloth and felt the table with his fingers. He pushed the cloth farther back. The table was oak and scarred.

Across the table, Claire Daussois turned back toward him, put down her glass, and brought her folded hands to her mouth. She seemed to be studying him, making a decision.

After a time, she stood up.

"Would you like to meet my daughter?" she asked.

He sensed it was not really a question. She waited for him to stand, and indicated he should follow her. The narrow corridor into which she led him was darkened, but he was aware of an elaborate wallpaper of street scenes, a crucifix on the wall, and a shallow bookcase with framed photographs. She stopped at the threshold of a room, softly called a name, and said a few words. He heard a television in the background. Gently, Claire pushed open the door. She held the door back and leaned against it, an invitation to him. He turned and looked into the room.

The woman in the chair had his father's face and his eyes. The resemblance was so acute, he felt a stab of pain, as though he'd stumbled into a room and found his father still alive. He put his fist to his mouth.

Her hair was cut short and graying slightly, the way dark blondes tend to do. She was sitting in a rocker, her hands folded in her lap, and when she looked at him, her face melted into a sweet and girlish smile — the smile of a child. Her eyes were guileless with that unique color Tom had seen only in his father; and those eyes, combined with the smile, suggested to him a serene spirit. Though she wore a sweater and a pair of slacks, he had the sense that she was wrapped in a cocoon, and he thought it was perhaps that sense of being surrounded and protected that gave her a nunlike quality.

"This is my daughter, Charmaine. Charmaine . . ." Claire spoke up when she addressed her daughter. "This is Tom Brice."

He walked to where the woman was sitting. The images from the TV screen were flickering in the window beside her. She held a hand up to him, and he took it. He could see, even though she was sitting, that she was nearly as tall as he was. Her face was pale and smooth, untouched by the years.

"Bonjour," he said.

The woman looked a bit flustered.

"She is not speaking very much," Claire said from the doorway.

He held her hand longer than he needed to. He was bewildered to realize that all the years he'd been alive, she had been alive. Here. In this house. She was forty-nine, he quickly calculated. Three years older than himself. His sister. His half-sister. He bent down and kissed her on the cheek.

She colored instantly and shyly withdrew her hand. Like a child might, she put the flat of her palm on the place where he had kissed her. She murmured something he couldn't make out and looked toward her mother.

"They are starving me in the prison," Claire said. "When she is in the womb."

There was a chair behind Tom. He backed up to it and sat

down. Claire came and stood beside him. Charmaine turned her attention back to the silent TV screen.

"I'm . . ." He couldn't continue.

"Yes," said Claire. "I know."

"He never knew he had a daughter," he said slowly.

"When the war is ending, we are trying, all of us, to put those years as far behind us as we can."

"When my father was liberated from the POW camp," Tom said, "they brought him out on a stretcher. They shipped him straight home."

It seemed almost more than Tom could take in. And he knew that if he thought about the sadness of it — of his father never having known he had another child — he would not be able to remain in that room.

"You've been alone all this time?" he asked Madame Daussois.

"Oh no," she said quickly, leaning against the wall. The room was small. It had a daybed, the TV, a lamp, a dark oak armoire, a table that Tom could see doubled as a tray. Another crucifix. "I am raising the boy, Jean, along with Charmaine."

"He never told me, when I met him today at the ceremony, about finding my father in the woods."

"No. He would not. Is not his way. He is beautiful child growing up. His father is shot after the war, and his mother is leaving the village. And then I am meeting a man, a teacher, from Charleroi, and we are married. We are on holiday in Spain this month, and at first I am not coming to the ceremony. There are many bad memories, and there are some persons in Delahaut who remember Henri as traitor. And though I am living here and am well remembered for what I do in the war, is best, I think, I do not come to the ceremony. But then I change my mind. I am wanting too much to see the monument. And to have the chance of meeting you. My husband is still in Spain."

She looked at Tom and then looked down. She wrapped her arms around herself.

"I have something," she said.

She left the room and returned with a photograph in a silver frame. She handed it to him.

It was a picture of his father in a white shirt with a poorly knotted tie. His evasion photo, Tom guessed.

"I am keeping this," she said. "Sometimes I am showing it to Charmaine and telling her the man is her father. I am never holding the truth from her or from anyone."

She took the photograph from him, flipped it over to its back to remove the frame. In the backing was another photograph. She offered this picture to him as well.

"It's my mother," he said with some surprise.

Claire almost smiled and nodded her head. "He is marrying her, then. I am thinking this."

He looked at the young woman in the picture — his mother a half-century ago. Had his father once told her about Claire Daussois? Or had she somehow guessed?

"They are loving each other?" Claire asked.

"Yes," he answered, "I'm sure of it." He gave her back the photograph. "They broke his arm in prison camp," he told her. "After he went back to America, he flew cargo planes for a while, and then worked as a flight instructor at a small airport near where he grew up. It was hard for him to keep a job, though. He had problems with his lungs as a result of the prison camp. He died in 1960 of pneumonia. Actually, his name isn't on a marker anywhere but here."

She held the pictures to her chest with both hands. "I have never know," she said, "if your father is all this time thinking it is me who is betraying him. And I am always sorry about this."

"I'm sure he didn't believe that," Tom said quickly.

She made a small movement toward the door. It was late, nearly midnight. But he didn't want to leave the room.

"I always knew that the war had changed my father," he said, "but I was just a boy when he died, and I never really knew why. My mother died in 1979. Luckily the invitation somehow made its way to me."

"I'm glad."

"May I come back someday?" he asked. "To see . . ." He tilted his head toward the woman in the rocking chair, who, all the time that Claire and he had been speaking, had watched the TV screen. He could not yet say her name.

"Yes, of course," Claire said. "You are welcome always."

Tom stood up and walked to where his half-sister sat. He touched her on the shoulder and said goodbye. She looked up at him and smiled again, but didn't speak. He wanted once again to kiss her, but he didn't.

Outside her room, Claire and Tom made awkward progress toward the door.

"You have children?" she asked.

"Yes, I have two boys. But I'm divorced."

"What do you do?"

"I teach high school English — in the town where my father grew up."

"You don't fly?"

"No."

"When you are coming here next time, you must bring your boys. Charmaine is aunt?"

He nodded.

"Oh," she said suddenly. "I am forgetting. On your father's plane is drawing with the name of the plane, *Woman's Home Companion*. When the plane is crashing, as I am telling you earlier, I am hearing of this drawing, and your father is saying he will tell me what it is, but then he is taken. . . ."

"*Woman's Home Companion*," Tom said. "It was the name of a popular magazine then."

"Yes. And the drawing?"

How was he to describe the drawing to this Belgian woman? His father had told him when he was twelve, and he had blushed furiously at the time.

"Have you ever seen much of the nose art that was on the war planes then?" he asked.

"Yes. I know these drawings. They are like cartoons, yes? And the women, they are not wearing too much clothes."

"Well. Yes. But in this drawing . . ." He stopped, trying to think of a way to put this. "It's a picture of a man's . . ."

He waited.

"Oh," she said suddenly, getting it.

"A very large . . .?"

"Ah, yes," she said, nodding. She looked a bit shocked. *"Woman's Home Companion,"* she repeated thoughtfully. Then she put her hand to her mouth and looked at him. She began to laugh. It was a wonderful laugh — tickled and scandalized at once. The laugh lit up her face, and he saw that she was beautiful.

He laughed with her, but what he was really thinking about was of all the things our fathers couldn't tell us.